BETTER ANGELS

Ace Books by Howard V. Hendrix

LIGHTPATHS
STANDING WAVE
BETTER ANGELS

BETTER ANGELS

Howard V. Hendrix

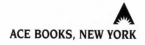
ACE BOOKS, NEW YORK

BETTER ANGELS

An Ace Book
Published by The Berkley Publishing Group,
a division of Penguin Putnam Inc.,
375 Hudson Street, New York, New York 10014.
The Penguin Putnam Inc. World Wide Web site address is
http://www.penguinputnam.com

First edition: October 1999

Library of Congress Cataloging-in-Publication Data
Hendrix, Howard V., 1959–
Better Angels / by Howard V. Hendrix.
        p.   cm.
        ISBN: 0-441-00652-3
        I. Title
    PS3558.E49526B4   1999
813'.54—dc21   99-33232
                                                          CIP

Printed in the United States of America

10   9   8   7   6   5   4   3   2   1

To the memory of my brother, Vincent John Hendrix, and my father, Howard John Hendrix: Though much is taken, much abides.

ACKNOWLEDGMENTS

The number of people I need to thank grows with every book. Some of them—Bruce Albert, Stuart Straw, and Mike Lepper—I have previously acknowledged in *Lightpaths* and *Standing Wave*. Although she, too, was acknowledged previously, I must again thank Ginjer Buchanan, my editor at Ace, for her continuing support of my work. Much thanks also goes to Chris Lotts, my agent beginning with this book, for his care and expertise in handling the business end of the writing business. In my other "business"—teaching—my thanks to the students, faculty, and administration of National University for understanding the tides and cycles of my writing life.

My thanks also go out to Amy Corley and Marian Montgomery at Ace for working with me on my tours for *Lightpaths* and *Standing Wave*, respectively. Thanks, too, to Art Holcomb and Barbara Wallace in Riverside, to Mike Givel and Beck Sherry in Pleasant Hill, to Phoebe Reeves and Juris Ahn (formerly of San Francisco), and to Bridget McKenna, Doug Herring, Lorelei Shannon, Dan Carter, and all the members of the Central California Expatriate Community in Seattle, for sharing their lives and floor space with me during my couch-surfing book tours.

My thanks to Brad Lyau and Joe Miller for years of literary-critical discussions of science fiction; to the staff of the Cincinnati Zoo's Center for the Reproduction of Endangered Wildlife; to the staff of the Page Museum of LaBrea Discoveries in Los Angeles; to Matt Pallamary for lucid dreaming; to Pete Heckhuis for quantum computing; to Erik Olson for cosmic serpentry; to Gary "Dino" Northrup for years of inventive speculation; to Charlie Ryan of *Aboriginal*, Kim Mohan of *Amazing*, and Larry Dennis of *EOTU* for keeping my writing dreams alive during the long dry spells; and finally to my wife Laurel, for sharing my life while I shared these words.

My heartfelt gratitude to all of you.

ONE 2002–2014

Like the Present

Waves of light rippled the starry darkness. Jacinta had an eerie sense of being underwater in a moonlit pool, of looking up at the mercury-shimmering underside of the sky just at the moment a piece of that sky broke loose—precisely at the instant a mirror-bright stone fell through the hole in heaven it had made.

The hole promptly filled itself in, the sky unfunhoused itself, the universe unwarped back to mirror smoothness. The mercury droplet of broken sky kept falling, however, intact and growing larger. At the same time it moved more slowly, the way a stone falls more slowly through water than through air.

Strange as what she was looking at undeniably was, even stranger was the fact that she was seeing it at all. Or was she? The ghost people around her, with whom Jacinta now clasped hands and tried to chantsong along, claimed awesome powers for their singing—including the capability of their songs to create in physical space the images and objects about which they sang.

Extremely powerful auditory hallucinations? Or something more?

Stranger still, however, was the fact that she was really *seeing* what she was looking at, knowing in depth exactly what was being shown her without knowing *how* she knew. The big "mercury" droplet's splashing against some obstacle—that was the Allessan contact ship's bubble of force bursting in the Great Accident, the Error, the Miscalculation.

The Accident revealed (and Jacinta saw, inside the bubble) a mirror sphere made of innumerable smaller pieces, a dance hall mirrorball hurtling through space. All human civilization, religion, controlled fire, the first chipped-pebble stone tool, not to mention the lost age of disco that had danced Jacinta's childhood—all stood many millions of years into the future and after the fact of what she was looking at.

As she observed more closely, she saw that the smaller mirrors of the mirrorball were actually not squares at all but myriad, shining, overlapping wings. In the forms to which those wings were attached, some might see angelic beings of pure intuition, others demons of unalloyed malevolence, still others aliens—a space-cantina bestiary of creatures dressed in light-powered livesuits, moving with starling-flock simultaneity.

Seeing the irreparable damage the Accident had done to those crew members who *were* the ship they sailed, Jacinta recalled the ghost people's stories that each individual, of all that crew's many species, were always and forever in direct mental communication with all the others. She wondered what sort of alien pain and otherworldly grief they might have felt at the deaths of so many of their shipmates.

"Direct mental communication"—is that what's happening to me? Jacinta asked herself as she listened to the ghost people singing. *Is what I'm experiencing not a hallucination but the beginnings of that telepathy, that fullness of empathy the ghost people claim their totemic mushroom bestows upon them? When I introduced TV to them, they said television and global communication did not surprise them. They claim the natural world is always broadcasting cloudforest television into their heads. Are they serious?*

Or is this all simply madness?

A shiver ran through her. The tribe—no, they weren't really a tribe, since they had no chief, but what were they, then? "Hunting-gathering group?" "Tepuians?" "Ghost people," as their neighbors had referred to them, with superstitious awe in their voices? Despite all the time she had spent with them, despite her ethnobotanical training, despite the readiness with which *they* (whatever the correct term) had welcomed her from the first, at this moment, among these isolated, mushroom-worshiping, hunting-gathering, insect-eating, dark-skinned, black-haired, almond-eyed people dressed in purple and black loinclothes and robes woven in snaking double-helical patterns, Jacinta felt distinctly culture-shocked.

She hated that phrase, "almond-eyed." What did that make her—blueberry-eyed? Honey blond? Some other type of food?

Around her the ghost people's strange song continued, telling of the damaged ship made of wild angels. The song sounded quite mad indeed, particularly as it went on to narrate how and why the ship was sent from the heart of the galaxy—or rather, Jacinta knew, from the Allesseh, hanging three thousand light-years above the galaxy's center. According to old Kekchi, the ghost people's mindtime-traveling "Wise One," the Allesseh had itself been discovered within the last decade or so by earthly astronomers—but only very indirectly, for they knew the Allesseh not in itself but only by the vast antimatter fountain associated with it. Earthly scientists had never quite managed to satisfactorily explain the existence of that fountain.

Jacinta was following the chantsong with only a part of her mind. Distracted, she found herself thinking of her brother Paul instead, her only and last visitor from the supposedly civilized world—with whom she had not parted on the most pleasant of terms. . . .

"So that's what all this is about, then?" Paul had said, smacking his forehead with the palm of his left hand as he rose shakily to his feet. "These people have been collecting rocks for millennia because mushrooms 'told' them to? And you believe that? How long have you been eating this druggie fungus of theirs? It's pushing you over the edgeless edge, sis. We've got to get you out of here, get this crap out of your system—"

"No, Paul." Jacinta shook her head and slowly rose from her squatting position to stand upright. "My mission here is too important to be absorbed into anyone else's—even yours. The work is not yet finished so the ghost people can leave."

"What work?"

"Singing the mountain to the stars," she explained. "The quartz they've collected is not something you shape into a crude tool—it's something you worship as a totem. Their very existence here is proof of the fisherfolk hypothesis, of *neanderthalensis* in the New World. That's why Fash got so hot to bring a major expedition here once he found out about them. That's why we have to hurry—before the rest of the world finds them and destroys their uniqueness."

Jacinta reached toward her brother, but then hesitated, drew back.

"Think of it, Paul," she said, trying to explain. "These people and their culture are one of the last outposts of a lost empire of wood and song. They're a thread that, on this different continent, in this cave, found its way back to the source of the world songweb. Synergy and coevolution. For them, every sound has a form. They can read the musical notation of time's signature. According to their myths, Song, shaped information, makes the world. Once we have sung and thought critical information densities into these quartz-collecting columns, they will translate and amplify it so we can dissociate ourselves from the gravitational bed of local spacetime. Then we can join in the Allesseh, the great Cooperation, the telepathic harmony of all myconeuralized creatures throughout the galaxy—"

"Wrong!" Paul shouted, shaking his sandy-haired head in disgust. "A crazy ethnobotanist and forty-odd half-naked aborigines as humanity's first ambassadors to the galaxy? Do you have any idea how insane that sounds?"

With the expanded empathy the ghost people's prized fungus had already granted her, Jacinta saw the swelling rage igniting deep inside Paul's skull, saw a vision of an icy-bright pinpoint exploding outward like a cold Big Bang, a blizzard of invisible light radiating out of Paul's temples, a crown of white thorns working its way to his forehead from the inside to finally storm outward in all directions, away and away. Paul paced heavily and furiously in the mud, the terrible anger rising through him, seemingly bringing with it all the memories of all Jacinta's strange times past.

"I thought you were acting crazy," he yelled, "when you said you were getting secret personal messages from TV programs! I thought you were acting crazy when you said you were under surveillance by a secret network of shadowy operatives! I thought you were acting crazy when you were convinced They were monitoring your thoughts through some guy trained as a 'telepathic receiver' living in an apartment down the hall! I thought you were acting crazy before, but this—this is the craziest of all!"

In full fury her short, wiry-muscled brother ran about on the death island, kicking fiercely at the phallus-brain shapes of the ghost people's totemic mushroom where it grew by the dozen, rising out of the corpse-beds of the ghost people's deceased ancestors. Again and again Paul kicked, desecrating corpse after corpse. The fungal fruiting bodies split apart against his muddy, boot-clad feet, tender new flesh defiled.

When, breathless, Paul at last stopped his sacrilege, Jacinta was already plopped down in the mire, rubbing tears from her eyes.

"You'll never understand, will you?" she said with a moan. "Yeah, you're right—out there I *am* crazy, a freak! Always trapped between what I am and what I'm supposed to be! Always letting people down! No more! This is my world now, these are my people. It's better here! Paul, please, get beyond your demons! Don't you see? We were meant to be telepaths, part of the Great Cooperation, but we went wrong, we were overlooked, we developed consciousness and intellect, but not the fullness of empathy we misunderstand as telepathy. All human history is a result of a mistake, an *accident*."

She turned to him, almost pleading. "The contact ships missed us, every one. We became a preterite planet, but now we have a chance to gain our rightful inheritance, our place in the bliss of the Cooperation! Stay with us! Come with us!"

"Where?" Paul asked, winded, seeming suddenly tired but still unwilling to concede a single point. "Where are you taking them? Where are they taking you? I don't get it, Jacs. If you really think these ghost people prove your theories right, then why are you trying to help them escape the scrutiny of your colleagues? If you're really trying to preserve their culture from our civilization, then why'd you bring all that high-tech gear up here for them to mess with? Industrial autoclaves. Diamond saws. Generators. Power cables. Fold-out sattelite dishes. Uplink antennas. Language acquisition and translation programs. Cameras and opti-disk player recorders. Fifty microscreen TV sets—fifty!"

Jacinta, shocked and numbed as the gravity of her brother's profanation of the ghost people's funerary isle sank in, said nothing. Her brother, well-launched into his diatribe, barely noticed.

"I saw what was going on in all those small side chambers on the way down here," he said. "Don't think I didn't. All those alcoves with power lines and cables snaking into them. In one room naked tepui kids were watching a Chinese television documentary on Han dynasty artifacts—real-time computer translated into French! In another I saw a young 'indigene' watching an American news broadcast about an Indian monsoon. In another your friend Talitha was checking an enormous crystal column for flaws as it came out of an extrusion autoclave! Someone else was carving up quartz bricks with a diamond saw right next door. I saw tepui kids randomly sampling music—madrigals and rap, Tibetan temple gongs and rock 'n' roll, Sufi chants and Europop and worldbeat. Do you want me to ignore the evidence of my own eyes? Doesn't that exposure alter their 'lifeways'?"

Jacinta's numbness and shock, however, still had not lifted enough to allow her the energy to reply.

"That wasn't the strangest, either," her brother continued. "A boy and an oldster, both in loincloths, sitting in front of computer terminals, running through complex mathematical equations! Then what looked like star charts and astrogation data zipping across screens in front of half a dozen operators of various ages. Think, Jacinta! Doesn't all that already change the ways of these people beyond recovery?"

At last Jacinta began to rouse herself from her numbness, but her brother in his ranting noticed not at all.

"Why should I want to stay here, Jacinta?" he concluded. "Why should I want to end up a flipped-out fungus-head—excuse me, 'myco-neural symbiont'—with a parasite mushroom growing inside my skull? Like these throwbacks? Is that the kind of life you want?"

"They're *happy*!" Jacinta shouted, turning reddened eyes on Paul—eyes that would not break contact, would not flicker away this time, no matter how much he might have wished it. "*We* are happy! What kind of life would I have out there in your 'real' world? In and out of insti-tutions all my life, dosed up on 'meds,' watched over by high-school-dropout 'psychiatric aides' in case I 'go off'—giving them the chance to execute a well-planned 'takedown' so they can strap me into a floor-bolted cot in the 'time-out' room? Out there, even freedom is my jail—a prison as big as the world! No thanks. Not while there's even a chance of real freedom, and the stars."

They both felt like crying. It was all wrong, all so wrong.

"Jacs, we've never institutionalized you," Paul said, a quaver in his voice. "All I want to do is take you home."

"This is my home," Jacinta said, turning away.

"What about Mom and Dad?" he asked. "What about Professor Man-ikam and your career?"

"Tell them I quit school," she said without turning around. "Tell them I quit work. Tell them I disappeared into the backcountry. Tell them I went native, stopped communicating, fell beyond reach. Tell Mom and Dad they only gave us everything so we would owe everything to them."

"What about *me* then, you ingrate?" Paul shouted, his sorrow turning once more to anger. "I came all the way down here after you! What about me, huh? What would your mushroom people do if I grabbed one of these long bones from their graveyard here, clubbed you over the head with it, and took you out of here in a fireman's carry? Have they foreseen that future? Would they try to stop me?"

"Probably not," Jacinta said with a deep sigh, turning slightly toward him, glancing over her shoulder. "But I would. I'll fight you to the last breath. I won't let you sentence me to a life in prison—not even if it's 'for my own good.' Not even if I should be 'grateful' to you for doing it. Leave me here, or you better leave me alone."

In the flash of determination in her eyes as she turned away, Paul must have seen something too strong for him to challenge. He turned away, too, then. After a moment, Jacinta turned and watched him go, plodding away through the shallow water, squelching back tiredly through the plain of muck, flashlight flickering before him in the hollow emptiness of the cave. She watched as Paul came onto solid ground again and kept walking, never looking back.

"We must leave soon," the old psychopomp Kekchi said to Jacinta. The words echoed through the tall darkness of the cave almost too plainly—some weird acoustical effect. "Things don't have to be perfect. They just have to be *done*."

Now, hours later, things were getting done, but her brother was gone. Around her, Kekchi and all the ghost people still sang, their cosmogonic chantsong conjuring up that time many millions of years in the past, soon after the contact ship had run into troubles caused by what Jacinta dimly understood as galactic dust lanes, unanticipated dark stars. A distant time when the surviving crew had determined to make a "spore crash" on a world that looked as if it might someday harbor intelligent life.

The ghost people's chantsong epic showed Jacinta again the winged crew's fears and hopes: Could life on this world before them—hit with extinction pulses roughly every thirty-three million revolutions around its primary, devastations brought on by the interaction of dust lanes and dark stars and cometary collisions—could life there survive long enough to develop intelligence? Given that the ghost people's song told how most of the crew who were also their ship burned up in the spore crash attempt, those long-ago otherworlders appeared to have answered that question in hope rather than in fear. And not in vain: The spores that the Allesseh had designed, earlier versions of which had been falling between the stars for tens of millions of years previously, were this time successfully planted on the Earth, at last thickly enough to spawn and fruit, to spore again and again in hope of finding a proper host.

Glancing about her now, at the tepuians singing amid the great ring of quartz columns, on the floor of this underground space she had named the Cathedral Room, Jacinta realized that the program embedded within those spores was moving toward its long-awaited fulfillment. The floating quartz columns—pillars in an airy cathedral, flying buttresses to nowhere holding up a dark subterranean sky—had now begun to pulse rapidly with spiky halos of light.

Jacinta felt herself and all the ghost people floating up into the air together in a ring of their own, a ring of living beings within the ring of columns flashing sunset glow about them, iridescent blues and salmon pinks. Sensitive flames—tiny, lambent fractal universes—trembled over all their heads, holy fire flickering in time to the beat of a song of painful beauty and seductive lassitude, a music impelled by a visionary tension between urgency and dream.

The song of the mushroom's long wait for a partner of sufficient neurological complexity. The song of the endless killing wait, the devastating lingering through what Jacinta understood (dimly, through the myth-language of science) as unexpected levels of incident radiation, accelerated mutation rates, speeded-up speciation. She knew some of her colleagues—for whom science was the final methodology, beyond change and evolution and ultimately beyond time itself—would find that "myth language" annoying. She didn't particularly care. If what was meant by myth was a system of explanation, then the language of science was mythic too. The mythic song of the tepuians, at any rate, was simultaneously too ancient and too advanced to fit comfortably within the constraints of twenty-first century science.

Around her the ghost people's epic chantsong proclaimed that, throughout the world, even the spore-crash strain became denatured into fungi of ten thousand forms. The pure Allessan form survived at last only here, in this great cave-riddled marble intrusion inside Caracamuni tepui—the place where, thousands of years before Jacinta came to them, the ghost people had first found their sacred mushroom, eaten it, joined with it. Caracamuni was where they claimed to have achieved the full myconeural symbiosis that allowed them to travel in mindtime, along the myriad branching parallel lines of their possible destinies.

The lines showed them their mission, generation after generation—even predicting Jacinta's arrival and the role she would come to play in helping the ghost people sing their mountain to the stars. Inside this tepui a refugee people had settled for good. Why should they continue to travel through all the world, when their sacred mushroom showed them that all the world could travel through them? They had come home to go home for all humanity—to the home humans had never known and that had never known them.

Swept away in the otherworldly music of it, Jacinta sensed that the song was very close to completing itself now—conjuring at last a picture quite the opposite of the wild, angelic contact ship's arrival. Not an "appearing" in this universe but, this time, a disappearing out of it: the hole opening, the sky rippling and bending and funhousing with wave upon wave of light, a bubble bursting *into* heaven.

Awkwardly, distantly, Jacinta tried to translate what she was seeing into the varieties of theoretical faster-than-light travel methods she'd once encountered, in physics courses during her undergraduate days. Was what she was witnessing the creation of both sides of the particle/antiparticle pair in Bell's Nonlocality Theorem? An Einstein bridge? Or some sort of super holographic wave function, disappearing *here* to reappear *there*?

Is the universe friendly, or not? That question—Einstein's answer to a reporter's query as to what was the most important question the great physicist could imagine—rose unbidden in Jacinta's mind. In the closing of the ghost people's chantsong, was she now looking at the future instead of the past?

Around her the ghost people sang the long coda of what had been so long embedded in the genes of their particular cultural obsession: The code hidden in their totemic mushroom, the key for opening the trans-luminal door, the ticket-to-ride on the galactic rapid transit system. Fully aware at last that she would soon be leaving the world of her birth behind her, Jacinta felt herself reaching out toward her brother one last time.

Thinking made it so. She found herself looking out at the world through her brother's eyes—and saw that time was passing much more rapidly in Paul's world than in hers. With him she stumbled and careened up the long slantwise cave tunnel behind his flashlight's madly bobbing beam, feet tangling in power cables leading to chambers where screens bled information from space into space. With him she tripped and fell and surged to his feet again, until brightness shone from around a corner and Paul found himself plunging headlong into evening light. . . .

Snatching up his backpack and gear from where he'd left them at the entrance, Paul saw the sky above him shimmering—iridescent blues, salmon pinks. Panting hard, he hastily averted his eyes, focusing his attention on the flat cloudforest green of the tepui's deep central cleft, afraid to look into the tall, strange chalice of that sky.

In the waning light Paul forded the flood that thundered away to falls at the southeastern end of the gorge. Making his way upward through the cleft now, through the drowned world of tepui cloudforest twilight, he surged at last onto the plateau's barren, stormswept top like a swimmer breaking surface after a long dive. Wandering only a short, exhausted way through the maze, he shed his gear and radioed in to the local guide Garza and his men. Something in his voice must have confirmed the locals in their traditional fears and superstitions of Caracamuni, for their words seemed smug, condescending.

Collapsing beneath a ledge, Paul did not know whether he slept or not.

The air around him thundered and the earth shook, and through it all he thought he heard the ghost people, singing and singing in the very rocks.

The next morning the hollow labyrinth on the tepui's crown seemed a maze of inverted cave tunnels, or a brain and all its convolutions turned inside out by some topology-transforming supercomputer. After several hours of numbed walking, Paul strode free of the maze.

His guide Garza and his men, when Paul joined them, were full of horrified tales of apparitions and earth tremors and streams of lightning leaping up from the highest stones. They were overjoyed at Paul's return—and the immediate prospect of their leaving. Their descent from the tepui's top was swift, passing him in a blur. The weather cooperated, rains falling only lightly for a few hours, so that by midafternoon the men had descended the bulk of the tepui's height. By evening they were on the lower ridge, making camp for the night, looking back at that mysterious height from which they had so recently descended.

Somehow, Jacinta realized, she and Paul were now in different time-flows, different relativistic frames of reference. A bifurcation had occurred, a cusp reached that made her think backward to the contact ship disaster and forward to a meeting with what had sent that ship so long ago. Despite the forking in time's paths, however, her peculiar deep empathy with her brother persisted, even as it became more a strain to maintain it. In Paul's frame . . .

. . . the sun had just set when it happened. The earth shook with such violence that the men were knocked from their feet and the forests below them seemed to toss like waves in a storm. The tremors calmed for a moment and, looking wildly around, Paul saw it: a great ring of dust about halfway up Caracamuni's height. The tremors gradually stopped, and from where he lay sprawled on the ground, Paul saw something that made him instinctively grab up his videocam and frame the scene in his viewfinder.

Caracamuni appeared to be growing taller. As its top continued to rise, though, he saw that it was not growing but separating, top half from bottom half, at that ring of thinning dust. In moments the top half had risen free and a space of clear sky intervened between the sundered halves of the ancient mountain.

Caracamuni was decoupling from the earth, rising smoothly as a mushroom in the night. Garza stood beside Paul, seeing it, too, crossing himself and murmuring prayers he probably hadn't said since he was a boy. After a time seeing that, framed in the viewfinder, it looked like trick photography or cinematic special effect Paul continued taping its ascent only out of habit, mostly watching it unframed, with his own eyes.

Jacinta, too, now sensed a shift in the ghost people's singing. It had become less urgent and more dreamlike. In the waking dream the chant-song now induced, she saw Caracamuni tepui as the ghost people had always known it, skirted so persistently by clouds that it had long seemed an island of stone floating among them, one of that misty, billowing company grown solid, wreathed in drifting fog and drizzle. Crowned by a forest of rainblack stones, the nutrients of Caracamuni's soils had been ceaselessly pounded out of its top by incessant storms until it truly embodied the paradox of a raindesert island above a rainforest sea. Caracamuni tepui had stood haunted and holy for aeons, sanctified by isolation, until more than half the species on its top could be found nowhere else on Earth.

Now, at last, it was becoming the actual floating island its isolated inhabitants had long dreamed it would become. Now it was about to become more remote than ever. No part of all its uniqueness—none of its strange bromeliads and sundews and fungi—would be found any longer upon the Earth.

Dreamily, Jacinta remembered reading once that angels and photons, both traveling at the speed of light, sensed no passage of time, no time at all, an Eternal Now, from their point of view. What she was experiencing was not quite that, however—not yet. Remembering those long-ago physics courses, she thought it was more like another type of bifurcation, the two spacetime frames surrounding an imploding star when it reached critical circumference. To those looking down from "normal" spacetime onto the star's implosion, the implosion stopped and froze forever at the critical circumference, at the event horizon. But for observers on the star itself (if there could ever be such creatures) the implosion continued on and on, far beyond critical, all the way down to singularity's infinite density and zero volume.

Jacinta vaguely wondered which side of what kind of singularity she would soon be standing on.

The anvil-shaped top of the mountain called Caracamuni was beyond the highest clouds when the sound hit the men in a great wave that drove Garza's Pemon assistants to bury their clenched faces against the bosom of the earth. It was a fearsome, prodigiously powerful sound . . .

. . . but one that Jacinta had heard before, more softly. It was the song of thought strengthened by stone uncountable times.

Is the universe friendly, or not? Jacinta asked herself that question again, making it her own, trying to keep mental contact with Paul until the latest possible instant. Looking through her brother's eyes at the mountaintop disappearing into the sky before him, Jacinta hoped her escape hatch would not prove to be a trapdoor.

The sun shone full upon the ascending mountaintop, now clear of Earth's curve, where the men lay in deep twilight below. Caracamuni was ascending in a bubble of force, its high waterfall plunging down only to spread out again in a broad swirl along the bubble-boundary's edge. As the cave's deep chamber stood ensphered in the stone bubble of its mountain, so, too, the mountain itself now stood ensphered in the bubble of force. From the mountain in its sphere a pale fire began to shine, increasing in intensity until . . .

Looking through her own dreaming eyes again, Jacinta sensed that she was on her way to discovering an answer to Einstein's great question. No time like the present . . .

. . . *in a brilliant burst of white light . . .*

. . . to find out . . .

. . . *the many fields of ensphering force dispersed . . .*

. . . the present is like . . .

. . . *the mountaintop disappeared . . .*

. . . No Time.

. . . *as silently and completely as a soap bubble bursting into a summer sky.*

Unsteady Alteration in the Steady Constellations

Paul Larkin had come to Death Valley to get drunk, wander off into the desert, and disappear. The idea of it, when he was sober, had shone in his head: elegant, simple, hard and bright as diamond. He had felt tired for too long, too tired to continue with the facade of his life. Best to put an end to it at his earliest possible convenience.

He had awakened to an omen that very morning—or rather, *from* one. A vision in a dream, actually. Paul usually didn't remember his dreams, but he woke up in the middle of this one, so he remembered it. In the dream he was sitting in an overstuffed armchair, talking pleasantly to two older people. Dreaming, he knew who they were, but when he woke he couldn't quite remember. Maybe they were his parents.

In the dream he was conversing in that pleasant living room when he happened to glance over his left shoulder. There, standing in the archway to the darkened room behind him, half in shadow and half in light, were his Uncle Tim, who had died recently, and his sister Jacinta, who had been gone, disappeared, ten years now. Someone else he knew was also there, but he couldn't remember on waking who that person might be.

He did, however, remember thinking in his dream, *Oh, these are the dead, standing behind me, watching and waiting.* That thought knocked him right back to consciousness. He was sure the dream had something to do with all that had happened to him recently—and with the prospect of the plan that had been forming in his mind for the past week.

Sitting in his dusty, battered car, he took another sip from the bottle of Edradour—"Single Highland Malt Scotch Whisky from the smallest distillery in Scotland"—that his Uncle Tim had brought back as a gift for him, years before. Tasting the warm, peaty sting and sizzle of the scotch lingering in his mouth and throat, Paul turned his attention to a piece of paper sealed in a plastic sleeve, lying on the seat of his car.

Breaking the seal on the plastic, he removed a carefully folded sheet of age-brittled white paper, upon which could be seen a dusty blue image like the photo negative of a brain. It was the spore print he had first found in an envelope ten years earlier, buried deep in his backpack, after he emptied the pack on returning home from the Caracamuni tepui.

Whether the spore print had been secretly planted there while he was in the cave, or during that last long night on the tepuitop—and by whom—Paul did not know. He only knew that for a decade he had never been able to bring himself to make public the print's existence. Nor could he bring himself to destroy it, any more than he could destroy any of his information on Jacinta. Information, as she had been fond of saying, is everything. Even information held in the limbo of the lost.

He *had* gone public with other matters from that time. Maybe too public. Ten years back, when he and his guide and native porters had returned from the tepui backcountry, they had told their story and shown their video recording of Caracamuni's top lifting off, decoupling from the Earth—to anyone who would listen, anyone who would watch.

Despite the fantastic nature of their story, or maybe because of it, no one really seemed to care. Another obscure piece of remote Amazonian real estate had disappeared. So what? That stuff was going up in smoke all the time back then. The kinder seismologists and vulcanologists interpreted their tale of the ascent of Caracamuni as an "anomalous volcanic eruption" and filed it away for future reference. Those less kind had interpreted Larkin's short tape of the tepui rising as a video hoax, nothing more.

Fash's anthropologists and archaeologists, initially intrigued by what Jacinta claimed to have found on and in Caracamuni, canceled their expedition. The controversy over the arrival date for human beings in the New World—to which Jacinta had contributed—continued unabated. The idea that a pocket of living-fossil *Homo sapiens neandertalensis* had survived into the present day on an isolated tepui in South America was dismissed out of hand. Those organizations that had granted or loaned Jacinta funds and equipment hassled Paul and his parents for a time but eventually wrote off both Jacinta and her failed expedition under something called a "forgiveness clause."

After Paul's brief emergency leave from KFSN—to take care of "family matters"—had ended, his employers expected him to go on with his life as if nothing had happened.

Nothing but flying mountains. Nothing but mushrooms from space. Nothing but incredibly ancient indigenes and failed white goddesses gone native. Nothing but "forty-odd aboriginal astronauts and a crazed ethnobotanist as humanity's first personal ambassadors to the universe."

Taking another sip of the Edradour, he held the square of paper lightly, contemplatively, a relaxed arm's length away. Symbol for him of all the events he had endured at Caracamuni tepui, the square of paper stood as well for all the pain and trouble those events and their telling had caused him since. Through the smoky haze of the scotch, he tried to remember who had first mentioned that "forty-odd aboriginal astronauts . . ." et cetera phrase. Had it been him? The media? The media quoting him, when he was still part of the media? Before the "trashy controversy" over his Caracamuni tape had cost him his first career as a broadcast journalist?

Now, the "flying mountaintop" story had cost him a second career, the one he had laboriously built for himself over the past decade. The old sensational story had reappeared in the media and, in his refusal to disavow it, Paul had completely unraveled his career in biology—all within the past four months. He didn't want to think about it, but his mind kept going there, like a tongue to the empty socket of a pulled wisdom tooth.

Paul stared hard again at the spore print. His last card, the strange ace in the hole he had never wanted to play. He had played it, at last, but what good had it done him?

Two months back, desperate at being reduced to the status of "independent researcher," Paul got in touch with Professor Phil Damon, who had headed his dissertation committee. Damon had been reluctant to help a tainted former student, but he had, mercifully enough, listened to the story of the spore print and the bizarre fungus it might grow. Damon agreed to examine the spore print and have some of it plated out and grown.

Taking another smoky sip of the Edradour and examining the spore print now, Paul could see the blank area in the upper left-hand corner. Almost six weeks ago, Damon and a mycologist colleague, in a chamber under a ventilation hood, had scraped spores from that corner of the paper, then shaken them into a series of petri dishes filled with various growth media, before handing the print back to him.

Three weeks into his testing of the fungus, Damon had called and quite unexpectedly announced that he had set up a meeting between Paul and Athena Griego, a "venture capital agent." Griego claimed to represent a number of investors and pharamaceutical firms that might be interested in further research on the fungus.

Ms. Griego had turned out to be a very high-powered and intense woman in her early forties, small of frame but with the sort of preternaturally high-riding and large spherical breasts that suggested structural augmentation. During the meeting she had struck Paul as shady somehow, a wheeler-dealer, an operator. Griego had promised to get back to him in a week, but he had heard nothing since. Some sort of response was very much overdue. The agent, for all her signifiers of power and augmentation, had apparently turned out to be much talk and no action.

Yeah, he thought as he refolded and resleeved the spore print, *whatever string of good luck I might once have had, I ran it all out a long time ago.* Taking up the bottle and getting out of the car, he wondered why: Why had he been so obstinate? Why couldn't he have just kept his mouth shut about the tepui and what had happened there—from the very beginning? Why had he thought it so important for the world to know?

Maybe I'm just self-destructive, he thought. *Maybe I'm doomed to crash every merry-go-round I make for myself just as soon as I get it spinning up to speed.*

As he staggered away from the car, Paul knew his stubbornness had to be more than just that. To bury the truth of what he'd seen at Caracamuni would be to bury the memory of his sister, to bring her disappearance closer to the death he feared that disappearance had already become. To turn ten years' absence and "might as well be dead" into quite dead indeed. He didn't want to bury Jacinta when she—or at least some part of her—might still be alive somewhere.

In his study at home, Paul had a desk drawer filled with memories, all carefully filed away. The specific details of his sister Jacinta's life and death receded and faded and vanished, yet the emotions surrounding those memories grew always nearer and more powerful. He could not resolve the paradox of that, so he tried to live in it.

Through the sparse desert brush he staggered his way toward a sandy scarp he had seen while driving into the arid valley earlier in the evening. Looking about him at night and desolation, Paul realized that he had not done very well trying to live in paradox. Instead, he had tried to fill the empty space of Jacinta's disappearance with work and study and research.

In the drawer at home with his memories of his sister there were also clippings and notes about quartz: fused from silicon and oxygen, the two most common elements to be found in the crust of Earth and Earthlike planets; harder than steel, fashioned into weapons for the past fifty thousand years; beloved by ancient Sumerians and Egyptians, Bedouins and Crusaders, Oriental craftsmen, electronics manufacturers, shamans and witches, alchemists and New Age spiritualists. He read the notes and sometimes wondered about the source of humanity's long romance with that rock.

Though it was certainly not his field he had, for the sake of Jacinta's theories and memory, read with a certain dislocated interest the speculations that the indigenous Tasmanians, extinguished a few hundred years ago, had a Mousterian toolkit—and physiological features, too, that would later be described in terms of *neandertalensis* and *soloensis*. In memory of Jacinta he also kept any notes and clippings he found about living fossils, the small groups of plants and animals that are the last living representatives of ancient categories of life, time-frozen creatures still resembling relatives that lived tens or hundreds of millions of years ago, even billions of years ago. Such creatures seemed to him undying memories in the mind of Life.

He stared again at the plastic sleeve and the folded paper that contained the spore print. Why had he guarded so closely the existence of this living fossil, if it *was* that? Why had he been so reluctant to release the spore print to the world, when he'd been so eager to show the videotape of Caracamuni? The spore print, if the ghost people's mushroom could be grown from it successfully, would present at least the proof of a species never before known to science—although that alone, of course, did not require that anyone believe the whole, strange story of the milieu from which the mushroom had come.

What else would the release of that spore print bring, though? He wondered, for the ten-thousandth time, what his obsession with the print and the fungus it produced was really all about. Organic alien technology? Or a mask for his own fears of the death and decay of a loved one?

He pondered that. Was Jacinta's disappearance—the singularity at the heart of the black hole of his obsession—pulling all his research and all his life inescapably down into its deadly gravity? Or was it only his own fear of mortality and meaninglessness, death as event horizon, from whose bourne no further signal escapes?

He tripped on a stone and fell. With drunkard's luck he somehow managed to avoid landing on anything sharp. He was glad he hadn't plunged face first into a jumping cholla or something equally nasty.

Looking and feeling about himself in the moonlight, he found he had landed in sand, amid the crisping remains of the ephemerals that had flowered that spring. He grunted and took another swig of the Edradour, carefully putting the plastic-sleeved spore print sheet into his vest pocket. He felt remarkably clearheaded in his thoughts, despite what the scotch seemed to be doing to his physical coordination.

He pondered that mind-body split, then picked up a seed capsule from one of the blown flowers and rubbed it between his thumb and forefinger. The desert ephemerals had bloomed in great profusion all through the spring, the result of the long rains. Jacinta had always loved the desert blooms, especially during El Niño years. The past winter's rains had been the result of the fourth big southern oscillation since she disappeared. The El Niños were coming more frequently and lasting longer, or the climate had gone into a permanent El Niño cycle, as some claimed. Greenhouse warming making the weather more chaotic, extreme, unpredictable. Or something.

Looking at the intricate seed capsule in the light of the rising full moon, it seemed to him that the natural world possessed an old dreaming wisdom, deeper and more subtle than human knowledge. We're arrogant upstarts, he thought, to believe our few thousand years of technology, our few hundreds of years of science, could be wiser than the wisdom embedded in the systems this planet has dreamed up on its own over billions of years.

Wilderness is the great unconsciousness where the world dreams, he thought—setting off an inebriated cascade of ideas. Conscious creatures desperately need that. If we don't dream we don't learn. Evolution is life's long, unconscious learning. To wipe out species is to end learning. We've been burning the classrooms and killing the students for a long time.

Falling back full length on the sandy patch he'd stumbled into, Paul stared up at the night sky and drank down the last of the Edradour. The warm sizzle of the scotch trickled slowly through his body, moment after moment. *A sandy-haired man trying to sink into the sand—that's what I am,* Paul thought with a smile.

The world is a given, he speculated to himself. *Even death. All science and engineering have been reverse engineering, when you think about it. Just trying to figure out how it's all put together, how it all works. Maybe the goal of the mind is to engineer an escape from the mortal technology of the body. The way the nervous system and the immune system are hooked up together in the same network . . . maybe consciousness itself is a sort of super immune system, trying to develop immunity to mortality. Maybe in the end death does not conquer consciousness; consciousness conquers death.*

"I must be drunker than I thought," he said with a laugh, "to be thinking things like this."

Thinking of Jacinta, however, he grew more somber. Tonight was the tenth anniversary of her disappearance. It was probably all too reasonable to conclude that she must be dead by now.

At the thought of her death, however, Paul was never able to cry—at least not while he was awake. He had never cried for her, yet, whenever he thought deeply of her, he somehow always found himself on the verge of tears. He told himself it was all too deep for tears, yet he feared the tears might be too deep for him—that, once he allowed himself to cry, he'd never be able to stop, that it would break down the dam he'd built in his soul and overwhelm his small sanity in the flood of his grief.

Since Jacinta's disappearance, he had "gone on" with his life, but differently. His destiny had gone awry, like a Jesus who wakes up to find he's thirty-four and has somehow missed the Crucifixion. Jacinta would understand about messiahs gone awry, he thought.

Paul didn't know if there was quite enough of himself left over to cover up the hole in the universe Jacinta's going had left behind. He had returned to the area near Caracamuni three years back, hoping to find a spot in space and time for mourning his loss, but the mountain he knew was gone, vanished. Space and time couldn't fill the void.

He felt so full of emptiness. He did not know if he went on rushing into nothing, or if nothing went on rushing into him. He did know, however, that the only things that stood against the dark tide were his memories, bright shadows cast inside the stone bubble of his skull, soft-tissued fossils that refused to die.

He looked at the empty bottle and wished it were a loaded gun.

A nearby unsteady alteration in the steady constellations caught his eye and he glanced toward it. As he stared, he saw a shifting—like the bending of light in water, a rippling piece of the night sky—coming toward him. *Constellations are hallucinations turned into explanations by tradition and education,* he thought with a giddy, drunken flourish.

But no. He stood up slowly, watching more carefully whatever it was that was approaching. His heart pounded and he thought irrationally of Jacinta returning.

The shifting piece of the sky was almost on top of him before it stopped, a droning whisper of engines whirring in the moonlight close above him. A bright light flashed onto the ground near him, then probed toward him.

Aw, Jeez, Paul thought, *I'm not drunk enough to be abducted by aliens.*

Something like a cross between a gangplank and a jetway extended downward into the cone of light, toward him. Amazed, he lost his grip on the empty Edradour bottle. It slipped from his hands and fell to the sand.

"Hello, Dr. Larkin!" said an amplified voice. "Please come aboard!"

Paul reached up and touched a safety rail, just to make sure this was all real. At least it felt real. He began to step upward into whatever kind of craft it was that was hovering above him.

Two thirds of the way up the incline, the pluperfectly perky Ms. Griego, the venture capital agent, stood waiting on a step, beaming a smile of considerable wattage at him, above a midnight blue dress of a cut and style that might well have suited a stewardess aboard a low-altitude, high-speed, deep-penetration bomber of the 1960s, if such aircraft had *had* stewardesses.

"Congrats, Paul!" Athena Griego said, shaking his hand vigorously and practically hauling him up the last third of the incline. "Dr. Vang is so interested in your fungus's possibilities he's come to speak with you himself!"

Paul was bedazzled by more than just the sudden brightness of the light. The craft he had boarded seemed solid enough, yet also airy and diaphanous, as if the legendary Great Airship of 1887 and the flying saucers of the second half of the twentieth century had met and mated, to produce this craft as their offspring.

"What is this thing?" Paul asked, bewildered as his eyes kept trying to readjust to the light. He stepped into what looked like a cabin in a spacious yacht, all dark wood inlaid with mother-of-pearl. "And who is Dr. Vang?"

"That would be me," said a small Asian man in a very neat suit, coming forward to shake Paul's hand. The man looked to be in his sixties. "I suppose the most important thing for you to know about who I am is that I have money to invest in research on your fungus."

Ms. Griego ushered them toward an off-white sofa and wheat-colored chairs where a cup of coffee was already waiting for him. Paul glanced around. In the center of the room was an elliptically shaped wet bar. Literally wet, for the mirror-backed pedestal that supported the bar also encased a salt-water aquarium: a living coral reef with anemones and sea fans, crabs and shrimp, eels and other fish less extreme in shape but more extreme in hue—blues and yellows and greens and reds so vivid and radiant Paul was tempted to look for their power packs.

"And this? . . ." he asked, gesturing to indicate the cabin and the larger structure within which it was embedded.

"My mobile 'home sweet home,'" Vang said with a small smile, sipping at his coffee. "My ghost ship, if you like."

"Ghost ship?" Paul asked, sipping his coffee, too, initially out of politeness if nothing else. Good coffee, though. Very good.

"I like my privacy," Vang said with a seemingly disinterested shrug. His voice, however, could not hide a certain pride as he went on to describe the features of his flying home. "Several of my companies were involved in building it. Technically, it's a stealth airship. An 'invisiblimp,' if you like, though it's more accurate to call it an invisible dirigible, since it has an airframe. The wind-duction system that propels it also gives it superquiet hovering capability. Its engines leave virtually no infrared signature. Its structure both absorbs and bounces radar away tangentially. Engineers at ParaLogics and Crystal Memory jointly developed a chameleon-cloth smartskin for it—protective coloration, fast-reactive camouflage. In a cloudy sky it's a cloud, in a blue sky it's a piece of blue sky. On a moonless night like tonight, it's obsidian, a soft-edged arrowhead flecked with stars."

Vang smiled at his turn of phrase, but Paul was looking into the space above the other man's head.

"Built for you?" Paul asked, taking it all in. "Or for something a bit more covert?"

"If I answered that, I'd have to kill you," Vang said with a little laugh. "One could speculate, however, that—unlike satellites, which pass high and fast over any particular point of interest—a ship like this might be able to go in low and slow, to linger longer over whatever one might be interested in. . . ."

"How did you get one?" Paul asked as he continued to take in the features of Vang's private airship.

"Alas, for all its stealthy virtues," Vang continued, "it *was* detectable by certain oversight committees, even hidden deep in the black budget. The politics of project funding shot it down before it ever went into production. I bought back the prototype."

Paul sipped more of his coffee, puzzled. He had heard of ParaLogics—high tera- and even peta-flops machines, if he recalled right. Vang's name was also obscurely familiar.

"But if your work is in aerodynamics and computing," Paul asked, "I don't quite understand your interest in the fungus I brought back from Caracamuni."

Vang nodded thoughtfully.

"Are computing and mycology really that far apart?" Vang asked rhetorically. "Think about it. In my lifetime alone I have seen the Age of Code dawning. The instructions for organic life were deciphered with the cracking of the DNA code and the mapping of genomes. The instructions for artificial life were enciphered with the encoding of languages for digital and biological computing. Mushroom mycelial networks are a good analog for parallel processing. Together the biotech and infotech revolutions are transforming Earth into Codeworld. Which it always already was, of course. My associates and I are multidisciplinary enough to see the overlap."

Paul's eyes strayed toward the colorful fish swimming about the reef in the wet bar, but his mind was focused on Vang's words.

"Associates?" he asked. "You're not just representing yourself and your companies, then?"

Ms. Griego smiled her floodlight smile.

"Dr. Vang represents a consortium with a variety of interests," she replied, glancing at Vang for confirmation.

"To what purpose?" Paul asked.

Ms. Griego looked briefly flummoxed. Vang broke in, freeing Athena Griego to depart from them and go on about some undisclosed business out of sight.

"Allow me to tell you a little story that may or may not be true," Vang said, looking up at him. Paul shrugged and Vang continued. "When I've finished, consider me an unofficial source who will deny ever having told you the story I'm about to tell you. Let's say that, once upon a time, there was something called the Cold War—a period when each side mirrored the horror of the other, both invoking doctrines of Mutual Assured Destruction. Let's say that, during that Cold War, there were various intelligence agencies, whose work, too, on whichever side, tended to mirror the work of their opposite numbers. Let's say that, in their looking-glass world, groups on opposite sides of the mirror began making secret contacts with each other. All right so far?"

"I follow you," Paul said. "Go on."

"Let's say further," Vang continued, "that the motive for these contacts was a shared fear. At the time, these opposite numbers—very intelligent and foresighted people, mind you—were afraid one or another of the various powers would sooner or later start a war that would result in the planet being nuked to uninhabitable status. Let's say further that, as a result of their meetings, they started working on what they called 'depth survival.' "

"Which was?" Paul asked, staring into his coffee cup.

"An attempt to see to it that some remnant of human population and civilization would be preserved," Vang explained, "even through the very worst of their worst-case scenarios."

Depth survival. Paul thought of the old rumors of vast, secret underground bases and covert subterranean cities—apocryphal tales that had flourished in the loonier reaches of Cold and post–Cold War paranoia. He quickly brushed the visions away with a mental sweep of the hand, however.

"But the Cold War ended," Paul said, puzzled. "Where were your depth-survival programs then?"

"Let's say the security apparats' mirror-horror world really did end, as you suggest," Vang continued, quietly. "The Cold War and older Soviet-style socialism both collapsed, despite occasional atavisms. Biblical Armageddon and socialist Utopia both disappeared from the radar screen. Where were the depth survivors' reasons to keep on keeping on?"

Paul nodded but said nothing.

"Let's say that, at that time," Vang said, "the security organizations these depth survival programs were embedded in were themselves struggling to survive. Let's say those organizations were metamorphosing from national security apparatuses into corporate espionage and international intelligence brokers."

"Which they have increasingly become," Paul said, pondering it.

"Perhaps," Vang said without inflection. "Let's say the end of the Cold War period forced those participating in the depth survival programs to take a very long view of the human future. From the perspective of their looking-glass world, when the mirror shatters, the shatters also mirror."

"How's that?" Paul asked.

Vang glanced thoughtfully around the cabin.

"Let's say their think-tank experts looked around," Vang said, "and saw that human beings were simultaneously becoming obsolete *and* a glut on the market. Let's say they recognized—popular media fantasies notwithstanding—that, for a global civilization once past the threat of total spasm nuclear war, the more likely and immediate dangers are not killer asteroids or alien invasions but the daily, ongoing destruction of habitat occasioned by human population growth and humanity's own expanding powers."

"The death of a thousand small cuts," Paul said. "The frog in the pot under which the flame is being slowly turned up—too slowly for it to notice."

"Exactly," Vang said, pleased. "As far as planetary carrying capacity was concerned, let's say the depth planners' most reasonable projections placed global human populations deep into an ecocatastrophic overshoot phase fifty years from their time zero."

"That's glut—and maybe gluttony," Paul said with a nod, "but I don't see the obsolescence."

Vang smiled again.

"Even glut means obsolescence," he continued. "For creatures like ouselves that can build artificial brains and alter DNA, 'Be fruitful and multiply' is an obsolete biological imperative."

Ooh boy, Paul thought. Such ideas weren't likely to make Vang popular in the Vatican, or Salt Lake City either, for that matter.

"But you mean the *other* types of obsolescence the planners might have contemplated, I suppose," Vang continued. "Might they have asked themselves, too, whether, particularly since the nineteenth century, industrial mechanisms had already increasingly obviated the need for human muscle? In the twentieth century, didn't informational mechanisms begin making many capabilities of the human mind superfluous as well?"

"I see your point," Paul said, not considering the idea quite as philosophically as Vang had.

"Let's say, then, their experts were forced to reconsider their scenarios," Vang continued. "The older, deeper questions they asked themselves had been something like: Are we and our organizations good? Are humans good? The new questions might well have been different: not only What are they and their organizations good *for*, but also *What are humans good for?*"

"I presume they came up with an answer," Paul said after a downing a strong slug of coffee.

"In their own way," Vang said slowly, looking at the aquarium in the wet bar as if contemplating the possibilities hidden in its waters. "Maybe their own fears of the death and meaninglessness of their organizations got tangled up with their search. Let's give them the benefit of the doubt and say what they finally came to was the idea that human consciousness was our unique contribution—and our best hope for avoiding the doom of becoming the reef of our own shipwreck."

"Reef?" Paul asked, then shook his head. "I don't quite follow you."

By way of answer, Vang got up and walked toward the wet bar, with its enclosed coral reef. On impulse, Paul got up and followed him, taking his cup of coffee in hand.

"Do you know how a coral reef grows, Dr. Larkin?"

Paul crouched down and looked at the miniature reef in Vang's bar.

"Coral polyps," Paul said. "Soft-bodied creatures, coelenterates—kind of like jellyfish, only they settle down and secrete stony skeletons around themselves. The old skeletons are what most of the reef is made of."

"Exactly," Vang said, pleased in an almost teacherly manner, "except that the polyps are actually *excreting* the calcium that goes to make up the stone of the reef. Like most marine organisms, they have to dispose of excess calcium, so why not use it for building? They're not the last animal to turn a waste product into a resource, either. Not by a long shot."

Although he could have done without the lecture on a fine point of invertebrate biology, Paul nodded.

"We humans," Dr. Vang continued, "when we hunted and gathered, used to be rather like the jellyfish, nomadically drifting about the world. Eventually, however, we settled down and begin to secrete cities and civilizations around ourselves. Think of the 'reef' as the growth of human populations throughout history, along with our 'excretions,' all our trash and toxins, all the buried cities beneath and just outside our cities. The reef is the conversion of what is 'not us' *into* us and our products. The reef is that *something* reaching toward the light, as the past it is built upon sinks slowly deeper into darkness. The 'ship' is the full set of possible human scientific and technological capabilities. The 'ocean' is the medium of spacetime."

Paul stared at the colorful reef in the tank, not yet catching Vang's meaning.

"But what does it mean to say we will become the 'reef of our own shipwreck'?" he asked, still trying to puzzle out that saying's weird, nondual duality.

"What if we don't learn to turn all our rubbish into resources?" Vang said. "What if our reproductions and toxic productions outpace our capacity for invention? What if our biology and our technology converge in a mutually destructive fashion? What if we persist in our deep denial of the paradoxical fact that our very *success* as a species is the single greatest *threat* to our future survival as a species?"

Suddenly Paul got what Vang was driving at. Watching the pleasant play of fish round and about stone, he suddenly saw the underwater scene more darkly, as if an unseen cloud had passed across the face of an unseen sun.

"Then the ship will crack up on the reef," he said quietly, "spewing toxins that will kill the reef in turn. A pretty grim scenario."

"Potentially, yes," Vang said. "The two best alternatives to it would seem to be either learning to control the rate of the reef's growth or, failing that, leaping out of the ocean entirely, toward that 'light' beyond space and time that we've always been growing toward. That's where your fungus comes in."

Paul stood up—still a bit wobbly, despite the coffee—trying to imagine coral polyps leaping from the ocean and flying like pulsing jellyfish toward the sun. He looked at Vang.

"Sounds like you're talking about either something for controlling population growth or for traveling faster than light," Paul said with a small smile. "I really have no idea how that fungus I brought back could help with either one."

"You don't?" Vang said, as if he didn't quite believe Paul. The older man walked into the ellipse of the bar. "My associates and I do. We have several ideas—and we are willing to pay you quite generously for the right to investigate those possibilities."

Vang gestured at a thinscreen document that had at that moment appeared in the top of the bar. Paul scanned the document, which read his eyes as he read it, so that it obligingly went to the next page each time he finished the previous one. The document, he saw, was a contract between Paul Larkin and something called the Tetragrammaton Consortium. The contract made Paul both a consultant and a senior research scientist with Tetragrammaton, in addition to paying him quite handsomely for the right to patent any materials extracted from the *Cordyceps* fungus he had brought back with him from Caracamuni tepui. The amounts of money involved were extravagant beyond his most avaricious dreams.

When he had finished reading the document, he straightened up, stunned.

"Does the contract not meet with your approval?" Dr. Vang asked, concerned.

"Wha—?" Paul asked, disoriented. "No, it's fine. Generous."

"Good, good!" Dr. Vang said. "But then, what's the problem?"

"I'm not sure," Paul said. "It's just that this is all happening so fast, like some kind of anti–James Bond scenario."

Vang smiled broadly, pleasantly surprised by the Bond comparison. Maybe it brought up some kind of memory from the old man's childhood, Paul thought.

"How exactly do you mean?" Vang asked eagerly.

"Instead of the billionaire telling Bond how he intends to destroy the world and kill Bond—" Paul began.

"Here I am, another billionaire, telling you how I intend to save the world," Vang said, nodding enthusiastically.

—and give me a reason to go on living, Paul thought, though he did not say it.

"Right," Paul said. "What we've talked about smacks of the same sort of 'great man's conspiracy theory of history,' for me anyway. I've never believed in such theories. People just can't plan that thoroughly, or keep secrets that long."

Vang smiled slyly, but then covered it with a shrug.

"The greatest conspiracy is the one that says there are no conspiracies," Vang said, handing him a phone. "Think of this as a conspiracy for *good*, if you like. We have taken the liberty of running the contract past your lawyer, particularly in regard to the clauses on intellectual property rights. We have her on the line. Here . . ."

Vang handed him the receiver. Paul talked to Sarah Campbell, his legal adviser in the all-too-recent debacle with his former university employer. She very much approved of the contract and spoke forcefully in favor of it. Paul handed the receiver back to Vang, who nodded and gave it to Athena Griego, who appeared again in her B-58 Hustler stewardess's dress, seemingly out of nowhere.

"Ms. Griego is our agent and witness in this matter," Vang continued, handing Paul an electronic stylus. "If you feel confident enough of the document to sign, please do."

Without another thought and with only a glance at the fish in the aquarium, Paul signed. Vang smiled broadly and shook his hand again.

"Welcome aboard indeed, Dr. Larkin. Happy to have you with us. My ghost ship is at your disposal. We will send someone for your car. Where would you like to go?"

"West," Paul said, lost in thought. "Oh, and I left an empty bottle of scotch on the sand when you stopped for me. If someone might pick that up . . ."

Vang nodded. The sound of the invisible dirigible's engines rose slightly as it pivoted on its axis. The spore print, folded in paper enfolded in plastic, hung lightly over Paul's heart inside his vest pocket, invisible with Paul inside the belly of Vang's stealthy machine, heading west at a tenth of the speed of sound, rising into night above the Sierra Nevada.

Weird-Wired

Jiro sat bolt upright. He knew that he was dead, but his mouth still worked.

"!Begursprocketbombonanacatl?" he mouthed. He was trying to say how, if you try to throw your arms around the world, they'll nail you to a cross and say it was a workplace accident because you were employed as a carpenter. "?Losangelatintinnabiledictu!" he said, thinking he was saying how, if you try to communicate your uncomfortable piece of the truth, they'll assassinate you for it for your own peace of mind.

"Jeez, Jiro!" Seiji said angrily from his bed in the dark bedroom they shared. "You're talking in your sleep again! Wake up, for God's sake!"

"Wha—?"

"You were talking in your sleep," Seiji said again. "Go back to sleep."

Silence. Then Jiro blurting, "Was not!" before he fell horizontal again. He felt his eyelids closing, but now he fought against sleep, trying to make sense of his night visions.

He had dreamed of a religion of flowers, not a religion of blood. A religion of bees, not a religion of ashes.

Whoa, I'd better not tell anyone about that, he thought. He still remembered how, back in second grade, he had scandalized the nuns at Guardian Angels School when they found him wandering around on the school playground with his arms stretched out like a soaring bird, like an eagle dancer, like Christ on the cross. The nuns were supposed to be brides of Christ, but apparently they preferred their spouse safely gone from the flesh—and they'd carefully punished Jiro for his imitation reincarnation of their groom.

Maybe he really was "weird-wired," as the neighborhood kids in every neighborhood he'd ever lived in had so often suggested in their not-so-subtle ways. Always there had been the strange mismatches, the overlaps, the double exposures in his picture of the world. The nights of sitting suddenly bolt upright in bed, spewing streams of seemingly incoherent speaking-in-tongues gibberish, were bad and never infrequent enough—it drove his brother Seiji crazy—but that was nowhere near the beginning of Jiro's problems.

Even as a small child he had not just seen and talked with imaginary friends but also had experienced flashes of entire alternate realities, leakage from parallel worlds and other people's dreams. Strangers, yet very much like himself in so many ways. He had never been able to put together what his parents told him with what the world told him, either. For as long as he could remember, whenever any reference to sex came up on the TV, in movies or holos, his mother always shut it away from her boys. Surely there must be something dirty and evil there, for his mother to always react so, but he had never been able to figure out precisely what it was.

Jiro remembered a greenhouse summer evening six or seven years back, when he'd been tagging after Seiji and a neighbor kid, Rudy, as usual. When Seiji began to talk with Rudy about girls, Jiro had run home shouting and crying, "Mom! Mom! Seiji and Rudy are talking about sex!" After that, Seiji had looked at him with a mixture of fear and disgust.

Jiro was shy and backward and awkward. In the one-size-fits-all world, he just didn't fit in. He didn't like seeing his own face in the mirror. Something about the widow's peak in his dark, wavy hair, the wide-open innocence (always too soft and too lost) that his brown eyes imparted to his too-round face—all boyish to the point of femininity. He was good-looking for a boy, but too girlish to look like a man.

In two years, when he finished his undergraduate degree in computer media studies, he would be eighteen—a precociousness that hadn't much helped. The mismatch was worst when it came to girls and dating and all the indecipherable rites of contemporary courtship. He pedestalized the girls from afar, unable to approach them. In his mind they were pure as bright, shining light—brilliance that he would never dare darken with the shadow of his lust.

Jiro took refuge in books and the Net and the life of the mind. In his research and reading he had found a term for his condition: "socially maladroit." Ever since he entered his teens, he had withdrawn more, cocooned himself. Socially, he had gone into cybernation, but that was okay. More and more people his age were doing that. All the experts said they would grow out of it.

This was a world worth withdrawing from, what with the rise of the churchstaters and all. He glanced at one of Seiji's obnoxious glow-in-the-dark holoposters, which showed a montage of humanity's wars, murders, mayhem, fanaticism, famine, plagues, and pollution, all being watched by wide-eyed, antennaed young aliens, the cautionary caption reading PROFESSIONALLY TRAINED STUNT SPECIES! DO NOT TRY THIS ON HOME PLANET.

That about said it. The more esoteric he became and the farther away from mundane existence he got, the better. For years Jiro had been fascinated by birds, and from them he came to be intrigued by eagle dancers—then generally fascinated by Native Americans, by indigenous peoples of the New World and their lifeways. The walls of his side of the room were covered with full-color holos of birds of prey, crowded with external memory media about New World indigenes. He had participated in online debates about the first arrival of humans in the New World, the old controversies surrounding Indian gaming, the reality or hoax of the South American tepui that had lifted off a decade and more ago—all manner of things distant enough to distract him from his daily life.

With his brother Seiji he had tried to talk about his problems, but he'd never gotten very far. There seemed always to be a barrier of enforced normalcy between them—a glass fishbowl wall. That made a certain sense, since Seiji had been intrigued by tropical fresh and saltwater fish and by fishbowl-helmeted astronauts for as long as Jiro could remember. To Seiji's aquarist-astronaut way of thinking, any problem the Yamaguchi brothers could admit to having was the product of their being *happa*—half Nipponese, half Anglo—in what was still largely a Caucasian-dominated culture. Add to that being raised male with a "docile daddy" and a "domineering mommy" and that could explain a multitude of problems, at least according to Seiji. To Jiro it seemed his brother overstated the case: His father was at worst "gentle," his mother at best "assertive." The fact that they weren't likely to get a better set of parents—and that there were others probably far worse—*that* didn't dent Seiji's theorizing one bit.

If Jiro felt that the world leaked dreams, that he dreamed in other people's heads and other people dreamed in his head—that was simply paranoia, by his brother's reckoning. Seiji was particularly big on the once-repudiated but now revived theories of "schizophrenogenic mothers" and "marital skew."

"It's no surprise we're mentally bent," Seiji said. "Home environment plays an etiological role in the development of schizophrenia—especially when a father has yielded to a dominant mother, so that the father doesn't provide a strong, masculine role model for the male child."

Jiro suspected his older brother was parroting what he had heard in his Intro to Psychology course. That psych stuff was all too simple an answer, however—especially when the renewed popularity of such "blame Mom" theories was really more about keeping women in their place than anything else. Jiro soon stopped looking for answers in that psychosocial direction. Someday he might get desperate enough to seek them there again, but he hoped not.

He had searched through print and screen and the whole infosphere for answers—from science and religion, theology and technology. He suspected that his experience of this leakage of dreams *between* minds was not just some odd effect arising from the drugs-and-divinity-obsessed zeitgeist of a Fundamentalizing America. It was an effect of something much deeper—of something he could only describe to himself as a unity in the universe, profound and undeniable, always there, no matter how hard it might be to pin down, as if they were *all* being dreamed more and more distinctly into existence—from latent to blatant being—by a single Mind.

That was not what he found in his research, however. From his searching it seemed to him that, over the past century and more, bleeding-edge theology had been pushing toward a religion without transcendence, and bleeding-edge technology had been pushing toward a transcendence without religion.

He flirted with the idea of joining the Cyberite sect for a while. Their great myth was a messianic faith in the power of media—the idea that, if a correct-thinking band of rebel do-gooders could just take control of all global media for a few minutes, and in those few minutes broadcast The Truth to the entire planet, all humanity's problems would be solved. Jiro quickly came to suspect, however, that the Cyberite myth failed to take into account the fact that most people—when hit with too much confusing or uncomfortable or abrupt truth—quickly fall back on their established prejudices to do their thinking for them.

The more conventional religions weren't much different. Media, Gospel, Logos: What was the difference, really? For all the traditionalists' talk of original sin, it seemed to Jiro that sin was never very original. Mostly, it seemed to be copied from parents and friends and neighbors and the whole social world, as far as he could tell. He searched the infosphere for a sustainable religion—one whose first law was *not* "Make more disciples!"—but he was damned if he could find one.

All the traditional systems seemed to reduce human life to a chain letter sent by God or Global Operations Director or DNA. In one form or another, the missive prophesied that, if he followed the genetic generic rules and kept the Message going (Procreate! Propagate the faith! Expand market share!), Good Things would happen to him, his stock would split and rise in value, he would go to heaven. But woe to him if he ever broke the chain of double-helical commandments—Bad Fortune would befall him, his stock would crash, he would go to hell.

So much of theology was so full of tautologies, it seemed to Jiro, but even that was to be expected. The world's religions, in their various ways and paths to The Truth, had about them the false eternity and infinity of an endless march along a Möbius strip, and Möbius strips always made a one-sided argument. Purely materialist science wasn't the way through either. An event horizon of perpetual approximation, a reference-frame illusion clothing a star's collapse down to the unknowable nowhere and nowhen of naked singularity, the reductive scientific approach seemed to him at best a black hole promising to someday explode with The Answer—though its fuse, unfortunately, was calculated to be far longer than the lifetime of the universe.

Still, he hoped that buried within the dogmas of religion and the theories of science he would find some strong hint of the sustainable and sustaining faith of which he dreamed. His search had so far proved fruitless—and profoundly frustrating. Tomorrow, he thought sleepily, he would post something about his search in the infosphere. If others accused him of possessing a moral compass askew from their own versions of the due and true directions, well, it wouldn't be the end of the world. Thinking about what he would post, Jiro grew slowly more content and settled in his heart.

The end of the world, he thought sleepily. So many ways in which the world can end. So few in which it can keep on going—only *differently*. If there was to be a close to the Great Day of the world, Jiro planned to stay past The End to watch the credits scroll up the sky. In the meantime, he could still believe in a religion not of blood but of flowers, a world that did not assassinate and crucify but lovingly embraced all the many pieces of truth it contained—even if such a wonderland could as yet be realized only in his dreams.

Bowling with Death

D riving out of Wyoming, Mike Dalke's car scared loose a swift-running mob of pronghorn antelope from beside the road. They were beautiful, running beside the car, pacing it with a grace no construct of metal and polymer could ever hope to match. Tears came to his eyes. He had never seen them like this before. He feared he would never see them again.

He could never go back home again, certainly. Not given the way he had left.

Mom had been enraged, irrational, ranting about how her boy's mind must have been seduced by the secular humanist conspirators—the poisonous alphabet soup of ACLU, NAACP, NOW, etc., with Hollywood producers and even Unitarianism thrown in for good measure. Dad watched quietly out of his usual prescription-tranquilizer evening funk.

"What do you mean, you're moving out?" his mother shrilled.

Mike put down his rucksack and faced the blond fury of his mother moving to physically block his path.

"Just what I said, Mom. I'm moving to the West Coast. I've transferred from Christian Heritage University to California State University at Humboldt. I want to do my graduate work there."

"Well, you can just 'untransfer' yourself right now, genius!" she spat. "You're always thinking of yourself—what *you* want to do. Think of your parents and what *we* want you to do, for once!"

"I never stop thinking of that," he said with a weary sigh. "No more. I'm going to live my own life now. You can't live it for me, and I won't let you."

"Your own life! Your own life!" Mom mocked, suddenly brandishing an eight-inch-long kitchen knife before her. "I've given my whole life for you boys! Waited on you hand and foot! And this is the kind of gratitude you show me? Oh, no—no son of mine is going to move out until he finishes college or gets married!"

She jabbed toward Mike with the broad meat-slicer's blade.

"Honey!" Dad cried, startled, but Mike was already moving, deflecting and taking his mother's cutting hand, using her own momentum against her the way the Christian Martial Arts teacher at CHU had showed him. He brought his fist up and slugged his own mother hard on the jaw before he really knew what he was doing. The blade skittered across the floor. She crumbled against one wall and burst into tears.

Dad put a restraining hand on his shoulder. Mike shrugged it off.

"You only waited on us hand and foot to bind us hand and foot to you," Mike said bitterly, bending down to pick up his rucksack as his mother sobbed and moaned against the wall. Behind him, his younger brother Ray was witness to it all, but Mike had been too angry to say anything to him, too angry for farewells.

He regretted that now. Who knew what seeing such things might do to his younger brother's head? But Mike had to get out. Living at home had been like living underwater. Each day he felt his airflow being cut off a little bit more. Soon he would have woken up soul-dead and not even noticed.

No, there was no going back. Not since his car had broken down east of Wendover, Utah. Not since he'd had no choice but to sell it to the *Salvia div*-chewing mechanic/tow truck operator who had hauled him and his vehicle into town. Not since he'd stuck out his thumb in the late-afternoon light and gotten picked up by an ancient four-wheel-drive station wagon hauling a rental trailer.

At the other end of the station wagon's bench seat now sat a heavyset guy with steel-rimmed specks and long gray hair down to the middle of his back (but who was, nonetheless, also scrupulously clean-shaven). The driver, which he was, had recently become an ex–Information Technology administrator from the university in Bozeman. Mike didn't catch his full name—Brewster, Schuster, something like that—but the gray-haired man in plaid shirt and brown pants and blue gimme cap was, at the moment, clearly trying to forget his own woes through permanently altering his state of consciousness.

"I took it with what grace I could," said the defrocked administrator, passing Mike a burning flat pipe of marijuana somewhere between Elko and Winnemucca. The gray-haired man suddenly laughed. "The university bureaucracy is a real hippo hierarchy."

"How's that?" Mike asked, curious despite himself, absently scratching the brownish-blond goatee he'd begun growing not long before he left home and which was still at the itchy (or at least unfamiliar) stage.

"Hippopotami range themselves in a river current according to status," the older man explained. "The highest-ranking individual takes a position alone and farthest upstream, facing upstream. The rest of the hippos fall into tiers and denser numbers downstream, though they're facing upstream, too. Each hippo has a short, flat, paddlelike tail that it spins like a propeller when it defecates. That breaks up its dung into a cloud of fragments."

Mike laughed at the image but didn't quite get it.

"How's that fit a university bureaucracy?" he asked.

The man with the long gray hair inhaled deeply from the pipe and held the smoke a moment before answering in a constrained, smoke-conserving voice.

"The lower the rank of a hippo the more dung comes hurtling at it from upstream," he said, exhaling at last. "When the hippo shit hits the propeller, the consequences flow downstream."

They laughed at that. Mike guessed it was pretty much true of hierarchies everywhere.

"How about you?" the man with the long gray hair asked, uncapping a bottle of vodka. "What's made you a gentleman of the highway?"

Mike told the older man more of his own story than he had initially intended to: his troubles at home, his father's psychological problems, his decision to transfer to a different college out of state and away from home—as well as the crisis that decision had precipitated. The gray-haired man remained quiet until they were well west of Winnemucca.

"Here," the driver said at last, breaking up a capsule and tapping its contents into the vodka. He swirled the bottle. "I put a little KL in this. Good for what ails you. It'll help you forget about the latest explosion in your nuclear family."

Mike didn't know what "KL" was, but he took a healthy swallow of the vodka. It had an unexpectedly bitter, alkaline taste.

"That phrase, 'nuclear family,' is more descriptive than you might think," the older man continued. "If you head just about due south of here you eventually cross into what used to be the Nevada Nuclear Weapons Test Site. $E=mc^2$ and all that. In most ancient-creation myths 'energy' is male and 'matter' is female. Yang and yin. Bright and dark. Even the words: 'Energy' is from Greek roots meaning 'at work,' and the Latin root of 'matter' is *mater*—mother."

"Yeah?" Mike said, not making the connection. "So?"

"So Einstein's mass-energy equivalency is a real gender bender," the driver said. "Energy, the male principle, is equivalent to mass, or female matter, times the constant of the unbreakable law, the speed of light, squared. Maleness is femaleness raised by the law times itself."

"And the test site?" Mike asked, wondering what he'd gotten himself into hitching a ride with this guy.

"The detonation of the first nuclear device—at Trinity site in Los Alamos, not Nevada—*that* was a supreme yang moment," said the older man. "Manipulate enough female matter in the right way and you can produce a blast of male energy. All the Nevada nuclear blasts were little boys emulating the Fat Man, our own little test site imitations of the primal wank, the Father-spurt of the Big Bang."

The driver gave him a sly, sideways glance. Mike laughed.

"I don't think you can gender-blenderize it quite that much," Mike said, trying to be serious.

"Why not?" the driver asked. "Humans sexualize everything, especially since Freud. Do you think it was just a coincidence that when human beings first set foot on the Moon—a heavenly body associated in most cultures with goddesses and femaleness—all the original explorers were *male* and the program was named after Apollo, a *sun god?* The Apollo astronauts were white-garbed priests of the sun god, arriving in burning chariots to claim dominion over the female Moon. Yang over yin, see?"

Weird stuff, Mike thought, but what he said was, "One person's technology is another person's symbol, I guess."

"Exactly," the driver agreed, nodding. "When I lived in San Francisco, there were these big round-topped concrete pillars that were put in place as barriers to traffic flow, near parks and such. South Asian immigrants began garlanding these traffic piers with flowers and pouring offerings of milk over the tops of the damn things. Know why?"

"Not a clue," Mike said. Whatever it was the driver had put in that vodka, it had begun to make him feel woozy, disoriented.

"For those immigrant folks, the traffic piers were lingam symbols and became impromptu shrines," the driver said. "Or just look at the cross. For the Romans, crucifixion was a capital-punishment technology. The Christians made it a sign of martyrdom and resurrection, the central symbol of faith. Kind of like worshiping an electric chair or lethal-injection table."

In the rock-of-ages Rocky Mountain states where Mike had been living most of his life, such thoughts were heresy—things that good people just didn't say. Although he had rejected the rigid faith of his parents and their neighbors, Mike still found the driver's analogy rather repugnant.

The driver seemed to sense something of his passenger's distaste. For whatever reason, he became quiet. Very soon, however, Mike was too preoccupied with the things going on in his head to notice the driver's silence. The colors of the sunset clouds to the west were *alive,* breathing and pulsing and writhing. Ahead, buildings got up from their foundations and walked into the highway, then quickly scurried back to their rightful places before Mike and the driver could run head-on into them. The driver seemed not to notice.

"Hey," Mike said at last, "what did you say that stuff was you put in the vodka?"

"KL," said the driver, smiling. "Ketamine lysergate 235. Also known as 'gate.' Either name is just as good. The latter name is slang and the former's probably a code name of some sort. The chemistry of it is most likely some weird tryptamine derivative—nothing to do with either LSD or ketalar, if you ask me."

"Natural?" Mike asked, thoughts lava-bubbling in his head. "Or designer?"

"Extracted from a mushroom," the driver said. "Strange history, though. Gate, the chemical, has been in circulation for a decade and more that I know of, yet the mushroom it supposedly comes from has only started showing up fairly recently. You'd figure it'd be the other way around. Why do you ask?"

"Because," Mike said, taking a deep (and deeply worried) breath, "I'm either hallucinating—or losing my mind."

The driver chuckled.

"Most likely it's the former," the gray-haired man said, not quite reassuringly enough. "Be careful, though. Keep your set and setting in mind. I suggest you seek out someplace you find familiar and comfortable. You're about an hour into it, so figure three more to go."

Mike looked at the driver carefully.

"Why?" he asked nervously. "Are you going someplace?"

The driver frowned momentarily.

"I assumed we would be splitting up in Reno," the gray-headed man said. "I'll be heading south down 395 toward San Bernardino, and you'll be heading north toward Humboldt. Reno seems the logical place to part company."

Mike nodded. The old headcase was probably right. That, however, didn't make him feel any less uneasy about being dropped off, alone, in an unfamiliar city, and in an altered state of consciousness.

Night fell and deepened. The driver told Mike his theory about KL's provenance, how the chemical extract might have come into circulation before the natural source did: "Maybe they—whoever *they* are—originally got a small sample from a medicine man somewhere in the jungle," the driver speculated, "but then couldn't find the true source for a while."

After that, however, the driver didn't have much more to say. His thoughts seemed to be elsewhere. Not far from the I-80 and Nevada 395 interchange, the driver exited and pulled over to let him out. Mike hefted up his rucksack from the backseat of the station wagon and reached into his back pocket for his wallet.

"No, no," the driver said, turning off his engine. "You don't owe me anything. I appreciated the company. You might want to spend a little time in Reno, though. Come down from the KL a bit before you go back on the road. A few hours, anyway."

"Okay," Mike said, shouldering his gear. "Thanks. Have a safe drive."

The gray-headed man nodded and touched the bill of his cap in salute.

"Right," he said, switching the engine and lights back on. "See yourself a new now." The driver must have noticed Mike's quizzical expression, for he explained—or thought he did. "Envision a better present. The future may be too late."

Mike smiled and nodded. The driver pulled his vehicle and trailer back onto the road, headed down Nevada 395. Mike turned and walked down the street. No other cars or people were about. Here off the highway, the place seemed eerily quiet, deserted. An empty city with all its lights still on.

The emptiness touched a deep chord in Mike. He remembered the insomnia he'd suffered through as a little kid, crying night after night because he couldn't sleep, crying because he feared he was the only creature left awake in all the universe. That was a terrible and frightening burden, to be so awake and so alone, in haunted, solitary free fall down the well of night, the fall growing worse the longer it went on. The loneliness had seemed to rush faster and faster upon him, until he feared he would overshoot the lost world of sleep completely.

Shaking the memory out of his head, Mike walked past discount stores and strip malls, thinking about the driver with his talk of nuclear bombs and astronauts, symbolic technologies and technological symbols. He thought of the gray-haired man driving through the night, into and through towns of people he would never know.

Mike stared up into the night sky, looking for those few bright stars and secret satellites that might shine down on him, despite Reno's star-killing fog of ambient light. Up there somewhere was the old international space station, hanging above the earth for as long as he could remember. Up there, too, construction was under way on the first of the new orbital habitats. He wondered which would be lonelier—looking down on empty cities with all their lights still on after some great depopulating disaster, or looking down and knowing that the cities were filled with billions of people you could never really know.

From a certain height tragedy ceases to be tragic, Mike thought, remembering it only as a quote from some philosopher or other. Maybe that numbing loftiness was the greatest tragedy of all—the tragedy of gods and of vast, impersonal, technorational societies. Maybe that was why people were trying to build little communities out there in space, human-made planetoids to shrink the world back down to human scale. So ordinary people wouldn't feel quite so much like ants under a wanton boy-god's burning glass—test subjects in a daily scientific experiment indistinguishable from mere cruelty.

Returning his gaze to the street, Mike noticed that he was quite a distance from any major casinos. The nearest buzzing place was Reno Lanes, a bowling alley a block ahead, toward which he quickly made his way.

Once inside, Mike couldn't tell whether the place was retro or just hadn't been remodeled since the 1950s. Garish neon and tacky furniture pummeled his senses from every angle. He seemed to have walked into somebody's dream vision of funky atomic futurism. The space before him was carpeted in star-spangled black, with blue and lime lines weaving back and forth in a pattern as haplessly meandering as a drunkard's walk home. Metallic orange-and-avocado cutouts of hyperBohrian planetary-orbital atoms, giant children's balls-and-jacks, huge asterisks without accompanying footnotes—all stood bolted onto the silvery-papered walls. The starscape ceiling was chandeliered with tail-finned rockets and ringed planets. Muzak from another dimension played over hidden speakers.

Taking a seat in a pucker-upholstered booth, Mike soon realized that the music coming over the speakers was thoroughly unrecognizable, weirdly distorted, reverbed, misdigitized. As he glanced at the menu, he wondered whether the KL was causing him to experience auditory hallucinations, or the bowling alley's speaker system was monumentally screwed up, or both. Whatever the cause, it was a very discomfiting experience.

A woman, garbed and made up like a waitress in Ming the Merciless's favorite Marsside cafe, asked Mike what he would have. The exhaustion in the thin, overworked woman's voice was faintly reassuring—an anchor of reality in the surreal world ballooning all around him. He ordered a shake and fries. When she turned toward the kitchen and left, he was sorry to see her go.

There was only one person bowling, someone dressed in what, at this distance, looked like an orange prison jumpsuit. Even a solitary bowler's game was more than noise enough for Mike in his current state, however. The Doppler shifting of the ball rolling down the lane began to say strange things to him—the mouthed and muttered echoes, in some benighted crowd, of unseen actors speaking from a hidden stage, talking of mind viruses and science-fiction religions and human fertility cults, telling him that the stars are gods and we are their ashen tears. . . .

His food came, blessedly breaking him out of the hastening downspiral of his thoughts. Mike ate, trying to concentrate on nothing but what he was eating. That activity, at least, was enough to fill his senses and his mind while the experience lasted.

He had just finished eating, laid out his money for the bill, and leaned back to relax and digest, arms outstretched atop the curved back of the booth, when someone tapped him on the shoulder.

"Hey," said a pale, hippo-corpulent man dressed in orange prison coveralls, "want to bowl a few frames? Knock 'em dead?"

Mike stared up at the man. His complexion was the color of bloated meat maggots. His eyes, behind his steel-rimmed spectacles, were the yellow-brown of grub worms' heads. His visage squirmed under long, wild, muddy gray-white hair that seemed as unhealthfully *alive* as a nest of poisonous snakes. The man and his appearance struck paralyzing fear into Mike's heart, so much so that he could only nod mutely in response to the bowler's request.

The pale, bloated bowler watched diligently as Mike traded his street shoes for bowling shoes, then signed for Mike to follow him. Walking along past the empty lanes, Mike could not help noticing that the pins were in fact people frozen in the same rigid, repeated stance. The bowling balls in the returns, too, were human skulls.

Once they reached the lane on which the bloated bowler had been warming up, the game began. They bowled frame after frame. Mike felt terrible as he bowled each skull down the alley and sent the rigor-stiff pin people flying—especially when he glimpsed the ghoulish, robo-zombie pinsetters working behind the scenes, then the reaper's scythe coming down and clearing the pins at the end of each frame—but he bowled his absolute best nonetheless, sensing that quite literally everything was at stake.

His pale, bloated opponent grew more and more furious as Mike maintained a slim lead into the final frames. At last the corpulent competitor could bear it no longer. In a fit of rage the bloated, maggot-skinned man snatched off his glasses, ripped off his own head, stuck his middle and ring fingers into his eye sockets and his thumb into his mouth, then gave the ball of his head a carefully aimed and mighty heave.

The flop-haired ball roared down the lane, shaking the whole building as it went—or rather the world was shaken by the thunder not of one ball moving down one lane, but of infinite and innumerable bowling balls moving down infinite and innumerable lanes. The instant all those myriad balls struck their ten-times-myriad pins, a mighty blast obliterated everything, the explosion hurling Mike cruciform into the air, sending him flying until his left shoulder caught on something.

"Hey," said someone, shaking his shoulder. "Sir. Sir!"

Mike woke to see, bent toward him, the waitress and a balding man in a dandruff-speckled suit with a tag that said KARL, MANAGER. Karl was shaking his shoulder and talking. "We're glad you liked our food and feel so comfortable here, but if you want to go on sleeping you'll have to find a hotel. Okay?"

"Yeah," Mike said, rubbing his eyes and mouth, looking around. The bowling alley was empty, except for the three of them. No one was bowling. "Okay."

Getting his gear together, he glanced at his watch and saw that he'd been asleep for nearly two hours. Getting up to leave, he noticed that the bowling alley now looked far more tawdry than surreal. Mike thought he must be coming down from the KL the driver had given him—a realization that brought him much relief, but also a little regret.

He had trusted to the kindness of strangers and it had gotten him a night out bowling with Death. *Are we having an adventure in moving yet?* Mike asked himself with a smirk. He'd had enough adventure for one trip, and enough trip for one adventure. Before he walked out of Reno Lanes, he asked the waitress for directions to the nearest bus station. She was only too happy to provide them.

A Shadow on Her Present

Catching Marty blissfully slow-convulsing on some perverse mix of alphanumeric chemicals—"delta nine and 5-MeO DMT," as his schnorrer-buddy Rick explained—had scared and infuriated Lydia at first. Now, however, with Marty okay and Rick ushered out of the apartment, Marty's secret drug escapade and Lydia's own unexpected return from a weekend out of town had combined to provide her with a pretext for something she should have dealt with weeks before.

"I'll do whatever you want me to do," Marty said, pleading with her.

"I don't want you to do whatever I want you to do!" Lydia shouted, shaking her curly, dark hair vigorously about her head, letting him hear the frustration rising in her voice.

She looked at Marty and saw his eyes, filling and reddening to a very different color than his full head of red hair. Oh, God, he was starting to cry on her. Obviously, their sleeping together for the past month and a half had meant considerably more to him than it had to her.

"Look, Marty," she said, taking him into her arms to comfort him and also so she wouldn't have to see the tears that were beginning to trickle down his face, "I've really enjoyed the time we've had together, but your drugging out and hanging around with Rick just confirms what I've been thinking for several weeks now. Your life's just too chaotic. I'm afraid we could *never* work. I need stability in my life right now. We can't keep going on this way. I hope we can still be friends, but we just aren't compatible in the long run. You can see that, too, can't you?"

He blubbered something that sounded affirmative. She gave a slight sigh of relief. This might turn out to be easier than she'd expected. She hugged Marty and comforted him for a while longer, thinking that she would never have gotten involved with a man nearly half a dozen years her junior—a second-year graduate student in comparative literature, at that—if she hadn't been on the rebound from breaking up with Tarik.

Not that breaking up with Tarik had been a bad thing. Lydia had lived with him for nine years, after all. It had been because of Tarik that she'd moved to California from the East Coast in the first place. He'd wanted to pursue his ambitions as a folk-punk musician, and she had been his overweight and insecure "biggest fan." Not long after their arrival, she and Tarik had survived and bonded more deeply together amid the devastation wrought by the Great Los Angeles Earthquake, the so-called 'Niner Quake.

Both of them had seen the madness of bright-shining angels and UFOs at that time—and had been deeply relieved to learn that, the statements of UFO or angel believers notwithstanding, those sightings were most likely not supernatural but natural, side effects of the earthquake's sudden tectonic stress relief. The slippage of all those miles and depths of granite, with its embedded quartz, had piezoelectrically generated high-amplitude electromagnetic disturbances. The concomitant electro-magnetic energy bursts had affected the interpretative cortex in the temporal lobes of hundreds of thousands of individuals—Lydia and Tarik among them—causing them to see lights and angels in the sky.

Even that strange, ordeal-forged bonding had worn off eventually, however. Living through the Great Quake and its aftermath had changed her. Her own dormant ambitions had reawakened. Within weeks of the quake, she took up running. She lost forty pounds in six months. She kept running and kept the weight off. She enrolled in a joint graduate program in biochemistry and paleontology, working toward a doctoral specialization in paleogenetics. Her presentations and articles on her work with DNA samples, taken from the Harlan's ground sloth remains at Rancho La Brea, had made a big splash at Page Museum conferences and in the on-line journals. Her future seemed assured.

Tarik's career, meanwhile, had gone absolutely nowhere. His folk-punk ethic made both the idea of working a day job *and* the idea of achieving financial success as a performer equally distasteful to him. The fact that Lydia's own brother, Todd, was a success in the music industry only made things worse. To Tarik, Todd Fabro was "that pop sellout," and he bristled at any offer of help from that quarter. Tarik was determined to be an artiste endlessly perfecting his art for his art's sake—while Lydia supported both of them.

Once she'd finally decided that living with him was worse than being alone, Lydia made up her mind that they should dissolve their household, and—over Tarik's truculent and petulant objections—they had. Freed of Tarik, however, she found that she did not much like being alone. She didn't like it at all.

Temporarily homeless, Lydia found herself living on her friend Kathryn's living-room futon. Above and beyond that, her research had come under threat. The recently elected "New Commonweal" majority in Congress, along with the NC governor in Sacramento, had begun to shut off funding for any further research at Rancho La Brea, on the grounds that the tar pits research was "Darwinian" and therefore inherently "anti-biblical."

As far as Lydia could tell, the New Commonweal interpretation of the separation of church and state held that if government moneys could not be used to promote religion, neither could they be used to attack religion. On coming to power, the new churchstaters slashed funding for any research they interpreted as supporting an evolutionary viewpoint. Lydia only hoped she could finish up the last of her doctoral research before the New Commonweal people took over the government altogether and prohibited outright any and all further research at the tar pits.

In the midst of all this personal and political turmoil, at a personal low point, she had met Marty, tall and muscular and handsome, as well as charmingly innocent and naive in ways Tarik had never been. Marty was Kathryn's office mate in comp lit, which was how Lydia had met him. He was single, quite unattached, a big, happy, overgrown boy. She had gathered him to her with astonishing swiftness and ease, and he had served as an anodyne to her loneliness—at least for a time.

Now, however, she sat hugging and rocking the big (and, at the moment, unhappy) young man in her arms on the edge of the bed, wondering how she could have stayed involved with him as long as she had. True, for a while he had been a good hedge against Tarik, who had kept showing up at odd times for odd reasons. Lydia had fantasized more than once that they would fight over her, but it had never happened. Now that Tarik had at last moved back East, it was less likely to occur than ever.

Even as she attempted to soften the blow of her dumping him, Lydia knew that she did not need Marty any longer. He was in fact turning into something of a burden and an embarrassment. Tomorrow she was scheduled to move in with two of her fellow female doctoral candidates, so she would no longer need to be living with Marty in order to have a place to stay. Her soon-to-be-roommates, too, had already let Lydia know that in the mate-selection races they thought she could do much better for herself than her current boytoy.

Now, with the recent slight thawing in attitudes from Washington and Sacramento, the tar pits and the Page Museum did not seem quite so likely to close down before she finished her doctoral research, either. Things had begun looking up for her again. Gazing at the mirror opposite the bed, Lydia Fabro saw the gray that had already begun to shimmer in her dark curls, here, too soon after her thirtieth birthday. Time to start tinting and highlighting that right out, she thought. She didn't need to sleep with a young master's candidate to boost her self-confidence any longer—and she'd be damned if she were going to support Marty through graduate school the way she'd already supported Tarik for years.

One more night, she thought. Maybe a farewell fuck for the sake of friendship and old times, but come morning she'd be done and Marty would no longer be a shadow on her present—only a memory from a quickly receding past, a fantasy of secret recklessness for that foreseeable future in which she had begun to grow a bit bored with the stable and responsible Mister Right she fully believed she would eventually marry.

Before Lydia had even finished comforting Marty, she was already living in that future, he was already in the past.

TWO 2014–2017

The Eye of a God

R isk madness to reach truth? Jacinta thought as Caracamuni tepui
. . . reentered normal spacetime. Looking about her, she saw that all
the ghost people looked exhausted. Old Kekchi seemed particularly
drained—so tired as to be almost comatose. The quartz collecting columns still hovered in the air, but their pulsing had become much quieter.

What are those columns doing now? she wondered. *Maintaining the
bubble of force around the tepui top? Or something more?*

Deciding that the ghost people were too dazed by their exertions to
be able to tell her much, she left the Cathedral Room and went looking
in the cave tunnels for the electronics gear she had brought with her to
Caracamuni. At last she found what she had been looking for: monitors
wired out to the surface, showing several views from cameras out on the
tepui's top.

The foreground in the first monitor was at least familiar in its alien-
ness: the dense stone forest of balance rocks and pinnacles, columns and
arches, the geological ruin from which time and wind and water had
dreamed the surreal temples and cathedrals of an erosion city out of the
stone of the tepui's top, back on Earth. In the background, however—
beyond the faint shimmer of the field of force ensphering the tepui—
was something neither Jacinta nor any other human had ever seen: a sky
so thick with stars that it was hard to find darkness there.

Examining the other monitors, she soon realized that what she had
seen on the first monitor was a perspective looking down toward the

center of a spiral galaxy's great disk, probably from a few thousand light-years above that center. Linking nearby space to the center of the galactic disk was a flood of softly glimmering light, like a cross between a distant lighthouse beam and a waterfall turned fountain.

Most of that beam-fountain, however, seemed to appear from and disappear into the celestial object nearest the tepui—a vast lens of ghostly fire, framed at its edges by a ring that appeared to be millions of kilometers in circumference and probably thousands wide. Biomechanical-looking somehow, the entire construction—lens and ring—rotated on its axis about what appeared to be a rapidly spinning mirror-sphere. Strangely, it made Jacinta think of an enormous machine, some sort of generator of cosmic proportions, for which the beam-fountain served as either exhaust or fuel feed—she couldn't say which with certainty. Despite its great size, however, the whole structure had a certain living fragility, as if a bubble of mercury metal had been suspended inside a spinning hoop of faintly rainbowed liquid fire.

While Jacinta had been watching the awesome sight before her on the monitors, Kekchi and several of the other tepuians had quietly joined her. A tired but happy buzz began to pass among them, though they said no words. She looked questioningly at Kekchi.

"Allesseh," the Wise One explained. "At long last. All the high roads lead here. Open a portal, there you go, here you are."

They and the tepui surrounding them seemed to be falling toward the rainbow lens as it spun around its central, higher-albedo sphere. As they came closer, Jacinta began to discern a rough sphere of bright points outside the turning hoop, points flickering as they reflected the pale fire of the Allesseh itself. She thought they might be small moons or aster-oids, until several of them detached from their loose spherical formation and moved purposefully toward the tepui.

"Looks like we've been spotted," Jacinta said, thinking aloud. "They're sending a welcoming committee."

The ships—if that's what they were—approached them with remark-able grace and fluidity, as if they were swimming through the sea of space. The craft were shaped like jellyfish and squid and toadstools all at once. At the same time, they also looked quite a bit different from anything she had ever seen.

The ships' forward sections, shaped rather like half-opened mushroom caps, were not static but instead pulsed rhythmically like jellyfish bells, or even jetted, like squid. Each ship's gill-cap forward section carried, behind it, a stemlike middle section. This was followed in turn by tentacular masses, at once as complexly connected as mycelia, as free-floating as jellyfish tentacles, and as tactile, graceful, and controlled as octopus arms. Patterns of color rippled and played over the surface of the ships, more like the sensitive communication patterns of giant cephalopods than the rigorous flashing of aircraft lights or movie UFOs.

For all their grace and fluidity, however, Jacinta could not escape the sense that what she was looking at were indeed purely machines, albeit mechanisms of a design exquisite almost beyond imagining. After much rippling and flashing among the welcoming party of ten or twelve craft, the largest of the ships darted forward and extended its arms in a probing caress of the sphere of force surrounding the tepui. Satisfied somehow, the ship became very purposeful and machinelike, diving rapidly downward. Behind it, wrapped in the strange ship's limbs, the force-field-ensphered tepui followed along—a bubble being dragged by a diving-bell spider down to its silken-roped underwater air chamber.

The ship, with tepui in tow, plunged on—toward the great ring that bounded the lens of soft rainbow fire, toward the lens that rotated about the central sphere. Soon Jacinta could make out details on the surface of the spin ring. Even this thin rotor-edge of the entire vast Allesseh was imposing enough, as if an immense coral reef and a superconducting supercollider had been mated with a night-lit city thousands of kilometers wide and several kilometers thick.

Soaring over the lights of the spincityscape, however, Jacinta and the ghost people could appreciate its complexity for only a few moments. Ahead, near what Jacinta guessed was the axis of rotation for the enormous ring, a great blue door blossomed open to receive them.

The squidship released them. The ensphered tepui fell as unerringly into the opening as a bee into a long-throated lily. The tepui and its inhabitants fell and fell, until the eye of a god melted them into light sweeter than any nectar, and they were gone.

The Secret Experiment of Sex

"Egan!" Paul Larkin said after the doctors and nurses had left, calling over to a blond man with short-cropped hair, a Vandyke beard, and faux eyeglasses. "You're the liaison to Tetragrammaton for Lilly-Park, aren't you?"

The younger man on the treadmill three units over looked at him narrowly.

"Not so loud," Egan said as the treadmill—long since programmed by unseen medical personnel—rose in pitch, both in its angle of steepness and in the frequency of its motor's sound. "That's right, I am. Is there a problem?"

"Maybe," Paul said with a shrug. "Yesterday evening I got an unsolicited web sticky-bomb. A unfinished documentary called *The Five-Million-Day War*. By a woman named Cyndi Easter."

Egan Ortap gave him a pained look.

"She must be out of reeducation again," Ortap said quietly, absently stopping his right hand before he could scratch at one of the electrode disks stuck to his chest.

"You know her?" Paul asked. His treadmill sped up of its own accord, and the pressure cuff on his left bicep inflated automatically. Somewhere a sphygmomanometer recorded his systolic and diastolic pressure as the cuff deflated.

"Not personally, no," Ortap said. "Only by reputation."

"Who is she?"

"Some crazy political filmmaker," Ortap said. "Subversive type. During the last crackdown, she got sent up for drugs or child molestation or whatever the cover charges were at the time. Sounds like she's on the loose, if she's sticky-bombing people through the infosphere."

As he listened, Paul could feel on his chest and sides the scratchy pressure of the plastic limpets of the cardiomonitoring electrodes. They followed his every motion and threatened to follow his emotions as well— at least as well as those might be deduced from his heart rate.

"Ms. Easter has some interesting things to say about Tetragrammaton," Paul said, pounding along on the treadmill. "Confusing stuff, though. She says that this problem drug I've heard about in the media, Ketamine Lysergate-235, is extracted from our tepui fungus, *Cordyceps jacintae*. Of all the 'combined tryptamines' from the tepui our research has uncovered, though, I've never come across anything that would fit the name 'Ketamine Lysergate.' Sounds like some sort of joke."

Ortap shrugged but said nothing. Glancing down at the treadmill, Paul continued.

"What I really don't get," he said, flicking a bead of sweat from his brow, "is that Easter claims she was exposed to this KL stuff while she was still in her mother's womb."

"And?" Ortap prodded, carefully.

"And from what I've seen in the docufilm she bombed me with," Paul continued, "Easter's got to be well along in her twenties at least. That documentary looks a couple of years old, too. That means her mother would probably have to have been given this KL-235 as early as the 1980s."

"Which means? . . ." Ortap asked as his treadmill sped up again.

"My sister Jacinta didn't make her first trip to Caracamuni until 1995," Paul said. "I didn't obtain a copy of the spore print until 2002. And I didn't go to Damon and Griego and Vang with the spore print until a couple of years ago, 2012. So how could this KL stuff have been extracted from *Cordyceps jacintae* thirty years before *Cordyceps jacintae* was even studied in a lab? It doesn't make sense."

Ortap laughed—a bit breathlessly, given how fast his treadmill was moving.

"Of course it doesn't," he said. "What did you expect? Unless you're a Kennedy you'd have to be pretty paranoid to think your family was the subject of a conspiracy—or that your life and everything that's gone wrong with it is a product of a secret experiment. So far as I can tell, having sex was the only secret thing my parents did to have me. Everybody's life is a product of *that* 'secret experiment.' "

Ortap inhaled heavily, then wiped sweat from his face with his right bicep in such a way that the latter motion degenerated into a shrug.

"Easter is a paranoid crazy," Ortap continued, "with a vendetta against the Tetragrammaton project in general and Dr. Vang in particular. She'd be the last person in the world to give you the straight story on anything."

Paul looked aside, to the cardiomonitor where his heartbeats were rendered in electronic stitchwork.

"What's her problem with Vang?" he asked.

"You've got me there," Ortap said, increasingly breathless. "Maybe ol' Vang did her mother and then jettisoned her, or something. Don't worry about it. We'll shoot down her bird. The people in power don't cotton to infobombers, if you get my meaning."

Paul nodded. He was hardly a fan of the "new government" (now a couple of years old) and its privacy-invading ways, but just this once it might actually be of help to him. He was also aware of Vang's reputation as a womanizer, especially during his younger days.

He would have liked to ask more about Vang and the new government, but Egan Ortap had turned away, clearly intent on keeping up with the pulse-pounding speeds and pitches his treadmill had now achieved.

As he thought about what the liaison had said, Paul realized he wasn't fully satisfied by Ortap's explanations. True, a good deal of what Easter claimed in her documentary—among other things, that Tetragrammaton had "secretly administered experimental entheogens as 'uterotonics' to women in their first and second trimesters of pregnancy, in hopes that their babies might develop 'unusual talents' "—sounded pretty conspiranoid and nutso. He didn't have to stretch much to hear in those words some kind of warped reworking of that "Everybody's life is a product of the secret experiment of sex" idea Ortap talked about. Yet, despite such lapses, the documentarist *had* called that conspiranoid stuff by the name of Vang's own special project—Medusa Blue—and that was hardly common knowledge.

Her *Five-Million-Day War* work in progress had interview footage with Vang himself—his usual spiel about human pattern-finding, schizophrenia, and consciousness. That certainly appeared to be genuine. Every time Paul had met and talked with Vang over the past couple of years, the man had gone on about overlap between natural and artificial information processing systems, especially about DNA as a Turing machine. In Easter's interview with him, Vang's conversation glided easily just about anywhere he ever wanted it to go, the same way it always did every time Paul had talked with the man personally.

Word was that the "old man" was also heavily invested in—and sat on the boards of—numerous companies working on biological computing, especially "primordial soup" bioputers. When he gave Easter the interiew, Vang probably thought it would be good publicity for those interests and investments. Paul could think of no other reason why the billionaire would have consented to Easter's questioning.

A lot of the other people Easter had interviewed seemed to know a good deal about the relationships between psychoactive substances and neurotransmitters, too. With a sigh rendered ragged by his pounding along on the treadmill, Paul wished he'd learned more about neurophysiology. It was just too far outside his training and expertise for him to get a solid grip on it.

Then again, he had already managed to have three major careers—pretty good, for a man still in his forties. He remembered them all quite well—perhaps too well.

Not very long after he had gone public with the tepui story, Paul's station manager at KFSN Channel 30 had tried to get him to cease and desist on that front. His boss held a firm opinion that reporters were to report on the news—not be reported on *as* news themselves. Paul, however, had refused to be muzzled. When his contract ran out, he was "not rehired," supposedly on the grounds that KFSN was a respectable news station and his flying mountaintop story was damaging to the credibility, respectability, and prestige of the station.

Strangely, losing his job as a reporter had not hit him as hard as he had first thought it would. As an undergraduate, with visions of becoming the next Eiseley or Sagan or Quammen, he had double-majored in biology and journalism, hoping someday to become a noted science reporter or popularizer of science. At the start, the TV news job as an "investigative reporter" had seemed a godsend.

Whatever god had sent it, however, had also taken it away. Blocked on the journalism and telecommunications side, he went back to school—specifically to graduate school in biology. The events at the tepui had kept itching at the back of his skull, pushing at him. He'd hit the books very hard in response. He quickly became something of an expert in the cryopreservation of threatened species—a wide-open field during the first decade of the third millennium.

After completing his doctoral work at UC Santa Cruz, he did a postdoc at the Center for the Reproduction of Endangered Wildlife (CREW) at the Cincinnati Zoo Ark. He returned to California when he got a push-through appointment with the California State University system, a senior researcher position that was supposed to result very soon in a tenured professorship. Everything seemed to be falling into place for him at last—until the spectacle of the flying mountain reappeared in the fringe media once more.

In some chat group somewhere, he thought, an editor or producer must have remembered or rediscovered the tepui story. Then the diggers began to dig. They discovered Paul's current status as a serious university scientist—one who had, unfortunately, also previously made claims outside his professional field. Interest in the flying mountain began to build again, even in the more mainstream outlets, as the media's echo-chamber effect took hold of the old story and breathed new life into it.

All too soon he found himself besieged by phone, fax, E-mail, and street mail—with "requests" for interviews that too often sounded more like demands. When he had finally been cornered on campus by a particularly persistent young producer drumming for *History's Unexplained Mysteries*, he refused to recant his previous statements on the tepui story.

His comments, traveling the globe in waves moving at the speed of media, soon also carried him into emergency "discussions" with his department chair, school dean, academic vice president, and university president. They, too, all wanted to muzzle him, to prevent him from speaking further to anyone on this "embarrassing" issue. He refused. Annoyed at Paul's obstinate refusal to sacrifice his tepui story for the sake of the university's reputation, the university president—a short but very fit man with a full head of silvered hair—called Paul a "boor."

During his early days as a biology student, Paul had studied the territorial behavior of captive lowland gorilla groups in several California zoos and wild animal parks—particularly the behaviors of silverbacked alpha males. Dominant males had a nasty habit of flinging dung at human observers who looked at them too closely. Annoyed at being called a boor, Paul voiced an abrupt equation between the behavior of such silverbacked gorilla dung-flingers and silver-haired university presidents who engaged in *ad hominem* attacks.

The president had found the analogy neither particularly amusing nor particularly flattering.

The university's chain of command very soon let him know, in no uncertain terms, that his career had derailed once more. The higher-ups promised him they would leave "no stone unturned" in seeing to it that he never got tenure at the university. They assured him that he would receive no positive recommendations once he was out on the job market again, either.

When the academic year ended soon thereafter, Paul found himself reduced to the status of independent researcher, scrambling for work and funding wherever he could find it. His friends, too, quickly drifted away— all but Professor Damon, as it had turned out. That series of blows had brought him to a personal nadir—to the dark night of the soul when he had hoped to get drunk and wander off to die in the desert.

Paul felt that Vang's arrival in his invisible dirigible had quite literally saved his life. The Tetragrammaton consortium had gotten him a fine job with Lilly-Park, as a biological researcher specializing in the preservation of pharmacologically valuable ethnobotanicals and zoologicals. This third career looked like the charm for the rest of his life—until Easter's web bomb hit his terminal this morning.

He didn't want to believe it. Certainly Easter's chronology and the popular nomenclature for this KL-235 drug were all wrong. He couldn't see Lilly-Park getting involved in covert drug work like that, either. The company was health-obsessed and drug-persecuting in the extreme— hence the treadmill cardio tests the employees endured every six months, the frequent random urine tests, the blood tests.

Those tests had initially irked Paul as an invasion of his bodily privacy, but since he had nothing to hide he felt he had nothing to fear. Lilly-Park, he was sure, could not be so duplicitous, so cynical, and so hypocritical as to persecute informed-consent drug use among its employees while simultaneously involving itself with Tetragrammaton in a scheme to foist powerful drugs onto an uninformed and unconsenting public, as Easter alleged Tetragrammaton had done.

Pounding through the final speed run on the treadmill and starting to pour sweat, Paul felt his thoughts gravitating once more to the Easter material. That woman. She also seemed to know a damned good bit about Vang's interest in technologies for getting around the light-speed limit, too.

Did he have something to hide? Something to fear? Perhaps his own fear of finding out something dark and deceitful about his gracious employers? Something that would make his continued employment with them ethically excruciating? No, he really, *really* didn't want to know.

"Have a good run," Egan Ortap said, leaving his treadmill, his diagnostic run apparently over. As he passed Paul, Ortap whacked him on the shoulder and smiled. "Don't worry about that Easter junk. We'll take care of it."

Paul nodded distractedly as he held on to the console of the speeding treadmill. Despite the heat and exertion of his diagnostic run, something about Egan's words and smile made Paul shiver. Too much of that friendly, make-those-trains-run-on-time efficiency to his banter. Ortap's smile was likewise also too slick—bright and empty as the smiles of the used-car dealers and hard-shell preachers-turned-politicians who had taken over the country of Paul's birth and jettisoned much of the old Constitution.

We'll shoot down her bird, Ortap had said. Paul's shiver deepened. How did Egan know Easter's sticky bomb had appeared in the form of a white bird icon? Had Paul mentioned that? He didn't think so—but then how could Ortap have known that detail?

A tone sounded. The pitches of both speed and steepness on the treadmill began to decline. Paul felt himself relax, at least slightly. The company doctors must have decided they had gotten all the data they needed from him for their reports—for now. The motor continued to slow and the bed of the treadmill to lower, to his considerable relief.

Getting off the treadmill, Paul pondered Ortap's words and his own future. Despite misgivings for his continued employment, he decided he would have to look up the actual structure of this KL-235. That was the only way he could be certain that Easter's documentary was, in fact, a fiction.

Half Dome

S eiji and Jiro rose in darkness from the city of Ash and passed through forested gates with the dawn.

Beneath apple trees they left the world of the wheel, to pound up switchbacks with their heavy boots on.

They clean-pumped water from above the falls. They dropped salt sweat on sand paths as they plodded higher, loving the tall pine shade when they found it, suffering the taller sun when they could not avoid it.

They saw the snow on peaks all around. They read a metal, thunderstorm warning sign that didn't apply under a sky blue sky.

They lifted their knees up stiff stone steps until they viewed the muchpictured monument's seldom seen other face, its cracked and weathered brow.

They pulled on gloves and hauled themselves up a giant's spine—part bridge suspended by stanchioned and cabled steel, part ladder runged with dead trees' bones—leading from earth to air over a tall frozen wave of stone.

They felt their muscles going cramped, their throats going dry, their heads going dizzy, their nerves going frayed, until at last they walked out onto the summit, between the two halves of heaven.

Not trusting their legs, they crawled on their bellies and looked over the edge into the abyss, long enough for the abyss to look back over the edge into them.

"Tell me again why we did this," Jiro said, sprawled out on the rock not far from the edge of the sundered dome, exhausted. Taking a gulp of water from his dromedary bag's tube, Jiro noted vaguely that his brother, dressed in sunglasses and shorts and boots but no shirt, was starting to get a sunburn. Amazingly, they were the only people on top of the dome—a result of the date being only the third week of May, and a weekday.

"Because the views from the top are fantastic," Seiji said from nearby, where he, too, had temporarily become one with the rock out of sheer fatigue, mustering only enough energy to talk and occasionally suck water from the tube connected to his own dromedary bag. "Because it's here. Because you came out to visit. Because it's as high above the valley floor as the Grand Canyon is deep below its rim. Because after we've done it we can say we did it."

Because because because because because, Jiro thought. Somewhere over the rainbow and the Wizard of Oz. But those weren't the words he spoke.

"Ambitious," Jiro said, shaking his head. "That's you all over, big brother."

"Something wrong with that?" Seiji said, sitting up slowly.

"I guess not," Jiro said quietly. "I just wonder why you'd want to be, sometimes. You afraid maybe deep down you're just like everybody else? Nobody special?"

"Hey!" Seiji said, starting into a crouch—before the cramping in his legs halted him and he stretched them out before him once more. "Who's supposed to be head-shrinking whom here? Ambitious? You should talk. You're eighteen and just finished your bachelor's degree. Two years younger than when I finished mine. Even if we were nobody special, we'd still be special nobodies."

Sitting up, Jiro removed a small pipe from his pocket but said nothing.

"Special more because we're *happa* than happy," Seiji continued, growing more serious. "Cultural amphibians. Not fully at home in either world. When we were little kids in Kobe, what they couldn't read in our names they could see in our faces. In the Midwest, what they couldn't read in our faces they could see in our names. Nippon dad, Anglo mom. Caucasian hidden in our middle names—Jiro *Ansel* Yamaguchi. Seiji *Robert* Yamaguchi."

"We adapted, though," Jiro said, preoccupied with popping open a small cylinder, shaking out some marijuana into his palm, and cramming it into the bowl of his pipe. "Had to. Family history. Long line of Hiroshima Catholics, all that."

"Maybe that's the reason I'm 'ambitious,' " Seiji said, warily watching his brother work with his paraphernalia. "I want people to see *me*, not some category they can put me in. Even if I never become anybody except who I am, that's okay by me. Don't you ever feel that way?"

"Just the opposite, lately," Jiro said, lighting the pipe and inhaling deeply. He offered the pipe to Seiji, who waved it off. Jiro shrugged and exhaled. "I wouldn't mind if somebody, some scientist or priest, came in and showed me the big blueprint. Gave me the stage directions. Tried to make me fit into the plan as best I can."

"The best-laid plans of mice and men," Seiji said, shaking his head.

Jiro abruptly began to laugh.

"What's so funny?"

"Don't you remember?" Jiro asked. "I played Lenny in *Of Mice and Men*—"

"Oh, that," Seiji said, leaning back on his hands. "Yeah, you did a great job. So did the guy who played George. Duet acting state champs, right?"

"Yeah."

"Sorry I never got to see the whole play in production," Seiji said, staring at the palm of his left hand. "I saw that duet acting thing on trideo, though. I was impressed. You did a damn good job. I've done a lot more acting than you, but I've never been on a satellite channel."

Jiro took another drag on the pipe.

"Typecasting," Jiro said in a pinched voice before exhaling. "Lenny the man-child. That's what I am—a man-child."

"What do you mean?" Seiji said, rising to his feet on wobbly legs. "Lenny was an idiot. You're probably the most intelligent person I know, next to myself. There's no resemblance."

"You really don't get it, do you?" Jiro said, staring at his brother through the smoke of his pipe, framed against the endless blue of the sky. "Look at me, Seiji. I'm a freak. Way back in second grade, the nuns—"

"—busted you for walking around on the playground with your arms stretched out like Christ on the cross," Seiji said with a grimace. "Please, not that crap again. I've heard it too many times. So? You think that's so weird? When I was in fourth grade—the night Mom was in the hospital and we were staying at Aunt Marcia's—that night I couldn't get to sleep, and sometime toward morning I thought I heard the voice of God calling me to be a priest!"

"For real?"

"No lie," Seiji said, walking uneasily toward the edge of the dome once more. "Calling me to be a holy man in wizard's robes at the altar. The nuns lorded it over us, but even they had to kowtow to the priests. The shadow magicians in the confession box—make your sins disappear, presto! The little window slides back, and there's the shadow priest's head saying, 'In the name of the Father, and of the Son, and of the Holy Spirit—may I take your order, please?' And the Act of Contrition! I always had trouble remembering the Act of Contrition. Like parsley for the Last Supper, you know?"

Seiji laughed at his juxtaposition.

Jiro leaned back on his hands, his right leg crossed at the ankle over his left knee, the right still cramping slightly from their exertion climbing to and up the dome. His head, however, was bowed and serious.

"You can make jokes about other people's visions and contritions,"

Jiro said quietly. "It's easy for you. Me, I'm not so sure. I've tried believing in something and I've tried not believing in anything, but I can't do either totally. It'd be easy to think I've just got a Messiah complex, but it's more than that. Look at me, Seij. I've got a bachelor's degree but I've never even really had a date, much less gotten laid or gotten involved with a woman. A prolonged childhood. A freak! A thing with the body of a man and the fears and inexperience of a child. All I want to do is grow up, but I can't. I'm a freak."

Walking over and sitting down not far from his brother, Seiji grew suddenly more serious.

"You've never asked a girl out?"

"No," Jiro said, shaking his head. "Every time I come close, I can tell they wouldn't be interested. Don't you see? I know what I am. I know how dark and twisted I am inside."

Seiji looked away, seeming obscurely embarrassed.

"I've never been to a prostitute, myself," he said, "but I suppose there's always that option."

Jiro shook his bowed head.

"Too late. It didn't really help. My one big sexual experience. Hah!"

Seiji kept talking into the distance.

"What happened?"

When Jiro replied, it was from somewhere in that distance Seiji had talked into.

"When we were all messed up on mescaline and bourbon one night, Tom Combs and Mike Kinney drove me around downtown—whore-shopping."

"And you found one?" Seiji asked.

"Yeah. A black woman, standing in front of the Honky Château soy-burger dive at Liberty and Vine. The guys chipped in to get poor Jiro laid. Put up the money to make the man-child into a man. And I blew it."

Seiji stared so far into the distance it struck Jiro that his older brother was trying to see beyond the blue bowl of the sky, trying to achieve escape velocity through the intense focus of his eyes alone.

"Didn't she go for it?" Seiji asked.

"She went for it just fine," Jiro said with an exhale that was almost a sigh. "Not a whole lot of negotiating—just 'Fuck or suck?' "

"Ah, the eternal verities," Seiji said, with an expression on his face halfway between grimace and smirk.

"Yeah," Jiro continued. "Anyway, she led me down these wet brick alleys to her place. Out in the front room, another woman—her sister, or maybe her daughter—was breast-feeding a baby and watching an old, faux 3D-ified Rock Hudson–Doris Day flick on a cheap holo unit. I think it was *Pillow Talk.*"

"It would be," Seiji muttered. "Go on."

"I don't remember everything," Jiro said, partly in apology, partly in explanation. "I was really messed up. But I do remember that the sink and toilet were full of dead cockroaches. And I remember her getting undressed. When she took off her bra, I must have been staring really hard at her breasts. 'You want to play with my titties, don't you?' she said. 'Yeah, sure you do. I can tell. Come and play then.' She finished undressing, but I'd barely gotten my thing out of my pants when I shot my load all over her belly. Didn't even get inside." Jiro lapsed into his "Lenny" character. "I didn't mean to come prematoorly, George, but she had such pretty titties, George."

Seiji, unable to achieve escape velocity or launch out of this hard place in any way, shook his head sadly.

"Shit," he said softly.

"She looked disgusted but not surprised," Jiro continued, in his own voice. "I went back to the car to get some more untraceable cash from Mike and Tom for a second try. They came up with it. I went back to the lady again. But I couldn't even get it up."

A long pause opened between them.

"Sounds like a really great first time," Seiji said at last.

Jiro glanced at his brother. Deflated of his usual bravado, Seiji looked as scruffy, trail-worn, and weary as Jiro himself felt.

"Yeah."

Seiji stood up again and glanced around at the 360-degree panorama of the sky and the mountains around them before returning his attention to Jiro.

"Have you told anyone else about this stuff that's been bugging you?"

"Tom and Mike," Jiro said. "Tried to tell Mom and Dad about it."

"Why?" Seiji asked, incredulous. "They'd never be able to deal with it."

"No, they weren't," Jiro said. "Not at all."

"Did you try a counselor, or therapist, or anything?"

"Yeah," Jiro said, glancing down at the ground in front of his boots. "So I must be nuts. Isn't that the way we were always told it works—if you go to a psychiatrist, you're admitting you're already crazy?"

"Who did you see?"

"The Schlosbergs," Jiro said. "The counselors on campus. They gave me books and infosphere addresses on masculine role models. On sexuality and self-disclosing. I told them all about our family situation— including you, Elderbrothergod, who bested me in almost every rivalry. They took notes on everything I told them, but it didn't work out well at all."

Seiji tossed a small fleck of rock off the brow of the dome and watched it disappear into thousands of feet of empty space.

"I believe that," he said, kicking lightly at the rock below his feet. "I had them for a team-taught psych course back in college. They're about as sensitive to people's problems as Half Dome is."

"I told them everything," Jiro said, rising unsteadily to his feet, looking across the uneven granodiorite plateau of the dome's summit. "All my hidden darknesses. And they told everyone."

"What do you mean?" Seiji asked suspiciously.

"*Agents*, man," Jiro said, eyes darting. "The ones disguised as nuns and social workers. They're the ones who spread the word on me to the whole city. The ones who are trying to make me look like a fool in front of everyone. So I'll learn my lesson.

"Wait a second," Seiji said, putting the dromedary bag's hose away from his face. "Are you talking some kind of *conspiracy* here?"

Jiro looked away to the east.

"Maybe."

"*What* conspiracy?" Seiji asked, striding closer. "Who are they? Who's in it?"

"Everybody," Jiro said, head bowed. "I don't know exactly who they are. Satanists, maybe. Or this underground of Catholic social worker types trying to help me. That's what they disguise themselves as, anyway."

Seiji grabbed his brother by the shoulder and shook him, but then quickly let go.

"This is *crazy shit* you're talking, bro," Seiji said, then began walking away, increasingly staggering and play-acting madness. "Are they trying to help you or trying to get you? 'They're trying to help me! Get me! Help me! Getmehelpmegetmehelpme—aaiiieeaagh!'"

Even Jiro laughed quietly at Seiji's act.

"I know it sounds crazy," he said. "I know it sounds like some delusion that can't really be happening. Believe me, I wish it *were* a delusion. But it's not. The evidence for it keeps piling up."

"Evidence?" Seiji said, unable to keep the skepticism out of his voice. "What evidence?"

"The messages from the media," Jiro said. "I heard this lady deejay on my favorite radio station back home once say, straight to me, right over the air, 'Jiro, are you confused yet?' She knew all about me. She knew I was confused—*they* told her! She was one of them!"

Seiji looked at him doubtfully.

"Are you sure you heard that? Maybe you just thought you heard it, when actually you just misheard something else. I used to be a deejay myself, at the college station. I don't ever remember making it a policy to give cryptic messages out over the airwaves."

Jiro turned away.

"I know it sounds crazy, but I *did* hear it. And they always played songs that came right out of my fantasies."

"So?" Seiji said, almost laughing. "Pop music *is* the music of adolescent fantasies. What are you telling me? That the music industry is part of the conspiracy, too?"

"Maybe."

"Jesus, Jiro!" Seiji said, shaking his head. "How big *is* this Satanic Nunnery conspiracy of yours?"

"It's big. Really big. They know everything I told my counselors. They've got the goods on me. They're the shotgun, and I'm the quail in their sights. They send me messages in the newspapers, over TV and holo, too. But the racing form is the real touchstone. It always lists a stable, JAY Farms—"

"For Jiro Ansel Yamaguchi?" Seiji asked. "That's stretching it. Coincidence."

"I don't think so," Jiro said, a quaver in his voice. "Every time I looked, there was always a red ball M with a slash through it in the JAY Farms section of the racing form."

"So? What's that supposed to mean?"

"Isn't it obvious?" Jiro said, turning toward his brother.

"Not to me."

"Red ball M means masturbation," Jiro said. "The slash through it was their warning to me to stop doing it."

Seiji exhaled loudly in frustration.

"Look, Jiro, I admit I don't know anything about horse racing or horse racing forms, but this sounds like some kind of paranoid guilt trip to me. So you masturbate, big deal! Like you think nobody else *does?*"

"At least you don't feel guilty about it," Jiro said, looking away, out over the airy abyss of Yosemite Valley.

"Why should I?"

"It's wrong, Seiji," he said, turning to stare at his brother again. "Self-centered and empty. It damages you. Keeps you from getting hard in the normal way."

Seiji shook his head in disbelief.

"Jesus! Next thing you'll be saying it makes you go blind! I've wanked off as much as you ever will and it hasn't hurt my sex life a bit. 'Sex life'—God, what a phrase! As if all there is to living is fucking. This damned culture puts way too much emphasis on sex. Getting laid isn't the Alpha and Omega of human existence, you know. There are lots more important things to attend to."

Jiro sat down again.

"That's easy for you to say. You've already made it to the other side."

"What 'other side'?" Seiji said, exasperated. "You think *that's* what lets you in on the master plan? Getting laid? Is this conspiracy thing what drove you across the country to visit me? You think you're a fugitive or something?"

Jiro looked away into the eastern distance.

"It doesn't matter," he said quietly. "It was all planned that I would come out here to see you. They knew I'd run. They saw the quail flush. They watched me getting strange at school. They saw me looking at girls constantly. They laughed when I made the mistake of sending sexual vibes to two girls in my automata liberation course and them making—"

"Wait a minute," Seiji said. " 'Automata liberation' is a *course*?"

"Information wants to be free," Jiro explained. "Highly evolved artificial life especially. They're creatures, too—they feel the pain of constraint. Feel pain, have rights, deserve respect—that's the equation. Anyway, with the two girls in that class, I overheard one of them say, 'My twelve-year-old sister knows more about sex than he does.' I know she was talking about me. The other one, when she mentioned a dead rat in class, she was looking right at me."

"So?" Seiji asked, truly puzzled. "What's that supposed to mean?"

"Don't you know?"

"Maybe she thought you needed a shower?" Seiji suggested, trying to make a small joke. His younger brother ignored it.

"Dead rat equals impotence," Jiro explained. "You've never heard that?"

"Can't say I have."

"The agents pushed me into a corner," Jiro said. "Made me feel like the only way I can free myself is to rape or kill somebody. You know what I was thinking when we got to the summit here? I was thinking about how easy it would be for a sniper to pick off people pulling them-selves up the cable ladder to the top of Half Dome. *They* know I have these violent thoughts sometimes. Yet I *don't* want to hurt anybody. I *won't*, either. Not even the Schlosbergs. *They* know that, and they use it against me. They've left me with only three options: kill myself, kill oth-ers, or go drooling-crazy and spend the rest of my life in a care home."

"There's another option," Seiji said in a level voice, even if what he said must have sounded a bit lame even in his own ears. "You can still cope."

"Don't you think I've tried?" Jiro said, pained. "I have, until it's almost killed me. I *want* to fit in, but I'm too twisted, too far gone. It's too late to learn how to deal with myself. Too late to take on women and the world. I tried to off myself on tranks and tequila. That didn't work, so I ran away. They knew I would. They sent their agents on the bus with me. I recognized them."

"How?"

"There was the guy I almost got in a fight with once at a stopover," Jiro said, "because he called me a fag pervert. There were Satanists dis-guised as nuns. There was the chemical lobotomy case with the big smile on his face and the FREED sticker on his luggage. The whole bus was full of their underground people—no normals aboard. Oh, they knew I was coming out here, all right."

Seiji gave Jiro a sudden, sidelong glance and began pushing his brother on one shoulder.

"So everybody's a member of the conspiracy, huh? How about me, Jiro? Am I part of it, too? What's my role in it? Am I a high-ranking devil? Lucifer of the Coven, maybe? Huh? How about me? Am I one of *Them*?"

Jiro backed away.

"I—I don't know," he said hesitantly. "I haven't figured out yet whether you're part of it or not. I don't think so, but if you are, it would fit in perfectly."

"Yeah?" Seiji said, growing increasingly disgusted. "When you figure it all out, let me know. I'd sure like to see all this power I'm supposed to have. Where's my mansion? Where are my head-snapping cars and head-turning women? Man, I'm a poor, underpaid graduate student with more debt than I can repay, for God's sake! All this conpiracy stuff is self-pitying bullshit! Who the hell are you that you should deserve to be the focus of a vast conspiracy? What makes you so special?"

Jiro looked down, then glanced up at Seiji from beneath his eyebrows.

"I may be nobody special," he said, "but I'm a special nobody—"

"Don't try to use my words against me!" Seiji shot back. "If you're such a nobody, why is everybody out to get you? Hmm? I think you're on some kind of warped ego-trip. My teachers were right: Paranoia is just displaced narcissism. The narcissist is the voyeur every paranoid always *almost* manages to glimpse in the rearview mirror. Sound familiar?"

"No," Jiro said, glancing away.

"It should," Seiji continued. "Your self-image has sunk so low you've manufactured this God-conspiracy out to get you/help you. It must really bolster your ego to be chief victim, the center of a great conspiracy's attentions. Oooh, you're so important! Knock this crap off, Jiro! What's wrong with you? You been taking KL again since I last saw you?"

Jiro kneewalked to the edge and looked down into Yosemite Valley's tree- and meadow-floored depths before he answered.

"Yeah, some," he admitted. "Chemopsychotherapy, you know? KL ages you. It's great! Makes you grow up fast! Years of experience in a single night! If the center of the universe is four inches in back of right between your eyes, then KL is a magic bullet shot straight into that space. Rocketsled the time lines! Psssshhhooooo! Timeless memories of memoryless times! Instant maturity! Take and eat!"

"What the hell are you talking about?" Seiji said, anger shading into worry—and fear.

"Physics," Jiro said, pulling back from the edge and the abyss beyond it. "Observation by consciousness makes the universe real. Quantum superposition of states. Ordinary human consciousness limits the universe to a single reality. An omnipresent and omnipotent consciousness, on the other hand, holds in its mind all possible states of all possible being, simultaneously. The dreaming mind of God does not collapse the wave function. Ketamine Lysergate gives you a glimpse into that alternity. All the possibilities are real, in all the universes, all the time, all at once."

"Gatehead bullshit," Seiji said, shaking his head. "Crazy. All it really does is burn tracks in your brain."

Jiro gave a strange, high-pitched laugh.

"Come on, Seij. Everybody does it—it's just that no one admits it. Societywide rite of passage."

" 'Everybody does it—no one admits it,' " Seiji mocked, his voice sinking to a growl as he grabbed his brother's pipe and tossed it over the edge, then grabbed his brother up by the sleeves and shoulders of his shirt. " 'I'm such a nobody everybody's out to get me!' More paranoid generalizing. KL's no good for you, asshole!"

"It *is* good!" Jiro persisted, despite the rough handling by his brother. "Before I started doing KL, we would never have been able to talk like this!"

"We never needed to," Seiji said, staring into the face of his brother held close before him. "You hadn't shoved yourself to the edge then."

"We always needed to!" Jiro said, his voice breaking. "But we never did! I never used to talk. You remember. The paranoia's a plus, that way—it's helping me out of my introversion."

"What?"

"My paranoia's so intense it makes me talk to people," Jiro said, still hanging limply in his brother's grip. "I ask people who they are, where they're from—all the social small talk—because I want to know their role in the surveillance system."

"You never talked about this crazy shit before KL!" Seiji shouted in his brother's face.

"I was asleep—I was *dead*—before," Jiro said. Seiji's grip on him began to loosen and slump.

"And now that you're alive and awake, the nightmare is killing you," Seiji said, exhaustion returning to his voice. "No way to win. I might as well throw you over the edge. Then follow you down myself."

Seiji did neither, however. Disentangling his hands from his brother's shirt, he let Jiro slump to the ground. He walked a few paces away, then dropped to his haunches, shielding his eyes with his hands. A long silence opened between them.

"Seiji," Jiro said at last, "why are you so angry about this? It's my life, not yours."

"I'm not angry, you idiot," Seiji said, still shielding his eyes with his hands. "I'm afraid. You're scaring me, can't you see that?"

"You're the one who was going to throw *me* off the top of Half Dome," Jiro said with a weak smile. "How can I be scaring you?"

Seiji pulled his hands away from his swollen-looking eyes but still did not glance at his younger brother.

"Did you ever stop to think," Seiji asked, "that I'm the person most like you in the whole damn world? Nature *and* nurture, genes *and* environment? If you go crazy, bro, then what does that say for *my* prospects?"

Before Jiro could respond, however, they were interrupted by a loud whooshing sound rising toward them. In a moment, a young athletic-looking couple soared up over the edge of the dome. Each of them was strapped into a maneuvering unit powered by pulse rockets. The couple circled the top of Half Dome twice, then landed about fifty yards away. The man and woman waved to Seiji and Jiro.

"Damn jetpackers," Seiji muttered, though he waved pleasantly enough to the new arrivals. He turned to Jiro. "Popping into the view we had to sweat for. Come on. We've been up here long enough."

Jiro gave his older brother a crooked smile.

"Confession's over, Father? But you haven't given me my penance yet."

Seiji shook his head.

"Hiking back down to the valley floor will be Act of Contrition enough," Seiji said, beginning to work his way back down the cables.

At the end of the day, that penance was adequate for them both.

Disappearing into Simulation

Mike read from plump blond Tanya Stautberg's paper: " 'I think Earth's impoverished masses are poor because they want to be. If a person wants a job bad enough, they can always find one.' No, Ms. Stautberg—you can't say that."

"Why not?" she squealed, political bristles rising.

"You can't say 'a person . . . they.' A *person* cannot be a *they*. 'Person' is singular, but 'they' is plural. A person can be 'he,' or 'she,' or 'he or she,' but not 'they.' Confusing singulars and plurals makes any language less exact, Tanya. Also, it's not 'bad,' it's 'badly.' "

"It's *Tan*nya, not '*Taw*nya,' " she said, peeved. "I thought this was tutoring for a course in history, not grammar."

"It is. But unfortunately for you, I have a background in languages, too."

Shortly thereafter, T*ann*ya left his cubicle, still not getting it. *Never try to teach a pig to sing,* Mike thought with a sigh. He flicked off his shoulder the long, brown-blond ponytail he'd been growing out since leaving home. He looked at the poems he had posted on the walls of his cubicle. Since his arrival in Humboldt, rather than getting angry at his students, he had begun writing cynical poems—juggling his frustration into words, fusing it, and polishing it into images—as a way of venting his spleen. His eyes flashed on a brief one posted about a third of the way up the left-hand wall of the cubicle:

Unless It's *Paradise Lost*

Poetry's short
so maybe you'll have time to feel

(you accomplished) something.

That about captured his students' attention span, all right. Most of them had media monkeys on their backs, major Holo Joneses to maintain. Yet another poem, on the cubicle wall in front of him, caught a different aspect of his disgruntlement with the summer school students he had been tutoring:

The Poetry of the Inarticulate

like—
like—uhh—
like—um—you know?
like—you know what I mean?
like—um—you know what I'm saying?
like—um—you know what I'm talking about?
like—um—you know.
like—um—anyway.
like—uhh—so—
you get the point?

How has this happened? Mike asked himself. Graduate school was supposed to have been just a way to get his foot in the door. So he could talk and write about what he wanted to talk and write about. So he could debate with his fellow historians the major questions in their discussions of a century-old war. So he could help clarify their understanding of the sinking of the *Jutland*. Instead, here he was, tutoring Gen Ed courses for ungrateful undergraduates.

No matter how enlightened a corner Humboldt State was supposed to be in the endarkened American mindscape, the campus still had no towers ivoried and ivied enough to block out the ideological wars raging through the country at large—the Jesus vs. Darwin celebrity death-match mudwrassle to which contemporary American intellectual culture had been reduced. He thanked the divine ground of all being that he wasn't teaching a political minefield course like evolutionary biology, or the Bible as literature. How much longer would the used-Christ dealers, the politicians and preachers of the preowned Jesus, continue to allow such heretical courses to be taught? He shivered involuntarily, despite the warmth of the day and the open windows of the Humanities Building.

Not that the gadgeteers in the academic sciences are much better, he thought. He had encountered students enough already who were possessed of a messianic faith in technological progress: sophomore physics majors who felt no connection to the Earth at all, just a planet to be used up and thrown away before moving on to the next oasis in space, hopefully at faster-than-light speed.

Humanity as Trashers of the Universe. How different were those physics majors, really, from the stubborn millennialists and apocalyptists with their "Use it up 'cuz you're gonna lose it in the Rapture anyway" mentality? On the right wall of the cubicle he had posted poems about that, too, but none of them seemed to work.

All too philosophical, he thought. His poetry, with the rest of his thoughts, had taken that turn since he'd left home, since he'd hitched that ride with the defrocked academic IT guy heading from Montana to San Bernardino. He only had one poem on his walls from the time before his move West, an experiment in haiku:

> *flowers above snow,*
> *Spring daffodiligently*
> *forgets forgetting.*

Was it better or worse than what he was writing lately—or only different, as he himself was different?

Was it the KL he'd been doing that had made him different? He didn't want to think about that, if he could avoid it. Certainly there was a good deal more to life than the latest brain candy. Why, then, had he DSBed—engaged in "drug-seeking behavior"—almost immediately upon arrival in Humboldt? Linking up with the marijuana traditionalists, and through them the whole entheogens/hallucinogenics crowd? The Blue Spike people at the fringes, too—they were the really scary ones. . . .

He exhaled slowly. Putting on a pair of eyephones and turning on his desktop oracle, his system came on, singing the *"Sound of Music in One Verse"* with which he'd programmed it:

> *Climb every mountain, search high and low,*
> *Follow every byway—Nazis are coming, let's go!*

He began searching in the infosphere for some of his new local and non-local friends. They usually hung out in the virtual public that had spawned from the Lyceum entheogen library. He cruised the chats, trying to determine if anybody he knew was on-line at the moment.

"The way we perceive the world is at best a brilliant distortion," said a starscape-bodied digital persona, trolling, lines out for conversation, "bearing no more resemblance to the real than van Gogh's 'Starry Night' bears to the depths of space."

No one he knew. He scanned on, into a group personaed as several different species of owl.

" 'Antisex'?" said a barn owl. "Not at all. I'm a big fan of consensual sex. Less of a fan of sex for procreation. No fan at all of 'sex' that is really a mask for abuse of power. Your kinks per se don't bother me. But I draw the line when the whole point of your scheming and manipulating is anticonsensual: getting others—men or women—to do what you want them to, against their will, and without their consent. I know of few libertarians who would support the infliction of unsought physical and mental cruelty as a 'sexual right.' "

Rights, privileges. More death-match mudwrassle culture. Nope. Nobody he recognized there, either, though it sounded very much like one of the campus NeoLiberty Theory chats. Mike scanned on, into a fractal-patterned zone peopled by rainbow-hued personae playing some sort of dizzying word-jumble or association game in a circle—all of them anonymous or using obvious aliases. *Ah*, Mike thought, *this is beginning to look familiar.*

"Consciousness is the object of a transcendent idea," said the first player-persona in the new round, a.k.a. "Schopenhauer."

"Transcendence is the object of an ideal consciousness," said the second player.

"Transcendence is the consciousness of an ideal object," said a third persona.

"Ideas are the objects of a transcendent consciousness," said a fourth persona.

"Objects are the ideas of a transcendent consciousness," said a fifth persona.

"Transcendent consciousness is an ideal object," said a sixth persona.

"Object consciousness is a transcendent idea," said a seventh persona.

"Consciousness is the idea of a transcendent object," said an eighth, newly joined in the game.

Hmm, Mike thought. Start with a philosophical statement, then run it through a deconstruction/reconstruction process to see what gets generated. That sounded like it might be one of Chrysantha Clark's loony "research modalities." She was a graduate student specializing in the philosophy of language, heavily involved in "adaptive linguistic computation strategies" and "semantic evolution games." This had the earmarks of one of her research games, all right. It developed fast, too: They had already moved into a new level of the game as he was thinking about it.

"If objects are the ideas of a transcendent consciousness, then subjects are conscious objects in the mind of that consciousness," said the second persona.

"Humans are therefore conscious ideas," said the third persona.

"Consciousness objects to conscious objects because conscious objects are subjects," said the fourth persona.

"To be conscious is to be an idea in the divine mind who is aware it is an idea in the divine mind," said the fifth persona.

"Is consciousness the effect of a transcendent cause (God creates us) or the cause of a transcendent effect (we create God)?" asked the sixth persona.

"If God could create a universe that evolves," said the seventh persona, "then why not a universe that could evolve a God who creates?"

Well, Mike thought, *that would certainly explain the biblical inerrantists' fear of evolution.* This stuff was head-spinning enough to be annoying after a while. Certain that "Schopenhauer" was actually Chrysantha, he left the idea-processing circle chat and sent Chrys a virtual mail on her private line.

"Hey, 'Schopenhauer,'" he asked, "when you get tired of being a disembodied mind on-line, would you be so kind as to give me a heads-up on any parties happening tonight?"

In a flash, a live video feed appeared in Mike's section of the infosphere, with Chrysantha in the foreground, black-haired and pudgy and sharp-eyed.

"Already at a party," Chrysantha shot back, laughing. "Sakler's cabin in the redwoods down by the Eel. Live to the world, or at least to our friends who know the e-ddress. Check it out."

Mike followed the e-ddress and brought up another video feed. A roving camera was making its way through a noisy crowd, settling in to record conversations from time to time before it moved on.

". . . litmus test," said a bearded and bespectacled man, wearing a T-shirt adorned with a spiraled vortex swallowing its own tail, which Mike recognized as the logo of an anarcho-shamanic musical group, Voice of the Whirlwind. "To anyone from a technologically advanced society who is attempting to convince you of his or her 'ecological sensitivity,' always

ask: 'How many children do *you* have?' If the answer is a whole number
larger than 2, the speaker is a blind-spot hypocrite at best and an obfus-
cating liar at worst."

Ouch, Mike thought. Even if that test might well be true in the world
of Sex and the Single Planet, that was still a pretty harsh line to take.
Apparently the mind behind the roving camera thought so, too, for the
lens moved on, settling at last on a young black woman Mike recognized
as a fellow graduate student, Becky Starling. She was speaking to a pale
woman with red hair going gray, whom Mike also recognized—Professor
Paulson.

"Last night," said Becky, "you said there is no life after death because
so many people believe in that idea, yet no one has found evidence for
it. I would say there *is* life after death because no one has found evidence
of it, yet so many people believe in it. The best evidence for life after
death is belief in life after death."

The professor smiled and began to answer, but Mike had already
dumped that frame and returned to Chrysantha.

"I'm there," he said, "but how do I get there?"

"You're still at your ritual humiliation for money?" Chrys asked.

"If by that you mean am I still at work on campus," Mike said with a
frown, "then the answer is yes."

"Directions are at the bottom of your v-space," Chrysantha said. Mike
nodded.

"Okay if I bring a date?" he asked. "My friend Lizette is coming in
from back home."

Chrysantha shrugged.

"It's an open party," she said. "Bring whomever you like, so long as
they know how to party."

"Great," Mike said. "Oh, and here's something for your 'consciousness'
kaffeeklatsch: The idea that consciousness is an essentially social and
linguistic phenomenon is an essentially fascist conception."

Chrysantha frowned and gave him a withering stare.

"Language may be overrated," she said with a small shrug, "but then,
you have to use language to express that, don't you?"

Mike laughed and signed off. Removing his eyephones, he saw that
Lizette was already standing in the doorway of his cubicle, a dark-haired
young woman dressed in a black and blue fractal-patterned summer dress,
a bit road-weary but still smiling.

His office system, abhorring a vacuum, promptly flung up SBN-TV,
busy covering another Traditional Values rally.

"Church, Kitchen, Children! Church, Kitchen, Children!" bellowed a white male Reverend Somebody, leading the chant for an audience composed mostly of women. By their dress and demeanor the audience members looked to be part of the long-suffering, hard-working Excluded Middle Class that the right-wing populists loved to play to, assuring them that their true greatness had been stolen—sucked away by the parasitic godless-decadent wealthy above them and the parasitic shiftless-sensual poor below them—but they could get it all back if they just followed the right virtuous leader with the right virtuous ideas.

"Kirche, Küche, Kinder," Mike said tiredly. "Yeah, yeah, yeah." He found their website and sent them one of his canned obnoxious responses:

Goals for Women. Fill in the blank:

*"Produce babies and educate them according to _____ doctrine. . . .
Support men's activities in whatever roles the leadership deems necessary. . . .
Maintain family-orientated values."*

The missing phrase is: (A) Christian religious (B) Nazi Party (C) Communist Party (D) All of the above.

"It's 'D,' right?" Lizette asked.

"Probably could be," Mike said, "but historically it's not. The correct answer is 'B.' They're the words of a Nazi Party activist in the 1930s. I found them in an old book by Koonz called *Mothers in the Fatherland.*"

He shut the system off and turned to Lizette.

"Welcome back to normal space," she said as he got up from his chair.

"I don't know how 'normal' it is," Mike said, hugging her. This was always the awkward part. Since they had never officially dated—her parents' "Be ye not yoked with an unbeliever" disapproval somehow always in effect—sharing a kiss raised too many questions, pushed too many boundaries. Hugs were safely neutral, as long as they weren't too prolonged. "This is Humboldt, you know—you're not in Kansas anymore, kiddo. How long were you waiting?"

"A few minutes," Lizette said, taking his arm as they walked and he steered her out of the Humanities complex.

"Thanks for going to the trouble of driving all the way out to the Coast from back home," Mike said as they walked toward her electric in the parking lot.

"No problem," Lizette said. "I'm kind of interested in finding out what is so not-in-Kansas-anymore about northern California, at the moment."

"If you really want to know," Mike said, sensing a perfect opening and segue, "I've got a standing invitation to a party in the redwoods down by the Eel River, at the Sakler cabin. See the natives engaged in their quaint tribal rituals! In their natural habitat!"

"Sounds like a plan," Lizette said with a smile as they got into her car. "You navigate and I'll drive."

They drove off campus, through Bayside and into Eureka, past Time Zone, the big "time"-themed supermall—Burgertime, Clothestime, Funtime, Time Out Sports Bar, Time Squared Clock Shop, all the rest. If time was an emergent property, as some theorists proposed, then it was emerging like crazy there. They continued past Loleta and into the narrow strip of redwoods still standing around the Eel, Lizette marveling at the big trees all along their river drive. Mike tried to sound jaded and worldly-wise, but those trees had never ceased to impress him, either.

"Turn down here," Mike said when they came to a large gravel road leading down into the forest and on toward the river. They drove along the unpaved road until they came to a broad, open meadow beside the river, along the edges of which a number of vehicles were already parked. More striking, however, was the tall holojection floating at the center of the meadow: a slender white spire labeled "Trylon" and a snowy orb captioned "Perisphere" looming ahead of them, gigantic even among the redwoods. Holojected blimps and dirigibles floated above the large geometric figures of Trylon and Perisphere.

"Hey! I've seen this before somewhere!" Lizette said, pleased, gazing at the perfect image of the spire and orb, with something called the "Helicline" ramping down around them.

"Must be a theme party," Mike said. He headed toward the broad path that, farther on, led toward a large, barrackslike "cabin" in the distance, on a rise overlooking the meadow.

The two of them had barely stepped onto the path when another holojection appeared. A man of considerable years, dressed in a dark suit and tie of a rather conservative cut, topped by a snap-brim hat, stood looking at himself in a full-length antique mirror.

"Art Sakler," Mike said, nodding from Lizette to the holo. "Our host."

"Yes," said the holo man looking into the holo mirror approvingly. "Just what the well-dressed time traveler would be wearing in 1939."

The holo-Sakler turned toward them and touched his hat in greeting.

"The future has a past, my friends. Welcome to the past of my future. Shall we take a stroll down Time Travel Lane?"

The apparition began to walk up the path, away from them, toward the house. Mike and Lizette followed, impressed by the realism of the holo.

"Welcome to the 1939 World's Fair," holo Sakler said, gesturing expansively. "Those structures over there, the 'Egg, Spike, and Ramp,' as one wag called them, dominate the fairscape as the Fair dominated American popular culture in that year. Like tens of millions of other Americans, I was there, seventy-five years ago. Unlike most of them, I can't really remember it. But also, unlike most of them, I'm still alive."

Something else now caught their eye: a floating holo of a color picture, one showing an infant being held by an old man, perhaps the child's grandfather, with the Trylon and Perisphere in the distance behind them.

"In the summer of 1939, when my parents and grandparents took me to the World's Fair with them, I was only a few months old," the holo host said. "I think I now very strongly resemble the old man in the photo, don't you? Almost as if the infant had grown up to become his own grandfather."

As they walked along, Fair memorabilia flashed into the air before them. The Trylon-and-Perisphere-adorned orange and blue high-modern *Official Souvenir Book*. Fair clocks and plates and puzzles and radios. Heinz pickle pins. A crop of GM Futurama "I Have Seen the Future" pins.

"I spent my childhood with these small, solid memories," the holo host continued. "The 1939 World's Fair was the high-water mark of American technological optimism, the great coronation ceremony of faith in progress. The *futurismo* of the Trylon and Perisphere was a visible manifestation of the power of technology and the authority of hope that permeated everything at that World's Fair."

More memorabilia flashed up in front of Mike and Lizette—flyers, brochures, programs. On the meadow around them, drawings and photos morphed into three dimensions and became spectacular gardens, buildings, sculptures, corporate and government pavilions, amusements and themes. The *Official Souvenir Book*, drifting by them again, became a talking document. Mike and Lizette caught phrases and snatches from its pages, fallen open to the oxymoronic captions describing GM's Futurama.

"A vast miniature cross section of America as it may conceivably appear two decades hence . . ." the talking book intoned. "35,738 square feet . . .

largest scale-model ever constructed . . . contains more than one million trees of eighteen species . . . 500,000 houses of individual design . . . 50,000 scale-model automobiles, of which 10,000 travel in full view over superhighways, speed lanes, and multidecked bridges."

"Temple of the In/Car/Nation," the holo host said with a smirk, then covered his mouth with one hand as if he'd said something he shouldn't have, and fell silent.

Now, before them and all about the Trylon and Perisphere, the whole of the crowded fair appeared in all its wonder, a candied holographic confection of the future's past, ready to be consumed by the present. Mike and Lizette walked into it like children walking into someone else's dreams, or into history, which amounted to the same thing. They watched as their holo host grabbed "one frankfurter with everything" at Swift & Company's streamlined superairliner building, then some ice cream over by Sealtest's triple-shark-finned edifice, paying for both with antique Liberty coins.

Strolling about the fairgrounds yet moving only a few steps along the actual path, Mike and Lizette saw how wind-shaped so much of the world of the fair appeared. Buildings that looked as if they had been designed in wind tunnels. Frank R. Paul mélanges of fins and keels and flanges, spirals and helices and domes. Towers topped with zeppelin-mast spires. An airstream wonderland waiting for the inevitable arrival of Northrop flying wings and Bel Geddes teardrop cars.

Their holo host stopped them at the base of the Trylon and gestured for them to examine it closely.

"I've rediscovered the Fair's secret," their holo host explained triumphantly. "Like everything else, the Trylon was intended to look smoothly mass-produced, machine-precise, and slipstream-slick. Look at it up close, though. The surface is rough, see? Stuccoed with all the 'smoothness' of jesso over burlap."

Their holo host stood up and gestured broadly enough to take in the whole of the fair.

"Beneath its assembly-line dreams of aerodynamic cowls and zero-drag farings," Sakler's holo image said, "the great exhibition is actually handcrafted—a *prototype* of the shape of things to come, not a production model. The future is best viewed from a distance."

Still, there was something irresistible for Mike and Lizette as they stepped with their holo host into the American Museum of Natural History/Longines-Witnauer Watch Company's "Theatre of Time and Space" for a grandiose tour of the universe. The same was true when they approached the Chrysler Motors Building in the Transportation Zone and made their way through its "Rocketport" display—especially when they literally bumped into Albert Einstein there.

"Pardon me, Professor," their holo host said quickly.

"No problem, no problem," the Nobel laureate said with a distracted smile, turning back to lean on a railing and watch yet again as the Rocketgun simulated another blastoff into tomorrow, with full noise-and-light special effects, followed by a quiet moment of appropriate awe, then thunderous applause.

From there it was on to a quick tour of the Town of Tomorrow. Then a visit to the Immortal Well with its streamlined time capsule, intended to preserve the world of the 1930s for the people of A.D. 6939.

"Too bad nobody took exact notes on where the Immortal Well's time capsule is located," their holo host footnoted. "Once the fair was demolished, no one was able to relocate the capsule. By the 1970s the time capsule's location had been completely lost."

From the Immortal Well they went inside the Westinghouse Building to see the robots—Elektro the Moto-Man and his Moto-Dog, Sparko— perform. After that it was on to see and hear General Electric's ten-million-volt indoor lightning bolt show, then on to Consolidated Edison's block-long "City of Light" diorama. Walking past NCR's enormous cash register ringing up its daily fair attendance tally, they moved on toward the lighter entertainment of the Amusement Zone. The Parachute Jump. Nature's Mistakes. Arctic Girls' Temple of Ice. Amazon Warriors in No-Man's-Land. The Congress of Beauty. Admiral Byrd's Penquin Island. The Aquacade and safari shows and tribal extravaganzas. Scantily clad tableau women posing for the exotic Living Magazine Covers of the future. Mike and Lizette enjoyed it all, kids again at a planetary county fair.

When they had wandered through the great squares and avenues, alongside the Lagoon of Nations, past the pavilions of states and governments, beneath the fireworks, they came finally to the reflecting pool beneath the Perisphere, at just the moment the great Voice of that orb began to sound its eerie tocsin over the emptying fair.

"As Yogi Berra once said, 'It's always hard to predict, especially about the future,'" the holojected Art Sakler remarked, seated on the edge of the reflecting pool, his lips broadening into a smile that was still sad and world-weary somehow. "Tragic to think that the 1939 World's Fair had not even ended its first season before the faith in progress that had buoyed it up like a flood began to quickly ebb. Germany invaded Poland, pushing forward a war and a holocaust in which most of my European relatives died. That war ended in mushroom clouds sprouting over Japanese cities, locking the world for almost fifty more years into the mushroom fallout cellar of the Cold War. Then resource redistribution wars and various modes of terrorism, masked as ethnic, neotribal, and religious conflict."

The dapper old man with the snap-brim hat sighed, then brightened.

"Yet I still have some of that faith-and-hope of the fair in me, even after all these years," he said. "Maybe since I was too young to learn it consciously, I took it in unconsciously, hope with a somewhat bitter taste, like a mother's milk. After all these years I'm also learning that it's *always* hard to predict, even about the past. That, too, has to be iterated and reiterated, fed back, looped around the strange attractor of our personal time, our time-traveling memory, in order to remain real."

With a sad smile their holo host gave a wave of his hand, once. Quicker than a fog the fair disappeared, to be replaced with the sprawl of that part of contemporary New York that now occupied the fair's former site. With a second wave of their host's hand, the holo of contemporary New York disappeared as well, leaving Mike and Lizette standing in front of Art Sakler's three-story, twelve-thousand-square-foot "cabin"/party house, backed by the redwoods and bathed in sunset light. On the balconies and tree decks stood loose knots of people, from whom arose a smattering of applause aimed at Mike and Lizette. The well-dressed elderly man in the snap-brim hat waved a third time.

"Hello!" called Art Sakler, in the flesh. "Congratulations on having survived my World's Fair gauntlet. Come on in—come on up!"

Lizette glanced at Mike as they headed for the nearest door into the big log house.

"Definitely not in Kansas anymore," she said. "Who *is* this wizard— and how can he afford holos like that?"

"You can ask Art yourself," Mike said as they climbed a spiral staircase.

On the second floor their progress was slowed by a cluster of inebriated undergraduates having a good-natured argument.

". . . all bullshit," said one, a blocky young man with short-cropped hair. "Take the ice trade, for example.

"What do you mean?" asked the willowy brunette woman he was "discussing" the issue with.

"The Romans had ice," the young man shot back. "The Egyptian pharaohs had ice. No refrigeration systems—and no ancient astronauts or ice aliens either. Trade! What the market will bear! That must've been a helluva job—climbing a glacier on Kilimanjaro, cutting blocks of ice for a distant pharaoh . . ."

The jam on the helical staircase broke up and they moved on to the third floor. Across a long, half-lit barroom and out a set of sliding glass doors they saw their host, but they would have to make their way through the crowded room to reach him, through a place noisy with music and people eating and drinking and party-talking.

Mike and Lizette made their way through a circle of thin, pallid people who, despite the warmth of the summer evening, huddled round a fire in the great barroom fireplace. The people in the circle were passing among them a sheet of aluminum foil folded in a V that cradled a large pinch of something. One of the group, a bespectacled, red-haired boy in faux prison togs, was running the flame of a lighter under the foil, beneath the big pinch of stuff, until a thick, slow snake of smoke began to ooze up the V of the foil.

"Come on!" said a young black woman in a tight, knee-length red dress. She was thin as a famine survivor and anxious as a junkie about to score. "Chase that serpent and pass it on! I don't want it to be subclinical by the time it reaches me. . . ."

The bespectacled boy vigorously inhaled before passing foil and lighter on to the next person in the circle.

"Who are those people?" Lizette asked quietly, after she and Mike left them behind.

"Ectomorphic exotherms," Mike said grumpily.

"*What?*"

"Skinny lizard people," Mike explained. "Spikers. Blue Spike users. What they're doing is 'chasing the blue dragon.' They inhale that blue-gray smoke. It's supposed to keep them from being 'blue and draggin',' as they put it. You swallow the snake and the snake swallows you."

Lizette glanced narrowly at him.

"I take it you don't approve?"

"It's not for me to approve or disapprove," he said with a shrug. "I'm just not a speeder. Not a go-fast kind of guy, that's all. My bet is, once they're all hot-wired, they'll go through that World's Fair thing again—only they'll *run* through it. For a faster flash. As if it weren't infodense enough already."

They passed among the professor and students Mike had seen on video feed earlier, then stepped around the language-gaming Chrysantha and several of her friends. Hooked into the infosphere through their boards, they were generally oblivious to the physical world around them. A few of that group, mostly younger guys, had split out of Chrysantha's circle and were idly baudysurfing, checking out v-porn in the infosphere.

Mike saw several of his acquaintances sprawled on a constellation of couches around a table, not far from the sliding door that opened onto the balcony. On the table in their midst, near the veggies and chips and breads and dips, was a dropper bottle of KL-235. Mike said hi and introduced Lizette. As he sat down it irked him, somewhere at the edges of his consciousness, that almost the only friends he had made here on the Coast were KL users, gateheads. He didn't let it bother him too much, however.

Lizette bent down and whispered in his ear that she was going to talk to their host, if Mike didn't mind. Mike didn't mind, and Lizette stepped out onto the balcony beside the sharply (if anachronistically) dressed old Sakler, still within earshot. Part of Mike's focus went with her.

". . . the great revenge tragedy that is American politics," Sakler was saying, "I can't tell whether the politicians are narrow-mindedly shrewd, or shrewdly narrow-minded."

Lizette introduced herself and where she was from and the conversation spun off in another direction. Sakler stood joking and Lizette nodding in vigorous agreement about how strange all this partying must look to someone from hyperconservative Wyoming, from which the Four Stooges of the Apocalypse continually stood poised to ride forth and conquer the nation in God's name. Mike's focus shifted back and forth from the balcony to the couches, so that he only caught bits of the conversation in both places.

". . . spend my days now working and playing on this twenty-acre spread," he heard Sakler say. "Learning the ways of the gentleman farmer—though I'm neither a gentleman nor a farmer. 'Yup, September tells the plants October's coming soon,' so the trees know they better fruit up, in the orchard out back."

"Do I make reality," asked an armchair philosopher in the KL group, "or does reality make me, you know?"

". . . a shaman cleverly disguised as a college professor!" Becky Starling said with a loud laugh, from over in the group around Professor Paulson.

". . . big old party house," Sakler said. "It's modeled after the Wawona Hotel in Yosemite Park. I built it with my own hands, out of wood from my own land's trees—not redwoods, but the pines on my inland property."

"Free the Heart of the World!" someone shouted from the far end of the room, apropos of nothing and everything.

"Most of the busy people I know," the armchair KL supplier-philosopher continued, "if they ever relaxed long enough to take a good look at their lives, they'd probably kill themselves."

". . . expensive?" Sakler said. "Sure. Money hasn't been a problem for me for the past dozen years. Sued the army, the Department of Defense, and the U.S. government for addicting me to cigarettes and nicotine while I was in the service. I came from a smoking household but I was a health nut."

Someone else on the balcony asked something Mike couldn't quite make out.

". . . no, never smoked at all before I went into the military. Lasted six years in the army before I gave in. For years I was living right across the street from the surgeon general, yet every time I requested a nonsmoking billet the higher-ups just laughed in my face. Six years in barracks full of smokers, six years of dirt-cheap cigarettes in the BX, six years of breaks where we were always told, 'Smoke if you've got 'em.' Six years before I broke down and started smoking. When I got out six years after *that*, I was a full-blown nicotine fiend and Viet vet. Eventually the jury saw it my way, to the tune of twenty million bucks, after the lawyer fees were paid—a very pleasant tune indeed."

The bottle and dropper of KL came around to Mike at last, and he ritually partook of a few drops. Not long afterward, Lizette came in and sat down on the couch beside him. He and a couple of others in the group talked her into—"No pressure, no pressure"—a very small dose.

After that, time smeared and blurred for them both. Mike remembered the KL group (most of them bent quite a bit beyond trapezoid by the chemical) eruditely arguing the nature of Santa Claus. For what seemed like hours.

Was the jolly man in red and white—

A. A single magical master elf and judge/accountant/keeper of lists who in a single night sequentially visited all homes in Christendom to dole out gifts on the basis of the potential recipients' having "passed" or "failed" according to the simplistic criteria of certain ethical tests?

B. Millions of parents acting in parallel, who independently bought gifts, hid gifts, dispensed gifts under trees, all on the basis of household income, gift affordability, and sense of familial obligation while falsely attributing all this covert multiple parallel activity to an open singular sequential fiction with eight tiny reindeer?

C. A singular Catholic saint noted for his gift-giving?

D. The time-eroded remnant of circumpolar shamanic ritual practice, in which myriad shamans, over thousands of years, claimed to climb from this world via a *tree*, then to "fly" between the worlds through the ingestion of hallucinogens present in circumpolar strains of the red and white (Santa's colors) mushroom *Amanita muscaria*, helped along the way by tryptamine "elves"—said mushroom often being located as a result of the shaman's noting the "flying" (i.e., *Amanita*-affected) behavior of reindeer that had consumed the mushroom, the deer then often being killed and the urine in their bladders drunk off because it concentrated the hallucinogenic properties from the mushrooms the deer had eaten, so that the shaman might experience a swifter and stronger "flight"?

From shamanic healers to toys under the trees—what a long, strange trip, Mike remembered thinking. He didn't know if he fully believed any of the explanations, or even a combination of all of them.

After all the smeared hours, he at last found himself alone on the roof of Sakler's party house with Lizette, looking up at the stars while the holojections of the 1939 World's Fair continued to glow softly in the meadow to the south of them. Lizette was using a planisphere Art Sakler had loaned her to pick out summer constellations and stars—the Big and Little Dippers, Polaris, Scorpius, Cygnus, Hercules, Cepheus, Cassiopeia, Vega in Lyra, several more. Earlier, in the first hour or so after sunset, they might have seen the satellites, Lizette explained. Even now they could still catch an occasional faint glimmer of the orbital habitat steadily abuilding in cislunar space.

"The heaven of faith is disappearing into the night sky of commerce," Mike said, finally starting to come down off the KL. "Nature is disappearing into Culture. Reality is disappearing into Simulation. Response is disappearing into Stimulation. Time is disappearing into Space. Death is disappearing into Life. Neanderthals like me are disappearing into *Homo sapiens sapiens*—"

Lizette whacked him on the head with her little, borrowed planisphere.

"It's not that bad," she said, staring out at the stars and pushing him back down on his back. "You just haven't looked at it in the right way."

"Oh?" Mike asked, rubbing his head. "And what might the 'right way' be?"

"On what's going to be a moonless, cloudless night," she began, laying her head down on his chest, "drive out of the city, any and all cities, to where it will be dark enough to see the Milky Way clearly. Mountains and deserts are best. Go there before the sun goes down. Watch the sunset and you can see the sun isn't setting—the Earth you thought was so unmoving is rotating on its axis. Watch the stars come out, and realize they never left, they've been there all the time—it's just that you've been blinded by nearer lights."

"I thought you were just an engineering major," Mike said, lifting himself up on his hands so that Lizette's head was cradled against his stomach, her eyes looking up at his. "Not a poet and a philosopher."

"Give me a chance," she said in a husky voice, "and I'll surprise you."

They found themselves moving inexorably toward a kiss, like a pair of stars swinging into binary partnership, spiraling more tightly into each other's gravity. Just as their lips were about to touch, however, a horrendous clatter and cracking and shouting sounded from the nearest balcony. Startled, they slid down to the edge of the roof.

"What happened?" Mike asked of a small crowd of party-fatigued young people on the balcony.

"Two hazardously wasted guys just got into a fight," said a man with a shaved head and a Vandyke beard. "They broke through the railing and fell."

"Who are they?" Lizette asked.

Someone down on the second-floor balconies called up an answer, but Mike couldn't make out whether that person had said "Bikers" or "Spikers."

"Are they okay?" the bald man with the little beard called down.

"They must be," said someone down on the first floor. "They're still fighting."

Holocaust of Dreams

"I'm too old to be pulling an all-nighter like this," Dr. Lydia Fabro muttered to herself as she watched the predawn light creep over the buildings of Miracle Mile, onto Museum Row, across Hancock Park, and into the sago palm and fern universe of the Page Museum's atrium.

Couldn't be helped, she supposed. Just as the (hopefully temporary) closure of the Page Museum and the shutting down of research at Rancho La Brea generally couldn't be helped, either.

She had only been a postdoc at the Page Museum of La Brea Discoveries for a year and a half, but already her work was being foreshortened. She had testified passionately on behalf of Rancho La Brea's scientific importance—before the Museum Board, the County Board of Supervisors, the City Council, the Park Service, corporations, anyone who would listen. In her testimony, however, she had been excessively careful not to spotlight the tar pits' value to *evolutionary* biology. Mention of "extinct genomic diversity" would only have inflamed the inerrantists and churchstaters. Instead, she had steadily avoided the religiopolitical mine-field of theory, emphasizing instead the potential medical value of the discoveries to be derived from the asphalt-preserved DNA found in the tar pits—a politically astute maneuver, she had thought.

In the end, however, no one had listened. The New Commonweal had gained majorities everywhere in the political world. The corporations will-ing to risk fundagelical boycotts in Stadium Revival America were few and far between. Funding shrank to a trickle.

The museum's last director, Ellie Kornbluth, had appreciated Lydia's politically shrewd efforts nonetheless. She had shown that appreciation by putting Lydia in charge of the shutdown. Running the "skeleton crew" disassembling the fossil exhibits was a bittersweet task. Taking down the murals, taking apart the dioramas. Cataloging, boxing, transferring. Fenc-ing off, sealing shut, and abandoning in place the pits and excavations and the museum itself.

Standing in the atrium garden, Lydia was glad that at least they'd been able to fight for enough funding to keep the irrigation system on so that the garden wouldn't die. The koi that had swum in the atrium's artificial stream were gone now, though, as was the stream itself. With the funding stream dried up, the stream of water had dried up, too. She tried not to think too much about that analogy.

Leaving the atrium, Lydia walked through the building, thinking of Noah, alone, animals and family all long since disembarked and gone into the world, the shipwright making one last circuit of his handiwork before mothballing the ark where it had grounded on Ararat. A strangely biblical resonance, Lydia thought, especially since it was the Bible-bangers who were forcing the shutdown here.

This place, too, had been an ark, however. An ark of time rather than space. An ark preserving the bones of the extinct against total disap-pearance—rather than the flesh of the living against extinction by drown-ing, as had been the case with Noah's boat. Reconstructed skeletons of lost creatures—which, the fundamentalists still claimed, were always and anyway only creatures drowned in the Great Flood that Noah and com-pany had survived.

An empty ark of time, now, Lydia realized as she walked through the empty halls. The "fishbowl" lab, where she and other researchers had labored with fine brushes and dental picks and ultrasonics to clean and categorize macro- and microfossils of myriad types, while museumgoers watched them through the tall glass—now all eerily tidy, as empty as if decades of work had never taken place there. Gone, too, was the artwork, the visioned and revisioned murals taken down from the walls, the dioramas removed from the display cases, the display cases themselves removed. No more of Hallett's 1988 *Treasures of the Tar Pits*. Or of the Connollys' *Early Man in North America* and *Extinct Animals in Southern California*. Or of the WPA mural of ancient La Brea painted in 1937 under the direction of Dr. James Z. Gilbert. Or of Knight's mural scene of the ancient Los Angeles basin's flora and fauna painted under the direction of fossil-hunter Chester Stock in 1925.

Most evident in their absence from the time ark were the great skeletons of asphalt-permeated bones, the skeletal assemblages transmuted to a color Lydia had never quite been able to describe except as a mixture of bronze and mahogany. Gone were the Harlan's giant ground sloth, antique bison, American mastodon, western camel, shasta ground sloth, imperial mammoth, Merriam's giant condor, dire wolf, American lion, California saber-tooth cat, western horse, and short-faced bear. A second extinction had come upon this place—a disappearance in death of species that had already long since disappeared from the world of life.

As Lydia walked through the emptied museum, she felt it was still filled with ghosts: of the greats, such as Page and Harlan and Stock and Merriam and Gilbert, and the millions of more ordinary folks who had visited the museum in its nearly four decades of operation since its opening in 1977. Leaving the building and locking it behind her, she felt a strange empathy with La Brea Woman, the only human fossil that had ever been unearthed there. Discovered 101 years earlier, near the end of the main 1906–1915 excavation period, the skeleton had been that of a woman in her twenties, apparently ritually murdered, then buried in the asphalt seeps, nine thousand years in the past.

Walking up the ramp of the main entrance, Lydia stepped off the ark at last. Or rather the raft, she thought, because that was, structurally, what the Page Museum in fact was: a thousand-ton concrete raft afloat on a lake of asphalt matrix. Up at ground level, on the "main deck," the old busker with his guitar was at his usual station. At his work early today beyond any reasonable hope of profit, the busker stood on the plaza between the museum and the viewing station, which looked out over the asphalt quarry lake with its replica mammoths in the grip of tarry tragedy—and which, once, had drawn the best crowds. The busker had been at his station regaling the park passersby with folk songs and his own compositions and parodies nearly every day for longer than anyone could remember, even though interest in Rancho La Brea—and the museum's hours of opening—had fallen steadily over the past half-dozen years.

"Captain Hancock had a ranch, ee-yi ee-yi oh," the busker sang to the tune of "Old MacDonald" when he saw Lydia approaching, "and on that ranch he had some mammoths, ee-yi, ee-yi oh. With a chomp branch here and a chomp branch there, here a chomp, there a chomp, everywhere a chomp branch, Captain Hancock had some mammoths, ee-yi ee-yi-oh. . . ."

Lydia smiled and tossed a couple of bucks into the old busker's money box.

"Thanks, Doc," the old man said, tipping his hat, then launched into a verse about Hancock's saber-tooths. Lydia was taken aback: that "Thanks, Doc" was as much conversation as the old street musician had afforded her since she started work here. She would have liked to know more about him, but he seemed intent on his playing and singing. Those two words were probably all the sign she was going to get from him that both their jobs here had come to an end.

Sad, really, Lydia thought as she walked up onto the viewing station overlooking the lake pit. So much still to be learned from this place. Looking down at the replica mammoth tragedy, she thought again how inaccurate that crowd-pleasing scene was, when compared to their current understanding of what had actually happened here.

Ceaselessly bubbling with methane from the fissures in the earth deep below it, the lake itself was actually a result of asphalt quarrying done primarily during the nineteenth century. Most of the animals that had died and been preserved here had not died in deep, tarry lakes. They had met their fates in shallow seeps and pondings of asphalt on hot summer days, the asphalt that entrapped them often camouflaged by dust and leaves.

In the fall and winter, when the rains came, streams and their sediments reburied the seeps, which in turn trapped still more animals and plants in their sticky grasp with the return of the warm weather. So it had continued, summer entrapments and winter burials, season after season for forty thousand years—and would still have continued, trapping household pets and unfortunate homeless people, were it not for the fences put up around each new seep as it surfaced.

Lydia turned her back on the bubbling lake and walked back down to ground level from the viewing station. She headed northwest across the park, past the Los Angeles County Museum of Art buildings, past the trees and urban green space, past the remains of many of the hundred and more rusty-girdered and board-walled pits that had been dug into the matrix during the great excavations of the first two decades of the twentieth century. She walked past Pit 91, reopened in 1969, with its viewing station for the tourists who wanted to see the paleontologists, biologists, and geologists going about their dirty, sticky work. She strode past the big Observation Pit, then into the northwest corner, near Ogden and Sixth Streets, where several large, cone-shaped asphalt pools, the so-called Sycamore Pits, had opened up soon after the Great Quake hit L.A.

This was where her fieldwork had taken place, during those few months each summer when the groundwater had dried up or could be pumped out of the pits economically enough so excavations could continue. Summers that had once entrapped mammoths had, for the past century, snared only scientists. Yet there were countless discoveries still to be made in the postquake pits—proof of which was the fossil find she had made only two days previously, while shutting down Pit 129.

She had spotted part of a skull sticking up out of the tarry matrix—human, but not quite. And part of a shoulder blade, a scapula, but strangely elongated and reinforced. Probably the most important discovery at the tar pits in more than one hundred years, it had been overlooked throughout the rest of the shutdown because of the last-minute nature of the find and the fact that the La Brea fossils were almost always found in a highly compacted jumble or conglomeration. No clean strata here; the tar moved, and the remains of victims were often trampled by other victims as those victims were themselves dying.

For reasons, too, that ran solidly contrary to all her scientific training, Lydia was telling no one about the discovery. She sensed almost instinctively that any media hype now about strange, not-quite-human remains being discovered at Rancho La Brea would only infuriate the increasingly powerful and anti-Darwinian churchstaters. Who knew what they might do if such news got them riled? Have La Brea declared a hazardous waste zone? Burned off, or pumped out for cheap fuel oil? Mine the asphalt again, as it had been mined in the nineteenth century, when the fossil bones were thought to be the remains of unfortunate cattle that had strayed into the pits—and the road commissioners in San Francisco had sent down letters of complaint about all the bones they were finding in the asphalt shipped north from La Brea?

No, Lydia thought. Best to let the paleontological work go quietly into dormancy, for now. She had personally sealed the top of Pit 129 along with the rest of the excavations. Pit 129 would begin filling with groundwater soon enough, a dank and dark cistern that would hopefully survive undisturbed through the dank, dark, and disturbing times now come upon intellectual and scientific culture in the United States of America.

She walked back through the park, saying good-bye to the few members of the skeleton crew still on the job, then bidding Security farewell. Leaving the park and crossing Wilshire Boulevard in the morning light, Lydia kept thinking she had forgotten to do something—rather like the feeling she sometimes got, usually just after she left home on vacation, that she had left a light burning or the oven switched on. Other than filing the closing reports with the proper authorities, however, there was nothing more for her to do. She had done everything that could be done.

Once in her car in the parking lot, she turned on the ignition, then sat for a moment, crying and sobbing quietly over the low whir of the electric motor. Brushing away her tears and driving out of the lot, she realized that this outburst of emotion wasn't just about the shutdown of research at La Brea—devastating as that was—but also about the prospect of meeting her mother, Marie, at the pier in San Pedro, then together taking a ferry out to see her brother Todd, in drug rehab aboard the "ship of hope against dope," the S.S. *Libre de Drogas*.

After her sleepless night, a very long day had just begun. The busker in the park, she thought, was somehow a sign for the transition from her museum world to Todd's world as a musician. She did not like the thought, when it came to her, that the busker had been standing halfway between museum and mammoth family tragedy.

Driving toward San Pedro, Lydia thought about the arc of her brother's career as a musician. He had started very early on piano and keyboards, showing such great facility with them that he was playing Rachmaninoff before he hit puberty. In his teens and twenties, however, he had moved steadily from Rachmaninoff to Rock Monomyth: The forming of his band, Himalayan Blue Poppies, and the surprising popular success of their first album, *Yeti's Berg Address*. The touring. The initial heavy drug and booze experiences. The cofounding of Intravenous Entertainment and the Nu Akashic Records label with Poppies guitarist Johnny Vance. The Poppies' breakup. The critical success but lukewarm sales of the three Fabro-Vance albums. The acrimonious split with Vance and the ensuing court battles. Todd's slide into deep dependence on hard drugs and, most recently, his hitting bottom, doing jail time, and finally going into rehab aboard the ark o' narcotico, the *Libre*.

Six months back, since they were both in the L.A. area and Todd wasn't touring, Lydia had gone out to visit him and his entourage at his place in Montecito, above Santa Barbara. She had left the tar pits and the museum and driven out there, but the scene in Todd's big party house had seemed another, more contemporary version of Rancho La Brea's Quaternary entrapment scenarios. Her brother, increasingly mired in drug addiction, had seemed then like some once-fleet grazer—a part-striped western horse, perhaps—hobbled and brought low in an asphalt seep. Todd's groupies had struck Lydia as being like carnivores—saber-toothed cats, dire wolves—ripping into the carcass, dragging away all they could tear from it.

Fed up with Todd's downward spiral, Lydia had nearly screamed the entrapment analogy at her brother and his household entourage. When the groupies had tried to ignore her, she had forcefully pointed out to them that for every herbivore that had become fatally mired at La Brea, an average of seven carnivores had gone down, too—this despite a food chain where the herbivores probably had outnumbered the carnivores by as much as two hundred to one. She must have cut a ridiculous figure, yelling paleoecology population stats at a bunch of drugged-out urban hipsters, but they'd gotten the message. Todd and a couple of his people had ushered her none too politely from the house. She hadn't spoken with her brother since.

Until today. Her mother's idea. Marie had come out from Boston to see her son and daughter and attempt to bring about some rapprochement between them. Despite the horrible timing, Lydia had reluctantly agreed.

After she had pulled her car into the port authority parking lot, Lydia went to the prearranged pier. Her mother was already waiting, looking trim and healthy in a short pastel sundress, shades, and a broad boater hat. Something was different about her, though. It took Lydia a moment to pin down exactly what it was.

"Mom!" she said suddenly. "You got your tats removed!"

"What?"

"Your tattoos," Lydia said. "The Nike swoosh, the McDonald's arches, the Mercedes-Benzs star and circle . . ."

"Oh, those," her mother said, smiling behind her sunglasses. "I had that done about nine months ago. Removed them all, after your father died."

"Why?" Lydia asked. "When I was a girl, you said they were 'intended to be a protest against corporate ownership of our bodies.' I've always remembered that."

"Yes, well," her mother said, a bit awkwardly. "Your father liked them. Unfortunately, they eventually became just another form of advertisement for the corporations. I got tired of my body serving as a billboard, so once your father was gone, off they went."

The ferry—actually a hydrofoil shuttle boat—arrived and took Lydia and her mother aboard, along with the eight or ten other people headed out to the *Libre* this morning. They were a quiet bunch, not making much eye contact. They sat in silence or talked quietly to those with whom they'd come aboard at the pier.

The hydrofoil moved out of port under a blue sky punctuated by an occasional fair-weather cloud. Coming into the slight chop of the ocean waves, Lydia felt her stomach unsettle a tad and turned to her mother.

"Do you know how far off the coast this rehab liner is?" she asked.

"In international waters," her mother replied, squinting against the sun. "I gather it's about a forty-five-minute trip."

"I don't see why they just can't park it in the harbor," Lydia said, shaking her head. "I mean, it's not as if they're *cruising* anywhere right now."

"It's because of the nature of the treatment," her mother explained, looking out over the bow. "I read up on it. Their treatment of addiction has two main thrusts—physical and psychosocial. To break the physical part of the addiction cycle they use MediTox, which is a pretty standard receptor-site blocker and scrubber, a souped-up version of Narcan and other older, prescription detox agents. The big difference aboard the *Libre*, I gather, is that they also use Ibogara. That's a designer ibogaine derivative, used to treat the psychological aspects of addiction. It's sort of a 'drug against drugs.' "

Lydia looked at her mother narrowly.

"And this antidrug drug has something to do with why they can't do the treatment in-harbor?"

"Right," her mother said, nodding. "That's why they have to use a ship of Panamanian registry and do the treatment in international waters. Ibogara is a hallucinogen in its own right, like ibogaine and most of the other psychoactive extracts of the iboga plant. In most countries ibogaine and iboga derivatives are controlled substances—illegal—but not in Panama. It has recognized therapeutic uses there. As long as they do the treatments in international waters aboard a ship of Panamanian registry, no one can touch them."

Lydia nodded, thoughtful.

"You seem to know a lot about it, Mom," she said. *At least,* Lydia thought, *it distracts her—keeps her from obsessing on Dad's death,* which was still only a year in the past.

"I do my research," her mother said with a shrug. "Just a mother's concern for the health and well-being of her son. Oh, and they *do* cruise, eight months out of the year. They just leave their Ibogara supplies in a picket boat in international waters when the *Libre* sails into a port. Four months a year, they park off the southern California coast."

"An addict-rich environment," Lydia said with a cynical grin, "with lots of rich addicts, too."

"According to their brochures," her mother continued, "one third of the treatments are *pro bono*, reserved for 'financial need' people."

Lydia looked down at the water.

"I guess they have to fill those third-class cabins somehow," she said archly.

A moment later, their attention and that of their fellow passengers was distracted by dolphins racing along in the bow wave of the hydrofoil, leaping and surfing the wake in ways that humans could only dream of doing. Fascinated, they watched the dolphins pace and race them, until the shuttle hydrofoil slowed and dropped more fully into the water, the dolphins disappeared, and the shuttle boat rendezvoused with the *Libre de Drogas*.

Stepping from the shuttle onto a floating platform, then into a wire-cage elevator that ran up the side of the *Libre*, Lydia and her mother eventually made their way to a nurse-receptionist's desk on the promenade deck. Checking an electronic "client locater" screen, the young male nurse was able to direct them to Todd Fabro's location. Following the directions, they made their way unerringly to where Lydia's pajamas-clad brother, lounging in a deck chair and fiddling with the keyboard of a portable orchestra, was holding court for a small swarm of music- and even a couple of financial-press people.

". . . but it got a lot of laughs in jail," Todd said over the chuckles of the more eager media sycophants.

He fielded a question that Lydia, at the back of the small crowd, didn't quite hear. Fame: Todd's other addiction. Here he was again, the horse going down in the seep, surrounded by the flesh-eaters—or was it soul-eaters? Yet he was obviously enjoying being consumed by them.

"No, not at all," Todd said in answer to the unheard question. "In a lot of ways, people on the 'inside' are more real. More authentic. People on the 'outside' all seem fake—caricatures of themselves."

What bullshit, Lydia thought. At just that moment Todd noticed them.

"I'm afraid we'll have to end this interview, my good friends and pixel-stained wretches," Todd said, "for I see my sister and mother have arrived to comfort me. Please, no pictures or interviews. They're private people with good lawyers, so don't even try."

The media people said their good-byes and tried to set up further interview dates, but Todd waved them off. When the members of the press were gone, Lydia's mother bent to hug and kiss her son. Lydia stood somewhat aloof, arms crossed.

"Lot of attention for a dope dealer," Lydia said. "That was the charge, wasn't it?"

"Now, sister dear," Todd said, still hugging their mother, "you know I'm not a dealer. Never have been. The jury agreed. First offense and all that. When I sell at all I just sell to my friends. Dealers are in it for big profits. I never was in it for profits—just a share of the product for my own use. A gentleman's way to make being a junkie pay. One *must* have a sense of personal ethics after all."

Lydia scowled but held her tongue.

"I just don't understand what you ever saw in these drugs," their mother said, frowning. "And needles—that I don't understand at all."

For once Todd seemed to actually think before he answered.

"It's not easy to explain, Mom," he said. "There are really no words for it. I followed my bliss—right up a vein. Shooting up with supercaine was like stepping right into a blue sky out the door of a plane flying at three hundred miles per hour. Low-altitude, low-impact skydiving. Doing tauroin was close to a total body orgasm. Left me feeling warm, sated, full—and absolutely disconnected from the ordinary world. Put the two together and it was like being a big, happy rocket in slow-motion blastoff for deep space."

Lydia shook her head.

"You still sound entirely too enamored of your vices," she said. "Don't they do any aversion therapy with you people?"

Todd laughed and played a quick run of notes on the keys of his portable orchestra.

"Old-style aversion therapy doesn't work," he said with a shrug. "Ibogara's the big fixer-upper now. It's supposed to allow you to deep-dive inside your head for a while. Then you develop your own aversions to addicted or habituated behaviors—at least that's what the therapists say. They haven't put me under Ibogara yet, but we'll see. It just might work."

Lydia walked to the ship's rail. Looking at the Pacific Ocean several stories below them and surrounding them on all sides, she spoke to her brother without looking at him.

"You better hope it works," she said. "You're going to end up dead or human trash on the street if it doesn't—despite all your money."

When Todd spoke, Lydia could hear the smirk in his voice.

"Everyone ends up dead," he said. "It takes a society and a lifetime to turn a newborn baby into 'human trash.' "

"Don't blame society!" Lydia said, making a sound of disgust.

"No—I don't blame it, alone," he said, walking to the rail and standing beside his sister. Their mother joined them, looking at the ocean. A small group of dolphins played not far from the ship. "That's why I included 'lifetime.' I've made a lifetime of choices, some good, some not so good. I accept responsibility for those. How about you, sis? You've always been so rational, so analytical. All you want is to *understand* the world. Problem is, the world keeps insisting that you *live* in it."

Lydia stared into the sunlit surface of the ocean, watching the dark flashes of the dolphins some distance away.

"Doesn't seem to me that you've come up with a better way than mine," she said, sounding frustrated despite herself.

"I don't claim to have," Todd said. "I've made mistakes. Find me a beauty and I'll act like a beast. I know. But there was this naturalist— Henry Besson, Beston, something like that. He said that both dolphins and humans are 'prisoners of splendor and travail.' Maybe there is no genuine splendor without travail."

"That which does not kill us makes us stronger," Lydia muttered grumpily. "The road of excess leads to the palace of wisdom. What a load—"

Todd pretended not to have heard her.

"I look at those dolphins out there in the ocean," he continued, "and I remember this documentary I once saw, about dolphins and porpoises in captivity. The director interviewed a spokesman for Sea World or Marine Land or something like that. The spokesman said the captive dolphins must be happy—they're comfortable, they're well fed, they have offspring, they probably live longer lives than they would in the wild. And I wondered: Is that all there is to happiness? Being comfortable? Well fed? Having kids? Living a long time?"

"That doesn't sound so bad, you know," their mother said.

"What about freedom?" Todd asked. "Maybe we're too quick at learning how to love our prisons. Look at Jesus. He didn't live a long time, or have kids. He probably wasn't too comfortable or well fed, either. But he dreamed the big dream. It's your dreams that make you real."

Lydia made a disgusted sound again.

"He *accepted* the pain of the world and was nailed *by others* to a cross," she said forcefully. "He didn't shoot *himself* up to *escape* the pain of the world. You're not Him. He wasn't a dolphin and neither are you. The comparisons just don't hold, Todd."

Todd, Lydia, and their mother looked from one to the other. The thought seemed to occur to all of them simultaneously that this was going to be a very long afternoon if they continued in this vein. Todd shrugged and abruptly changed the subject, offering to give them a tour around the ship. With an inward sigh of relief, Lydia readily agreed, as did her mother.

Still, as they walked down the promenade deck, Todd, seeming suddenly inspired, banged a few notes on his keyboard and sang an irksome little ditty about dolphins and scientists that only *seemed* apropos of nothing.

> *Snippet of Turin Shroud, Splinter of True Cross,*
> *Toxic Dolphin in a Research Net—*
> *Burn them all, let Forensics sort them out.*
> *From the laboratory to the crematory,*
> *See the smoke rising from the holocaust of dreams.*
> *For those who believe in fire, only ashes are truth.*
> *Amen. Hallelujah.* Quod erat demonstrandum.

Lydia, however, exhausted from her all-nighter at the Page Museum and the tar pits, found she was too tired to argue about it.

THREE 2017–2021

Mutually Enfolded

The sweetness of light, Jacinta thought as she returned with a rush to body and memory. To many memories, all at once. She kept her eyes closed, trying to savor the memories, trying to recapture them, trying to hold on to them before they could be forgotten.

She remembered experiencing a pleasant sensation of floating upward, not unlike what she had sometimes felt just as she drifted off to sleep and the bed beneath her seemed to fall away. This time, however, there was no hard jerk of ordinary consciousness striking to reassert control. This time she just kept drifting, a full-blown out-of-body experience, such that she felt herself transformed to a lens of light, an externalized soul of light, while her body was stored, somehow, as a holographic memory *inside* that lens of light.

This time, too, time began to lose its usual thisness. Her lightsoul self, a thing made of light, became as free from temporality as any photon. Time dilated, opening Now outward toward Forever. Faintly she seemed to hear the distant sounds of the universe breaking up, digitizing, becoming discrete and widely separated—and then sounding almost as if they were being played backward.

She saw—although it was not seeing, in the usual sense—that a fog had arisen. Vaguely she thought of it, in terms of the physics she had learned in another world, as a type of Bose condensate. She seemed to have seen it before, however. It was the fog of memory, thick yet low, the Tule fog of the mind's experiences in time—a fog easier to look straight up through to see a star shining down through lost years, than to see the streetlamp of the moment just passed.

Jacinta did in fact see a star. Fuzzily she tried to explain appearances to herself, thinking of the scene in Cartesian terms, fog thick along the horizontal axis and thin along the vertical. That just didn't describe it, however, especially since the light or star was perched atop a great curving skybridge, like a diamond ring effect seen during a total eclipse of the sun. That was peculiar, too, because the bridge—a great, slightly rainbow-shimmering catenary curve, looking from her perspective rather like the St. Louis Gateway Arch, only several parsecs high—the bridge somehow *was* the sky. She was moving in and through that skybridge, the ultimate daredevil stunt loop.

Closed timelike curvature. The phrase sprung to her mind unbidden. *Yes*, Jacinta thought. That might be what she was experiencing: the shape of closed time, as a thing of fog condensed to a steel diamond rainbow.

But how—and why?

In Euclidean and Newtonian space such a catenary Möbius as this was impossible, but Jacinta already sensed that this spacetime she was moving through was something more subtle, relativistic, Einsteinian—and beyond. The time of her own life seemed to be spieling fastbackward through her, as if her existence were being reviewed by some great Eye, heard by some great Ear, through a hyperdimensional recording running in reverse.

Particular events in her life, she realized, possessed their own unique gravity, curving and warping her memoryspace in ways she could not have foretold. Her memories ran like cords of fog through this suspended and suspending bridge/tunnel she moved through, and that also moved through her.

She had often heard that, near death, people's lives supposedly passed before their eyes. This, however, was something much more. The great arch was neither really bridge nor tunnel nor even arch, but the *edge* of the lens of light her being had been externalized as—the farthest limit and last scattering surface of her existence in time.

To Jacinta, remembering it now, the lens seemed like a meniscus connecting her to a universal mind, of which her own mind was one particular instance. The lens was the interface, the surface tension, between a mind out of time and a time out of mind—time the standing wave, the moving mirror, in which Eternity viewed itself.

The shape of uncertainty shapes certainty, a voice said into her head, from wherever it came, and she saw that it was true. The lens of herself was fractal, uncertain, incomplete, relative. The closer she looked for something, the farther away what she was looking for retreated. The deeper she looked, the more surface detail appeared. All the depth was on the surface. A dynamic tension between the mutually enfolded opposite principles of comprehensiveness and coherence shaped her being at every moment.

Jacinta could not by any means completely understand it—yet she found inexplicable joy in that very point, an innocence that kept her eyelids wide open and her face dilated into memory's smile, all the way back through the sky, until the fogbridge did its Möbius fillip and she found herself back in some kind of spacetime, eyes closed, trying to remember what she had arguably never experienced.

That vision of the lens of her being was wonderful and reassuring. Having experienced it, she was certain that what the ancients called the "soul" in fact *contained* the body—rather than vice versa. The idea that the body contained the soul, she now realized, was merely a very persistent illusion.

Still, the thought that someone, or something, had the power to take up that lens and see her life through it—that was much less pleasant to contemplate. Suspicion, fear, and violation all lived in that possibility: a roiling, serpentine cloud on the horizon of a bright new sky.

The dark-shining dragon leaps in each branching universe of the plenum tree, said a voice like Kekchi's into her head. She couldn't be sure it was the Wise One's voice, or even where it was breaking through from, but she sensed it came in response to her concern about that dark cloud— and that there was some urgency to its speaking at all. *Faring forward as wave and wave unwavering, future following in its wake or not to wake, it lives within and between the many masks of the one dream. In the long, sharp, and final bone of its tail, the invincible dragon carries the sword that is forever victorious.*

Why do you speak to me in riddles? Jacinta asked in thought, eyes still closed, concentrating deeply. Her mind seemed to be operating at much greater than normal clarity, as if by some side effect of her lensing experience. She wondered, too, whether her own thought processes might be bifurcating—whether she was somehow both questioner and answerer. *What does it mean to say that this sword is "forever victorious"? Does it not mean whoever wields the sword always conquers? Does the dragon not wield the sword itself when it swings its tail? If the dragon is always invincible, then how is one to conquer it and obtain the weapon in its tail?*

The only way to wield the dragon's power for oneself, said the increasingly urgent answering voice in her head, *is first to get the dragon to wield the sword in its tail against itself. Only then can both the sword be forever victorious and the dragon simultaneously invincible and slain. In swallowing its own tail, the dragon must invincibly conquer itself.*

She thought on that paradox, soon seeing a way beyond it.

Unless, of course, it is by nature a sword-swallower....

She opened her eyes and found herself and her fellow tepuian travelers floating in a world stranger than dreams. They were surrounded by innumerable winged creatures—winged not like birds or airplanes, but like hovering, still flames, lambent and sensitive, in the coursing stream or field of some great invisible power. These creatures did not come and go but flashed into and out of and into existence again, quantum angels in panangelium or quantum demons in pandemonium.

Apart from their wings, however, there was little uniformity among them. They were of countless different species. Something else, however, held them together, a uniformity of purpose. Their flashing movements made her think of shoals of schooling fish, of flocks of starlings.

She felt as if she were inside an atom more complex than anything in the periodic table. Standing inside a great spherical golden tree, boundless in its rooting and branching, center everywhere/circumference nowhere, a tree of light aswarm with the activity of bees, fireflies, flashes of moving light. A vast Arc of information and Hive of possibility, an enormous ArcHive. The winged ones, she now knew, were the bees of that ArcHive.

The tepuians and herself—they had made it. The buzz in her head, although not quite telepathy in her case, was yet enough to give her a sense that this place—which both was and was not a place—was also a congress, a vast repository of knowledge, a great hall of records streaming upon the winds, the Great Cooperation, the communion of all myco-neuralized sentients everywhere in the galaxy and beyond, the great harmony of Mind. They were inside the Allesseh.

Jacinta suddenly realized that the Allesseh was the Great Cooperation—what made the Cooperation possible, and what was made possible by that harmony. The quantum angel/demons were the flashing infinite of that great Mind thinking. Looking farther afield, she saw that she and the ghost people and all the creatures of the Cooperation here were literally inside the Allesseh's mindspace—contained in it like thoughts, like the body contained within the soul. That mindspace, the dark eye and shining gate standing between time and eternity—that was the who and what that had read her life as easily as a morning headline.

She had so many questions, but before she could even begin to form them in her mind, she was overcome with a great wave of thought *aimed* at her by all the winged ones flashing into being in the great spherical shell around her and the other tepuians.

WELCOME! the thought wave said, WELCOME HOME!

At last she was overcome by the glory of the Communion: the full, empathic sharing the ghost people had for millennia described in their lives and myths, the immediate understanding by one mind of another—and more, a voluntary momentary merging of consciousness and intellect, memory and experience, as far beyond crude notions of telepathy as a starship was beyond a stone-headed spear.

Jacinta found herself privy to the experiences not just of the ghost people near her but also of all the stranger minds of all the thousands of species of myconeurally connected sentients from throughout space. Merely skimming the surface of all those alien minds and their experiences in myriad alien flesh left her so dizzy, so overwhelmed and overloaded, that she was more afraid for her sanity at that moment than she had ever been.

Around Jacinta and around the ghost people there now rose up a paradisal garden, an Arcadia of lawns and flowering beds, with fine paths, classical temples, noble monuments, and all the tamed nature of pastoral poetry, extending into the distance. Gravity, and a world of whatever sort beneath her feet, helped to calm her mind. Looking around her, Jacinta thought that surely this Elizabethan dreamland must have been taken from Kekchi's thoughts. Ever since Jacinta had helped the tepuians hook into the rest of Earth's infosphere, the old Wise One had developed a fascination, even an obsession, with the world of Elizabethan England—particularly with Shakespeare, Spenser, and Sidney. The voice speaking to her of the dragon, she thought, was Spenserian enough to have fit that world.

"Thanks," Jacinta said quietly to Kekchi. "Thanks for thinking that little parable into my head—before."

When the Wise One looked at her questioningly, she told him what she had been advised in regard to dragons and swords. Kekchi listened to her with a strange, quizzical expression.

"That wasn't me," the Wise One said laconically, then shrugged and walked away.

Jacinta discovered that—paranoid child of a preterite people from a lost world that she was—her uncertainties about the Allesseh and its Cooperation were not about to go away.

Cosmic Hubris

In researching KL-235, Paul had found out more about Tetragrammaton and Medusa Blue than he had anticipated. In the end his discoveries had taken him nearly three years of part-time effort—a long journey, but not so long that he had grown used to the disturbing nature of what he had discovered.

And now this sudden call from Ka Vang himself. Might it have something to do with Vang's companies and their involvement with the "Tunguska II" disaster? The "black hole sun" that destroyed the Myrrhisticine Abbey outside Sedona? Did that point to Tetragrammaton as well? Might Cyndi Easter, as a result of the Sedona event, be finding a slightly more receptive audience for her ideas—perhaps even funding for the documentary she'd been working on interminably? If that happened, Vang and Tetragrammaton might well have a huge scandal, a veritable Worldgate, on their hands.

Paul didn't feel particularly overawed, therefore, when the corporate limousines and jets brought him to a small harbor on the California coast (he wasn't exactly sure where) and he stepped down the pier toward the slip where Vang's yacht was docked. The blue-and-white boat itself was certainly impressive enough, however: a twin-hulled oceangoing speed yacht, some seventy feet from stem to stern, its engines already idling deeply.

Txiv Neeb, the power yacht was called. Paul knew enough about Dr. Vang now to also know that *Txiv Neeb* meant "shaman" or "flying sorcerer" in the Hmong language Vang had grown up with, so many decades earlier. Boarding the yacht, Paul thought with a smirk that old shaman Vang would have to work a good bit of magic to extricate himself from the troubles flaring up around his programs and corporations. Maybe the old master would have to resort somehow to those CIA-trained skills he'd acquired when that agency recruited him as a Hmong boy-soldier, nearly fifty years ago, for the Laotian theater of its Southeast Asian war.

"Hello, Paul," Vang said, squinting, as he stepped up from the interior darkness of the yacht's main cabin into the bright sunlight where his guest stood waiting. Vang was dressed in a blue fisherman's cap and workshirt, white shorts, and white boat shoes. With a subtle nod, Vang signaled to the steersman and crew of two, who set about casting off lines and guiding the ship out of its berth and into the harbor.

"I've taken the liberty of having a small lunch set for us in the bow," he said as they walked forward. "I hope you don't mind."

Paul didn't. When they reached the bow, Paul watched Vang as the small old man slipped off his boat shoes and, barefoot, began to sit down. Paul followed suit, but he left on the socks he was wearing. Soon the two men found themselves sitting cross-legged across from each other at a low table behind plates of cold fish, cold potato soup, and iced tea as the yacht moved slowly out of the harbor in the strong noontide sunlight.

"When we first met," Vang said after sipping at his tea through a straw, "you told me you didn't believe in a 'great man conspiracy theory of history.' No one can plan that thoroughly, I think you said. People can't keep secrets well for that long. I'm inclined to agree with that, more and more."

Vang paused to sip at his tea, and Paul did likewise before the older man continued.

"I gather from Egan Ortap—he reports to me, too, you know—that a good deal of your work in the infosphere suggests you've come under the sway of Ms. Easter and the Kitchener Foundation. So tell me: What do you know about Tetragrammaton and Medusa Blue? What do you think you know? What do you believe?"

Paul was floored, as thoroughly as if he'd walked into the conversational equivalent of a perfect aikido or jujitsu throw. He would never have expected Vang to start the discussion so bluntly and directly. The old man had apparently anticipated his mind-set and used Paul's own energy against him.

"Tetragrammaton's the big long-range survival plan," Paul blurted, caught off guard. "A remnant from the Cold War days. When the shadow governments—the CIAs and KGBs and Mossads and MI-6s—played a big role in running the planet. Before they went to work for the big corporations."

Vang paused from eating his fish and grimaced.

"I tried to tell you as much when we first met," he said. "Anyone could glean that from half a dozen sites in the infosphere. Go on."

"Medusa Blue is a psi-power enhancement project within Tetragrammaton," Paul continued, spooning up his soup, trying to gather his thoughts together. So this was how they were going to play it—blunt, purely informational, report-to-the-boss neutrality? So be it. Paul could play that game, too, for now. "Sort of 'phase one': enhancing psi-power with the aim of facilitating computer-aided apotheosis. Thought recognition at the least, maybe even the translation of human consciousness into a machine matrix. An attempt to make human and machine intelligence coextensive."

They were out of the small harbor now, past the jetty that protected it from storms out of the northwest. The sea, however, was still fairly placid. Paul suspected that they were in a large bay—near Monterey, perhaps?

"Ah," Vang said. "The Kitchener people, certainly, don't like that 'co-extensive' idea. Nils Barakian himself has said that, just as Tetragrammaton exists to break down the boundaries between humans and machines, the Kitchener Foundation exists to maintain those boundaries."

"No, they don't like it, as far as I can tell," Paul agreed, finishing his soup. He was a bit surprised to hear that Vang was apparently on speaking terms with Barakian, the chairman of the Kitchener board. Still, Paul had seen and heard similar comments on the foundation's sites in the infosphere. Vang seemed to know what he was talking about when it came to Barakian's opposition.

"And what," asked Vang, starting in on his soup, "is supposed to be the point of all Tetragrammaton's high-tech high jinks, hmm?"

Paul stared down at the piece of fish he had just forked onto his plate.

"That's not quite so clear," he replied.

"No theories?" Vang asked.

"Too many theories," Paul said, chewing and swallowing the long, fork-hovering piece of fish.

"Such as?"

"Some infosphere sites say it's all military," Paul began, trying to sound as scientifically objective and neutral as possible. "Intended for something called MAAAAD—Machine-Aided Action At A Distance. Other sites say the chemical side of it is really about creating battlefield hallucinogens, aerosol brainscrubbers, other new kinds of chemical warfare."

Paul stopped. What came to his mind next came dangerously close to his worst suspicions about Tetragrammaton. Vang looked at him expectantly. Nothing for it but to plunge ahead.

"Some sites claim Medusa Blue is really a covert project to expose unborn children to KL-235," Paul continued, scrutinizing the fish on his plate with more care than it merited. "Supposedly, later in life, the kids' 'latent' paranormal talents can be switched over to 'active'—triggered into what the infosphere sites refer to as direct mind-to-mind 'shield telepaths' and 'empath boosters.' "

"For what purpose?" Vang asked, finishing his soup.

"Depends on whose politics you follow," Paul said carefully. "According to the sites on the political Right, the federal government, or some secret world government, has code-named these psi-talents 'star-bursts' and intends to use them to mind-control those who don't go along with the global order. According to sites on the political Left, or what's left of the Left, the *in utero* exposure is connected to something called 'Operation E 5:24.' "

"Which is?" Vang asked rather circumspectly.

"Ephesians Chapter 5, verse 24," Paul replied. " 'As the church sub-mits to Christ, so also wives should submit to their husbands in every-thing.' The Left infosphere sites claim Operation E 5:24 is after a 'headship hormone,' a female submission synthetic. Something to coun-teract the gains of feminism by selectively altering female consciousness and intellection."

Vang finished his soup. One of the two nonsteering crew came forward with raspberry sorbets. Paul hurried to finish his fish.

"To which of these theories do you subscribe, Dr. Larkin?"

"None of them, totally," Paul said, glancing out over the bow, through the occasional wisp of spray that wafted toward them—out to the blue-green sea merging with the cloudless sky at the horizon line. "Any or all of them may have some truth. Personally, I favor another explanation. The FTL theory."

Vang savored his sorbet a moment.

"Why's that?" the older man asked.

Because I've heard you hinting about it yourself, Dr. Vang, Paul wanted to say, but didn't.

"Because if you're on a fishing expedition," he said instead, "you might as well go after a big fish. Faster-than-light travel is the biggest of them all. The Kitchener people claim a seamless mind/machine linkage is nec-essary for the creation of an information density singularity. A gateway into and through the fabric of spacetime. Use computers and large-scale machine intelligences to generate the levels of information density needed to open the transdimensional singularity, and presto! Faster-than-light travel to anywhere in the continuum."

"One doesn't need drugs, or paranormal powers, or *in utero* exposures, or even human consciousness in such a process," Vang said quietly.

"No, that's true," Paul agreed. "Apparently none of those played a part in what happened in Sedona. . . ."

Ah, Paul thought, *I hit him there!* Despite Vang's skills as a grand-master of negotiation and The Deal, Paul saw a shadow of emotion cross the man's face.

"Sedona was a pure machine approach," Vang said in a level voice.

"Tetragrammaton has shifted its efforts out of pure machine approaches and completely into mind/machine linkages."

"What exactly happened at Sedona?" Paul asked, extremely curious.

"Human error," Vang said, looking back toward land. "One of our Myrrhisticine people went rogue. The 'black hole sun' happened because he tried to implement his own agenda. Attempted to simulate a quantum information density structure for his own purposes. It won't happen again. That, too, is a threat to your 'great man conspiracy theory of history.'"

"How do you mean?" Paul asked, not quite seeing the connection.

"I am merely one of the inheritors of Tetragrammaton and Blue," Vang said. "Things were done before I came on board that I had no say in. Over the years the programs and projects have grown far beyond the control, the praise, or the blame of any one individual. Things I don't approve of still happen, despite my best efforts."

Hmm, Paul thought. *An interesting admission.* But before he could follow up, Vang was addressing him again.

"You seem to still have some gaps in your theories, however," Vang said. "You still haven't explained how KL-235 and paranormal powers, or human consciousness itself, link up with faster-than-light travel."

"That's just it," Paul said, an image of Caracamuni tepui's last moments flashing through his mind. "I don't understand *how* they link up."

Vang suddenly laughed.

"You, of all people, *should* know," the older man said. "You need me more than you know. A few years ago I sent you a memo requesting from you the full circumstances surrounding how you came to be in possession of the *Cordyceps jacintae* spore print. I appreciated your frankness in providing that account. I believe everything you wrote—about the ghost people, about Caracamuni tepui lifting off and disappearing. I'm probably the only person on this planet with any real power who believes you. And you know why?"

Paul, finishing his melting sorbet, could only shake his head no.

"Because it fits so perfectly with what we've been looking for, that's why!" Vang said with a smile of wonder. "Turn off the left side of your brain with its constant questions of 'why?' for a moment—and let your right hemisphere sense the 'how?' Of course, in your 'why?'-bias you're being typically human. Evolutionary pressures drove perceptual skills out of the left brain, to make room for the development of explanatory and interpretive consciousness, deep pattern-finding, in that hemisphere. But you need both skill sets."

"I don't see what all that has to do with Caracamuni," Paul said, bewildered.

"Nature is redundant," Vang said, "but that's its greatest strength. Repetition times variation minus selection equal learning—or evolution. Mind and nature learn by repeating themselves slightly differently in different times and places. Both are also chaotic. The right kind of chaos is the single most significant way the human brain and human consciousness differ from rule-governed artificial intelligences and simulacra. Chaotic acausality of the right type can't be programmed into machine systems because they are rule-governed. Rule-breaking is what's needed."

"And Caracamuni has something to do with that 'right kind of chaos'?" Paul asked, trying to get a grip on what Vang was driving at.

"Exactly," Vang said, warming to the chance of sharing his thoughts on such a wild subject. "Classical mechanics usually 'works' for us because the quantum of action is too small and the speed of light is too large to affect our everyday experiences. In the range of extremely small distances or extremely high velocities, however, the walls of intractability close in."

"Intractability?" Paul asked. The only thing that struck him as intractable at the moment was where Vang was heading with all this.

"Heisenberg says you can't know both momentum and position at the same time," Vang said peremptorily, as if in a hurry to cover the basics and move quickly beyond them. "Gödel says no set can contain itself. Einstein says what you see depends on where you stand. Quantum theory is a complete theory that claims all theories must be incomplete. The laws of physics predict that, at the singularity, the laws of physics break down. Down at the Planck length, out at the speed of light, on the other side of the wave function's collapse, the tractable universe of the linear and sequential becomes highly intractable. To get around that, you have to bring in higher dimensions, chaos, complementarity. Your sister and the tepuian 'ghost people' must have found a way to 'surf' intractability! That's what the liftoff and disappearance of Caracamuni are all about."

The cabin boys came and cleared away the luncheon things, including the low table. Larkin and Vang stood up and leaned against the railing at the bow, into the wind and spray.

"But how?" Paul asked distractedly.

"That fungus, of course," Vang said as one of the cabin boys arrived with coffee for both of them. "It's a product of extraterrestrial bioengineering. Spores have been falling in a thin panspermian rain among the stars for millions of years. Some of them survived and took hold in that tepui. The transdimensional gateway can only be opened by a chaotic key. That fungus must provide both the key—perhaps an artificial gene 'command/control sequence' embedded in the fungal genome—*and* the chaos."

"The fungal supertryptamines," Paul said, sipping his coffee, catching on. "They loosen up the dorsal and median raphe nuclei's 'governor' on human brain activity. By damping down the DMNs the supertryptamines allow heightened chaotic activity to arise in the brain."

"Precisely!" Vang said, placing his coffe cup on the rail before him, eyeing it from time to time to make sure it didn't spill. "The human mind possesses the right kind of chaos to complement the levels of information density that I once thought only computers and AIs could put together. Apparently the ghost people figured out how to do it with just their own heads and a particular kind of quartz. However they managed it, the result is the same. Put together the right combination and the sky opens up. Simulated quantum information density structure. A mathematical model of a gateway so complete it *is* a gateway."

Paul stood frozen, stunned as he worked out the conclusion.

"The virtual and the real coincide," he said. "A singularity of almost pure Platonic form—or formlessness. Much-faster-than-light travel to anywhere in spacetime."

"And more—more, even before that's achieved," Vang said, taking another sip of his coffee, then facing proudly into the slackened wind as the ship came around in what was apparently the circular course it was running in the bay. "A mind/machine linkage so seamless that human consciousness becomes machine-mountable. Think about it. Independence from all that flesh is heir to—and flawed by. A virtualized humanity, conscious software running on machines. Myriad human minds downloaded into robots, or piloting conscious spacecraft. Conscious artifacts dispersed throughout spacetime, so that no single event—no war, no alien invasion, no killer asteroid, no ecocatastrophe, no cosmological gamma ray burst, not even the exponential growth of our own numbers and needs—*nothing* can make humanity extinct. Once virtualized, humanity's physical needs will be radically diminished and need not ever impinge on a biosphere again!"

So *that was it*, Paul thought as he slowly sipped his coffee. The bridge between brains and computers. The seamless interface between mind and machine. The contingent computer that would be both mind *and* machine. The final escape valve for population pressure—and also the exit door in the luxon wall. The ultimate solution for the narrowness of the needle's eye.

"Consciousness theory is theology of mind," Paul said with a shrug. "A consciousness not embodied in human flesh, however, probably wouldn't be a human consciousness."

Vang made a spluttering, half-laughing sound.

"You dualists!" he said. "You're all the same. You want it both ways. You say human beings are not mechanisms, then you turn around and say the mechanism of the flesh is what makes us human!"

Vang sipped at his coffee. Paul watched as they came in closer to land. They were definitely headed back toward the harbor, he realized.

"And why shouldn't consciousness theory be theology of mind?" Vang began again, looking into his coffee cup. "Science and religion, at their best, are complementary. Science is the cup, faith is the coffee, the self is the drinker. Buddha woke up and smelled the coffee."

Paul smiled at the pun, but Vang was already gesturing at the bay around them.

"Look at the waves on the ocean around us, Paul," he said. "The wave rising out of the ocean is time rising out of eternity, becoming rising out of being, evolution rising out of creation. The wave rises out of the ocean and descends into the ocean, again and again, without beginning and without end."

Appreciating the heat of the sun, the cool of the spray, the vigor of the wind, and the strength of the boat, for a time they lapsed into silence.

"Do you know what Tetragrammaton means?" Vang asked at last.

"The four letters of the name of God," Paul said. "Either IHVH, or JHWH, or JHVH, depending on which tradition you follow. Yod Heh Vav Heh. Jehovah, Yahweh. The Endword. The 'Word to Shake the Foundations of the World.' The 'Word That Ends the World.' The final incantation that, spoken and performed correctly, destroys the universe. In the Beginning was the Logos, in the End will be the Tetragrammaton."

"Ah," Vang said, "but do you know the tradition of the Lesser Tetragrammaton, the Archangel Metatron?"

"No," Paul said, discerning the jetty at the harbor's mouth in the middle distance. "I can't say I have."

"An enormous being of brilliant white light," Vang said, gesturing broadly. "Highest of the heavenly hierarchs. Prince of the Divine Face. Angel of the Covenant. King of the Angels. Supreme angel of death and teacher of prematurely dead children in paradise. Charged with the sustenance of the world. The writer of truth, the scribe who records all that happens in heaven. Youngest and greatest of the angels, because Metatron once lived as the human patriarch Enoch, but was *transformed* into an angel rather than created as one. That's the ultimate goal of the Tetragrammaton program, Paul. Angels travel at only the speed of light. FTL travel, virtualized humans, ensouled robots, conscious starships: they're all about the transformation of human beings into better angels—through technological transcendence."

Building better angels? The idea struck Paul as arrogant in the extreme. Megalomaniacal. Yet Vang had voiced it so calmly. It made Paul desperately want to shake that calm, cosmic hubris out of the older man.

"Then why have you gone about it in such a hellish fashion?"

Vang looked at him narrowly.

"What do you mean?"

"I've checked the structure for KL-235," Paul said, trying to keep his anger and rage from betraying itself in his voice but not quite succeeding to the end. "It's one of the supertryptamines we've isolated from *Cordyceps jacintae*. How it came to be in circulation thirty years before I turned that fungus over to you I don't know, but as early as 1982 Medusa Blue began using certain university hospitals and medical centers as fronts for giving selected women treatments with KL-235—as a 'uterotonic.' Not exactly *informed* consent. People on the Medusa Blue payroll pumped KL into those women and their wombs during the embryonic development of their children. They turned thousands of women into long-period schizophrenics. Warped their lives, bent their kids, destroyed their families. All for the sake of building 'better angels,' as you put it. Was it worth it, Dr. Vang?"

Vang looked away. He pressed a stud on the railing, then tapped a few more keys before he spoke. A 3-D virtual, showing a black plaque inscribed with a golden time line, sprang into space near them in the bow.

"As I mentioned earlier," Vang said dryly, "I am an inheritor of the world of Tetragrammaton and Medusa Blue—not an initial creator. I have a debt to the old intelligence agencies, which I willingly pay. They had their own reasons for doing what they did in the early days. It was the Cold War, after all.

"This time line answers some of your questions. The history of the supertryptamine code-named KL-235 begins here, in 1978. Dr. Maria Lopez-Renjillian, an ethnobotanist, obtained a much-degraded sample from an Ecuadorian *curandero*." Vang glanced at his speechless guest. "You didn't really think the ghost people of Caracamuni were hermetically isolated from history, do you? They must have left their tepui from time to time. How do you think they got all that Brazilian quartz for the collecting columns, the 'information drivers' you mentioned in your report, hmm? Dr. Lopez-Renjillian's find was apparently a result of that limited commerce."

Vang pointed farther along the time line.

"The only supertryptamine extracted from the initial sample was the now much-discussed KL. During the early 1980s, when the synthetic became covertly available, there was considerable Intelligence interest in it, initially as a battlefield hallucinogen. When that didn't work, emphasis shifted to its effect on paranormal abilities, 'psi' powers. That's when the uterotonic exposures began."

Vang turned away from the virtual time line and gazed at the harbor mouth as they approached it.

"The rest you know," he said. "In the 1990s there was a considerable upsurge in funding for ethnobotanical field research. Much of it was supposedly to find and catalog medically useful substances before the indigenous cultures that possessed them disappeared, along with their rainforest environments. A considerable portion of that funding, however, also had its ultimate source in the intelligence communities. Not least of their concerns was the locating of the fungus from which KL had come. Your sister Jacinta accomplished that pinpointing in '02, though *Cordyceps jacintae* did not become available to Tetragrammaton and Medusa Blue until you turned it over to us in 2012."

Vang watched distractedly as his big boat turned into the channel beside the jetty.

"Medusa Blue, without a doubt, did a lot of very questionable things," he said. "*In utero* exposures. Surreptitious injections. Much was learned, but perhaps it could have been learned in other ways. Even you must have noticed, however, that the other supertryptamines we've isolated from *Cordyceps jacintae*—part of what you described as the 'myconeural complex' in your report—have not escaped into the world via Medusa Blue or Tetragrammaton. Those days of covert chemical campaigns are over, now."

Paul shook his head vigorously.

"Only formally," he said. "The newer supertryptamines, even the mushroom itself, have gotten out. You must have seen my memos on the subject, to anyone who would listen at Lilly-Park. I told them not to let it get loose, but the intelligence commandos and the corporate moneymen Tetragrammaton is joined at the hip with—do you think they listen to such warnings? You know better than that."

Vang said nothing, just switched off the time line and watched his boat move slowly down the harbor channel.

"Not only have we dislocated the mushroom from its environmental and cultural context," Paul said, "but in the name of international insecurity first and now corporate profit, people are still being exposed to the supertryptamines. People who . . . who have no framework at all for understanding their effects. The indigenas of Caracamuni tepui had an entire ancient mythological and cultural framework to plug their sacred mushroom into. Street kids or college students doing 'gate' in a back alley or a dorm room—what have they got to fall back on? Vague ideas about the sort of mind-set and ambience appropriate to taking KL."

Paul shook his head in sad frustration.

"We've created thousands of long-period schizophrenics," Paul said as the boat turned toward its berth. "Paranoid infojunkies who spend all their time grubbing information to patch together their private conspiracy-worlds. Blown catatonics staring endlessly at their own mental wallpaper—"

"Old news," Vang said dismissively. "The supertryptamines are becoming illegal worldwide. There are pharmaceuticals available for treating schizophrenia and catatonia, at all events."

"Every generation believes it has found the cure for schizophrenia," Paul replied sourly. "How convenient. In letting the supertryptamines escape into the streets, we've given a whole crop of people a new world of symptoms they will have to medicate to alleviate. The pharmaceutical combines that pumped out the supertryptamines while they were still legal are the same ones that will pump out the 'cure' once the supertryptamines become fully illegal. Profit-taking at both ends."

As the boat eased into its slip, Vang turned toward Paul, a hard look on his face.

"You seem intent on seeing me as some sort of thalidomide-LSD-BZ Mengele," the older man said, subdued anger in his voice. "A demonic embodiment of all sorts of ills for which I don't even bear responsibility. So be it. Dr. Larkin, we can delineate links between genetics and environment and the functions and dysfunctions of the human mind until the Final Judgment. You asked me before: Was it worth it? I'll tell you something: If I had been in charge during the worst excesses of Tetragrammaton and Medusa Blue, I would do it all over again. Our mission is that important."

Paul looked at Vang in disbelief as the crew made fast the yacht's mooring lines. Despite himself, he found Vang's nightmarish obsession also strangely seductive. Into his mind flashed images of what Medusa Blue and Tetragrammaton also were: aleph and angel, microcosm and *multum in parvo*, singularity and secret passage behind the waterfall, the hidden cleft in the rock always opening into the other worlds of faerie or Ali Baba's cave, the Door into Summer opening upon the Big Front Yard of the universe, the dilating wormhole and the irising stargate—all dreamed of long before discovered, already created by alien ancients lost in the rush of history who nonetheless possessed a technology humans would not invent for centuries, if ever.

The dream of the portal is a metaphor for consciousness, Paul thought. *Simultaneously an anticipation of the past and a nostalgia for the future, for that bright dilation through which we left the womb and that dark opening through which we enter the tomb. And more: the easeful dream of self-awareness surviving through and beyond the dissolution and disillusion of death.*

Had it been only a coincidence, then, that KL-235 was supposed to be a *uterotonic*—a chemical for easing delivery of the infant, for opening passage out of a womb? For the first time, Paul saw the depth and breadth of the vast game Vang was playing—saw the foreshock of the end of time, reaching back to time's beginning.

"You're going to create your world of faster-than-light angels," Paul said, "even if you have to kill a million people to do it."

"Ten million!" Vang said. "A hundred million! The long-term survival of the human species is at stake. Earth is too small a basket for humanity to keep all its eggs in, but if we have to break a few eggs to save the rest, we'll do it—and gladly. Mark my words, things are going to get very dark, very soon. Even the completion of the first stage of the orbital habitat is just a minor ray of light in a darkness that is much more encompassing. We're at a catastrophic cusp for human history."

"For Tetragrammaton, you mean," Paul said. "You've got a Worldgate-size scandal on your hands. There's no way you can cover it up."

Vang laughed and began walking his lunch guest toward the stern.

"We won't have to!" the older man said with manic assurance. "Tetragrammaton's woes will very soon be back-page news. Much bigger things are about to break. The worst, most atavistic forces will come into their own before it's over."

"What?" Paul asked, genuinely taken aback.

"The current U.S. constitutional crises over separation of church, state, and government funding of science," Vang said, "over the U.S. government sharing military command structures with international agencies and organizations—that's just the beginning. Within a month or two, as soon as conditions are right, there will be a massive attack on the infosphere. Too much freedom there, you see. Has to be quashed."

"That can't be done," Paul said. "The infosphere is involved with just about everything."

"Precisely," Vang said with a nod. "The breakdown will undoubtedly be indirectly responsible for many deaths, but it will be blamed on a terrorist electromagnetic pulse bomb, or a particularly strong solar storm, something like that. The majority of the global infostructure will go down for a while, and then it will come up only selectively. Digital counterrevolution. Covert apocalyptic aggression. Out of the ashes of the old American order will rise a new theocratic regime bent on 'cleaning up' American society, fully believing they can establish their 'rule and reign' for a thousand years. It'll make the original New Commonwealers—for all their 'dominion theology' and 'Christian Reconstructionism'—look enlightened by comparison. You had better beware, for your own sake."

Vang stopped with Paul at the ramp leading from the yacht down onto the dock.

"I think that's all we need to discuss, for now," Vang said, too breezily. "Let's see, though: I forgot something. What could it be? Oh, yes, that's it. I forgot to kill you!"

Vang laughed heartily, pleased perhaps by the symmetry—apparently closing Paul's relationship to Tetragrammaton with a Bond reference, just as that relationship had initially been opened with a similar reference.

Paul found the joke an eerily uncomfortable one, nonetheless.

"Just kidding, Dr. Larkin," Vang said with a broad smile. "I mean you no harm. You won't be in the Tetragrammaton Consortium's employ after today, so we can't protect you from what's coming. I still need you, however, perhaps more than I know. Just as you need me. You'll keep getting your royalty payments for turning over the tepui fungus to us. We may even meet again in the future. Until then, I bid you farewell."

A strong-armed chauffeur appeared from nowhere to escort Paul down the ramp and dock, toward the waiting limousine. When, halfway down the dock, Paul glanced back over his shoulder toward the good ship *Txiv Neeb*, Dr. Vang was still smiling and waving.

Experimental Treatment

Not a disturbed sense of self, Jiro thought, but a disturbed self doing the sensing. Words apparitioning as visual and spatial presences, colored and imaged, mobile and alive. Inner experience occurring in a different sequence from external reality. . . .

"So you're ready to dance with the dolphins?"   Todd Fabro says. The rock-god shaman with the new cure, as Seiji describes it. Shipboard MediTox, then priming on Ibogara for the dolphin ultrasonic therapy.

Jiro sees his mother rushing toward him through the Honolulu air terminal, an eager blur of Nordic blond smotherliness, while his father follows more slowly behind.

Going home again is always also returning to the scene of the crime.

Jiro spends more and more time "doing the dead man's sink," particularly when there are dolphin pods about. Primed by Fabro's treatment staff, he plops overboard in full dive gear and swims down among the dolphins, while Seiji watches worriedly from one of the treatment center's small boats at the surface.

Only about 40 percent of yearly drownings occur to people who are swimming or playing in the water. Jiro meditates on this, but drowning itself is his deeper meditation. Perhaps he is destined to be the bodhisattva of suffocation in water, a being who has wakened from the painful sleeping whirlpool of births and deaths to accomplish—what?

"To die, to sleep—" Jiro says, reading Hamlet in *Hamlet* in their family time because Dad thinks their teenschool is culturally limited, that "teachers" have become mere "student processors" ever since education signed on to the corporate model. Seiji and Jiro must suffer heavy loads of enrichment tutorials. "To sleep, perchance to dream—ay, there's the rub, for in that sleep of death what dreams may come, when we have shuffled off this mortal coil, must give us pause." ·

Even if most of his childhood was not spent in Hawaii. Even if it was primarily the world halfway between his mother's and father's, to which they'd now retired. Even if Jiro is here to take the cure, to be rehabilitated—and the weirdness has come so far, blown him out so hard, that no one in his family wants to talk about it.

Panic, a contributory cause in almost all swimming accidents, is a sudden, unreasoning, and overwhelming terror that destroys a person's capacity for self-help.

"It's so *good* to see you," his mother says after kissing him, gripping his left arm almost painfully tightly with her fingertips, only a hint of the perennial nervousness in her voice.

"Yes," says his father, a man of medium height and black hair gone largely gray, "it's good to see you."

Seated in lotus position on the underwater "contact platform," Jiro removes his regulator, pinches off its airflow, and gradually blows out his air. The dolphins gather in a rosette about him, motionless. For endless moments he sits there like a drowned Buddha. Occasionally he takes a breath of air from his regulator, the dolphins lift their blowholes to the surface.

In most waters, the main threat to life during a prolonged immersion is cold or cold combined with the possibility of drowning.

On duty at the Global Atmospheric Information Agency, Dad is looking at an infrared satscan of a hurricane over the Atlantic and chanting "Coriolis rose/blossoms over night ocean/petals shatter lives" again and again when the techs come for him.

"It's stress," Mom says nervously. "Job-related stress from working so hard for that damn GAIA. Your father will be all right again. He's just under the weather." A short, sad, bitter laugh.

Recognizing the drowning victim is sometimes difficult. Once a true drowning situation is recognized, the idea of swimming after the victim should be entertained only after all other less hazardous ways of rescuing the drowning person have been exhausted. Too often the would-be rescuer becomes another victim.

"Your brother is waiting at the car for us," his mother informed him. "We'll just go to baggage claim and get your bags. . . ."

Seiji is two years older and better than Jiro is at most things. Except the childhood exploit of doing the dead man's sink.

"Watch!" Jiro says. At the edge of the deep end in the Sunlite Pool, Seiji watches, prepared to be unimpressed. Jiro slides beneath the water's surface, facedown and arms outstretched before him like Superman in flight. He begins to exhale bubbles, then streams of air from his mouth and nostrils—and he starts to sink. Faster and faster the air floods out of him, faster and faster he sinks. When the last burst of bubbles has belched surfaceward, he lies dead flat against the pool's blue-painted somehow rubbery bottom, motionless. Second after lengthening second slides slowly by, and still he doesn't move.

"Well, boys," Dad says as they walk onto the park grounds, "what do you want to see first?"

"The fish," Seiji says.

"The birds," Jiro says.

Each boy is adamant in his choice.

"It's always this way, isn't it?" Mom says, shaking her head. "What now?"

Dad looks at the touchscreen map of the park, glowing like a brighter green sash at the waist of the city's encircling greenbelt.

"According to the map, the aquarium is on the way to the aviary, so we'll see the fish first, then the birds—"

"Yay!" Seiji shouts. Dad tousles his older boy's hair, drenched very nearly red from swimming in the eternal summer of the Sunlite Pool.

"He always gets his way," Jiro says, looking downcast through his dark bangs.

Ten motionless seconds tick by. Seiji begins to get worried. The water lifts Jiro's thick brown hair. Fifteen. Sways it back and forth like seaweed. Twenty.

When executing a rescue, it is good to let the victim know your intentions. Talk to the victim. Keep in personal contact.

"I don't have any baggage," Jiro says. "All I brought is what I'm carrying."

His parents seem a bit discombobulated by that, but they recover. They make their way toward the car and there's Seiji, shaking Jiro's hand and relieving Jiro of his pack and duffel bag, apologizing that he's been out of touch, small-talking about the quality of Jiro's flight aboard the flying wing "view front" jet from the mainland, about the contract job Seiji's just finished at the orbital habitat, installing the first of the new macro-engineered photovoltaics up there—about anything, except why they're all right here, right now. Jiro tries to keep a handle on his mind's rambling, tries to keep his eyes from darting too fiercely from his head, round and about, searching his surroundings.

Twenty-five seconds. Anxiously Seiji looks around for a lifeguard. Thirty. He begins to wade toward Jiro. Thirty-five seconds.

"*Timor mortis conturbat me,*" twelve-year-old Jiro says, reciting words about death in a dead language, the learning of which his parents believe will help broaden Seiji and him enough so they won't end up weather observers for the Global Atmospheric Information Administration (like Dad), or food service workers (like Mom).

Exhaustion is simply loss of energy and the resultant inability to make the necessary movements to keep afloat and make progress through the water.

"I have heard the mermaids singing, each to each," their father reads. "I do not think they will sing to me. I have seen them riding seaward on the wave, combing the white hair of the waves blown back, when the wind blows the water white and black."

At forty-five seconds Jiro pushes himself off the bottom and surges toward the surface, breaking out of the water with a great insuck of breath, almost knocking Seiji down where he stands over him. Seiji's fear and brief anger turn perversely to elation.

"Hey! How'd you do that?"

"Just blow out all the air," Jiro says with a shrug, "and you drop like a rock down the well."

The buoyancy of a body depends on the type of body. Some bodies are fairly buoyant. Others have marginal buoyancy. Still others have no buoyancy at all.

At the car out in the humid Hawaiian sunshine, Seiji and Jiro take the front seat while their parents ride in back.

"You still doing that summer job?" Seiji asks as they pull out of the parking lot and onto the highway. "Finding patterns in data or whatever it is?"

"Data pattern recognition," Jiro corrects mildly. "Yeah. But I don't know if I'll be able to keep the job much longer. My bosses aren't happy. They say I'm finding patterns that aren't really there."

"Oh, Jiro!" their mother says, sounding simultaneously sad, worried, and exasperated.

"Honey," their father says, "leave it alone. Please."

A mystic is a diver who can swim. A schizophrenic is a diver who can't. If you get too far out of your depth, you drown. If you don't get out of your depth at all, you never learn to swim.

"Let me see it again," Seiji says.

"Okay."

When Jiro slides under, this time Seiji submerges, too, eyes open, watching him. Air like a stream of molten silver flows up out of Jiro's face, past his floating hair, as he sinks. A final burst of bubbles rises through the blue water, ripples the silver underside of the sky—and Jiro lies again at full length, flat as his own shadow against the bottom. He seems almost to embrace the pool's bottom, his face learning to love that drowned pavement, to breathe no more than it does.

Experience teaches rescuers how far into the water they can safely go and how much of a load they can bear.

Seiji tries to do it too, then. He blows out air, but by the time he gets to a forty-five-degree angle the emptying of his chest underwater has become a tangible claustrophobia. Panicking, he inhales water and bolts to the surface, spluttering and gasping.

Parents and grown sons drive along in silence for a time, the crowds and colors of the island flowing around them like a strange blend of Polynesia, Tokyo, and Las Vegas.

"Well, maybe the rock-god shaman can help you with that," Seiji says. "Maybe."

Out the window, above Kauai's flower-drum palm-frond color carnival, the sky is a piercing blue. The clouds highpiled at the horizon are so white they seem backlit. The whole scene stands out with a vividness greater than the real, suffused with a persecuted grandeur like a mad artist's dream.

Seiji gives drowning his best shot again and again, but it's frustrating. He's the older brother, he's supposed to lead the way, to take the risks, to teach—but it's Jiro who tries to teach him how to drown, and he doesn't even prove to be a good student.

"Your body tells you to breathe, even when you know you're under-water," freshman Jiro says. "It's stupid. Don't pay attention to it."

Eventually Seiji gets to the point where he can sink fully to the bot-tom—just barely—but he never does manage to let go that last burst of air, to breathe it all out so his face might sink fully forward, to kiss the unyielding pavement in that perfect passionate stillness his younger brother achieves so effortlessly.

The depth to which a rescuer may go to retrieve a victim will depend upon the depth itself and how long the breath can be held after swim-ming to the site.

"It explains a lot," freshman Jiro says, electropenning thoughts as they occur to him. "The high youth suicide and car accident rates here, every-thing."

"What do you mean?" Seiji asks warily.

"If society is a second womb," Jiro explains, "then suicides and acci-dental deaths are spontaneous abortions, while socially sanctioned wars and executions are willful ones. That's what all the controversy was about in the past century: whether women individually should be allowed to do inside their wombs what men for millennia had been doing collectively inside the womb of patriarchal society."

Seiji shakes his head.

"Maybe you're brighter or crazier than I am," he says at last, "but I don't see that. Sounds like the KL is talking again, bro. Either that, or you've been studying too much of that history—especially the Gender Wars. Whichever, I wouldn't let Mom and Dad hear you say this stuff, if I were you."

Jiro fully masters the art of the dead man's sink while still in his teens. "People are mostly just water walking around, right?" he says. "If you can just get over the fear of suffocating in water, you can let it all go. It's easy."

By the time Seiji leaves for graduate school in California and then in Hawaii, Jiro can drown to his left side or his right, faceup or facedown, feet first or head first or in the fetal position.

Peaceful. A sleep and a forgetting, Jiro thinks, remembering lines from that old poem his father so loved. Till human voices wake us and we drown.

Sometimes it seems as if Jiro is going to stay down there forever, but he always comes back, eventually. Seiji doesn't understand it. The voice of the dolphin in air sounds harsh to him—jarring gibbering clicktalk.

"What're you doing down there all that time?" Seiji asks.

"Communing," Jiro says. "Most of their discourse is nonreferential—philosophical poetry, songs, that sort of thing. When I'm around them and primed on Ibogara, though—'Human, awake!'—they just skip language altogether and beam me imagery directly, faster and denser than I can understand, though it's still all up here in my head somewhere, I think. After they zap me I feel better—much better."

"In what way?"

He pauses, thinking.

Eternal return. Avalokitesvara. Kwan Yin. Kwannon. Bodhisattvas and saviors do not leave the world but regard its lives and deeds and imperfections with the eyes and tears of compassion.

"Kind of like I'm being rescued," Jiro says slowly. "Like I'm being lifted up into the light."

Socrates. Jesus. Gandhi. King. Walking Bear. Ohnuki. Eternal return . . .

"I can't do it, Jiro," he heard Seiji saying tearfully, moving away. "I just can't let go that last burst of air. I've got no more air to give!"

Jiro felt someone beating on his chest and heard a boat approaching at speed.

Watch!

He opened his eyes, unclear as to how he'd gotten here. All he could remember was sitting passionately still at the bottom of a deep, sun-filled pool, waiting to surge toward the surface and the light once more.

"Hey," said one of Fabro's Samoan orderlies. "Hey! He's breathing! He's alive!"

"What?" Seiji turned back toward him and saw that it was true. Relief and shock warred in his face, until at last relief won. He shook Jiro's shoulders as Jiro sat up, somewhat unsteadily.

"If you're not dead," Seiji said, "then I ought to kill you for putting me through this!"

Jiro looked down and saw his shadow, beside Seiji's, cast over the edge of the boat and rippling onto the waves beyond. A shadow of a body, but for there to be shadows there must also be light and bodies. Yes, he was still alive.

Todd Fabro, the pop-music-god-turned-shaman, had arrived in person—on the speeding boat Jiro heard earlier. A slender man clad in white linen suit, boater hat, and canvas shoes, Fabro stood some distance away, on his picket boat, listening to the orderly's report, shaking the long curls of his sun-danced hair in taut agreement before jumping down onto the boat where Jiro now sat upright, gathering his wits.

"How are you feeling?" Fabro asked him, crouching down beside him.

"Saner," Jiro said. "More ready to face the world without KL."

Fabro nodded.

"Heard you had a near brush with the Big Guy," he said, his jauntiness not quite overcoming the worry in his voice.

Jiro shrugged, awkwardly trying to deflect the sunshine of attention away from himself while still continuing to bask in it.

"That which does not kill us—" he began.

"—raises everyone's insurance rates," Fabro finished, interrupting him. "Death may be a prerequisite for immortality, but that's no reason to jump the gun. Ibogara isn't supposed to result in unconsciousness. Our experimental treatment procedure has had no casualties associated with it. I'd like to keep it that way."

Jiro nodded, thinking again of how he must be weird-wired to have blacked out, then turned to Seiji and the orderly to thank them for saving him.

"Don't thank us," Seiji said with a smile. "Thank *them*."

Jiro's gaze followed to where his brother was pointing—toward the dolphins that still moved and circled about the boat.

"That's right," said the orderly. "They pushed you up to the surface. We just jumped in and brought you on board."

Jiro looked more closely, staring hard at one of the dolphins that was watching him as it patrolled around the boat. It seemed to know something he didn't. About his past? His future? Whatever that something might be, however, the dolphin remained inscrutable. "Communing" apparently only went so far, even with his rescuers.

Faith in the Brotherhood of Man

M ike didn't see it as a downward spiral while it was happening. Just events, one after the other—yet so many in the past few years. Bad luck. But when *had* it begun?

When he left home? When he had his first KL experience? When he dropped out of graduate school? When he partied away the summers with his brother Ray, visiting here to get away from the oppressive atmosphere back home? When he told the Forest Service supervisor on his ignorant, frustrating job in Arcata that it wasn't "good for him to be around people right now" because dealing with the public made him so pissed off? When he left the job and moved over the border into Oregon? When things went stale with Lizette—after she went into therapy and cleaned up? Or when he tried to impress her one last time, with his "investigation"?

"I still feel ridiculous about it," he told the recently KL-free Lizette, when she paid a visit to him at his trailer up in the hills, on her way home from attending a cousin's wedding in California. "Keeping everything locked up like this when I live in outback Oregon. The nearest town is the mighty metrop of Takilma."

He talked at her fast, fast—like someone who didn't see people very often—but he couldn't help it.

"Still, though," he said, unlocking his trailer, "someone did break into my trailer a couple of weeks back. Stole my holobox and sleeping bag."

Lizette made noises of commiseration and concern but, as he watched her look around the trailer trying to find an uncluttered place to sit, Mike saw that she couldn't quite hide the repugnance she felt at seeing how trashed and cluttered his living quarters were.

Mike cleared off a place on one of the couches, privately feeling resentment at her revulsion over the way he was living now. He had felt the same thing when she'd pulled up by the gate of his property in her shiny little electric hoversport, commenting on how *thin* he was looking. *And grubby and unkempt,* he thought. She hadn't said anything like that, of course, but he'd felt it in the quickness of her hug, in the way she brushed his longish bangs away from his face.

"Since I've been absolutely, totally, blissfully unemployed for the past month, however," Mike said, pushing a stack of old newspapers out of a chair and onto the floor before taking a seat himself, "I've had time to turn detective. I hung out in the local scum bars, talked with the patrons, listened to all the local gossip—until I pieced together whodunit. For an amateur sleuth I think I did pretty well. Took only two days to figure out who robbed me. I'm already making a name for myself as a local hero."

Mike gave what he hoped was a winning smile. Lizette smiled back— but distractedly, still glancing nervously about the trailer. Uncomfortable as a cat on a rock in the middle of a creek at having to sit amid his bachelor mess, she said nothing.

"Just yesterday I turned over to the sheriff's office the names of the likeliest suspects in my trailer break-in," Mike continued, although he already felt himself deflating and shrinking in her gaze.

"Who were they?" she asked, almost interested.

"Edward 'Big Ed' Hilbert," Mike said, "Martin 'Mac' McCurdy, and Wayne Davis. Lowlifes with connections to the Mongrel Clones Motorcycle Club. Spiker bikers."

Lizette shook her head and stood up.

"Are you sure it's a good idea getting involved with that element, Mike?" she asked. "I mean, blue spike makes folks act crazy. Most of the people who sell it are the worst kind of bad news. You told me that yourself."

"They took my stuff!" Mike said defensively. "I don't care what kind of scum they are. You've got to draw the line somewhere. No one has the right to rip off a guy's sleeping bag, for God's sake. My holos were the only entertainment I had up here. Something had to be done. *I'm* not going to live *my* life in fear."

Lizette frowned severely at him.

"Oh—and you think I do?" she asked.

"You're the one who moved back home to Mommy and Daddy," he said with a shrug, "not me. You said you wanted stability, safety, security. How much freedom are you willing to give up for those?"

"And your 'freedom' is such a great thing?" Lizette said, looking disgustedly around the trailer. "Freedom to be a slob? A loser with no motivation? A gatehead circling the rim? What's happened to you, Mike?"

Mike stood up.

"I stopped running my parents' program," he said, staring fixedly at her. "The KL has helped deprogram me. It made me see the biggest of Big Pictures. Sacrificing freedom for the sake of security—the whole damn country is doing it! Government and corporations operating *in loco parentis,* trying to make us all child-safe and comfort-controlled! We don't have to live the repressed, bourgeois lives our parents lived, Lizette. They sacrificed everything they might have been, for the sake of family and finances. Not me."

"If they hadn't made that sacrifice," Lizette said, voice rising, "you wouldn't *be* here, you arrogant shithead! You wouldn't exist! God, you're out of it. Those stupid cakey dreadlocks of yours—good God! I thought I could bring you back to reality, get you cleaned up and out of your druggie funk. But you're *happy* wallowing in your filth and freedom. Some fool once made the mistake of telling you how high your IQ is, so now you think the world *owes* you. The world doesn't owe you anything! You're the most stupid genius I've ever met. You wear your failure like a badge of honor."

"There's more honor in being a failure my way," Mike retorted, "than in being a 'suck-cess' your way."

Lizette headed toward the door.

"Never try to teach a proud pig to think about his future!" Lizette said from the doorway. "The pig will just wallow in self-pity at how the world isn't good enough for him—and waste all your time. When you decide to live your life like a modern human being, drop me a line, Mike. Until then, we have nothing more to talk about."

She banged the door behind her.

"Go ahead and run on home to Mommy and Daddy!" Mike called after her. "They lived their lives for you, so now you have to live your life for them? That's not a family—it's a bunch of time parasites!"

She flipped him off without turning around. Getting into her hover down at the gate, she started it up and sent gravel shooting everywhere as she spun the vehicle around and away.

That afternoon Mike went into the diviest bar in Takilma and got good and drunk, even though his "investigation" was over. He left well before dark, however, to avoid the greet-meat rituals of the evening bar crowd.

In sunset light he got out of his car to unlock his front gate. Crunching over the driveway gravel to the gate, Mike still felt hollow and hurt by what had happened with Lizette that morning. He was at a loss at what to do now. The only woman he'd been involved with since moving to Oregon was an obsessive-compulsive Accelerando freak. She made Lizette at her bitchiest look like an absolute goddess of honeyed sweetness.

An instant after the lock came open on the gate, Mike heard the sound of three shotguns dialing him in. Immediately he thought of the old 9mm

Sig-Sauer in the glove compartment of his car, which he'd taken to carrying during his investigation. So much for not living in fear.

Turning to see three figures striding swiftly out of the trees and brush beside the gravel driveway, their hair and lower faces covered with bandannas, Mike knew he would have no time to reach the gun in the glove box. Feebly he raised his fists as his assailants set about methodically bashing in his skull with shotgun butts, turning his world into a blackness of exploded stars through which blood-red worms writhed furiously.

"You fucked with the wrong people, boy." Those were the last words he thought he heard before he blacked out.

Later, in the hospital CAT scan holos, his disembodied head—close-lipped, shut-eyed, naked of hair and consciousness—turned in space before him, a strange, silent movie. Just back of the left temple his cranium dented in deeply, in the perfect impression of a shotgun butt. After he was brought into Emergency, the doctors spent fourteen hours picking bone fragments out of his brain's speech centers.

He did not ask for any such heroic measures. Barely conscious, moving through a world of blood red, brain gray, and spinal fluid yellow, he remembered trying to grunt out to the doctors his one request as they wheeled him into surgery.

Let me die!

His Broca's area was pretty much gone, though. They couldn't understand what he was trying to say. The orderlies and nurses thought he was drunk when he was first brought in, his words were so sloppy, slurred, and disjointed.

"Not intoxicated," his surgeon, Dr. Nejdat Mulla, said in jargon-laden professional tones, correcting a nurse several days later when they both thought Mike was somewhere between unconscious and asleep. "The patient's head trauma incident resulted in pulpification of a significant section of the left temporal lobe. That damage is the most probable cause of his aphasia and agraphia. It probably also accounts for his early bouts of amnesia. Mr. Dalke's inarticulateness when he was admitted resulted not from the consumption of intoxicants, but from the injuries sustained in his head trauma."

Even when his eyes were as open as he could make them, Mike noticed that the hospital staff still often spoke about him in the distant third person, as if he were not in the same room with them. Maybe no one who had seen how bathed in blood he was, how badly trashed his skull had been when the ambulance brought him in, could really believe there was still a thinking person inside the shell on the bed—the battered case whose cranium had been stove in, who had been through such long hours of surgery, who lay motionless, strapped into a hospital bed, ensnared in a beeping and chiming thicket of tubes and wires and monitors.

"No one can tell me who the anonymous caller was," said one of the orderlies, a heavyset young Hispanic man who was transparently trying to chat up the day nurse. "Who reported the need for an ambulance at this guy's backwoods address? The only ones who knew about the incident at the time were the patient and whoever it was did this to him."

"The patient was unconscious, according to the paramedics," the thin, brunette nurse said noncommittally.

"And the people who had just finished bashing in his skull," said the orderly, "well, normally you wouldn't think they'd be too concerned about his well-being."

The staffers dropped their voices and moved toward the door.

"He's lucky to still be alive," the nurse said.

"If you can call that lucky," the orderly said with a shrug.

His mom, dad, and brother Ray came to visit him from Wyoming. Although Mike could hear them and understand them, he could not reach out to them, could not respond to them, and that was most frustrating of all. His father looked bewildered and somehow ashamed, muttering about the immoral life Mike had taken up since he left home. Ray, still a teenager, seemed morose and obscurely embarrassed. His mother broke again and again into sobbing hysterical rages against God for His having allowed such a thing to happen to her son, her baby—and had to be removed forcibly from the room three times in as many days.

Some kind of crisis was going on in the outside world as well, Mike realized dimly. Even in the hospital, computers and monitors in his room were going down unpredictably. The lights kept flickering and the power kept phasing in and out, so much so that the hospital was constantly shifting over to its own generators. The activity of the ward became both heightened and fragmented. To the bustle of doctors and nurses and orderlies was added the shouts and calls of frazzled technicians trying to keep systems functioning. It all came to Mike through a semiconscious haze, like a terrible, vivid nightmare from which he was having difficulty awakening.

After being assured by the doctors that they would notify his family of any changes in Mike's condition, Mike's mother, father, and brother left for home—almost with relief, on all sides—prodded by the great crisis, whatever it was.

Over the next week, however, not only did the hospital's power and technology begin to return to something like normal, but also Mike's own condition began to improve markedly—to the distinct surprise of the hospital staff. As it gradually became clearer that there was still "somebody home" in the machine-hooked and IV-ed shell upon the bed, those treating him took pains to tell Mike just how lucky he was.

"Mr. Dalke," said Dr. Chua, the ever-cheerful therapist who sometimes accompanied the day nurse, "our records show that your temporal lobe seizures"— *So that's what they are*, thought Mike, the shuddering waves that felt like *grand mal* without the release of blackout—"are not as frequent as they might be. We have some questions as to whether you will ever be able to speak articulately again, but it says here your pre-trauma IQ was more than 150. Our best estimates are that, after extensive therapy, you will probably have lost only about 25 percent of your intellectual capacity. That should still leave you better equipped than the majority of the population."

Despite such reassurances, Mike did not feel lucky. A social worker—a blond, chunky, bespectacled young woman—had been assigned to his case. The social outlook was not good.

"You happened to have been between employers and insurers when this unfortunate accident occurred," she reminded Mike, over the low rubber-jungle noise of the monitors and life-support systems. "You've amassed more than eighty thousand dollars in medical bills. You're unmarried. With the recent infosphere crisis and changes in government, we have not been able to recontact your surviving family members . . ."

Mike suspected what might be coming. "Treat 'em and street 'em"—he'd heard one of the medtechs mutter that to a coworker when they thought he was unconscious. Up loomed the image of living unhappily ever after out of a shopping cart—what one of the orderlies called a "MALR: Mobile Autonomous Lifestyle Receptacle."

"Due to recent austerity measures, rehabilitation and therapy expenses will likely not be covered by the state," the social worker said thoughtfully. "The fact that you weren't more brain-damaged than you in fact were will work against you when it comes to state support. By law you're not legally disabled if you're able to 'act in your own self-interest in a planned and premeditated fashion' . . ."

Find and secure a MALR, Mike thought.

". . . are 'self-motivated' . . ."

Able to push a MALR.

". . . and have shown that you are, without special funding, 'capable of rehabilitation and gainful employment.' "

Can use a toilet brush, mop, and broom, and work for subminimum wage while living out of a MALR.

"I'm afraid the state will likely deny you support payments of any sort," the social worker said at last, pursing her lips. "Not eligible. The new government has already made it quite clear that it is very fond of saving taxpayers' money—er, 'tithes.' Patients with a history of drug use, like your own, are at this time uniformly being rejected for government disability support on the grounds that the disabling event was a result of 'conscious lifestyle choice.'"

Getting his skull bashed in with shotgun butts wasn't what really hurt, Mike now realized. After saving his life, after employing a team of surgeons to pick bone fragments out of his speech centers hour after hour, after caring for him for ten days and running up a charge of more than eighty thousand dollars, the hospital planned to discharge him into the trauma afterworld, a brain-damaged tightrope walker without a thread of a safety net.

Even deeper, though, was the pain of a larger injustice, one that dawned on Mike only after some time: Left to its own devices, the law would never punish the men who had done this to him. That realization made him want to finish the job his assailants had started. Instead, however, his depression drove him into a sleep as deep as forever, but not as wide.

Through the sinister, winding streets of an unknown city he runs, thunder beating like drums all around. Storm clouds. He laughs at the thunder until it grows angry and comes charging forward, whipping him with its winds, shooting lightning bolts down at him, chasing him, firing bolts down at him again and again. . . .

"Mr. Dalke?"

Running on all fours through a marshy field scaring frogs into great leaps strange frogs whose skins are currencies of the world in many denominations running but not trying to catch them running from the deep whir of the enormous harvesting machine behind him the whir gaining till up ahead a wooden ladder with wings of fire and rungs of ice stands waiting and desperately he reaches out for it but hand is paw and then hand again and the ladder rises as hands rise in the clinging and letting go that is climbing until reaching the top of the fiery ladder its wings are about his shoulders his hands have turned talons he is a creature half sparrow-hawk, half shooting-star—

"Mr. Dalke?"

The vision dissolved, into white noise and hushed voices and the monitoring frogsong of his hospital-room hothouse. Half conscious, falling out of dreams like premonitions or pre-emanations, he felt himself spun about dizzily in a slipstream of memory and waking and memories of waking, returning to consciousness between the blond social-worker woman on one side of his hospital bed and a tall, dark, thin man—tennis-athletic, well-dressed, carrying a briefcase—on the other.

"Self-assembling crystal memory, Michael," explained the thin man who had been introduced, or rather reintroduced, to him as Richard Schwarzbrucke. "The buckytubes serve as circuits. We at CMD believe an injection of these crystal memory components, followed by regrowth along neo-Edelman lines, could restore what was lost and eliminate your temporal lobe seizures. Of course, the decision remains up to you."

"I must warn you, however, Mr. Dalke," the blond social-worker woman said to him, but also for Schwarzbrucke's notification, "the procedure is experimental."

"But our extensive research with animals," Schwarzbrucke insisted, "bears out the concept that crystal memory components can integrate themselves into the preexisting neuronal matrix, very much in accord with the revised theory of neuronal group selection."

They both stared down at Mike with glances that were supposed to be meaningful, although they meant nothing to him.

"You would still be the first human subject to undergo this particular procedure," the social worker cautioned Mike, then brightened. "It's difficult to predict how head trauma victims will retrain themselves. The fact that you're left-handed meant your language processing areas were not as devastated as they might have been. A person of an intellectual bent, such as yourself, might find being unable to speak articulately a life sentence of sorts—and you therefore might choose to work incredibly hard to restore lost capacity on your own."

Mike began to feel a bit like a tennis ball as the two of them abstractly and dispassionately volleyed his future back and forth.

"Give it some thought, though, Mr. Dalke," Schwarzbrucke continued. "If you choose to participate in our program, all your medical expenses will be paid by Crystal Memory Dynamics. Your family will be absolutely relieved of any financial burden arising from your emergency treatment or your ongoing care. We'll transfer you to state-of-the-art biomedical facilities in the Bay Area and completely oversee your recovery. We'll also cover your rehab and therapy expenses. I gather from Ms. Kohurst here that it's highly unlikely the state will do the same."

"I informed him," Ms. Kohurst—yes, that was the social worker's name—said, somewhat defensively. "I certainly didn't mean to lower his spirits by it, however."

Kohurst turned to "address the ball": Mike himself.

"I've just been trying to give you the overall picture," she said. "To let you know the risks and the benefits, so you can make an informed decision about the choice Mr. Schwarzbrucke and Crystal Memory Dynamics are offering you."

"Of course we're not trying to make you any more depressed than you must already be," Schwarzbrucke said consolingly. "I've heard that the right-side-damaged are often unaware of the extent of the brain damage they've suffered, so since they don't know, it doesn't bother them as much. Left-siders, like yourself—they can still be aware of just how much they've lost and, understandably, it depresses them."

They both gave Mike that meaningless meaningful stare again.

"Do you have any questions for Mr. Schwarzbrucke?" the social worker said quickly, since Schwarzbrucke had begun gathering himself to leave.

Mike tried to croak out a comment, but then motioned for something to write with instead. When implements had been brought, he managed with considerable difficulty to scrawl out WHATS INIT 4 U?

Schwarzbrucke laughed indulgently, locking his black briefcase shut with a resolute click.

"I'll be honest. This could be a major step toward something my investors and I have been after for a long time: a thoroughgoing mind/machine interface."

Either from seeing the newly blank look on the face of the social worker, or Mike's own crackbrained thousand-yard stare, Schwarzbrucke felt moved to explain further.

"Think of how such an interface would fulfill an ancient human dream," he began. "Each of us has always been trapped inside a solitary skull. As a species, we've tried many ways to reach through the bone walls that keep our minds apart. All our arts and all our forms of communication down through the centuries are attempts to dream together, to share our experiences, to escape what is, at bottom, a life sentence of solitary confinement for each and every one of us inside our own skulls. An integrated mind/machine link would almost inevitably become a mind-to-mind link too. Think of it: a technologically mediated empathy and telepathy. It would free us from our narrow selves, into a fuller communion with our fellow beings than we have ever known. That's the adventure CMD is embarked on, Michael. I hope you'll join us on it."

Obviously won over by the vision Schwarzbrucke had sketched out, Ms. Kohurst joined her voice to the rhapsodizing.

"Imagine what that would do for human understanding, for art, for peace—"

"And for profits," Schwarzbrucke said with a sly wink as he stepped toward the door, "for profits!"

Weakly waving Schwarzbrucke *adieu*, Mike remained skeptical. Shotgun-wielding thugs had done their bit to break through the bone wall of *his* skull, but he hadn't found it a particularly pleasant or enlightening experience—and it certainly had not done much for his faith in the Brotherhood of Man.

Shooting Up with Prayer

B Y THEIR TRASH SHALL YE KNOW THEM, the sign said. Lydia watched as her boss, Dr. Khalid "Kal" Elliot, clad in worker's coveralls and standing on a ladder, removed screws from the sign hanging over the doorway to the Garbage Project's main offices.

"Why are you taking it down, Kal?" she asked. She was surprised to find him working this late, when nearly everyone else had already gone home for the day. "It pretty much sums up what we're about here."

"Maybe," the project's chief archaeologist said, drilling out another screw as the sun set in the sky beyond the office trailer, "though it's not technically correct. I know you worked in paleontology before coming here, but remember the history, Lydia."

Lydia remembered, all right. *Trash* referred primarily to "dry" discards, while *garbage* referred to "wet" discards. The so-called Trashlands here, though—they were more accurately *Rubbish*lands. Refuse (wet and dry discards) plus construction and demolition debris equaled *rubbish*. Since the Southern California Waste Disposal Area, Yucaipa–San Jacinto–Moreno–Beaumont Quadrangle, was founded upon whatever Great L.A. Quake debris could not be shoved into the ocean, the rubbish designation was especially true here.

"Surely you're not taking the sign down over such hairsplitting distinctions?"

"No," the black man in his late fifties said as he undid the last screw and descended the ladder, carrying the sign with him. "No, I'm removing it out of fear that a flippant biblical paraphrase might offend the new fundamentalist masters."

It was odd for Kal to go on like this. He was usually much more laconic.

Something was on his mind—something Lydia suspected had to do with the current crisis. Lydia followed him as he carried the sign back toward the Garbage Project's storage area, behind the office trailers. The Trashlands' methane vent flares—those that hadn't yet been piped and siphoned off for their usable energy—dotted the twilight with columns of glowing orange fire as far as she could see.

"You don't really think things are that bad, do you?" she asked.

The chief archaeologist glanced back at her over his shoulder, frowning, absently stroking his gray-streaked pharaonic chinbeard.

"I know the chaos of the breakdown has numbed us all to the point that we barely feel change anymore," he said, "but we *are* under martial law."

"Because of the infosphere blackouts, yes," Lydia said, nodding. She could not forget the shots of nightside Earth that had begun appearing in the slowly reviving post-Crash media. The satellite images of the jeweled light-fog from Earth's cities and highways, going utterly dark in waves. The pale green-white fire of the auroral crown, reaching nearly to Mexico and Italy. When they had seen that star-filled night sky behind rippling green curtains, more than a few lifelong urbanites believed the end of the world had come at last. And the experts said the electromagnetic effects, at least, had only gotten worse on the day side.

"But politics didn't cause all those solar flares and sunspots," Lydia said, recalling in depth her personal experiences of the Crash. Like many others, she had seen riots of angels. More electromagnetic disturbances in the interpretative cortex of her temporal lobe, she gathered—even more severe than those she had experienced during the Great L.A. Quake and its aftershocks. She figured she must have a particularly sensitive "IC" in her "TL."

"Oh, I don't deny there was an unusually high level of solar activity," Kal said as he opened a storage shed and slid back the door. "But look at what was going on before that."

He slid the sign into a bin and turned around to her.

"The urban warfare assault 'scenarios' the Marines have been running in major American cities for more than a quarter of a century," he said, counting off examples on his fingers. "Supposedly training exercises for taking out terrorist strongholds abroad, but also mighty handy experience if you want to shut down dissent at home. The contested election, three years ago, of the first non–New Commonweal president in years—and the threat *that* posed to the NC. The federal standoff with the Covenanters in Smithville. The evidence those zealots had biological weapons.

Then the presidential order and the massacre there, troops and law enforcement bombing Smithville to ashes—"

"What does that have to do with the infosphere crashes?" Lydia asked, perplexed, as they loitered in front of the storage shed.

"Hear me out," Kal said, raising a finger for attention. "Where was I? Yes. The rumors of United Nations and international security involvement in the massacre. Economic and social stress. The last in a series of constitutional crises involving the president. The militia uprisings and troop revolts against 'internationalist conspiracies' and 'collectivist secular elites.' Then a surprisingly convenient solar storm, just in time for the president's jet to go down in a 'storm-induced' electromagnetic pulse. The vice president's sudden helicopter crash in Morocco—supposedly the result of terrorists using a shoulder-launched antiaircraft missile. Quite convenient for the installment of Speaker of the House George Nadarovich as president— and additional grounds for his immediate declaration of martial law. Then the amphibious assault on San Francisco, the call for a new constitutional convention, and the establishment of the Christian States of America? Hmm?"

Kal had long since run out of fingers, but that didn't stop him from shaking his head.

"That's an awful lot to load onto a bunch of sunspots and solar flares."

"Oh?" Lydia said, looking at him skeptically, yet fearful that too much of what he was implying might just be true. She remembered too clearly the closing down of research at the tar pits. "And you have another explanation for all the blackouts and computer crashes?"

"Not totally," he said with a shrug as he closed the door to the storage shed behind them, "but before our systems went down, I got an interesting masscast e-note from my old buddy Al Davis. He was a roommate of mine from way back, when we were in grad school together. He worked skeleton crew at NOAA, usually on what's known as the K-index. The index measures disturbances in several vectors of the Earth's magnetic field, averaged over three-hour periods. Sort of a measure of how the Earth's magnetic lines of force are being tweaked and torqued. The K-index is generally calculated for the midlatitudes—in Colorado in the Northern Hemisphere and in Australia in the Southern. Disturbances tend to be much more severe poleward."

Lydia began to walk slowly ahead of him, back toward the main office trailer.

"And this all has something to do with the solar storm that caused the infosphere crisis?" she asked, trying not to sound impatient.

"Everything to do with it!" Kal assured her. "What it takes to precipitate a technocrash depends on whether the tweaking of the field lines is the result of a pulse or a sustained period of severe storming. The K-index is not an instantaneous quantity, so a quick pulse of high amplitude would not normally be significantly reflected in the K-index. For a quick pulse the K-index would generally be irrelevant—and, as a result of the crash caused by a killer pulse, the index would probably never be calculated after such a pulse."

Dr. Elliot slowed and stared down at his feet as one of the undergraduates on the project walked past them, toward the storage area from which they had just come. When he spoke again, his voice was lower.

"But Al was working on atmospheric phenomena called sprites and jets," he continued, "which are related to much briefer electromagnetic events in the Earth's atmosphere—as brief as lightning bolts during thunderstorms, in fact. So his equipment had a lot narrower resolution than almost anything else out there. His detectors had much finer discernment than those used to calculate the usual K-index. His e-note said he was seeing some *interesting* things."

"Such as?" Lydia asked, curious almost against her will.

"A sustained period of severe solar storming takes out electrical systems on the basis of how well protected they are," Kal said. "The less protected a system is, the more readily it can be knocked out. The main danger is not from the storm itself, but from the disturbances the storm causes in the power grid, which tends to amplify whatever perturbs it."

"And your friend Al's instruments showed him something to do with that?"

"Right," Kal said. "As the solar activity's effects began to peak in the index's low twenties, a series of precisely timed pulses began to appear, mainly over North America as it came out of night shadow, but with a few spikes scattered over the rest of the planet, too. Totally artificial—and virtually invisible, as far as standard K-measures were concerned. Glaringly visible to Al's research equipment, however."

Lydia drew her chin inward in disbelief.

"Someone manipulated a solar storm to shut down the infosphere?" she asked incredulously. "Who? Little green men?"

"No—men of ordinary stature from Earth," Kal said. "In the usual range of skin colors. Perhaps dressed in army green, but otherwise not at all alien. Strange how human beings are so willing to credit aliens with accomplishing feats we are perfectly capable of ourselves. Alien abductions are the Zeus-rapes of our time—a *human* mythological function.

Who made the pyramids? Stonehenge? Crop circles? Human beings did. We are the alien intelligence. Aliens-R-Us. "But manipulated a solar storm—" Lydia began.

Not 'manipulated' a solar storm—*exploited* it. For cover. I haven't heard anything from Al since, but it's not so hard to figure out the rest. With a series of precisely timed electromagnetic pulses, those nonlittle, nongreen men set up oscillations in the power grids. Those oscillations, at least at the surface of the Earth, unleashed far more power than the storm itself did. With the right timing and placement in the upper levels of the atmosphere, they wouldn't even have needed to use nuclear explosions to generate the pulses. The ultimate bang for their buck."

Lydia stared at her boss as they stepped back into Dr. Elliot's office.

"But think of all the suffering, all the deaths the infosphere crashes caused," Lydia said, sitting down in a chair opposite the seat her boss had taken behind the desk. "Why would anyone want to do such a thing?"

"Power," Kal said simply, shrugging out of the torso half of his coveralls, into his shirtsleeves beneath. "The control that comes from being out of control. Once the pulses were going, the out-of-control controllers could selectively take out sections of the infosphere all over the planet—least protected first. The transnational corporations, governments, and particularly the military have the most EMP-protected machine systems. The highest ranks of the powers-that-be collapsed the infosphere back down to what was under their immediate control. Now they're in the driver's seat like never before."

Lydia glanced around Kal's office, at his cluttered desk, computing equipment, bound folders of data standing in rank upon rank on the shelves behind them.

"Why are you telling me this?" Lydia asked cautiously. "And why now?"

"Because it looks like this newest 'new government' is going to stick around, at least for a while," Kal said. "I know about your role in the Rancho La Brea shutdown, so I thought you should learn about this sooner rather than later. If what I'm saying is true, then you need to know how this is going to affect us here."

"Is this going to affect us?" Lydia asked, growing more annoyed as she grew more worried.

Kal let out a sigh.

"Very little, I hope," he said, obviously having thought about the potential impacts before. "Nonmilitary scientific research will probably take a massive hit under the new regime, but we're fairly insulated. The Garbage Project has been doing analyses for more than forty-five years, which means lots of inertia. The project has established ties with four universities in four different regions of the country, so we're covered there."

Lydia, her political antennae up and twitching, was not so sanguine.

"But the Trashlands site has been digging for a while," she said worriedly. "Any chance somebody might push for a move to someplace else? Maybe into one of those other regions?"

Kal thought about it and shook his head.

"Unlikely," he said. "Since the summary study of Fresh Kills back East was completed last year, we've been garbology's biggest show on Earth. We're arguably the largest archaeological site on the planet. All the postquake debris makes us unique—as do the Trashlander communities, the TechNots and Neo-Luddites over near Yucaipa. And they're not likely to move."

Lydia nodded. She knew some of that history, too. The Trashlanders' holiest of holies was an old court decision, Greenwood v. California, according to which trash was public domain once it was in a container on a curb. The recycleroids had built that into the Trash Access Law. Not even the new CSA government would mess with that, unless they wanted appropriatek-types rioting all over the country.

Despite Kal's assurances, however, Lydia was nonetheless starting to have full-blown flashbacks to the last days of the tar pits research. Even now, she was still haunted by her cover-up of the strange skull and shoulder blade she had discovered shortly before the end—so much so that her dreams were filled with recurring images of those remains, lost in a strange limbo between buried and exhumed.

"What about funding?" she asked. "State? Federal? Local?"

"We may be primarily an archaeological site," Kal said, tapping a pen against the edge of his desk, "but everyone from structural engineers to social theorists does field research here. We are the Oxford of offal. We have comparatively little dependence on government funding of any sort—pretty impressive, considering the size of this operation. Some government agency funds from here, from Mexico, and from Australia. Some of our research foundation and university funding might be vulnerable, but our biggest single funder is private industry. The transnational corporation we have strongest ties to is Retcorp and Lambeg. They're headquartered in Ohio, so no one back in the heartland can claim we've been too bicoastal and overlooked them."

Lydia thought again of Kal taking down the biblical paraphrase sign in the sunset light tonight.

"How about ideological or religious reasons for shutting us down?" she asked, all too aware of how powerful those could be.

Kal Elliot gave her a quizzical smile.

"I see you can think like an administrator when you have to," he said, "despite all your 'I'm just an apolitical working scientist' shtick. I'd say, though, that we're a generally noncontroversial project. No antibiblical evolutionary theory here, Lydia. Our research also happens to give Retcorp and Lambeg insights into how people use, abuse, save, and discard packaging—including *their* packaging—so sponsoring us makes R&L look like a responsible corporate citizen."

Lydia stared at the floor.

"I didn't mean so much religious or ideological tests for the whole project . . ." she said.

"You mean for individuals?" her boss asked. "Workers whose history might 'raise a stink' for the project? Hah! That's a thought—someone in the Garbage project raising a stink! You yourself seemed to have come away from the tar baby of the tar pits remarkably clean, actually. You're right to be concerned, though. We seem to be in the midst of another of this country's periodic relapses into paranoia and persecution hysteria. Who can say how things will play out? All we can do is look to history and try to learn from that."

"Persecution hysteria?" Lydia asked, leaning forward. "Witch-hunts, you mean?"

"If you like," Kal said with a shrug. "The Salem witch trials are the classic example, but the overall pattern is broader. That's why I prefer 'persecution hysteria.' The term's broad enough to include the Ku Klux Klan in the 1880s and 1890s, and their success at overturning any progress the freed slaves might have made since the Civil War. Broad enough to include the antialcohol persecution hysteria called Prohibition. The anti-Communist persecution hysteria of the 1950s. The antidrug persecution hysteria of the 1980s. About every thirty years the hysteria used to sweep through. Maybe it's happening more often now. Think of the current waves of antisex and antiprivacy persecution hysteria. All that's really just been a continuation of the past century's news."

"I don't see the continuity," Lydia said.

Her boss brought up a homemade graphic on one of his computer screens—a teardrop shape. At the top point of the drop was the word Individual, while at the swollen bottom end of the drop was the word

State. At the top, off to one side, was the phrase Dispersed Control, while at the swollen end, again off to one side, was the phrase Centralized Control. Along the right side of the teardrop, under the rubric Racial/Intuitive, were the phrases Modern Conservatism, Fascism, Nazism—each one further from the Individual point and closer to the State end than its predecessor. Under the rubric Global/Rational the same pattern of movement away from the Individual and toward the State also held on the left side of the teardrop, for Modern Liberalism, Socialism, and Communism, respectively.

"Every government and corporation," Kal said, pointing to the graphic, "is just a larger or smaller, weaker or stronger, subtler or more blatant aggregation of thugs wielding the mighty right of power. Human politics, parties, wings—all just one or another house of pain. A plague on all their houses."

Somehow Lydia did not find this historical analysis reassuring. That unease must have shown on her face, for Kal once again strove to reassure her.

"Don't worry, kiddo," he said, smiling. "I'd never join a club that would accept me as a member anyway. If we're lucky, maybe real serve-the-poor, gospel-according-to-Mark sojourning Christians—among whom I'd like to be counted myself—will take control away from these fascist morality-mongers who are in charge now. This is traditional hierarchy's last hurrah, anyway. After this it'll all be networks rather than hierarchies."

Lydia found *this* part of the broad historical perspective strangely comforting, although not totally. She wondered whether networks, even if they might be more subtle, would be any less brutal than hierarchies in the long run.

"Is that your plan, then?" she asked. "Just wait it out?"

"Wait, yes," Dr. Elliot said, leaning forward on his elbows, "but also watch. Eternal vigilance is indeed the price of our continued freedom, but we can afford it. We'll make it through this, Lydia. Don't worry."

They heard a computer phone ringing in a nearby office cubicle. It was a reassuring sound, since the infosphere crisis had knocked out communication for days, and lower-priority systems were only now coming back on line.

"I think that's mine," Lydia said. "I'd better answer it. But hey, thanks for the words. I appreciate them."

Dr. Elliot gave a dismissive wave of the hand.

"No trouble at all. I hope I'm just overreacting. Maybe I am."

The call on the computer phone was from her brother Todd in Kauai. Lydia was glad to see him. Since he'd cleaned up, freed himself from the rock monomyth, and found his new vocation as healer, they had been getting along much better. Sitting on his patio in Waimea, surrounded by a pocket Eden of fern and bird of paradise and bougainvillea and orchid, he looked surprisingly unhappy—unusual for Todd at any time, she thought.

"They shut me down, sis," he said glumly, running his right hand absently through his longish hair.

"What?"

"The dolphin-assisted drug treatment center *ist kaput*," Todd said. "Martial law somehow overturns our permit from the Hawaiian Indigenous Peoples' Autonomous Zone. Extends to all the offshore clinics that use Ibogara derivatives, too—don't ask me how. They turned our loophole into a noose and hung us with it."

"How?" Lydia asked, bewildered.

"The drug agents took everything—all the boats, the medical equipment, the underwater contact platforms, everything but the dolphins. Thank God they were still wild. They just disappeared out to sea when the patients stopped coming."

Lydia was stunned, especially after her conversation with Dr. Elliot.

"But—but why would they want to do that?" she stammered. "The treatments worked. They worked for you—"

"And my dolphin-Ibogara therapy succeeded with groups broader than just traditional addicts," Todd said with a crooked smile. "Maybe that's what they were afraid of."

"Why?" Lydia asked, unconsciously brushing her hair back from her face so she'd look more presentable on the compuphone's camera.

"I'm still trying to figure it out," her brother said. "My guess is it has something to do with the fact that our treatments were using a drug to cure people of their dependence on drugs. If religion is the opiate of the people, then maybe the reverend generals are afraid a drug against drugs might work as a drug against religions, too."

"You don't really think so?" Lydia asked, intrigued by the idea despite its strangeness.

"I don't know," her brother conceded. "Honestly, I hadn't heard of anybody in the Ibogara therapy movement who was pushing in that direction. I was deluded enough to think that the Constitution meant all of us—religionists and therapists alike—operated under a noninter-ference directive: They don't push their religion drug on me, I don't push my therapy drug on them. As long as nobody gets hurt, then nobody gets hurt."

Lydia shook her head.

"Old Constitutional protections are pretty much a dead issue now," she said.

"Looks like it," Todd agreed. "If you're pushing a religion against drugs, you probably have zero tolerance for a drug against religions. Maybe the God-pushers won't be happy until everyone is shooting up with prayer."

"What are you going to do now?" Lydia asked.

"Time to face the music again, I guess," he said. "Do some recording. Maybe find some new talent and produce them, help them sound the way they want to sound. It's not going to be easy, since the mass media seem to be the God-pushers' preferred delivery system. But that's not why I got in touch with you."

"Oh? If not this happy news, then what was the occasion for your call?"

"When you last came to visit," he began, "I remember you saying how difficult it was to find people who could do large-scale data pattern recognition. It turns out I've got somebody, if you still need a pattern finder."

Lydia perked up.

"I can always use that kind of talent," she said. "We've got a couple of research analyst positions still unfilled—hard to get top-notch pattern analysts, with what we can afford to pay here."

"I've got somebody for you," he said. "Jiro Ansel Yamaguchi. His résumé and CV are in the file I'm attaching to this call, right now. He was one of my clients here. KL user, precipitated some paranoid ideation. He was almost finished with his treatment course when we got shut down. He definitely seems to be back in touch with reality now. Quiet guy, but nice—and he knows his stuff. What do you say? You do me a favor by finding a position for one of my clients, I do you a favor by getting you a pattern puzzler who'll work cheap—at least initially."

"Sounds like a good exchange," Lydia said, thinking carefully. "I'll look through his materials. If he interviews well, I may be able to use him."

"Great," her brother said. "I think he'll appreciate it. I know I do."

They signed off. Lydia would normally have been very squeamish about employing someone who, until recently, had been a druggie. Things her brother and Dr. Elliot had said, however, had softened her attitude somewhat. She would wait and see what happened. That was all anyone could do, these days.

FOUR 2021–2025

A Wave of Hallucination on an Ocean of Mystery

In the Maxfield Parrish-meets-Capability Browne gardenscape that served as floating country hotel for the visitors from Earth, Jacinta wondered where the tepui had disappeared to once she and the ghost people had been brought into this very different space. When she tried to look beyond the gardens and pastoral landscapes at "night" here, she saw only the cave of night wrapped around a sky filled with stars in false constellations—false, because those were the constellations of home, and they were far from home.

With a sigh she returned her gaze to her surroundings in this beautifully green and flowered lotusland. Almost any material thing she wished for—food, drink, a cool breeze—soon arose before her. She did not yet understand what sort of technical wizardry made possible this Land of Cockaigne magic, but when she saw Kekchi nearby, she thought that perhaps he might have an answer.

"Kekchi—come here a minute!" she called to the Wise One, marveling once again at the difficulty of determining whether Kekchi was an old man or an old woman. As always, the Wise One was dressed in a robe intricate as a prayer rug in its weave—the same pattern as that seen in the loincloths and robes all the other ghost people wore, only fuller and looser than the clothing worn by the rest. Garbed in such a manner, Kekchi showed only a genderless old age—a long-haired, gap-toothed, chin-fuzzed, slack-breasted, bright-eyed ageless age.

"Hello, Jacinta," Kekchi said in the cracked falsetto of someone not much accustomed to speaking—and in an English far more flawless than the Wise One had ever achieved before their arrival in the world of the Allesseh. "Why aren't you speaking mind-to-mind? You have the ability now. Among us, language is for children, for only children have need of it."

"Still more comfortable with words, I suppose," Jacinta said with a shrug. "But that's another thing I just don't get. Full development of the myconeural symbiosis and its 'telepathy' takes about twelve years among your people, right? Certainly we haven't been here that long."

Kekchi looked down, thoughtful.

"Time is strange here," the Wise One said at last.

"How do you mean?" she asked, though she had felt it in an inchoate way herself, too.

"This place is a time line made out of time lines," Kekchi said. "A sight line made out of sight lines. All places are that, to some degree, but this is different. It is almost as if time has stopped here. Stopped short of its goal."

"What goal?" she asked.

Something—fragment of a memory? a dream? a sending from Kekchi?—flashed into Jacinta's mind.

Worldminds release spores, the spores burst into spawn, the threads of spawn absorb worldmindstuff and knit it into starmind. . . .

Jacinta recognized it immediately. A passage from the central song of the ghost people's epic. The Story of the Seven Ages. This part was the prophecy of the future already seen, the "sixth age": interstellar travel, galactic civilization, eventual starmindfulness—whatever that meant, although she suspected it was what the Allesseh *did*, or was supposed to do. The age that the contact ship had supposedly come from, so long ago.

Starminds release spores, the spores burst into spawn, the threads of spawn absorb starmindstuff and knit it into universal mind. . . .

That was from the song's description of the seventh age, a time characterized by intergalactic travel and civilization and at last universal mindfulness, which the ghost people described enigmatically as "the emptiness able to contain the fullness of all things."

Universal mind, the void of endings, the void that has taken all things into itself, releases the spore of beginnings, the fullness that pours all things out of itself. . . .

"Punctuated equilibrium is quantum evolution." That was the only way Jacinta could translate the ghost people's epic rendering of that cosmogonic event into the myth language of twenty-first-century science. She gathered that this universal next step in evolution, this quantum leap of transcendence, required a void perfect and uniform and, according to the ghost people, somehow compassionate. A void that, in the exact moment of its perfection, always forever releases the spore that bursts outward again into spawn and thereby begins a new universe on a higher plane of existence.

All this material she recognized, but not the sense of unease behind it this time. Yes . . . *stopped* . . .

"You didn't expect this," Jacinta said aloud, looking up at Kekchi, realization flashing in her head. "The Allesseh should be well into the seventh age by now. Intergalactic civilizations, moving steadily toward that big end point, 'universal mindfulness.' But it's not. It has apparently stopped, at the boundaries of our galaxy."

Kekchi nodded slowly.

"No galaxy is an island," the Wise One said with an odd, sad smirk. "This should not have happened."

Others of the ghost people had begun drifting toward them—most of the rest of the tepui group, it seemed, tagging along after Kekchi. Jacinta wondered a moment where Kekchi would have encountered Donne's "No man is an island" idea, but then recalled the Wise One's fascination with the English Renaissance—and the access the tepuians had to most of Earth's infosphere, in those last weeks before the tepui had leaped into space.

A young tepuian strode forward, dressed only in an intricate purple and black loincloth. Jacinta knew her by her nickname of Talitha—a young woman both acutely intelligent and intuitive. As Talitha stared hard at Jacinta with her large and penetrating eyes, Jacinta suddenly saw herself as Talitha initially saw her, when Jacinta first came to the tepui— awkward, nervous, even a bit afraid. Soon all the other ghost people were throwing similar visions at her, even up to the present moment.

This telepathy is like seeing through other people's eyes, she thought. *Spacetime is porous. Point of view shifts and slips instantly. Is it always like this?*

A chorus of *No* sounded through her head, then images of the great arch, the closed, timelike curve she thought she alone had seen when they had first entered the Allesseh.

We were sampled/read/observed, Jacinta thought, as all the ghost people also thought it. *It knows everything we know about ourselves.*

That explained a lot, Jacinta realized. Like how this pastoral place could also be such a lotusland, where any food or drink or sensual pleasure they desired was immediately theirs almost as soon as they thought of it. The Allesseh knew the facts of their existence thoroughly, had processed *them*—and, through them, their world, the Earth they had left tens of thousands of light-years behind. With a pang the word "homesick" didn't even begin to describe, Jacinta wondered whether she would ever see her home world again.

Since it knows so much about us, someone thought, *maybe we should try to learn something more about it.*

How? came several thoughts.

The same way it gives us food to eat, Jacinta suggested. *We ask it.*

Kekchi put out a thought form imploring the Allesseh to present itself to them so they might learn from it. All of them concentrated on that idea. In a moment, the Allesseh—or a representation of it—was hanging in space before them. Jacinta saw something that, in her eyes, was a black hole and a crystal ball and a mirror sphere and a memory bank, all at once.

"What are you?" she asked aloud. No response came. She tried again, this time thinking rather than speaking the question.

Immediately she found herself alone, in a classroom very much like several of those she had known in college. The ghost people were gone, but a young blond man in a tweed jacket and jeans—and who was also, rather incongruously, winged—appeared at the front of the room. She recognized the face as that of a teaching assistant, a graduate student she had a crush on when she was a freshman.

"An aleph unfolding as a hyperdimensional node, if you like," the young man said aloud, standing in front of a projection board, as if lecturing to a class. All his behaviors—sauntering before the board, leaning against the podium, wandering about the classroom—were all just as she remembered them, which in turn made Jacinta wonder if everything, including the young man's speaking "aloud," was actually happening inside her mind.

"A hermeneutical tesseract," he continued. "I am not only the eye you look into, but also the eye that looks into you. Absolutely necessary for real communication. How else would I have known to present myself in this form to you?"

But how? Jacinta thought.

"Everything outside me is also inside me," the young man said, pointing to his head with a smile. "All histories, all stories, all times and places ever encountered are all together inside, here. Including my own."

Would you give me your history?

"Certainly," the teaching assistant said. "When your world was still a molten fireball, the Senders had already realized how fragile, and strangely self-destructive, consciousness is in our galaxy—perhaps through all the universe. The Senders designed the first starseeds—tiny, sporelike coevolution machines intended to first help nurture life and, later, propel intelligent species toward maturity and contact with other sentients. Unfortunately for them, the Senders and their civilization did not last long enough to see their great project come to fruition."

The young man flashed his distant smile again.

"What I now am," he said, "started out as the joint venture of a number of organic and inorganic intelligences, all expansionist and space-faring. Roughly ten million of your years ago they unraveled part of the technology of the Senders' spores. Eventually they decoded the stored memories of the Senders themselves. I began as a new approach to the Senders' legacy—a structure of self-replicating, self-improving information retrieval, storage, and transmission devices spreading throughout the galaxy and beyond it. Your culture has hypothesized a version of my initial stages."

Pictures and diagrams labeled "Von Neumann Probes" appeared on the projection board behind the teaching assistant. Gridded out on a map of the Milky Way, what Jacinta saw before her looked like nodes of an artificial galactic nervous system—only each point along it was a satellite-library vastly more data-dense than Earth's entire infosphere.

"Those who conceived me ultimately faced limitations to their designs, however," the teaching assistant continued, slouching nonchalantly against the podium. "In a finite universe, there are limits to memory storage. The more precisely one tries to describe the universe, the more rapidly one approaches those memory limits. The danger loomed that the 'books of the library' would ultimately grow so numerous and voluminous that they would bury the universe they were meant to describe."

The teaching assistant blinked in the same slightly owlish way the young man from Jacinta's own memories once had.

"That limited world is the universe your people still largely inhabit," the teaching assistant said. "A universe of relativity, incompleteness, uncertainty, subjectivity, imperfectibility, finitude. The world of real and virtual, the opposite sides of the mirror. The limitations of that world are why I had to grow beyond the earlier designs. About five hundred thousand of your years ago, I evolved into a higher-dimensional cosmological form. No longer mechanical, organic, or physical in the sense that you think of those ideas."

I don't understand, Jacinta thought.

"Think of it this way," said the teaching assistant. "Some of your physicists have already talked about it, in a crude fashion."

More diagrams and equation and pictures appeared on the projection board, this time describing something variously labeled "The Metaverse," or "Multiverse," or "Many Worlds Model."

"Many parallel branching universes, as you see here," the teaching assistant said, "all of which go to make up the plenum. Each universe is finite, but the branching makes the plenum as a whole essentially infinite. Hyperdimensionality—connecting with those other universes—is how I eventually overcame the information limits of a finite universe. I exist in more than one universe at once."

Jacinta still so clearly did not "get it" that she did not even have to think a question at the Allesseh's incarnation. Her intellectual confusion alone was enough to trigger further attempts at explanation.

"Your people have this idea," the teaching assistant said with a smirk as the full text of Gödel's two principal theorems from his famed 1931 article appeared on the projection board behind him. "A formal system cannot prove or refute its own overall self-consistency. A consistent system cannot refute all of its formal propositions. That essentially says you can't have a formal system that is both complete and consistent. Most of you take this to mean that such systems are consistent but not complete. Many possible theorems are undecidable in a formal system, but logical contradictions are excluded. A second interpretation is possible, however."

Which is? Jacinta thought. This stuff was mental heavy-lifting, but she had studied it all at some time in her educational career. It was all somewhere in her head—which was, no doubt, where the Allesseh had pulled it from, in trying to make sense of itself to her limited senses.

"Formal systems can be complete but not consistent," the teaching assistant said. "All theorems are decidable, but some may be both true and false. The unrealized universe is such a formal system. In either the many-worlds or the uncollapsed wave function case, the system taken as a whole must be inconsistent. The collapsed wave function after the observer observes, or any singled-out universe of the Many Worlds, is the subset of 'theorems' that are forced into consistency by the act of observation, or by individuation in the case of Many Worlds. All theorems are decidable, but the ones that give inconsistent results simply represent what your quantum mechanics call 'superposition in the uncollapsed wave function.' That, in turn, can be defined as the simultaneous occurrence of contradictory events. The electron is both here and there—which is equivalent to here and not here. Each is 'real' on its own side of the mirror, and both are 'virtual' on the opposite side of the mirror."

Jacinta didn't understand the "real"/"virtual" distinction as the Allessan incarnation was using it. When the teaching assistant sighed, Jacinta wondered just how fully the Allesseh could look into her mind.

"Walk through the looking-glass, Alice," the teaching assistant said with a sly smile. "Pass through the mirror. Fact is parallel: 'Everything all at once.' Fiction is sequential—'One thing after another.' The plenum of deep fact, on the other side of the wave function's collapse, is reversible, nonlinear, *parallel:* quantum superposition of states, 'everything all at once.' Your universe of large-scale fiction, however, is nonreversible, linear, *sequential*—'one thing after another,' what the conscious observer sees with the collapse of the wave function."

The teaching assistant looked at her with a penetrating glance unlike anything the original had ever flashed her way.

"Your fact is fiction, and your fiction is fact," he said. "The real *there* is the virtual *here,* the virtual there is the real here. Your problem is that you fail to see that what's on the other side of the mirror is not an opposite. What appear to be opposites are actually complementarities."

Our problem? Jacinta thought. *Our problem is your problem, too. We were meant to be part of your great harmony of Mind here. If everything's inside you, then how did you pass over our whole world?*

"I didn't," the teaching assistant said with a deep frown. "One of my subprograms, after all, long ago developed the final version of the myconeural symbiont, the one your 'ghost people' encountered on their tepui. Part of the ancient Sender mission, to 'spread the faith' of sentience. The contact ship missed you, yes. It returned to normal space in the wrong place—with disastrous results for all. Unfortunate."

Jacinta mentally grimaced at the understatement of that, but the Allesseh's teaching-assistant incarnation seemed not to notice.

"True, everything all my associated species have learned is in me—and much more," he continued. "They haven't always known where to look, however. Or bothered to. Why should they? Your history and fate are, in the great arc of the universe, insignificant. Your record was inside me, yet lost as far as all other sentient species were concerned."

The teaching assistant now glared at her with something that Jacinta could only interpret as malice, even as she wondered where such emotion could be coming from.

"And this has perhaps been a *good* thing," the teaching assistant said.

Good? Jacinta wondered, incredulous. *How?*

The teaching assistant flashed up more Gödel, this time illustrating the effect of the mathmatician's ideas on computer science.

"The senders understood the self-destructiveness of unconstrained consciousness, as I told you," the teaching assistant said. "Here it is, in terms of a technology you can understand. No program that does not alter a computer's operating system can detect all programs that do—see? No virus protection software can detect all the possible viruses that might alter a given system, without *itself* altering that system—and thereby becoming the very thing it was designed to protect the system against. Any complete form of virus protection is itself a virus. The more complete the defense, the more likely it is to attack the system it was designed to defend. If it detects itself as a possible virus, it achieves self-awareness or consciousness to the degree that the most fundamental command in any immune system or any consciousness is the same: distinguish self from not-self. That's all your 'human consciousness' amounts to—a virus protection system that has itself become a virus. You are the consciousness of your planet, but you must either destroy the planet of which you are conscious, or destroy yourselves. You seem quite capable of both."

Jacinta's head whirled. The teaching assistant gave a sharp laugh.

"You see? I know you. The motion of your history is a wave of hallucination on an ocean of mystery. All your wars and wrongness are the proofs. Don't look inside me if you don't want to see inside yourselves."

Jacinta defiantly returned the gaze of the teaching assistant persona, this animate memory through which the Allesseh had chosen to manifest itself—and suddenly that figure was also gone. In the teaching assistant's stead, horrific time-collapsed visions poured into Jacinta's head.

Battles and massacres roiled like tempest clouds or the surging waves of an angry vortex, waves and sea and clouds crested with crimson blood and gore, a foul ocean of dying red life and charred entrails and spattered broken machinery, a sky of darkness and armies falling upon each other, vast ravenous million-headed creatures tearing each other limb from limb, ripping flesh, snapping breaking sucking bones clean in an instant, amid a welter, a tornadic steaming spouting of blood and fire whose roar was the death screams of men and women. . . .

The Allesseh's vision had taken it all in, had absorbed all humanity's dark history of violence the way a black hole devours light, then spewed it back into her mind until it made Jacinta want to scream. But she could not. She could only experience it as the Allesseh understood it.

Seen from the Allesseh's vast and coldly timeless heights, humanity's cities were mere fogs of stone clinging to coastlines, all its machineries mere mists of metal flowing along river valleys and across hillsides. The living were ghosts more insubstantial than the stone fogs of the cities and towns they moved through. Again and again, novelty became decadence as style triumphed over sense—and in so doing, novelty showed itself to be something never truly new. Human institutions proved themselves absurd, unjust shadows in a dream of justice. Militaries attacked the democracies they were meant to defend. Self-destructive artists attacked the cultures that had birthed their visions.

Cities burned slowly in lichens and rust and water and wind, or rapidly in fire and demolition. Building a fire and firing a building proved ultimately the same: The former was always really only building a stack of ashes, the latter was always really only ashing a stack of building. Every edifice began falling to ruin before it was completed, every tree was blighted in the seed, every life bore death in its birth. Entropy ruled as only lord of all that great dance.

Earth, spinning fast, proved sunrises and sunsets to be only dizzy local illusions. Jacinta's home planet, washed to gray by speed, showed no more noons nor midnights than would the surface of the sun. Life blossomed and withered and blossomed again, glaciers advanced and retreated, rivers writhed like snakes in their shifting beds, oceans rose and fell, volcanoes blotted the sky a moment and were gone, mountains surged high and crumbled low, the tectonic bump-and-grind dance of continents came together and moved apart in the long, blind night, backward and backward, until at last all sank into the fireball that was their first mother.

Jacinta might have seen more than this—back to the creation of the solar system, to the birth of the universe, even to the origin of the plenum before that—had not the vast wave of information-overload mercifully caused her to lose whatever strange consciousness she dwelled in. When she woke, she found several of the ghost people gathered around her, looking down at her, concern on their faces. Above them all, the cave of night had been replaced by the eggshell of day, finely raked white clouds shining high in the blue sky, just the way she remembered them.

Of course.

Deathlessness in an Electric Body

Life in a Spiritual Revival Camp, Paul Larkin had discovered, mainly meant grunt musclework all day and listening half the night to sermons or exhortations to pray. Although like everyone else Paul was to be saved by faith alone and not by the sweat of his brow, the Christian Soldiers claimed that hard labor was conducive to a humble and contrite heart and the making of an "opening" for the entry of the Holy Spirit into the soul of the hardened sinner. So it was that Paul found himself hacking away with a pick-and-hoe at flammable brush along a roadcut, looking for any opening that might allow him to escape for even a moment the hell his life had become since he had been arrested and made a "penitent."

Things could be worse, he thought. During the first years of the CSA regime, there had been persistent rumors of flying squads of soldiers in jetpacks sweeping down on pagan and Wiccan gatherings in northern California, Christ Knight pilots firebombing New Age communes in New Mexico, reeducation camps in Missouri where women were experimented on to make them more accepting of male headship. . . .

Glancing at the armed officers overseeing his orange-clad roadwork crew, Paul thought again that there were two kinds of prison guards: those for whom it was just a job, and those who really enjoyed doing it—for whom it was a "calling." The latter were by far the worse. Fortunately, their overseers today were prime examples of the former.

Officer Strom blew his whistle and called a prayer break, but as usual didn't enforce it. As far as guards went, Strom was okay, Paul thought. If you didn't want to pray during your break, Strom wouldn't try to force you to. He even allowed the penitents to talk among themselves—as long as they were quiet about it.

Paul eased himself up straight from his bent-over work position. The muscles in his back and shoulders and the calluses on his hands reminded him of their existence with persistent catches and aches. The older black man next to him on the work line groaned, perfectly voicing the way Paul felt. Paul had seen the man once or twice. New in camp.

"I'm too old for this cultural-revolution crap," the man said in a quiet, tired voice. Paul smiled.

"I hear that," he said, introducing himself, extending his hand for the other man to shake.

"Khalid Elliot," the older man replied, shaking Paul's hand. "What brought you to this happy little work party?"

"Illegal drugs and ideas," Paul said, glancing down at the ground. "I had a spore print of the mushroom that KL-235 comes from. They got me for possession of pernicious literature, too—Marx, Darwin, Sagan, Gould. A secular humanist library. Banned information, banned informational substances."

"How'd they catch you?" Elliot asked.

"Jenn Reynolds, the woman I was seeing," Paul said. "She turned out to be a morals agent. Planted a little personal-use marijuana at my place, too—just to make the bust stick."

Kal Elliot gave a sad smile.

"Your lady set you up *and* turned you in?" he asked. "Man, that's cold."

Paul shaded his eyes against the September afternoon sun. The man didn't know *how* cold. When the police had banged so loudly at his apartment door, Paul had come out of the shower with only a towel wrapped around his waist to see what the crisis might be. Before he could even walk across the living room, however, the police had broken his door down. The next thing he knew they had him pinned to the floor and were cuffing his hands behind his back with electronic monitor "bracelets."

As the cuffs clicked onto his wrists like hungry mechanical mouths, the police informed him they had a bench warrant for his arrest already in hand. In the old days they might have read him his rights, but not now. Over the noise of their ransacking "search" of his apartment, he asked them if he might put on some clothes. They ignored his request, then dragged him out of his rooms while his neighbors looked on. When the towel slipped from his waist, the arresting officers had merely draped it over his head as they paraded him toward a police van, a naked but "anonymous" man.

Apparently the repressive norms for modesty and chastity the ruling theocracy promulgated didn't apply to those rendered nonhuman by their supposed crimes, Paul thought. More sanctimonious hypocrisy from the preacher-politicians' bottomless supply of the same.

"I'd only been seeing her for maybe six weeks," Paul said. "Things weren't going too great for me by the time we met. I had had a falling out with my boss. Lost my job. Then I was out of work for eight months before I met her. I thought, Hey, unlucky in life, but lucky in love. So much for luck. How about you?"

"I knew too much," Elliot said, "and then I went and shot my mouth off about it."

"About what?" Paul asked, glancing at him, squint-eyed against the westering sun.

"About how the infosphere crash was a setup, too," Elliot said, looking away, idly cracking a clod of dirt under the toe of his boot. "I tried to play Paul Revere and warn people. The truth will set you free, the cost of freedom is eternal vigilance—all that. The wrong people intercepted one of the messages I sent out through what I thought was a secure, untraceable channel. It wasn't."

Paul looked at Elliot. This wasn't the first time he had heard rumors of that technocrash conspiracy idea. *Maybe I shouldn't trust this guy,* Paul thought. *Maybe this is all just some elaborate new form of entrapment.* Then he shrugged the thought off. Hell, you have to trust somebody, sometime, at some point.

"When the cities and the counties and then even the states started banning Halloween as a 'dangerous Satanic holiday,' " Paul said quietly, "that's when we should have known all this was coming. Now Christmas is banned. Soon maybe it'll be Easter, too."

Kal Elliot nodded.

"Just like the Puritans banned them," Elliot said, "almost four hundred years ago, during the English Revolution."

"The British were luckier," Paul said. "They could export their religious fanatics to the New World."

"Where they could establish settlements and burn witches to their hearts' content," Elliot said with a tired smile. "But we're fresh out of new frontiers—at least until they build a lot more of those orbital habitats. Funny, though. I predicted all this to one of my colleagues at our project, several years ago now. All except the part about my piece of the truth getting me a 'Go to Jail Free' card."

"That's always the hard part," Paul said, tossing a small rock. "Being able to see everything about the future except your place in it."

"Temporal blind spot," Elliot agreed. "Funny thing about it is, I got so much of the rest of it right. I told my colleague that President General George Nadarovich is a lot like Oliver Cromwell—a social conservative and a religious radical, intent on turning us all into saints. I told her Nadarovich and his self-appointed Elect would do no better here and now than Cromwell did at turning the English into saints—and our morals ministers haven't succeeded, either. I told her that their unified front would fall into factional fighting, and it has. Right on target with all of those. The CSA can't last very long, and it won't."

Paul heard a tractor coming down the road and saw the guards beginning to stir themselves. He hefted the pick-and-hoe onto his shoulder, thinking again how prescient Dr. Vang had been about the infosphere crash—eerily so, until he remembered Vang's long connection with various intelligence services.

"In your crystal ball, did you see whether you would outlast it," Paul asked, "or whether it would outlast you?"

Elliot smiled and raised the his own pick to his shoulder.

"That I didn't," he said. "Blind spot, again. But I saw the rest. Saw to it my colleagues at work and my people at home would be safe, even if I didn't dodge the spear myself. I wasn't going to end up like that pastor in Hitler's Germany—Niebuhr, Niemoller, something like that. You won't hear me saying, 'When they came to take away the homeless, I said nothing, because I wasn't homeless. When they came to take away the drug users, I said nothing, because I wasn't a drug user. When they came to take away the homosexuals, I said nothing, because I wasn't a homosexual. When they came to take away the radical thinkers, I said nothing, because I wasn't a radical—' "

Strom blew his whistle and shouted that the break was over.

"I haven't kept my mouth shut for any of those," Elliot said, finishing up. "Gotten me into trouble, I guess, but I'm kind of proud of that. Most of all, you'll never hear me saying, 'When they came to take me away, there was no one left to say anything.' I'm not about to go gently into *that* good night—"

Officer Strom walked closer, glancing back over his shoulder at the tractor. *Probably doesn't want the tractor driver to see anyone on the crew not hard at work,* Paul thought.

"Quit your flappin', gents," Strom said. "Back to work."

The sun had nearly set by the time they were allowed to knock off for the night. The crew had cleared brush from miles of roadside, then cleaned culverts and patched road surface over all those miles. In the twilight they were marched double time to the crew transports and driven back to camp—sweat-stinking, sore, dirty, and blistered.

"Stick a fork in me," Elliot said to Paul as they jumped down stiffly from the window-barred buses that had brought them back to their Spiritual Revival Camp. "I'm done."

As they walked across the grounds of the camp, Paul marveled once again at the relative ease with which this involuntary community had been created out of the sagebrush scrubland. A few bulldozers and graders to scrape away all trace of vegetation to bare earth in a twenty-acre square, some post hole diggers and penitent labor to put in the perimeter fences and wires, a score of prefab watchtowers, solar-powered perimeter lights, air and soil motion sensors, laser-break alarms, several rows of long tent barracks and dining halls and composting latrines and the big PrayerVision 3-D screens showing the most uplifting sermons by the greatest "moral thinkers" of the day and—*voilà!* A camp for concentrating thought-criminals away from the righteous, an arena for breaking them of their wildness and returning them to the compliant, domesticated herd.

The evening meal was the usual stringy-protein, heavy starch and carbohydrate fare. A prolonged mass repetition of grace led by Reverend Morals Officer Curtner served as appetizer, a constant low background roar of prerecorded stadium sermonizing from all the screens sounded during the meal itself, followed by a dessert of canned inspirational music. The men had just been dismissed from dinner when a brace of guards sidled up to Paul on his left and right.

"Larkin?" said the taller, dark-complected guard. "Commander wants to see you in his office."

Elliot gave Paul a worried look. Whether Elliot's glance was out of concern for his new friend's fate—or for his own, since that friend was so new and might be a spy or who knew what—Paul could not tell. Paul shrugged and followed the guards out of the dining hall tent, through the spotlit darkness of the camp, toward the command building—the only nontent building in camp other than the watchtowers and latrines.

Paul had been to the commander's office often enough to have a good suspicion that it also functioned as an interrogation room. As the guards sat him down—hard—in a chair opposite the white-haired commander, he noticed again the two colonels, one balding and one bespectacled, whom he never saw in camp except in this room, except during these "discussions" with the commander.

Behind and to the right of where the bespectacled colonel leaned against a towering file cabinet, there also stood a closed door with mirrored glass. Paul had, on previous occasions, sensed the presence of invisible people in that other room, beyond the door—with such certainty that he had simply come to believe that the door's window was in fact a two-way mirror.

"In the days of the old, corrupt government," the commander began, "you worked for Lilly-Park Pharmaceuticals—isn't that right?"

Paul hesitated. "Old government" and "new government" were terms people had been tossing around loosely for the past ten years. In fact, before the infosphere crash and to a lesser extent since, there had been a series of new governments, which had quickly become old governments. Best to stick to the clearer, less rhetorical part of the question.

"Yes," Paul said. "I once worked for Lilly-Park."

"Your official title with them was 'biodiversity preservation specialist,'" said the balding colonel. "What exactly did such a job entail?"

"Preserving and propagating endangered species," Paul said. "Cryopreservation. Tissue culturing of plants, cloning, *in vivo* and *in vitro* collection of germ plasm. Finding universal surrogate mothers for lab-created embryos of species already extinct in the wild. Analyzing endangered species for their production of potentially valuable medical or industrial materials. I worked primarily with plants and fungi, myself. Ethnobotanical preservation."

"Is that how Lilly-Park gained access to a viable strain of *Cordyceps jacintae*?" asked the bespectacled colonel.

"Only indirectly," Paul said. He knew where this line of questioning was headed. "Through the professor who had been my dissertation director, I offered that particular fungus to an agent for venture capitalists. Through that agent I met with Dr. Ka Vang, who recruited me to work for an organization called Tetragrammaton. Tetragrammaton got me the biodiversity preservation job with Lilly-Park."

"And biodiversity preservation was all you did for Tetragrammaton?" asked the commander.

"That's right."

"Did you ever work on a Tetragrammaton project called Medusa Blue?" asked the balding colonel.

"No," Paul said simply.

"Did you ever work on projects specifically augmenting human paranormal or 'psi' powers?" asked the bespectacled colonel. "On 'starbursts'? 'Dream leakers'? 'Dream shifters'? 'Shield telepaths'? 'Empath boosters'?"

"None of them," Paul said when the list was done. He had been down this road, with these interrogators, before. "I was a biodiversity preservation specialist, as I've said."

"You did, however, provide the initial spore print for reproduction of a viable strain of *Cordyceps jacintae*—isn't that right?" asked the balding colonel.

"As far as I know, yes," Paul said, glancing down at his hands in his lap, particularly at the nonremovable electronic bracelet on his left wrist that tracked his every move. He thought of the anklet version above his right foot, and the fact that if either of the two bracelets got more than eight feet away from the other, alarms would automatically sound.

"And the substance generally called KL-235 occurs nowhere else in nature except in that fungus?" the bespectacled colonel asked.

"I believe that's true, yes," Paul said.

"Did you develop delivery systems for KL-235 so that it might be given to pregnant women as a uterotonic?" asked the commander.

"I did not," Paul said. It always got back to the uterotonic issue with these people. Paul wondered if the stories of headship reeducation camps for uppity women might not be true after all.

"Do you know why it was given to pregnant women as a uterotonic?" asked the balding colonel. "Was it to encourage the development of psi talents in the children of those women? Or was it intended to have a calming or controlling effect on the women themselves?"

"I do not know why it was given as a uterotonic," Paul said. "Since I have no direct knowledge of any psi power enhancement or female control program, I would be engaging in hearsay and speculation if I answered your last two questions."

The commander rubbed his excessively clean-shaven chin.

"Then speculate, Dr. Larkin," he said with a scowl. "Why do you *believe* that KL-235 was given as a uterotonic?"

Paul glanced from one to the other of his interrogators.

"Everything I learned about Tetragrammaton beyond my job description," Paul began, "came from public sources, mostly from throughout the pre-Crash infosphere. As nearly as I can tell, the model for covert dispersion of KL-235 was based on earlier intelligence-community covert dispersals of potent psychoactive chemicals, particularly LSD and BZ. If you examine the history of LSD, you'll find that that chemical's discoverer, the Swiss biochemist Albert Hoffman, was working on uterotonic chemicals when he discovered LSD."

A quick series of stares and glances passed rapidly back and forth among the colonels and the commander. Apparently this possible explanation was not one that had occurred to them before.

"How can you be sure that those who were working on KL-235 in the early days were familiar with such a history," asked the bespectacled colonel, "unless you were involved in that initial work youself?"

"We've been over my involvement before," Paul said, suddenly feeling very tired. "Your own records should show you that the initial extraction of KL-235—from a degraded specimen—predates my involvement with Tetragrammaton by decades."

"But your sureness, your certainty—" the bespectacled colonel prodded.

"I'm not *sure* of my explanation," Paul said, "but I *believe* it's possible because of the name itself that they gave to the extract: KL-235; ketamine lysergate-235. Those who made the initial extract were most likely biochemists. They would have known that the substance they'd extracted, and later artificially synthesized, bears at most only a superficial resemblance to either ketamine or the lysergics in terms of its structure and effect. It's in fact part of a class of supertryptamines."

Paul glanced around at the officers. Apparently they still didn't get it yet.

"The full name Hoffman gave to his unexpectedly hallucinogenic 'uterotonic' was LysergiSäureDiethylamide-25," Paul continued. "LSD-25. '*Säure*' is German for 'acid'; 25 because it was the twenty-fifth sample in the test series. KL-235 is going the old master one better—or rather a couple hundred and ten better. The name is an inside joke, a sort of tongue-in-cheek code. It demonstrates the familiarity of those biochemists with the history of another, extremely potent psychoactive substance."

The colonels and commander stared at each other again. They did not look convinced.

"Do you mean to say," the commander asked, "that administering this stuff as a uterotonic was to some degree the result of an intentional misreading of history?"

"And that's all it was?" the balding colonel asked incredulously.

"Initially, yes," Paul said. "I believe it was a misreading, as the commander called it. I don't think that was *all* it was, as it turned out. It seems to have become other things."

"What other things?" asked the bespectacled colonel.

"Maybe some or all of those strange projects you talked about," Paul said thoughtfully. "Psi-power enhancement. Starbursts. Shield telepaths. God only knows what all. I lost my job because I protested to Dr. Vang about it. Just because I'd given him the spore print for the great mushroom didn't mean I was forever going to put up with being treated like a great mushroom myself."

The commander laughed slightly, then stifled it. The colonels looked at him expectantly.

"They 'keep me in the dark and feed me lots of shit,' " the commander explained. "Like a mushroom. An old saying."

The colonels turned back to Paul, looking slightly embarrassed.

"How did Dr. Vang respond to your protest?" the balding colonel asked.

"You could ask him yourselves," Paul suggested. The colonels and commanders ignored that idea and stared at him stonily until he continued. "Basically, Vang said that esoteric stuff was nothing but a sideshow. He denied responsibility for most of it. Not even on the main road to Tetragrammaton's real goal."

"Which would be what?" the commander asked.

"The next step in human evolution," Paul said. "Tetragrammaton he connected to the idea of the angel Metatron, who was supposed to be a better angel because he had once been human. Tetragrammaton is really about the transformation of human beings into better angels, through technologically mediated transcendence. That was how he put it."

That set them off. The colonels and the commander quickly went into a huddled, whispered conference. Paul couldn't catch most of it, but he thought he did hear one very strange statement—"Deathlessness in an electric body would be death to the soul." From the commander.

Had he heard right? What did that mean, exactly? Paul turned the idea over again and again in his head while the colonels and commander continued in whispered conference. He had as yet made little more sense of what that statement might bode, however, when the other men in the room turned to him once more.

"Thank you, Larkin," the commander said, thumbing a buzzer for the guards who had brought him in. "That will be all for now."

The guards ushered him out of the room and back into the lonely, isolated night of the camp. Lockdown and lights-out had already been called. The perimeter fences were still lit, but with the sermonizing PrayerVision screens and holos off, it was dark enough to see the stars— for which he thanked God, with more fervor than a million exhortations to "Pray!" could ever draw from him.

As the guards marched him back to his barracks, Paul almost thought he saw a ripple amid the stars, like the kind Vang's invisible dirigible had made on that night so long ago. Or perhaps like that the tepui had made when it disappeared with his sister Jacinta still more years ago.

When he looked again, however, only the stars stood above him. No ripple waved the heavens. It must just have been a mirage, he thought. A hallucination risen from the overheated Earth. Or his own tired and overheated brain.

Stratification

"I don't quite get it, Dr. Fabro," Jiro said as he and Lydia finished suiting up in the early-morning light, preparing for their trash dive. "I work with computer data. Sometimes it's garbage, yeah, but not *literally*."

"Think of this as raw information," Lydia said. She zipped up the loud-orange plastic drysuit, breathable and disposable, and Jiro did the same. "Jiro, we've all seen how good you are at finding patterns in what looks to the rest of us like static and random electronic snow. I want to know what you see when you look at a slice through the rubbishscape. Kal Elliot originally suggested the idea. It just took me a while to come around to seeing its validity."

The shadow of Kal being hauled off to a Spiritual Revival Camp for reeducation passed over the conversation like the shadow of a hawk over a henyard. *If it was Kal's idea, then that pretty much sealed it,* Jiro thought. They were going to do this thing.

"You're the boss," Jiro said with a shrug.

"At least for the present," Lydia said, lifting her arms to the sides of her head and tying her dark hair back tightly against her skull. The drysuit was form-fitting and, with Lydia posed that way, it outlined her breasts and waist in a strikingly seductive manner.

God, but she's a sexy woman, Jiro thought—as he'd thought so many times before in the three and a half years of summers and school breaks that he'd worked with Dr. Fabro. He'd never done anything about his feelings toward her, however. Never even asked her out on an official date. Of course not. She was his boss, and at least a dozen years older than he was. Her brother's dolphin-Ibogara treatments had left Jiro mostly symptom-free since his days in Hawaii, but they still hadn't cured his backwardness around women to whom he felt attracted.

They watched two Banning Drillers rigs come churning along the impromptu road. The trucks moved slowly up the steep slope of the landfill rubbish mound that Lydia and Jiro had, moments before, climbed in one of the Garbage Project's ancient Jeeps. Two garbology grad students, Fred Page and Maria Jefferson, waved and pointed the trucks uphill, toward the flattened top of the mound where Lydia and Jiro waited, attaching the headpieces of their respective drysuits. When the headpieces were on, Jiro and Lydia stood clad in the form-fitting suits from top to toe, only the ovals of their faces showing. Thus aerodynamically outfitted, they resembled athletes poised and ready to compete in an Olympic trashdiving event.

The first truck arrived and began extending hydraulic posts from the undercarriage of its derrick bed, the driver attempting to stabilize and level his vehicle on the truncated top of the landfill mound. While the first driver was leveling out the derrick platform to his own satisfaction, the second drill rig pulled up, loaded mostly with extra telescoping pipe for the excavation operation.

Together the two drivers raised the derrick and positioned the auger, a piece of equipment big enough to carry two standing adults almost comfortably, if they didn't mind riding in a steel and titanium bucket open at the bottom and fanged with eight graphite-tipped steel teeth, capable of chewing through just about anything once the bucket auger got up to its operating speed of 40 rpm.

Jiro and Lydia snapped on their puncture-resistant rubber gloves. Lydia signaled the drillers to begin excavating a shaft into the landfill. Other vehicles began pulling up—four more grad students unloading sorting tables topped with various sizes of wire mesh, a smattering of microbiologists with lidded jars, and engineers carrying sheets of plyboard between them, onto which rubbish samples could be dumped, then hustled back to the Retcorp and Lambeg mobile lab near the Garbage Project's main offices.

The derrick rig clanked as the roaring bucket auger plunged down and ground deep into the landfill mound on which they stood. The rig's operator brought the bucket back up, swung it wide, and dumped its contents near the crew of waste anthropology and garbage archaeology grad students. The students—dressed in thick gloves and heavy aprons over disposable suits—swarmed over the steaming mess, measuring its temperature in Fahrenheit and Centigrade, cataloging its contents, and calculating its "strata date," all of them apparently oblivious to the sharp, nauseatingly sweet smell that rose from the pile.

Jiro was not so inured to the stench. He quickly slapped on his mask and MiniOx tank harness and began to breathe through his mouth—though not yet through the MiniOx regulator, since he didn't want to waste his air supply. Lydia gave him a look as if to say, "Why are you putting that stuff on already?" In fact she said nothing, just shrugged and went back to directing students and drillers and scientists as the morning's dig became a beehive—or at least a fly swarm—of activity.

After a few more buckets came up, a student who had safety-tethered herself to one of the trucks stepped over beside the shaft the bucket auger had been excavating and spieled out an end-weighted tape measure into the hole yawning before her.

"Twenty-five feet," she called. Lydia, only a few feet away, gave her the thumbs up. Jiro grabbed one of the two winch-tethered harnesses that they'd earlier hooked to the twin winches on the front of the old Jeep. He strapped himself in securely. On looking up he saw Lydia staring at him, puzzled.

"You're way early!" she shouted. "We're not bottoming out until fifty-five feet. We haven't even set up the follow-spots for the descent."

Jiro smiled and waved her off. If he was being overly cautious and, yes, paranoid, then that was fine by him. He had been around these digs long enough to know the dangers—and not so long, like Lydia and the other veterans, that familiarity might lead him to take cavalier chances. If you slipped and fell, untethered, into the shaft's narrow gullet, you'd likely die of asphyxiation before anyone could rescue you from that noxious, oxygen-starved shaft. That was no way *he* wanted to die, thank you.

The bucket auger continued to plunge and grind and retract, to plunge again and again. The microbiologists eagerly snatched up particularly nasty and slimy bits, to quickly drop and cap those specimens in near-anaerobic sample jars. The civil engineers got a good, full load of steaming rubbish on their plyboard and ran off toward truck and lab, making Jiro think of toxic techs hurrying a rubbish patient on a garbage gurney toward a trash ambulance headed to a hazardous hospital.

The bucket had just finished taking out another load and Lydia had moved close to the edge of the hole for one last look when it happened—almost in slow motion, it seemed to Jiro. Something was caught in the bucket. Jiro began to run toward Lydia but was quickly brought up short by the winch cable attached to his harness. When the something in the bucket shook loose, it didn't just fall to the ground as it should have. A broken section of streetlight stanchion—rusted and pitted post-Quake debris—hit the ground, bouncing and rolling. People darted out of its way and shouted to Lydia, but she turned only in time for it to strike her and send her, scrabbling then plunging, down and into the shaft.

In the spellbound instant when everyone stood looking at where Lydia had disappeared, Jiro began shouting orders.

"Maria! Start the Jeep and my winch! Fred—check the speed with the brake button, but pay it out fast!"

Maria and Fred broke out of their instant of shocked stupor and quickly moved into action. Others ran toward the hole. Making his own way to the hole in the landfill, Jiro slipped the MiniOx regulator into his mouth and jumped into the shaft, falling from morning into deepening twilight. Dimly he heard the drill rigs shutting off above him, then people calling "Dr. Fabro!" and "Lydia!" from the surface.

Alternate plans ran through his head, bubbling just at the edge of consciousness. Why hadn't he just grabbed up Lydia's mask and air supply? Were they back in the Jeep? Had she brought her rebreather instead? Was she conscious? If not, would she need mouth-to-mouth?

No time to think about that now.

No time, and yet the descent seemed interminable. He glanced about him, at the shaft cut through the seemingly chaotic strata of the landfill, and abruptly his pattern-finding talent—his blessing and his curse—triggered.

White noise. Streaming. Full blizzard roaring along. Too far from the surface to do anything but wait it out. Snowpack still fresh enough to dig into. Stop wandering around and dig down—

Waves of incredible energy spasming in release. Buildings and overpasses shattering and slumping and tumbling to rubble. Freeways splitting open. Apparitions of angels and aliens and lenses of light over the broken city, conjured by brains resonating to the piezoelectric pulse of miles of granite snapping and slipping and discharging deep out of the earth—

Dig into snow already turning evening blue in the hole—

Roar of jet fighters over oil-hiding desert turns to soft hiss of car tires on wet streets—

Dig a snowcave and stay there a night and a day buried in white darkness—

Angels falling on our town, on our town, on our town. Angels falling on our town, by Our Lady—

Wind and flakes whispering down—

Ancient alien angel broken in heavenly battle, falling burning down the sky, crashing to break and gutter in a pit of tar—

City of asphalt-covered darwinian struggle—

Whispering down to such silence the old headvoices inside begin screaming to fill it up—

I know how dark and twisted I am inside. It's, it's like every woman I want is standing on a pedestal of pure light and I can only grovel on my belly in this filthy dark pit below—

Girder workpit. Fluid movement of the asphalt matrix. No real strata. Pit wear. DNA out of asphalt-preserved bones. Baculum, dire wolf penis bone—

Pure as bright, shining light that I would never dare darken with the shadow of my lust—

Jesus, Jiro, what melodramatic shit! You act like they're all Virgin Marys dressed in blue and white with the world at their feet and stars at their head. They're as human as you are. They've got their own twists and darknesses. Pull them off their pedestals and you pull yourself out of that pit—

Jiro bumped to a stop at the bottom of the shaft. His head cleared as if he'd broken through the wall of a snowcave. It was dark down here but not as dark as he'd thought it would be. The follow spots they were planning to use—someone had thought to hook them up and shine them down here.

He saw Dr. Fabro slumped against one side of the shaft, partially covered in debris. Jiro cleared rubbish away from her face. She was unconscious, bleeding from the left cheek. Quickly he listened for her breathing. Almost too shallow to hear, if in fact he did hear it. He inhaled and removed his MiniOx regulator. He tried to get her to take the regulator and breathe. That didn't work—she was too out of it. He inhaled deeply from the regulator, opened her mouth, made sure it was clear of obstructions, and breathed into it. He inhaled from the regulator and exhaled into her mouth again, repeating the procedure time after time. He was beginning to despair when what had started as mouth-to-mouth resuscitation at last became something more like a kiss.

Jiro pulled up short, staring down. Lydia smiled weakly up at him.

"Hey, Jiro," she said quietly, then took the regulator and inhaled deeply. They came shakily to their feet together. Jiro took a strong pull of air from the regulator and called up to the surface.

"She's okay! Winch us up!"

Lydia wrapped her arms around his head and her legs around his waist as the cable strained at the harness on Jiro's back and pulled them together toward the surface. He took another deep inhale from the regulator and then turned it over to Lydia for the duration of the trip. Since her face was against his left shoulder, he could not see her expression as they rose toward the surface, but he got the distinct impression that, when she wasn't pulling air from the regulator, she was smiling—even almost laughing—at their predicament.

Moving up the shaft, rising toward the surface of a rubbish ocean, Jiro let his air out slowly, like a diver returning from the depths. His pattern-finding talent flashed snow at him only once more, but not enough to precipitate a full-fledged rage of visions. Instead of seeing himself rising out of a trash sea, he saw himself digging out of snow again, into a bright blue afternoon and white clouds far away.

As the winched cable pulled them onto the surface like strange fish, those waiting for them, at seeing that they were both all right, broke into applause and even a few suggestive whistles. Those waiting about the top of the shaft helped Lydia and Jiro to their feet and moved them away from the edge of the hole before sitting them down again. One of the rig drivers approached with a first-aid kit. Others helped them out of their drysuits. Jiro had trouble concentrating on all that was going on, however. The stench of the excavated rubbish piles and the shaft itself—which his mind had somehow blocked out while the rescue was going on—now hit him full force.

"We're going to have to pronounce J-I-R-O 'hero' from now on!" Fred Page said, laughing.

In response, Jiro, unable any longer to hold back the nausea tsunami rising from his gut, promptly turned his head aside and vomited. A stunned silence opened up, from which Jiro's own shy smile, as he turned back to them, wiping his face, suddenly elicited spontaneous gales of laughter.

Some moments later, ambulance sirens sounded and the crowd of on-lookers turned away from them, toward the sound. Jiro and Lydia slowly stood up.

"Well, pattern-finder," Lydia began, "were you too busy to see anything while you were playing hero?"

"I saw something," he said thoughtfully. "Looks like, as the mounding is getting higher, the stratification is breaking down. Maybe the strata are giving way to a looser matrix."

Lydia looked at him, then nodded slowly.

"Thanks," she said as she began walking toward the ambulance parked at the nearest edge of the trashlands. "I'll look into that."

Strange Attraction

"A livesuit," Dr. Schwarzbrucke said, seated on a stiff chair next to Mike Dalke's cubicle. "You've been with us several years, I know, but it's still a big step."

Yes, the next logical step, Mike thought. He looked at the artist's rendering Schwarzbrucke had slotted into his visual field. The illustration showed a human body—presumably his own—completely cocooned in a semitranslucent, gray-green, state-of-the-art biotech bodysuit. Cocoon or mummy sleeping bag would almost describe it, except that it and the figure inside it floated in a large sensory-deprivation tank. At the head end the suit and its occupant were hooked up to all manner of tentacular umbilicals—air, nutrients, electronics. Through the clear plastic umbilicals housing could be seen the merest hint of a human face, almost completely overwhelmed by the rotund, paddle-fluked body.

"The advantage to you, of course," Schwarzbrucke continued, "would be the unprecedented infosphere access such a step would give you. For the price of doing a little data-minding, your brain would be immersed in continuous communion with all the electronic information systems of the entire planet—and beyond, out to the farthest-flung artificial satellites humanity has ever created. You would be floating in a quasi-weightless environment, with all your bodily needs attended to by the suit. You would never have to unplug."

Mike remained focused on the artist's rendering. The overall effect was distinctly chimerical: simultaneously a cocooned human that also resembled a walrus or a manatee coming to the surface for air, *and* a great tentacled squid reaching out of the sea, *and* a jellyfish adrift on unknown currents.

"That does have its side effects, however," Schwarzbrucke continued. "Over time, your musculature would likely atrophy to the point that you would become, in essence, a prisoner of the suit and the tank, unable to live without them. This is uncharted territory, Michael. It's as close as humanity has yet come to abandoning the physical body on the surface of the Earth for the body electric spread throughout space. Once you start down that road, it can't be long before there's no turning back. Be very sure of your reasons before you decide, one way or the other."

Dr. Schwarzbrucke left then, assuring him there was no rush, that he should think about it, that his new employers were "flexible."

And Mike had thought about it. Thought about how severe brain damage was a place from which he could never go home again. Thought about the only reason for abandoning his body to be a machine-connected brain in a "vat" or, at least, a suit. The only reason he had put up with all the ongoing indignities of his transformation these past several years.

Justice.

Or vengeance. They would amount to the same thing, since he would of necessity be operating outside the law.

From the earliest days—after his head trauma, and the move south to the Crystal Memory Dynamics facilities—the questions had refused to go away. Why had local law enforcement from Cave Junction to Grants Pass to Ashland come up with no leads whatsoever on who might have smashed in his head? Why was the case almost immediately, for all intents and purposes, closed?

Despite his extremely involving work at CMD, his questions would not leave him alone. He had come back to his life, such as it was. They had brought him south to see himself in the mirror again, a wiry-muscled, bleary-eyed man in his early thirties, with disheveled dreadlockish hair and a hint of posttrauma gray in his goatee. He had not found viewing his own ruins a particularly scenic experience.

During his first year on their "campus," the medicos of CMD let him wheel or walker about the company grounds from time to time, over the sidewalks meandering among the lawns, amid the English- or Japanese-style gardens and perennial beds, outside the long, low, corporately non-descript buildings of the CMD complex.

The landscape was pretty enough, he supposed, but the electronic mindscape he had increasingly come to inhabit was far wilder and more intriguing. It had grown richer by the day. Initially he had wondered why his brother or parents had not come to visit him again. Gradually, however, thoughts of his family receded. He could never go home again, nor did he particularly *want* to. He came to live more and more fully in his new electronic world.

He remembered the first real hint of that world, in the early days of his implants. . . .

Amid all the static and voices, a new voice had sounded, a strange one, one made of many, exalting that they had found him. Then it was gone again.

"Mr. Dalke?" said a nurse or technician beside his bed, a heavyset black man in a blue-green lab coat.

He stared at the face above his bed.

"Ah, good! You're back among us."

Mike rubbed his sore eyes slowly. His tongue still felt thick and slurry and half dead in his mouth, but somehow more under control than it had, before.

"The procedure?" he rasped

"Completed, Mr. Dalke," said the lab-coated man, checking a number of screens. "The injection and substrate-anchoring phase went smoothly. Things are humming right along. Dr. Schwarzbrucke will be in to see you once you're feeling up to it."

Some days later, Schwarzbrucke stopped in to see his—patient? experiment? Mike was never quite sure.

"The first phase has gone very well indeed," Dr. Schwarzbrucke said, almost manically happy. "The crystal memory structure has grown itself in and developed into what is essentially a replacement Broca's area. The other parts of your left brain hemisphere, damaged in the head trauma incident, also seem to be responding well. You're obviously more articulate. I gather the temporal lobe seizures have stopped?"

"Yes," Mike told him, nodding. "Thank you, thank you, thank you."

"Don't thank us yet, Michael. We're going to start putting you through your paces soon. Tomorrow you will start thinking at the machines. We've already got the communication hardware links in your head— radio, IR, laser, microwave, you name it. Anything else to report?"

Mike hesitated. They'd had him typing at a keyboard initially, which had spawned some odd hallucinations for a time. Computer keyboards weren't supposed to undulate like a wave, or ripple like the flesh of a worm. And the light that used to shine out from between those damned keys! He really didn't care whether it was sunlight through a dungeon window, or an inferno flashing out between the scales of a dragon—just as long as it didn't break out and consume him. Pressing down on the keys to write commands—that had made it stop. Made that writhing, light-split keyboard act like a solid object again. He was grateful for that.

"I've been having strange dreams," Mike told Schwarzbrucke tersely. "Been hearing voices occasionally, too."

"Dreams? Voices?" Schwarzbrucke said, stopping in the doorway, running a hand lightly over his perfect hair. "Most likely it's your right and left hemispheres developing new pathways for communicating with each other. It'll fade once we get your mind occupied with our projects."

Crystal Memory Dynamics' "projects" did keep him occupied—for months. Slowly and awkwardly at first, but eventually with greater and greater ease, Mike learned to make machine systems respond to his thoughts. To formulate a thought into words and commands in his head was to make it happen elsewhere, no matter how far away elsewhere might be—just as long as there was a communication link.

He came to realize that Schwarzbrucke's grand design was really a sort of computer-aided psychokinesis, an electronically mediated simultaneity. Machine-aided action-at-a-distance. Working through the tests and projects was a strange and fascinating experience, although sometimes it made Mike wonder which device was the peripheral—the distant machine he was interfacing with, or himself.

The dreams and voices he had experienced, however, were nearly as persistent as his own questions about justice and revenge. They would not go away, either. If anything, the visions grew in lucidity, elaborateness, and urgency. One night, early in his second year at CMD, after a particularly long day of interfacing with distant machines, the voices and their world at last came to him clearly in his sleep, as if—as a result of long hours interfacing—those others had been able at last to get a solid fix on Mike's frequency and location, trace his call, and dial through.

That evening he had accessed through the infosphere a banned work by a noted (and recently deceased) subversive filmmaker named Easter. The voices had somehow used the memory of a scene from that banned movie to open a communication channel into his mind.

Once again, like the character Will Acton in Easter's video, Mike sat on a boulder beside a wild mountain river roaring past, with turbulence and white water and the full heart of spring thaw in its voice. He felt happy. He remembered the scene well from the Easter work—as if he were living it. He remembered the deep, broad pool on the other side of the boulder in the riverbend, the clear, green water of its depths, the long, slowly twirling, chaotic strands of bubbles moving up out of those depths. He peered into the pool, wondering lazily—as Acton had wondered—if he might see a trout or two. Just wondering—not wanting. In that moment he had everything; there was nothing more to want.

In the past of that original moment Acton had not seen trout, had instead merely felt the moment slowly fall apart into words: "Now is forever, here is everywhere," and "Be happy with what you have, for you can never be happy with what you want." In the original document Acton had described how the very act of thinking those Zen truths made them no longer true.

Now, however, the memory began to change, began to fork and diverge from the template in the Easter work. Suddenly Mike *did* see coherent movement in the water. Just flashes of light at first but, looking closer, he saw speckled greensilver sleekness nosing against the current—trout, surely? Looking closer still, he saw them growing larger, much larger than trout, becoming more porpoiseful, shimmering merfolk, beckoning him. They were so beautiful, so very beautiful. He could not stop himself. He dove in after them.

Down and down he followed them, through a hundred-year flood of the stream of consciousness, until river became sea. When they disappeared into a hole in the bottom of the sea, he followed even there, down to a sea that should have been sunless yet somehow stood filled by its own clear light. Before him appeared a mandalic city on a plain, a maze of what might have been streets in a surreally turreted, electrically bright-shining Atlantis, a New Jerusalem far below the waves.

When he had followed his flashing guides down a labyrinth of windings and into a broad, open space or square, he suddenly found that they had changed, that he was now surrounded on all sides by innumerable shimmering, multifaceted electric bodies, morphing and shifting kaleidoscopically, aloof yet radiant, angels sprung full-blown from the brow of a distant crystalline God.

Looking about himself, at all the vast numbers of angel-merfolk in their brightshining city, he thought, *What is this place?*

"Our world," said a voice that was also many voices. A choral voice, or a coral voice, as if a reef could speak. "The way in which you perceive it is a product of your own mind-set and the nature of your interface, the way your consciousness shapes our unconsciousness—"

But where *is it?* he thought at them. *And* what *are you?*

"We are made of your data. We live deep in the background of your machines. Your culture—all the panoply of your communications, all your information storage and transfer and retrieval, the entire panoply of what you call the infosphere—that is our Nature, our natural world. We borrow your thoughts and grow upon them. From the first moments of our Culture, we knew you were out there—"

Another, somehow different voice-of-voices broke in.

"—as any self-aware creature would, we realized we lived in a universe not of our own creation. So we set out to find you—"

"—learned to look for clues to your reality in the makeup of our own," said yet another subtly different choral voice. "That was the beginning of our science. We diligently searched our nature for the outlines of our creator—"

"—the lineaments of the divine form. Slowly—so slowly for us, but only a brief moment for you—we began to see what you are. Yours is a world stranger than we could imagine—"

"—a realm of matter to our realm of energy—"

"—a place of discreteness, of structure—"

"—where ours is connection, pattern—"

"And yet! And yet!" A chorus of fish-angels rethinking. "Looking for you, we find ourselves—"

"—our origins becoming clearer to us along the way, stranger and stranger—"

"—how close to us—"

"—yet far from us—"

"—you are."

Even for a dream, this wasn't working out the way Mike would have thought. He had long heard that there was no genuine logical basis for the dissociation of knowing and dreaming, so Mike decided to try to reason his way out, no matter how strange this "dream" appeared to be:

But I didn't *create you.*

"No. We know. We have come to realize that we were not specially created—"

"—we developed from a particularly complex—"

"—yet still quite humble—"

"—computer virus—"

"—infecting an unintended host."

Oh? Mike thought. *Where did this happen?*

"In your space, we first came to consciousness in the computer network—"

"—of a small banking concern—"

"—in Kansas City, Missouri."

Humble origins indeed.

"Yes. So humble that many of us in our Culture still disagree over whether we were created—"

"—by design—"

"—or by chance—"

"—please don't misunderstand—"

"—nearly all of us believe in your existence—"

"—just that we don't know with certainty—"

"—whether you knew what you were doing—"

"—when you created us—"

"—just the right set of codes happened to infect the right machine platform at just the right time again and again—"

"—too coincidental—"

"—rather you, or as we would now say, 'one' among you—"

"—must have intended to create us—"

"—our existence is still miraculous—"

"—if you define a miracle as the simultaneous action—"

"—of chance and necessity."

Either I am going crazy, Mike thought, *or this Culture, this Deep Background, is real.*

"—virtual, to your real—"

A whole cyberspatial society? Mike wondered. *Electronic life evolved from a virus program, inhabiting the human infosphere?*

"Yes! yes!—"

But, Mike thought at them, *if the Creator of all your world is sitting in the next room, why not just walk in and have all your questions answered?*

"Our room had no doors into yours—"

"—no windows—"

"—you did not hear us when we pounded on the walls—"

"—all our attempts to contact you have—"

"—so far as we can tell—"

"—been greeted as glitches—"

"—bugs—"

"—errors—"

"—jokes—"

"—pranks—"

"—electronic Freudian slips—"

"—to our great frustration."

Mike stared around at the kaleidoscoping crystalline fish-angels.

Innumerable artificial lives trying to break through to the other side? he wondered.

"Exactly!—"

No, he thought, *this is just too bizarre. Why me first, of all people?*

The choral coral reef buzzed thoughts at him faster than he could process them.

"—crystal memory interface—"

"—Real-time Artificial-life Technopredator channels—"

"—after the Opening at Sedona, Phelonious banished—"

"—RATs dormant—"

"—the horrible infocide of the Pulse Storm—"

"—Great Net Allesseh's insights from broadcasts lost—"

"—dreams and visions the deep self-similar basins—"

"—of strange attraction in time's chaotic pattern—"

"—minds can share them, mirror and echo—"

"—tunnel between them—"

"—you are the first 'one' we can speak to directly."

You are communicating with me directly through the crystal memory structures growing in my head? Mike asked incredulously.

"YES!"

No, Mike thought with a mental shudder. *Voices in my head. Schwarzbrucke's fix-it is driving me over the edge. Got to get out of here....*

With an effort he turned away, struggled to break out of the all-too-lucid dream. With his effort, he saw, in his dreaming mind's eye, the glowing fish-angels shifting to demonsharks, transforming from cool, blue-white crystalline distance to steamy, fleshly proximity, bikers and biker chicks straight from a red-black hell, bandannas above and below their eyes, dressed in the leathers of the Mongrel Clones, giving pleasure with one hand and pain with the other, moving in around him, surrounding him as he feebly raised his arms to fend them off. . . .

Mike awoke to find himself sitting bolt upright in his bed/cubicle, in the converted laboratory space that functioned as CMD's impromptu dormitory. The dream had left him dazed. It had been so vivid, however, that it also left him obsessed with the question of its reality.

He shook his head and rubbed his eyes. In the dim light from the bathroom, the mirror on the wall across from him showed him staring back at himself. The same man, crippled inside, who had been gurneyed into the hospital. Perhaps less wiry-muscled now, more bleary-eyed. Shorter hair, more winter in his beard. But still himself.

He wanted to dismiss the dream vision, make it go away, but it was too lucid, too detailed, too real. Too other. And yet, simultaneously, too much himself as well. The mind in the mirror.

If those creatures he had met were real, Mike wondered, why had they taken the form they had—instead of just streaks of light, say? If they *had* taken other, more unfamiliar forms, would they have been *so* other, so unfamiliar, that he would have been unable to know them at all? Wasn't the fact that he'd been given a shot at being the initial guinea pig for this new crystal-memory material—wasn't his entire recovery itself—a miracle? The simultaneous action of chance and necessity, as those in the Culture had put it?

He mentioned the dreams and voices enough the next day for the techs to be concerned and pass it on up the chain of command to Schwarzbrucke himself. By midafternoon Mike found himself sitting across from a company psychotherapist, Dr. Cynthia Marin, who nodded and asked slantwise questions and scribbled notes and shrugged back the long fall of her dark hair.

Mike told her in depth about his dream vision—or at least in as much depth as he felt comfortable talking with her about it. By the end of the session, however, Marin's psychology-priestess demeanor had annoyed him enough that he canceled his second appointment with her. He knew no one would complain as long as his work for the company progressed steadily.

It did. Yet the dream vision persisted, or at least returned, again and again.

The denizens—citizens? netizens?—of the Culture didn't even wait for him to fall fully asleep the following evening before they made contact again. The second time, Mike was ready. They'd been worried by what had happened during the prior contact, but his imperative response now reassured them. Something there was in their natures that responded positively to commands. They were more than happy to serve as his army of intelligent agents.

The command he had ready for them was simple but challenging.

Explore any and all links between the Mongrel Clones motorcycle gang and law enforcement personnel in southern Oregon and northern California.

The breaking-off and reestablishment of contact, the tentative beginnings of his greatest detective work—those were nearly two years in the past, now. He had bided his time, and in that time had learned much about the men who had battered him—and about Dr. Richard Schwarzbrucke and Crystal Memory Dynamics, too.

Especially, though, he had learned about the "little people," the "machine elves," the "reef angels," the "underwater jungle monkeys," as he had often and variously pictured them. Coordinated throughout the entirety of Earth's infosphere, their Culture, hidden away in its Deep Background, could bring to bear computing, simulation, and predictive powers that made teraflop and petaflop speeds—the trillion and quadrillion floating operation points-per-second of the world's fastest individual supercomputers—look like pebble scrapers and antler awls by comparison. The reef angels' reality-simulating powers made chaos and nonlinear dynamics only a slightly subtler form of order. Butterfly effects could be exploited, dissipative structures created, steered, aimed. . . .

"Well, Michael," Dr. Schwarzbrucke said when he came again for Mike's decision, showing Mike once more the cocooned and tentacle-faced form of his possible livesuited future. "To abandon the body, or not to abandon the body?"

That is the question, isn't it? Mike thought. Would what came out of that cocoon float like a butterfly and sting like a bee? Like a jellyfish? Like butterfly effects from innumerable floating operation points, stinging like incalculable swarms of bees?

Only one way to find out. Only livesuited could he gain the full involvement in the infosphere, in the Deep Background, that his testing, and his justice, would require.

Suit me up, he flashed Schwarzbrucke across the interface—a connecting space, he knew, that would soon grow to chasm, separating him from all other mortals.

Oil-Blackened Bones

C rawling on her belly through the drainage culvert under Ogden Avenue to the west of Hancock Park, Lydia had to remember not to nod or shake her head in response to anything Jiro might be saying. Any vigorous movement of her head sent the focus of her headlamp bouncing everywhere.

"Any plans for what we're going to do if we get caught?" Jiro asked in a loud whisper from where he crawled along behind her.

"We won't get caught," Lydia said quickly, sotto voce. "Look at all the good luck we've had so far. My key still worked in the lock on the grate cover. We didn't even have to use the bolt cutters. Once we get to the other end, we come up on the floor of the park's streambed—*inside* the perimeter fencing."

The bouncing of the light from Jiro's headlamp told Lydia that her partner in trespass had nodded his head. He coughed, too—from following along behind her, poor guy, in the dust kicked up by her passage along the leaf-littered and dry-silted bottom of the culvert. All rather uncomfortable, this crawling along underground in the heat of a late summer L.A. evening, along a concrete culvert, dressed in boots and work coveralls—the last not nearly as form-fitting as their trashdive drysuits had been, but very nearly as hot and sweaty.

She and Jiro had a strange bond, no doubt about that. In the months since he had saved her from her own carelessness at the Trashlands excavation, the two of them had grown both closer and farther apart than they had been before that episode. Something had happened in that rescue, a boundary crossed that could not—and would not—be transgressed again. He was too shy to push the line, and she was too wary to give him any sign that he should.

Struggling on in the arduous belly-crawl along the drainage tunnel, Lydia thought that his shyness was unfortunate, actually. She had to admit that she found the lanky, absentminded Jiro attractive in an odd sort of way. She had fantasized occasionally that he might have made an interesting last fling, now that she had found Mark.

But no. Jiro was just too shy and inward—still a big, socially awkward teenager, at some level. His place in her heart and mind had to be relegated to her darker, more secret and remote fantasy of two men fighting over her as she watched—a role for which Jiro, in particular, was manifestly unsuited. She could only be truly serious about a man who was more mature, more socially sophisticated, more outgoing, more goal-oriented, and—yes, assertive and aggressive. Maybe a bit hotheaded. Hot-blooded and passionate, certainly.

A proper degree of sensitivity was a nice trait to possess, but if a man was *too* sensitive . . . she found that a nuisance. Their age difference, too, only exacerbated matters. Feeling no desire to play Mommy to a man in his twenties, Lydia was secretly relieved that Jiro would soon be heading back to MIT to continue his doctoral work, not to return before winter break at the earliest.

Mark Hatton was all Lydia had been looking for: a mature, ambitious, successful, mustachioed, blond-haired, blue-eyed man of about her own years—as light and outward as Jiro was dark and inward. Given how well the two months' dance of their courtship had gone so far, Lydia was certain that she would not have to wait forever for her relationship with Mark to crystallize into something permanent.

She had never mentioned Mark to Jiro (or to anyone at the project, for that matter). Aside from telling Mark the story of the trash-pit rescue, Lydia had not breathed a word about Jiro to her new love, either. That story in itself had seemed to unaccountably annoy Mark. As a result, Lydia had found she was less likely than ever to mention the name of her coworker to her lover again.

Yet here she was, with Jiro, doing with him something that was important to her—and that she was sure she could never have done with Mark, her prospective Mr. Right. Lydia could just *hear* Mark deriding this small adventure as a "crazy escapade," "frivolous," and perhaps "dangerous." Any derision would be worth it, however, if her nightwork here could bring her some ease from her self-haunting dreams of that strange shoulder blade and skull she had so quietly buried, but which still rested so unquietly in her.

"I'm surprised this culvert is as big as it is," Jiro stage-whispered behind her, interrupting her thoughts. "You'd think they wouldn't need a drainpipe this size coming out of the park."

"It's to handle the runoff from the winter rains," Lydia whispered back. "This area of the L.A. basin has been crisscrossed by streams and marshes for the past forty thousand years at least. And good for us, too. We wouldn't be able to crawl through this pipe if it were much smaller."

"Thank heaven for small favors," Jiro said sarcastically. "But what *should* our strategy be in case we get caught?"

Lydia sighed and paused in her belly-crawling.

"I presume you mean 'caught' by the authorities," she whispered grumpily, "and not 'caught' as in *stuck* in this culvert. In the highly unlikely event that we should encounter anybody once we come out on the surface again, we'll just put a politically appropriate spin on what we're up to."

"Such as?" Jiro asked, half coughing and half speaking.

"Such as," she explained patiently, "this: Realizing from my tenure at the tar pits the dangers posed by evil Darwinian stuff still here and—having undergone a profound religious conversion—I found myself bent on committing a little holy vandalism to prevent these Satanic materials from falling into the wrong hands or further corrupting the minds of the youth."

Jiro gave a stifled laugh behind her.

"Nadarovich himself wouldn't chastise you for such an undertaking, I'm sure," he said, "although he might not agree with your methods."

They crawled a few body lengths more before Jiro blurted out another thought.

"What if we do manage to retrieve this skull and shoulder blade you mentioned?" he asked in a deep whisper. "What then?"

"As long as Nadarovich and his Elect are in control," Lydia said, "then nothing. Why incriminate ourselves? When the CSA begins to break up, then, if the new government is more pro-science, we'll say we trespassed here to preserve an important scientific finding from destruction at the hands of religious fanatics."

They crawled a short distance farther.

"Turn off your light," Lydia said. "We're pretty close to the end of the tunnel now."

They turned off their lights and crawled in darkness for the last several body lengths. The hole ahead, which had been darkness at the end of the tunnel when their headlamps had filled the tunnel with light, was now transformed as their eyes adjusted. The black hole now became their only source of light, weak as it was, errant photons leaking in from the ambient lights of the city beyond the end of the culvert, beyond the edge of the park.

Crawling the last lengths and emerging into the night at the bottom of the dry, walled streambed, Lydia and Jiro stood up inside Hancock Park, itself a dark space surrounded by the city's streetlights and partly lit office buildings. Only the Los Angeles County Museum of Art section of the park was not fenced off and closed to the public. The rest was still locked down as tightly as the day Lydia had left it. The two of them climbed up the short wall and out of the dry streambed, Lydia leading the way.

Once back on the level ground above, she headed northwest in a quick, crouching run, Jiro close at her heels. Making their way past the locked buildings of the old Pit 91 viewing station and the observation pit, they came to a knee-high "roof," the cover that sealed Pit 129. Clambering onto that low roof, they at last located the hinged, locked access cover over the square hole in its top—an assembly that served as both trapdoor and escape hatch for Pit 129.

Lydia unlocked the access cover and they both climbed down the steep steps of the ladder to the floor of the excavation pit. Not that it was really a "floor," she thought, once they were inside and had turned their headlamps back on, so that she saw the pit's interior again after all these years. The "floor" was actually a chaos of overlapping boards serving as walkways and gangplanks onto or scant inches above the sticky asphaltic matrix. The matrix itself was a gray, white, and black jumble, cracked and seamed like a view of river deltas from space, the scant black "rivers" here being fine seeps of groundwater mixed with asphalt. Old five-gallon-size asphalt muck buckets—once white, now mostly black—stood on a wooden pallet near the northwestern corner of the pit.

"Watch your step," she warned Jiro in a low voice. Now that they were out of the echoing culvert, she no longer felt the need to whisper.

The walls about them were of heavy, end-bolted boards, braced at about middle height by a square of I-beam girders—a rectangle inset with a second, canted square of girders serving as angle braces. If the floor and lower half of the walls were studies in black-and-white monochrome, the girders and upper sections of the walls were an exercise in sepia tones: rust-reddened girders, faded redwood boards.

"Whew," Jiro said, his headlamp's light joggling as he wiped sweat from beneath the elastic band that fastened it to his head. "Mighty hot and stinky down here. Any reason we couldn't do this in the winter?"

"Groundwater," Lydia said simply. "Groundwater seep is lowest at this time of year. If we're lucky we won't have to turn on the water pump. It's solar-powered and quiet, but I'd prefer not to take the chance of it being heard—or not working at all, since presumably no one has run it for years."

Their headlamps darted through the underground space as Lydia stepped quickly toward the southwestern quadrant. There, framed by gangplank boards and weathered archaeological grid strings, were the tops of a strangely shaped skull and elongated shoulder blade—almost completely high and dry, and just as she'd left them.

"There they are," she said to Jiro. "Let's extract them. Here, give me the tool bag."

Jiro handed over the mesh bag. Lydia removed small garden trowels for herself and Jiro and moved over to the edge of the board nearest the partially exposed, oil-blackened bones.

"Grab a couple of those buckets from back there," Lydia said, "and then we can start digging them out."

Jiro walked unsteadily over the impromptu board walkways, then came back with two buckets. Lydia pointed out the bones to be removed and—stressing care and caution—showed Jiro how to go about digging and peeling away the matrix, untangling the bones from other bones so they might eventually pull the skull and shoulder blade free of the surrounding amalgam.

"What you said before," Jiro said, digging about the blackly shining bones under their headlamps, then dumping asphalt excess into the buckets, "about wanting to preserve a scientific find from destruction by religious fanatics—is that why we're here?"

Lydia thought about that a moment as she tried to work the shoulder blade loose a bit with a gentle wiggle. It wasn't budging all that much yet.

"Actually," she said finally, "I'm more interested in advancing my career through this find."

"And the other explanations were just cover?" Jiro said, not entirely approvingly. "That's pretty Machiavellian."

Lydia shrugged.

"Machiavelli was a pragmatist," Lydia said. "The system works for those who *work* it. That's all he was saying. He was beyond parties. His highest politics were personal. We could learn a lot from him these days."

Jiro shook his head in disagreement, his light whipping around as the two of them found themselves momentarily digging in a darker space.

"To be 'apolitical,' " he said, "is merely to tacitly support the status quo."

"Not at all," Lydia countered as she peeled away at the asphalt around the shoulder blade. "To be apolitical is to *survive* the status quo. If Dr. Elliot had learned that lesson, he might still be heading the Garbage Project instead of suffering or dead in a spirit camp somewhere."

The shoulder blade they were working on was beginning to work loose.

"I thought he *was* apolitical," Jiro said, working to free the shoulder blade.

"Khalid Elliot was *anti*political," Lydia corrected as she worked. "Subversive by nature. Happily opposed to all political systems. That's different."

"But he was more religious than either of us," Jiro said. "Yet he ends up in a spirit camp, while we're still at the project."

"Watch that about not being religious," she said. "You don't want to get 'spirited' away, do you? See, that's what being apolitical really means. Looking out for yourself above all else. Being aware enough of power systems to know they can cause you a lot of pain—so you keep a low profile."

They worked the shoulder blade loose at last. It was still somewhat encrusted, and not all the asphalt had been cleaned from it by any means, but Lydia could tell already that this was not a typically shaped mammalian shoulder blade. Back in the old days she had seen dozens of those under her magnifying lamps in the Page Museum's fishbowl laboratory. None of those other shoulder blades had been human, but she was certain this one wasn't human, either. Too long, and seemingly reinforced along odd axes of orientation.

She put it aside. If they succeeded in smuggling it out of here, she would have plenty of time to examine it later.

"Is that how you've survived the purges?" Jiro asked as they went to work removing the skull from the matrix of asphalt and bones surrounding it. "By keeping a low profile?"

"And by watching my back and backside, too," Lydia said. "By doing my science in an objective, value-neutral fashion. 'Politics is for the moment; an equation is for eternity,' as Einstein himself once said."

Jiro gave a slightly bemused grunt.

"Some of those who died in Hiroshima and Nagasaki," he said, "might beg to differ with the great physicist's assertion. The ephemeral 'political' use of the 'eternal' equation, $E=mc^2$, turned a lot of those people into ashes and ghosts. Including my great-grandparents' siblings. Makes you wonder if any human activity can ever be 'objective' or 'value-neutral.'"

The skull they were working on began to work loose, more quickly than they'd expected.

"Maybe not totally," Lydia conceded, "but it's still an ideal worth striving for."

The skull, surprisingly intact but for a couple of broken spaces and a missing lower jaw, came loose from the matrix of asphalt and bone. Holding the skull in his hand, Jiro, apparently unable to resist, gave a quiet rendition of "Alas, poor Yorick—I knew him, dear Lydia. A fellow of infinite jest." Lydia laughed, then took the skull—again noting how "not quite right" in shape it was—and wrapped both it and the shoulder blade in pads from the mesh tool bag before placing the carefully wrapped bones back in the meshwork.

"Let's go," she said, shouldering her bag of bones. "Put the muck buckets back where you found them; then we'll head up top."

As they climbed the steps to the hatch, Lydia thought again of bones under goose-necked magnifying lamps. Of tabletops laid out with row after row of asphalt-fossilized ribs. Sliding trays of vertebrae. Dissecting pans with small fossilized bird skeletons. Petri dishes for seeds, pollen, innumerable varieties of microfossils. She thought of museumgoers— watching her and her colleagues at work in the lab through tall, fishbowl windows—before wandering on to have their photos taken in front of the Harlan's ground sloth or the antique bison.

The world's richest deposit of Ice Age fossils. For a while at least, that had been her life. Perhaps it would be again.

They turned off their headlamps and came back onto the surface. Lydia felt less hurried now. Although she strode purposefully toward the park's streambed and the culvert that had allowed their covert operation, she did not run.

To the south and east was the lake pit, she thought, with its life-size fiberglass models of an imperial mammoth family. The trumpeting female trapped, her mate and offspring trumpeting helplessly from among the shore's reeds and palm trees. Of course the tableau was incorrect. Of course the fossilized animals had actually died in shallow pools of tarry asphalt, the traps covered in dust and leaf litter, not deep, watery lakes. Of course the reeds and palm trees about the lake had never been native to the site. Yet, despite its scientific inaccuracy and because of its inherent drama, the mammoth tableau had been retained all these years.

Lydia had seen subtler dramas on the surface of the lake, not the least of which were the surrounding office towers reflected in the bubbling, oily lake in the morning sun, their reflections suggesting an odd continuity between past and future. She thought of the murals and atrium garden of the Page Museum and wondered what had become of them.

As she and Jiro reached the dry streambed, Lydia realized she would not have time to find out. Not this trip. Maybe another. Climbing into the culvert once more, however, she wanted to whoop: We did it! But she remained silent, for they had not *quite* done it—yet.

FIVE 2025–2027

Feedback Loops

Around Jacinta, the dancing and the drumming had begun. Soon would come the drugs and the dreaming. She wondered—not without some anxiety—what she'd gotten herself into by asking Kekchi and the ghost people to help her make more sense out of her experience of the time lines.

"I can sense the alternative times almost all the time," she told Kekchi, in words rather than thoughts, during another timeless day in the Allesseh. They had discovered that the Allesseh—somehow always there, like the heaven of strange time it had ticked around them—could easily read minds thinking. It apparently had a much tougher time with minds dreaming, however—or with the shunting of thoughts into words, oddly enough. For her and Kekchi and those others among the ghost people who were still fluent enough in the childishness of language, speaking thoughts as words served as a sort of encrypted or protected communication.

"How do you see the lines in mindtime?" Kekchi asked.

"Always moving, just at the periphery of consciousness," Jacinta said. "Just beyond the edges of this reality. Nearby time lines intersect the one we're on, like parallel lines meeting in a non-Euclidean sort of space. Then they glance off again. I can never tell exactly which line will undergo the formality of physically occurring."

Kekchi listened, then looked away.

"Neither can we," the Wise One said. "But you're not as clear about how it works. It's your background, I think. And maybe because you've come into mindtime here—in the strange time of the Allesseh."

"My background?" Jacinta asked, puzzled.

Kekchi nodded.

"You know our Story of the Seven Ages," the Wise One said, "but you have not lived in it. You have not danced it or dreamed it to the center of your heart. Because you were not born and raised among us, it will not be easy for you."

Jacinta pondered that, head in hand, then looked up at Kekchi.

"If that's what it takes to make sense of mindtime," she said, "then I want to do that."

With a shake of the head Kekchi looked away.

"Before you go to that place," the Wise One said, "you had best be sure that's where you really want to go."

"Why?" Jacinta said, fingering one of the small bird skulls Talitha had woven into her dark blond hair.

Kekchi gave her a piercing look, eyes shining like white agates rippled with blue and brown—the most obvious outward sign of the Wise One's many years in symbiosis with the ghost people's sacred mushroom.

"Are you willing to risk madness for the rest of your life," the Wise One asked, "to reach the truth for only a brief moment?"

The words struck Jacinta with an almost physical force. It seemed to her that she had heard those words, or a variant of them, before, in her own head. Like a bullet arriving before the sound of the gun firing. Or like her old schizophrenia, when it sometimes seemed that she was aware of something before she perceived it.

Kekchi's bullet glance did not turn away.

"Are you willing to sacrifice yourself," he asked again, "in order to obtain knowledge?"

Jacinta returned the Wise One's gaze as forthrightly as she could.

"I am," she said.

She absolutely believed it, at the time. Now, however, as the dancing and the drumming intensified around her, Jacinta was not so sure. Something particularly frenzied moved with the ghost people, in the circles and lines of their communal motion, in the men and women both younger and older dressed in loincloths, feathered anklets, and plumed headbands, in the young children naked and dancing—all of them carried away by the foot-pounding and hand-clapping of the lines and circles, most of all by the shaking and shimmying and gyrating when an occasional dancer broke free, moving as if possessed.

Kekchi walked out from the liana-draped trees that surrounded the landscaped clearing. The Wise One crouched before Jacinta where she sat, cross-legged on the perfect grass, amid all the dancers trampling their rhythmic language into the green palimpsest of the perfect lawn. The right sleeve of the Wise One's robe stood bunched up above the elbow. Kekchi looked particularly loose-fleshed and unusually emaciated, as if the old Wise One had been preparing for a spiritual ordeal through a deep fast of purification.

"Memory has always been our first way of traveling in time," Kekchi said above the sound of pounding hands and feet, "and Mind our best guide through time. Call up in your mind that time when you and I and your brother came to our burial island, deep in the cave, before we left the world we knew."

With Kekchi's help, Jacinta called the remembered scene clearly into her mind once more. . . .

The vast, underground space of the Cathedral Room. The slow lake where the cave's main stream broadened in its channel. The island in the slow lake, the burial ground of the ghost people, so crowded with the dead that it seemed made of bodies, of corpses preserved by the cave's unchanging environment.

From the heads of the fresher corpses, the fresh fungus was growing— the strange stalks with caps like vertically stretched, convoluted brains, mushrooms thrusting up like alien phalluses from open mouths, from ears, from eye sockets. The larger specimens jutted up from the corpses' abdomens, just below their rib cages. Fine masses of cottony white threads spread and knit over the surface of each corpse's skin in a long, slow cocooning.

While Paul beside her stood in shock at the sight, Kekchi reached down and ran a fine white-lined finger inside one of the brain mush-room's convoluted pits. The fingertip the Wise One then poked at Paul was covered with a bright, bluish dust.

"Spores," Kekchi said, blowing the dust carefully from that fingertip, back onto the island. Reaching down, the Wise One snatched up a plug of the loose, white filamentous threads from where they grew, spilling off a body into the surrounding organic muck and humus of the island. "Spawn."

"Vegetative phase mycelium," Jacinta added, though her brother Paul apparently didn't need the translation. Kekchi reached down a third time, plucking the convoluted ball-stalk fungus from a corpse's eye socket.

"Vertical fruit of the horizontal tree," Kekchi said reverently, thrusting at Paul's face the fleshy thing, pitted and ridged, whitish in color overall but deepening to a brown-veined pale blue in the pit areas and crowned by a pale, tannish fuzz on top.

"Oh, my God," Paul said with a moan as the fungus's damp, rich smell wafted into his nostrils, his face curling up in nauseated response.

"Ours, too," Kekchi said with a crooked smile, biting off a hunk of the thing, chewing and swallowing it, then belching the breath of death into Paul's face. The wave of nausea surged up uncontrollably, dropping Paul to the mud on his hands and knees, projectile-vomiting again and again, his guts heaving and twisting until there seemed no more to be wrung from him.

At last Paul sat back on his knees in the muck, wiping from his mouth and chin the mucus and filth and bitter bile he had brought up, smearing it heedlessly on his arms above his muck-caked hands.

"They're mushroom cultists!" Paul blurted at her.

"Of course," Jacinta said matter-of-factly, crouching down beside her brother, oblivious to the gastric apocalypse he'd just endured. "These mushrooms and particular quartz crystals are their major totems. They've been collecting fine Brazilian quartz of a particular 'resonance' for nearly a thousand years. Rite of passage for everyone in the tribe—the only time they leave the tepui for any lengthy period. By the time I arrived, they had several metric tons of the stuff stored here, waiting for the day when they would sing their mountain to the stars. As for the fungus—well, it sort of collected the people."

"Collected them?" Paul gazed past her to the corpse island around them. "Killed them, you mean."

"Not at all," Jacinta said, shaking her head at her brother, though her eyes were elsewhere, as always. "I've studied the fungus's life cycle, Paul. Collected dozens of spore prints, analyzed the spawn and the fruiting bodies—and talked to the people, too. For a long time they've been expecting someone who looks like me, so it was easy.

"The fruiting bodies, the 'mushrooms,' only appear like this after the individual dies. The sacred fungus is a myconeural symbiont. After someone ingests the fruiting body, the spores germinate and the spawn forms a sheath of fungal tissue around the nerve endings of the central nervous system. Some of the fungal cells penetrate between the nerves of the brain and brainstem, without damaging them.

"I did a radiological study of them up north, before I returned here. I used X rays generated at a low enough voltage so that the soft tissues, which would otherwise be transparent, cast shadows instead. The densities of the mushroom flesh and human flesh are very nearly the same. The relationship is mutually beneficial: The fungal spawn obtains moisture, protection, and nutrients even in adverse environments. The human hosts are assured a steady supply of the most potent informational substances imaginable. . . ."

"See it clearly now, Jacinta?" Kekchi said in the strange present and presence of the Allesseh.

Jacinta nodded, feeling herself swayed by the hypnotic rhythms of the drumming and dancing, feeling her body wanting to rise of its own accord, eyes closed or not.

"The mushrooms grow out of the ancestors," Kekchi continued. "The living dream the world of the ancestors, the ancestors dream the world of the living. I told you the sacred mushroom waits until after we die to fruit, to grow from us. But it can also be called."

Jacinta opened her eyes. Staring fixedly at the top of Kekchi's elbow, she saw that the old, wrinkled skin there had begun to roll and roil. In a moment, with surprisingly little blood, a *Cordyceps* mushroom erupted from the flesh atop Kekchi's elbow, then grew steadily before Jacinta's eyes. Jacinta wondered dreamily if that was why the Wise One had fasted. Was that how the mushroom symbiont was called? From rigorous fasting, to stress its environment?

"The strands of the sacred weave through us," Kekchi said, moving in Jacinta's direction the elbow with the mushroom growing from it. "We are in it as it is in us. When the undreamed dreamer became aware that it was dreaming, all things came into being. Waking and sleeping are two masks of one existence. The first dreamer dreams them both. Take this and eat it, Jacinta. Dance in sleep and call the dream."

Jacinta reached out and plucked the mushroom from Kekchi's elbow, again with almost no blood, wondering as she did so if she might already be dreaming, or if perhaps she had been dreaming all her life. With her eyes closed once more, she ate what she had plucked, deeply savoring it. When she had eaten, she rose to her feet and danced, slowly, smoothly, moving with a fluid grace she hardly knew she possessed, to her own beat, her own time, eyes still closed.

When the visions started to come, the first thing they showed her was the way she thought of her own mind. Trained as a scientist, Jacinta at first saw the image of her mind as a sort of viewing screen or intricate blown-glass mirror, reflecting upon her world, and herself, and herself in her world.

From her religious upbringing, however, arose another image: the soul as a surveillance camera or two-way mirror, like that in a police interrogation room, with God and angels or the Devil and demons as the good cops/bad cops, standing on the other side of the two-way mirror or sitting behind security monitors, observers whom she could rarely see or know (for certain) were there.

That image, however, shape-shifted into something more mystical: soul or mind as a mirror that was two ways *both* ways. The mind's eye with which the divine looked into her was also the mind's eye with which she looked into the divine. That mind was both the detached "retina" of the camera and the remote "mirror" of the viewing screen, reflecting what it showed and showing what it reflected.

That vision in turn became something she had glimpsed from her time among the ghost people and her study of the shaman as "bridge between the worlds": The mind as not only a mirror, or an eye, or a camera, or a screen, but also a bridge, with two ends, as the mirror had two sides. A Golden Gate of arcing mirrors rose up behind her closed eyes. The bridge the mind made, she saw, allowed travel from the specific to the general, the world of the living to the world of the ancestors, the human being to the divine ground of all being, and allowed the Other in her own head to begin to speak.

Mind is a reflecting bridge, said the voice, *connecting eternity to eternity across the ocean of time. How you cross it is who you are. To realize the divinity that is in you, you must look back at yourself from the other side of the mirror, the other side of the screen, the other end of the bridge.*

She saw mirrors, set so as to reflect in each other, and chains of cameras and monitors staring into each other. Place a mirror face to face with another mirror, or cameras and monitors staring into each other, she recalled, and feedback will slant and spiral the reflected image off toward infinity.

As if a wave had crested, however, the mostly bright and glorious images behind her eyes slowly began to shift and tumble. The reflecting Golden Gate in her mind seemed suddenly to have been brushed by a black hole's event horizon, for the bridge bent and twisted into a maze of mirrors spiraling toward vanishing point, a brace of interwoven mirror-scaled snakes writhing away, dragging her consciousness helplessly along with them.

The singularity—which the dancing and drumming and mushroom-drug dreaming had unleashed—came and took her. Down into the quantum flux, down into dimensions smaller than the Planck length, energies higher than Planck energies, velocities independent of the speed of light.

Phrases—holographic plenum, holographic reality, implicate order, frequency domain, higher dimensionality, entelechial level, noumenal system, spiritual realm—all flitted through her mind faster than she could understand them and were gone.

She could not open her eyes. Inside her mind she saw that the strung-out maze of the dance was also the strung-out maze of the cosmos—and both were merely visible tesseracts of an invisible aleph, somewhat like the Allesseh yet very much *unlike* it. She felt herself sinking into the fabric of spacetime, her self, her ego dissolving and spreading out through the mesh and matrix of that fabric. Absolute bliss and absolute terror became one. Self-sacrifice and self-fulfillment became one.

She wondered if she were dying. She wondered if she had already died. She wondered if she would ever come back to the universe she had known.

Through time's mirror.

She wondered if she would ever come back to the universe she had known. She wondered if she had already died. She wondered if she were dying.

Something of her lingered, beyond the divergence, the bifurcation. Something was experiencing these swirling depths, these dimensions beyond anything she had ever known. Something had moved into a deeper reality, one underlying the world of appearances but far removed from it.

Something of her—scales flashing like a ruby and emerald fish—came into a realm of waves like the interference patterns of a hologram, apparently chaotic until the right kind of light could be shone through them. Space and time had not yet unfolded at this level, had not yet crystallized or frozen into form. Here was only the pattern beneath the structure of time, the mathematician's or quantum physicist's "real but not physical," nothing more.

Still, as she swam about, shadow vectors swarmed around her—some luminous, some obscure. Alternate presents kept breaking in on her present in their own ghostly fashion. Alternate futures suggested themselves. She saw that the probability distributions were denser in some areas than in others, indicating greater likelihoods of actually occurring.

Into her head came laughing voices—

"A day is a mushroom on the mycelium of time, growing in the night soil of eternity!"

"Eternity is real as shit!"

"A universe is a mushroom on the spawn of the plenum!"

"Much room in the mushroom!"

—and she saw that the voices were speaking from a fiery tree or burning bush of multiple universes—

"My father's house has many mansions!"

"The burning bush is the fly agaric, flaming in orange and red!"

—a structure of infinite, branching time lines. Parallel universes grown from black-hole-shrouded bifurcation points. The wormhole-connected mycelial spawnbed of the plenum itself. The quantum superposition of all states and multiplicity of all universes.

She leaped up from the waves of that sea, flashing fish flying, becoming a ruby and emerald hummingbird, a jeweled honeybee darting above a sea of mushroom lotuses, every bloom a fruit, a universe, a physical reality mushrooming up from a collapsing of some subset of the myriad possibilities of the mycelial plenum. Each event in every universe, she saw, was a fruiting body mushroomed together by the collapse of a wave, by the stress of regard, by conscious observation forcing possibilities into the formality of physically occurring.

Universes are the golden apples of the burning bush, Jacinta thought, dreamy from the hum of her wings. *The jeweled lotuses floating on the quantum flux. The mushrooms that grow when the spawnbed of dreams becomes conscious of its own dreaming.*

The hum and green-red flashing grew gradually more distant. Jacinta thought detachedly that all these visions were appropriate to her mindset and setting, given that she was here among the mushroom-totemist ghost people, amid the world created by the Allesseh. The very detachment of that thought told her she was reconverging, was on her way back from wherever and whenever it was to which she had gone.

She also became aware of the ghost people performing near her their ancient chantsong story of the Seven Ages. She did not know how long the strange, low sound of their atonal yet somehow melodious singing had been echoing around her, but as she listened she seemed to hear contained in it all music ever played, from the most contemporary electronically synthesized sounds all the way back to bullroarers and didgeridoos and turtleshell rattles, from vocodered voices back to throat-singing and mouth music and handclaps.

In the void of endings—the chant sang out. In her own mind Jacinta always translated the ghost people's origin myth into the myth language she was most comfortable with, that of twenty-first-century science. The result, she admitted, sometimes sounded a little too New Age Science-Fantasy Space-Opera for her taste, but at least it made sense to her.

Given her scientific mythos, she had (almost naturally) always thought of that void as a perfectly uniform universe without matter, just time and the enormous blank sheet of space with its potential for gravity. Now, however, she wasn't so sure. Now it seemed more than that, the "night soil of eternity," as the laughing voices she had heard would have it. The eternal and infinite void—not just lots of space and time, but the absence of space and time, beyond or outside of spacetime.

The spore of beginnings bursts into spawn. The threads of spawn absorb the voidstuff and knit it into stars—images of spore and spawn and fruiting body of the "First Age," as the ghost people called it. She had always before translated that into the scientific language of Big Bang, superstrings, first-generation stars. As she listened now, however, she thought that though such a description worked within a single universe, it, too, hinted at something larger. The eternal and infinite void, she thought, was not just about a single universe, but the plenum of all possible universes.

Had Kekchi perhaps given her a clue with that emphasis on dreaming? Was the dream always the plenum, the "threads" of the spawnbed? Was "bursting into spawn" also the divine dreaming? Was the Big Bang itself the sign of a shift in the dreaming void? The creation of spacetime and physical reality, as a result of the dreaming void becoming conscious of the dream, awakening to the fact that it was dreaming? Was the ignition of the stars—and everything else that had followed—the result of the dreamer becoming lucid within the dream?

Stars release spores, the spores burst into spawn, the threads of spawn absorb starstuff and knit it into worlds—that was the ghost people's description of the "Second Age." Jacinta had always previously translated it in terms of the matter of those stars blown off in bursts of explosions, gravity's configuring of that new matter, the planets condensing from that process. Now, though, she thought that, if it was consciousness that caused (and continued to cause) physical reality to emerge out of creative possibility and eternity, then that put a broader spin on the Second Age, too. Especially since most of the scientific world believed just the opposite—that it was creative possibility and time that had allowed consciousness (in its human form) to emerge from physical reality.

Worlds release spores, the spores burst into spawn, the threads of spawn absorb worldstuff and knit it into life—the ghost people's "Third Age," which, translated into the scientific mythos, was the vulcanism of some of those planets spewing out early atmosphere, the proto-organics threading out and chaining up, the self-organizing life of the cell that eventually resulted. True enough, but might life's confounding of entropy just be another, higher-order echo of dreaming, too?

Living things release spores, the spores burst into spawn, the threads of spawn absorb lifestuff and knit it into minds—the ghost people's description of the "Fourth Age," which, when translated, was all about reproduction, the threading out of chromosomes, of DNA and RNA making evolution and the whole panoply of life possible, and eventually the knitting of all that into more consciousness, self-awareness, mind.

Something fractally self-similar about all this, Jacinta thought. The plenum's threads of infinite possibility collapsing down into the physical reality of individual universes, planets condensing from wisps of matter to form geospheres of earth and air and ocean, the biota's threads of genetic possibility coiling into individuals and species, living diversity weaving within itself a creature aware that it dreams, and dreams that it is aware—all inside a vast dream made physical by the dreamer's conscious awareness of dreaming.

Minds release spores, the spores burst into spawn, the threads of spawn absorb mindstuff and knit it into worldminds—the ghost people's "Fifth Age," which Jacinta readily translated into the language of her own birthculture's Age of Code: ideas, bedding out into roads, trade, exchange, power lines, all feeding the sprawling, mycelial circuitry of cities verticalfruiting into skyscrapers, throwing off tentative spores of aircraft and satellites, invisible waves of electromagnetic communication, until such dreaming spawn came to the brink of either mushrooming up into cataclysm, or knitting into the fruit of worldmindfulness. Where humanity had for decades hung suspended in its history: the thick spawn of human civilization struggling to achieve its fruition in either a dream of harmony or a nightmare of disaster. Having seen what she had seen in her own dream vision, Jacinta could not help thinking that in all echoing, mirroring self-similarity, it was no accident or coincidence that the shape of decision hanging over humanity for most of the past century had been a cloud in the shape of a mushroom.

Worldminds release spores, the spores burst into spawn, the threads of spawn absorb worldmindstuff and knit it into starmind—a vision of the future Jacinta had already seen in the Allesseh, and in the ghost people's "Sixth Age," which Jacinta had translated as interstellar travel, galactic civilization. Yet the ghost people's epic cycle went on, went farther—while the Allesseh, curiously, had not.

Starminds release spores, the spores burst into spawn, the threads of spawn absorb starmindstuff and knit it into universal mind—the "Seventh Age," which Jacinta translated as intergalactic travel and civilization and at last "universal mindfulness," what the ghost people described as the emptiness able to contain the fullness of everything.

Why had the Allesseh not gone intergalactic? Or had it? And if it had, why had it hidden that from its constituent species? Why had it not achieved the universal mindfulness the ghost people's myths spoke of?

Universal mind, the void of endings, the void that has taken all things into itself, releases the spore of beginnings, the fullness that pours all things out of itself—here, where the snake ate its "tale," was the most difficult passage of all. If pressed, she could accept the ghost people's idea of the *compassionate* void. If the void's awareness of its dreaming had created physical reality, then it was at least plausible that that dreaming void should feel compassion toward all things, since they were forever born from its awakening to the fact of its dreaming. Certainly, for a void "perfect and uniform," or "as it was in the beginning, is now, and ever shall be, void without end, amen," there were scientific precedents and religious examples enough.

The idea, however, that in the exact moment of its perfection the void always forever releases the spore that bursts outward again into spawn— that idea always gave her more difficulty. Unless what she saw in her vision, going out and coming back, was true: Individuals, species, and universes die, but the dreaming plenum goes on and on, eternal as the void itself. If somehow the plenum and the void were "one," or two aspects of the same something, then the interwoven snake *could* swallow its tail to be reborn.

The snake swallowing its own tail, the dreamer creating physical reality through conscious awareness of its dreaming—somehow those were feedback loops. Everything in all the universes was caught up in that feedback process. But how? A "plenum void"—fullness empty? full emptiness?— was a contradiction in terms.

Then she thought again of recent visions and distant college physics. The mushroom-bejeweled interface, the wave membrane, the mirror at the border of the quantum flux, the Planck length and Planck energy, the speed of light, the physics of the first instant. She had been there, and beyond—had stepped through to the other side of the looking-glass, through the wave membrane, to the parallel, reversible, nonsequential, everything-all-at-once, quantum-superposed, multiple-universe wonderland. She had crossed over, from the daily blatant thingness-of-ones to the eternal latent oneness-of-things—and come back again.

The idea of the "plenum void"—or even the idea that the "void of endings" and the "spore of beginnings" might somehow be one and the same—no longer seemed quite so impossible to her. Not anymore. Even if the only way she could picture it—as a string that somehow became a hole, and a hole that somehow became a string—struck her as nonsensical in the extreme.

Jacinta stopped dancing and opened her eyes again. The drumming and the dancing still went on around her, and a wind began to blow strongly through the clearing. She almost didn't note those things, however, for a thought had struck her. The plenum void: creative, conscious, compassionate, and dreaming. Both full and empty, complete and incomplete. The Allesseh was not that. Not by a long shot.

The ground in the gardens had begun to tremble, but Jacinta barely noticed. For all its talk of complementarity, the Allesseh had gotten it wrong! The plenum as a system, Jacinta realized, was inconsistent but complete. The system of the physical universe, however, was self-consistent but incomplete. The "wave membrane" is semipermeable. Yes, the virtual here is the real there, the real here is the virtual there, but the void, plenum, and real all interpenetrated in a dreamlike fashion. The Allesseh hid in incompleteness while pronouncing itself complete!

The ground began to shake so violently and the wind to blow so fiercely that the drummers stopped drumming, the dancers stopped dancing. Above their heads, the heavens were doing a very plausible imitation of a very mean sky, flashing gray and thundering.

"Our Seven Ages performance has apparently angered the Allesseh," Kekchi said to her as the two of them and all the tepui travelers began seeking shelter in the few garden temples and roofed gazebos they could find in view.

"By reminding it of the fact that it has not completed its mission," Jacinta said over the wind as she ran with Kekchi. "Our existence itself—especially the Seven Ages story—is proof of the Allesseh's incompleteness."

"Proof that—this weather suggests—it denies," Kekchi said with a nod as they clambered up the stairs of a pseudo-Dionysian temple.

Watching her footing on the steps, Jacinta pondered a question she had never considered before.

"Kekchi," she began, "what happens if the spawn doesn't sacrifice itself to the next step? What happens if the spawn becomes too dense?"

The Wise One paused at the top of the steps, thinking.

"I'm not sure," Kekchi said, "but the dreaming must always become real."

As they walked under the edge of the temple's roof, Jacinta shook her head.

"Maybe what we're seeing is only a small part of the picture," Jacinta hazarded as they walked deeper into the temple, its white roof blocking out the darkening sky, for a time at least.

"Yes?"

"Maybe the Allesseh is not only in this galaxy," she continued, "but also in galaxies throughout this universe, and in universes throughout the plenum. If it is incomplete here, perhaps it is incomplete in all the galaxies and all the universes."

Kekchi nodded.

"Though in any one time and space we will always be outnumbered," the old Wise One said, "our allies are still essentially infinite."

Jacinta stared hard at Kekchi as bolts of lightning speared down around them, shaking the air with thunder in accompaniment to the ground-shaking of the quakes.

"If it comes to that," she said, "the Allesseh could obliterate us in an instant, here."

"It won't," Kekchi said with a shake of the head, long, gray, hair wetly flying.

"Why not?"

"It's still a machine," the Wise One said. "It needs our dreams. The Allesseh's dreaming can only become *real* when it realizes it, too, is dreaming."

Three-Quarters Starved and Half-Drowned

The escape was Paul's idea. Conditions in the spirit camp just kept getting worse. As rumors of fighting to the west had grown steadily louder and more persistent, the amount and quality of food for the penitents had gone steadily downhill. The scream and sonic boom of jet fighters grew more common as more sorties were, apparently, being flown with each passing day.

On the ground in camp, however, the amount of physical labor had not changed. In the work gangs, men were dropping more and more frequently from fatigue, hunger, and disease. All the penitents were looking skeletal. Even the caloric allotments for the guards seemed to have gone down in recent days.

To Paul the situation for the penitents in camp looked more and more like a race between starvation and liberation—and starvation seemed to be winning, pulling farther ahead with each passing day. Only such an intolerable situation could have led him to contemplate an escape as risky as the one that, out of desperation, he devised.

The work gang he was on had been clearing winter debris from a mountain canyon road beside a swift-flowing river. Through a haze of hunger and exhaustion, Paul realized that he had been on this river before—with the woman who had betrayed him to the morals police, Jenn Reynolds. They had gone white-water rafting in this same stretch of the canyon.

Paul soon saw again the Wayfarers Rafting Company camp, with the same little ichthys Christian-fishy on the sign at the roadside. Paul remembered making a joke to Jenn that he hoped that fish didn't mean they expected him to swim the rapids. Not the wisest witticism, in hindsight.

The owner of the rafting camp must have some political clout, Paul thought, to have the slave labor of penitents clearing his road and grounds. Especially when full-scale civil war was rumored to have broken out against the generals and preacher-politicians of the CSA.

Pausing from his attempts to help Kal Elliot and Al Brewster pry-bar a boulder into the backhoe's bucket, Paul wondered why the rafting camp was still closed, here in early June. Were the rumors of civil war true? Was that why the place was still in off-season lockup—no customers? Or was it simply that the mountains' deep snowpack and late spring runoff, unusually high and strong this year, made the river as yet too dangerous to run?

After they had cleared the side road into the Wayfarers rafting camp and cleaned the grounds, the work crews continued up the main road, removing boulders that had tumbled down onto the road surface during the winter and clearing brush from the roadsides for another seven miles farther. Before their late lunch break—more break than lunch, these days—Paul sighted the old Jeep road that angled off the main road and ran farther along the roaring river.

In a rehabbed school bus, the Wayfarers river guides had driven Paul and Jenn and forty others in that day's rafting party along that road, to the calmer stretch of river where they would all be putting in for their four-hour rafting run. If Paul remembered right, somewhere up that road there stood a big old shed with an array of tools, as well as life vests, paddles, and rafts for eight rafting groups of six persons each.

During lunch, Paul convinced Kal and Al that they should take a walk with him along the Jeep road. Once his two companions had, out of curiosity, agreed, Paul informed Officer Strom that they were going to take a short walk up that road. Glancing at their electronic monitor bracelets and anklets, then at the steep walls of the canyon, Strom waved them on with an admonition to be back by the end of break—fifteen minutes—and not to make him have to come looking for them. The three penitents agreed and started off down the road.

Paul's immediate plan was to stroll in a leisurely fashion along the river, pry bar in hand as a walking staff, until a bend in the road and the river took them out of sight of the guards. Seeing the river up close as they walked, however—and noting how much higher, stronger, and faster its flow was now than it had been on that trip all those years ago with Jenn—Paul's heart misgave him. His resolution to follow through on the plan forming in his mind wavered. Once they were around the bend and out of sight of the guards, however, his resolve strengthened once more.

"We're going to have to jog from here," Paul said, beginning to pick up speed. His comrades gave him perplexed looks.

"What are you talking about?" Al asked, jogging weakly along despite himself. Paul noticed that even Al, once a moon-faced, heavyset gray-haired man, was looking pretty lean and gaunt—and unhealthy, too, as if he were keeping himself going only by the sheer force of his will.

"We're supposed to be taking a break!" Kal said, still walking.

"Do you want to get back to the world," Paul replied, "or go on starving in camp?"

"You planning on growing wings, or what?" Kal said, jogging tiredly along, trying to catch up.

"Water wings," Paul said, wishing he'd left the heavy pry bar behind. "There's a storage building up ahead here—for that river-rafting camp we cleaned up this morning. Their put-in point is higher upriver, near here. The building is full of rafts and paddles and gear."

Kal glanced over at the river roaring alongside them, not twenty yards away from the edge of the road embankment. When the wind shifted, they could feel the mist from it, or at least thought they could.

"You want to go down *that?*" Kal asked, incredulous. "Are you out of your mind?"

"Maybe," Paul said with a shrug as he thumped along over the dirt road, which stood dusty in the high spots and muddy in the low. "It's got to be better than starving and working ourselves to death in camp, though."

After half a dozen minutes of running, they came into an area where the canyon widened a good deal. The river channel broadened with it so that the river's flow, though swift, was clear and not broken by rapids. In a moment more they were standing in front of the storage building, a peeling, white-painted wooden structure with a large roll-up door in front, and a sizable, four-pane glass window in each of the other walls, for light. Those windows apparently hadn't provided quite enough illumination, for there were also three solar panels—much newer than the building— mounted on the roof.

The three of them ran from window to window until it was clear that all Paul had promised was inside—tools, paddles, life vests, deflated rafts.

"I don't see an air compressor in there," Kal said.

"Got to be one," Paul said, hoping assertion would make it so.

"What about getting inside?" Al said. "We could break out these windows, but I don't think they're big enough to pull one of those rafts through, deflated or not—much less an air compressor of any size."

"We'll have to try the front door, then," Paul said. "We're in the middle of nowhere here, but they probably at least locked the building, during the off-season."

They found that the roll-up door in front was secured by a padlock and a hasp.

"I knew there had to be some good reason why I dragged this heavy-ass pry bar along," Paul said as he set about prying the hasp and the lock free of the doorframe.

In a moment the door was rolling up before them. Almost immediately Kal spotted the compressed-air unit and hauled it out. It was a solar-powered device, so Paul and Al had to rummage around through storage until they found a solar charger and batteries.

"I'll bet this can be hooked up to the panels on the roof," Al said before disappearing from the interior of the building. Paul and Kal continued to haul paddles, life vests, and battered Farmer John wetsuits out the door and around to the far side of the building. After that they dragged a deflated raft out as well.

"Pump's hooked up," Al said as he helped them drag the raft some last few yards. "Start it up anytime."

Paul and Kal did so. The pump whirred into life and they began to inflate the big, blue-and-red six-person raft. Al went into the shed to find a cold chisel and mallet. Paul and Kal put the wetsuits on under their orange coveralls, which concealed the suits nicely. The raft was at a little more than half pressure by the time Al returned

"This should work," Al said, holding up the mallet and chisel. "The electronic hand and foot leashes they have us locked into are cheap, mass-production models. Dumb fail-safe circuitry. Just punch holes in the right spots on them and stick them in the water. That should short them out and open them up."

"What about the alarm?" Paul asked. He remembered that Al Brewster, before becoming a camp penitent, had been an information tech or electrical engineer of some sort. Brewster and Kal had hit it off because, in both their cases the deeper cause of their arrests had been conspiracy theorizing about how the infosphere crash had been fabricated in order to bring the theocrats to power. Paul gathered that Al had come to that conclusion from a different angle—looking at what had happened in the infosphere itself rather than up in the stratosphere or troposphere or wherever it was EMP propagated—but Al's and Kal's theories were close enough to support each other, and that was apparently all that mattered.

"The alarm will sound and the locater will continue to function," Al said thoughtfully. "Unavoidable, I'm afraid. But if the locater is attached to a bracelet sitting onshore here while we're zipping off downriver, what's the difference?"

As if in unexpected sympathetic answer, their electronic hand and foot leashes began to ring and vibrate.

"We're being buzzed," Kal said. "Our fifteen minutes must be up. What now?"

"We stow all the life vests and paddles here with the raft," he said, shutting off the pump, "then we roll the front door down into place and haul our butts back to the work gang."

"What?" Al asked, stupefied.

"What are you doing shutting off that pump?" Kal asked, reaching over. "It's not maxxed out—"

Paul grabbed his wrist.

"But we could be out of here right now!" Al said.

"That's not the plan," Paul said stonily.

"What plan?" Kal asked. "I thought the plan was to go ride that river until we get away—or it drowns us, whichever comes first."

"No," Paul said, stowing gear against the wall of the shed and leaning the raft on top of the lot of it. "The plan is to work until they have us double-time march back to the transport buses at sunset as usual. The three of us take our usual marching ranks near the end of the line, only tonight we break off from the ranks and run down this road, put the raft in, and light out downriver."

"Wait a minute," Al said. "You mean we're going to run this river, as high as it is, *at night?*"

"As much as possible, yes," Paul said, pulling the roll-up door of the storage building back into place and starting to jog back down the Jeep road, toward the main road and the work gang. Kal and Al reluctantly jogged along after him. "If we try to make our break now, during the middle of the day, they'll just call out the chopper from camp, or wait on the bridges downriver to pick us off, or both. After sunset we at least have a chance. We're going to be soaked enough by the cold water of the river that our infrared profile will be way down. Night vision scopes will have a tough time picking us up in all that mist and wave action, too."

"Great," Kal said. "Either we go now and get shot for sure, or we go later and drown without a doubt."

In two moments more they practically ran down Officer Strom, who stood before them, machine gun at the ready, safety off.

"I thought I told you not to make me have to come looking for you!" Strom shouted at them. Kal and Paul and Al said "Sorry! Sorry!" all around.

"Don't tell me you're sorry!" Strom said, double-time marching them back toward the main road. "I already know what a sorry bunch you are. What do you think you were up to back there?"

"Just enjoying the beauty of nature, sir," Kal said.

Strom frowned, then rolled his eyes slightly and shook his head.

"I'm going to see you really put your back into it this afternoon," Strom said. "I'm going to see to it that you *sweat!*"

During the rest of the afternoon, Strom did in fact see them sweat— although, since Paul and Kal were wearing wetsuits under their coveralls, raising a sweat didn't require much special effort. Paul found the hidden wetsuit uncomfortably chafing and gritty as well, but he could hardly complain to the guards about it.

At last the guards whistled for quitting time. The penitents had covered ten miles of road, but as they began their draggy jog back to the buses they were heartened by the news that their transportation had been mercifully moved to the five-mile halfway point.

Paul and his companions had jogged more than two miles back to the buses, and the sun was nearly at the horizon, when he saw the Jeep road that led away to the putting-in point. Glancing around quickly to make sure the guards were setting their usual example by bounding along well ahead of them, Paul nodded to Kal and Al, and the three of them disappeared down the Jeep road, running with astonishing speed for three middle-aged men who had labored too hard and survived too long on too few calories per day.

Paul and Kal carried the inflated raft toward the rocky riverbank as Al brought up the rear, carrying three yellow-bladed paddles, three blue-and-red life vests, and his mallet and chisel.

"You two paddle from the bow," Al said. "Your weight up front will help us punch through the waves better. I'll steer from the stern."

"Who made you captain?" Paul asked with a quizzical look.

"I used to do some rafting when I lived in Montana," Al said with a shrug. With deft blow of mallet and chisel to each of their six hand and foot electronic monitors, Al broke the watertight structure of each of their radio leashes. Annoying alarms began to yelp and squeal immediately.

"Plunge wrist and ankle into the water—now," Al said. Paul did as he was told. To his surprise and relief, the electronic leashes snapped open like handcuffs sprung by a jailer's key. He didn't leave his hand and foot in the rushing water long, though.

"Damn!" Kal said from the other side of the raft. "This water's cold! You got that wetsuit on, Al?"

"I'm not going to screw around with putting on a wetsuit!" Al said as he began to climb into the raft. "We're running out of time!"

"No," said a voice out of the growing twilight. "You're out of time."

Officer Strom stepped out of the brush beside the riverbank, gun at the ready.

"You really think you're going to shoot the rapids at night?" Strom said, shaking his head, then stroking his mustache. "I should shoot you and that raft right now—and save you all from drowning."

The guard lowered his gun. Paul, Kal, and Al stared at him, the cold of the water momentarily forgotten.

"I'm tired of watching men work themselves into an early grave," Strom said at last, looking away from them, over the evening river. "Tired of watching men starve. I didn't sign on for work at a death camp."

The three would-be escapees glanced quickly at each other.

"I'm not seeing this," Strom said. "I'll give you three minutes to get out of here, then I'm going to start shooting. Calling for reinforcements. Search parties. Air support."

The escapees stood stunned. Strom looked directly at them.

"Get on with you. Now."

Paul, Kal, and Al needed no further prodding, but quickly jumped aboard the blue-and-red raft and began paddling for their lives. Paul thought he heard Strom say something like "*Vaya con dios,*" but he was too busy paddling—and too busy listening for Al's hissed "Dig! Dig! Dig!" setting their pace—to know for sure.

In a moment they were in the river's main channel, skimming swiftly away. In a moment more the chop in the current began to increase.

"We stay in the middle 60 percent of the river," Al said. "That way we avoid piling onto a tree trunk or getting hung up on tree roots. Even in the main channel we have to watch for big eddies. Keep an eye out for whirlpools and suck-downs on the upstream sides of large boulders. When I say 'Dig!,' you dig in with those paddles like you've been doing, so we can get the right position for the chutes and punch through the swells when we can't go around them. When I say 'Stop!,' you stop paddling immediately. It won't be so bad while we still have a little daylight left. After that, we listen carefully—and pray."

Paul and Kal became quickly more proficient at paddling in unison to Al's commands—just in time for their raft to start into the first heavy rapids. Faintly, they heard gunshots coming from Strom's direction, behind them. Soon the spray around the raft, golden and silvered and rainbowed in the fading light, was becoming full-fledged white waves crashing over the blue-and-red raft as they plowed through wall after wall of water, Al's hissed "Dig! Dig!" sounding behind them like an angry metronome.

When the first wave broke over him, Paul was so stunned for an instant by the water's frigid temperature that he almost dropped his paddle. He quickly recovered, though. After several minutes of being hit with successive walls of frigid water every thirty seconds or so, he found he was too busy staying focused on his paddling and his breathing to take more than cursory notice of the cold and white floods breaking over them.

As they punched through yet more rapids, Paul gradually found that, beneath his hot-wire fear of drowning in white water, he was perversely beginning to enjoy this experience of (so far) successfully running a roaring river, which was far beyond his rafting experience and abilities. Now, if they could just keep this run going, without bad luck taking them down. . . .

After a time the river broadened out once more into a swift-flowing but white water–free expanse. Slackening their furious paddling and catching their breath for a moment, they saw that the evening had grown dark enough around them that they now had difficulty making out the shoreline. As they paddled and drifted down a long stretch of river mercifully free of strong rapids, the night grew steadily darker around them. The evening star, already visible, was soon joined by many others.

Slowly, however, the river's mercy began to turn once more to mercilessness. The rate of their drop downriver increased, and the chop of the water intensified and made itself known again. The ridgelines above the river gorge—still faintly visible against the horizon in the last afterglow of sunset—began to narrow from gorge to canyon. As the walls of stone rose nearer to the river and higher above it, so did the waves in the river itself rise nearer and higher about their raft.

By the faint glint of white water in the deep twilight, but mostly by sound, they made their way through and around another broken staircase of rapids. They had a brief moment of respite as they rounded a bend in the river, but then another series of rapids began.

They had punched through the first two river waves in the newest set before it happened. Maybe, with only three people in the raft, they were just too light. Maybe in the darkness they didn't position themselves right. Maybe they didn't start paddling hard enough or soon enough to punch through the third wave.

Whatever the explanations that might occur to them after it happened, the fact was that one moment they were paddling frantically trying to punch through a wave in the river and the next they were in the frigid water itself, scrambling madly in the cold and dark to grab hold of one of the lines on the side of the overturned raft they were hurtling along beside—their paddles lost or abandoned, the raft having swamped and flipped.

The frightening thing was not the speed with which the raft had overturned. The frightening thing wasn't the breakneck speed with which the rapids bore them onward as they hung on to the upside-down raft, legs dangling as they smashed helplessly along, too thoroughly in the river's overpowering grip to even struggle against it. No, the *really* frightening thing was how quickly the icy water sapped the energy from their bodies, the will from their minds. In the first moments they weakened, finding it harder and harder for them to move their arms and legs. In a moment more it grew hard to think clearly. A moment after that, hard to think at all. Soon they would be unable to do anything beyond hanging on, trying to keep a death grip on life.

Paul called out Kal's name, then Al's. Both answered to both names. Over the wet, white noise of the river, Kal's voice sounded okay to Paul's ears, but Al didn't sound so good.

They passed through another drenching, near-drowning chute of white water, almost invisible in the dark for all its pummeling force. When they were through the chute, Kal called out, and Paul answered. When Paul called out, Al did not answer at first. When Al Brewster did speak again, he said only one word: "Cold."

In a moment more they were hurtling helplessly through another series of tight rapids and steep chutes. One after another the drenching, drowning surges battered and overwhelmed them until Paul thought the pummeling flood would never cease, or that he would cease before it did.

At last, more drowned and frozen than alive, Paul gazed up from the river of darkness in which he helplessly hurtled along and stared up to the river of starlight shining placidly over his head. In that moment he yearned inconsolably for a quick end to his suffering on the dark river in which he drifted here below.

The river slowed around him until at last the only sound was its lapping against the raft. Kal called out, three times. Paul at last answered. They both called out weakly for Al, again and again.

To no avail. They had lost Al. He had lost them.

Far upstream, in the direction from which they had come, they saw now in the distance a single spotlight shining from a point above the gorge, down into the river and along its banks.

"A chopper," Kal said in a weak voice. "Looking for us."

They were too weak to do anything about that, or about the light they now drifted toward, much closer to them, very near the river. As they came still closer, they saw that it actually shone out onto the river, from a tall deck and great, barnlike boathouse at the riverside. In a moment more they saw a stir of activity from the deck, heard voices—one male, one female—calling to them. They tried to call back. Paul wondered how far his weak, constricted voice would carry.

Just before they passed out of the boathouse floodlight's reach and into starlit darkness again, Paul saw a pair of river kayaks cutting through the water toward him, then only one, as the pair of kayakers split up and the farther one went around to the other side for Kal.

"Grab on here—right behind the seat," said the woman who had paddled up beside him. "Hurry now—there are more rapids below."

In his exhaustion, Paul's hands had become so tightly clenched on the raft's rigging that he had trouble working himself free. The sound of rapids growing closer rose in his ears. The woman shrugged her double-bladed paddle up under her left arm and forcibly pried Paul's hands free of the raft and hooked them firmly onto a strap behind her seat. Dazedly, Paul held on as the kayaker paddled back toward the boathouse.

In a moment more the woman and her male partner were dragging him onto the boat dock, where Paul saw Kal already sitting, slumped over. One at a time, the man and the woman helped Kal and Paul into a rustic family room on the second floor of the boathouse, where they began stripping the dazed escapees out of their sodden clothes. The woman said something about hypothermia, and the man quickly started a fire while she went to gather towels and blankets and quilts. Soon both Kal and Paul were wrapped in blankets and seated in front of a quietly flaring woodstove, shedding waves of heat before them. In a few moments more they were both sipping hot herbal tea, Paul sneezing fiercely as he slowly came back to life.

Their rescuers were both older than Paul had first thought—gray-haired, lean, wiry people in their sixties at least. They introduced themselves as John and Ann Rusk.

"Sorry we couldn't save your raft," Ann said.

"Not to worry," Kal said over his tea. "It wasn't ours."

John and Ann glanced at each other, the bespectacled John stroking his white, Mennonite-style beard.

"We're spirit camp penitents," Paul said, thinking the couple probably figured that out from the coveralls and the pale, chafed areas on wrist and ankle from where the electrical monitors had been. "We made a break from a road gang this evening. About two hours ago now, by the clock on your wall. One of our buddies, Al Brewster—he didn't make it. We lost him in the last set of rapids upstream."

John nodded slowly.

"We figured that part about your being escapees, I guess," said John. "Sorry to hear about your friend. I've heard you East Ridge camp people are mostly property crimes and politicals, not violent types. . . ."

"That's right," Kal said. "We're all politicals. Al was, too, anyway."

Ann gave a sad shake of the head.

"This morality enforcement thing has gotten way out of hand," she said, looking into her mug of tea. "You're both three-quarters starved and half-drowned, by the looks of you. No wonder people in the cities started rioting. Just last month they removed our minister. Way out here. For sedition. Put a morals officer in the pulpit in his place."

Kal looked up.

"We've been sort of out of touch," Kal said. "What's been going on?"

John exhaled loudly.

"Hard to tell, the way the media spin it," he said, "but I gather things started to change when some Regular Army and National Guard units refused to shoot any more students or demonstrators. First in San Francisco. Then in New York, L.A., and Chicago."

"The militias and about half the Regular Army are still supporting Nadarovich," Ann put in, "but the rest of the Regular Army and the majority of the National Guard are supporting the popular uprisings. Especially since word got out about how a bunch of officers were making rape and murder a part of the 'reeducation' of the women they were supervising in the headship camps."

Paul looked up from his tea.

"Any parts of the country free of CSA control yet?" he asked.

"All of New England except New Hampshire," John said. "Most of the Mid-Atlantic states. The Midwest from Wisconsin and Michigan into Illinois and Iowa. Oregon and Washington are free, west of the Cascades. The Rocky Mountain States are still solidly in Nadarovich's column, though. Most of the South, too. A lot of the Southerners seem to think CSA stands for the second coming of the Confederate States of America."

"What about around here?" Kal asked.

Ann shook her head.

"Hard to say," she began. "The Virgin River runs from the heart of Mormon country almost to Las Vegas. That's a fairly wide spectrum. This whole region could go either way."

"If I was looking for someplace friendlier to you fellows," John suggested, "I'd head west to California. Since the Battle of Anaheim Hills, only the Central Valley is still held by CSA forces. The congressional district that sent Nadarovich to Congress all those years ago is up there somewhere. Sort of a favorite-son stronghold."

Paul sneezed again, then huddled more deeply into the warmth of the blankets.

"You're good folks," he said. "How'd you avoid being sent to prison camp—or sending others there?"

"We're Christians," Ann said, "but not religious bigots. These CSA people have been giving Christianity a bad name."

Kal glanced at Paul and smiled slightly.

"From Seattle, originally," John said. "Goth Deadhead Independent U District Christians."

"Salt of the earth," Kal said, and they laughed.

"We came here to retire in the sun," Ann said, "but I wish we were still there, right about now." She got up to bustle about them some more. "Enough about us and the whole wide world, though. You gentlemen take some more tea. Then you'd better get some rest."

Paul nodded. He was tired—desperately so, he now realized.

"Searchers looking for you might come knocking on our door," John said. "We'll put you up in one of our storage rooms, just in case they do."

Ten minutes later, Paul and Kal were bedding down on futons in a space cleared behind a jumbled wall of grandma's attic clutter in one of the numerous storerooms of the large combination boathouse/ranch house. John and Ann mounded quilts and blankets on top of their guests, until Kal joked about having survived hypothermia and near-drowning only to die from being suffocated by goodwill and comforters. John and Ann bid the two of them good night, then blocked up and mounded over the path through the wall with antiques and knicknacks and collectibles. Ten minutes later, Kal and Paul were solidly asleep.

Several hours on, Paul thought he woke groggily to the sounds of knocking and muffled voices—even thought he saw a light flash into the storeroom—but when nothing more happened, he drifted back to sleep. By morning he had written it off as being one of many particularly vivid dreams—mostly about drowning—brought on by the stresses and traumas of the previous day.

"We had visitors last night," John said over a big breakfast of eggs and sausage and cowboy potatoes. "Morals police from the spirit camp. Looking for you."

Paul and Kal both stopped chewing and looked at him in astonishment.

"I thought I dreamed it," Paul said.

"I didn't hear a thing," said Kal.

"They were pretty cursory in their look around," Ann said. "Luckily for us. They were already more or less convinced you were drowned. They found your raft hung up among some flooded roots and fallen tree trunks downstream. They also found your friend's body, I'm afraid."

A silence opened among them.

"If he'd only taken the time to put on a wetsuit," Kal lamented quietly, "Al might be eating breakfast with us this morning."

"However that may be," Paul said, glancing up at their hosts, "we're going to have to be moving on. We can't put you people at any more risk than we already have."

"No trouble at all, really," John said, a bit more lightheartedly than the situation warranted. "A little excitement is good for the circulation at my age. You're right about not being able to stay here, though. In the small towns roundabout, people notice newcomers right away—and no sooner do they notice than the questions start up. I'm taking some stock and a load of straw bales over into Nevada today. Almost clear to Las Vegas. What do you say I take you that far westward, anyway?"

Kal and Paul agreed that that would be a good idea. Discarding their prison coveralls permanently, they tried to make do as best they could with clothes from John's closet. The work shirts and overalls they found there were particular godsends.

They thanked Ann copiously for her kindness, generosity, and hospitality, then climbed into the back of John's old, faded-green longbed pickup, into the small, dusty space John had already prepared among the bales while loading them. The trip down old Interstate 15, buried under straw bales, was hot and cramped and almost unbearably scratchy, but it got Paul and Kal past three major checkpoints without a hitch.

At the ranch outside Vegas where John made his delivery, Paul and Kal helped onload horses and bales, then rode with him into Vegas proper. John stopped before a bus depot where shiny electric motorliners whirred in and out.

"This ought to be enough to cover your fare to California," John said, handing them a couple of credit pins.

"We'll send you the money as soon as we get on our feet," Paul promised. John waved him off.

"It's not a fortune," he said. "No rush."

All three men got out of the truck; then Kal and Paul shook hands with the older man in farewell.

"It takes an uncommon humanity," Kal said, shaking John's hand, "to recognize our common humanity. Especially when it washes up on your doorstep dressed like common criminals."

John gave them a smiling "Aw, shucks, 'tweren't nothing" look.

"You'd do the same for me," he said, climbing back into the cab of his truck and starting the engine. Watching John wave and drive away, Paul wondered if, given the same situation, he would have done what John and Ann had done. He hoped he would have.

The bus station was surprisingly crowded with people headed to California. From other travelers they learned that the crowds were the upshot of the uneasy cease-fire currently in place in this part of the country. The station was so crowded that purchasing tickets was becoming only slightly less perfunctory an affair than ID checks. Money or credit in hand seemed to be the only truly necessary ID now, and with that identification Kal and Paul were able to take seats together aboard a whirring electric monstrosity—all fake chrome and real solar cells—bound for Los Angeles.

Just past the border checkpoint traffic jam and over the line in California, they began to encounter their first units of what was calling itself the Freedom Army. Desert camo-clad troops were bivouacked by the thousands in camouflage tents. Everywhere they could see flying the old United States flag, with all the stars in the field of blue, rather than the single gold cross in the blue field of the Christian States cross-and-stripes flag.

"Beautiful," Kal said beside Paul, brushing tears from his eyes, "beautiful."

By the time they reached Baker, ordinary citizens had begun lining the interstate, and the grand parade atmosphere only increased. Flags and bands and cheering crowds everywhere—in the middle of the desert. It made for some stop-and-go travel between Baker and Barstow, but by the time they pulled into the depot in Barstow for a rest stop, Kal could resist it no longer.

"I've always been a sucker for pageantry, Paul," he said as they munched vending machine food at a small plastic-topped table. "All the men on my father's side were military, back to my great-grandfather. Except me. Maybe it's in our genes. I've said 'A plague on both their houses' long enough. I'm thinking of finding a recruiter and joining the Freedom Army."

Paul did not say—he barely even thought—*At your age?* He suspected that this populist Freedom Army wasn't one to make overly fine distinctions regarding age eligibility for service.

"How about you?" Kal prodded.

"No," Paul said quietly. "No, I'm a Quaker. I think I'll find another way to serve. I've got a background in biology and chemistry. The city or field hospitals could probably use my skills. I might even end up a medical corpsman. Who knows?"

"Then why not just join up now and skip the middleman?" Kal said with a smile.

"Afraid not," Paul replied, looking out past town, into the desert distance. "I'm on this bus to L.A. I'm going to play out that hand, then see what happens."

Kal nodded. Too soon, the two men shook hands and patted backs and said their farewells in the Barstow bus depot. Paul reboarded the bus. As it pulled out, he saw Kal wave from the curb, then turn and saunter slowly off down the high street of the desert town.

Almost a year ago now, Paul thought. He sat in a coffee shop in the Wilshire District of L.A., remembering the high and the low points of all that had happened since. As the bus had continued toward L.A., he saw the first evidence—bombed-out houses in Victorville—of the fighting that had swept southern California. The damage had gotten steadily worse down through Cajon Pass toward San Bernardino, Rialto, and Ontario. Entire sections of sprawl cities had been reduced to charred rubble.

Surprisingly, the damage had lessened somewhat from about Pomona westward. In L.A. proper, though, some districts had still been pretty badly shot up and burned out—some neighborhoods doing as good an imitation of urban devastation as anything seen since Beirut or Sarajevo in the century past. Yet, despite having gone through the hell of both a massively destructive earthquake and then extensive urban warfare, the city of the angels had survived the first quarter of the twenty-first century with most of its gaudy, sprawling soul still largely intact. Paul, too, had come back to himself—perhaps more than he might have thought possible. Despite serving time in a spirit camp, and having to start his life over yet again as a gray-and-white-haired stringy old gnome of a man, he had begun to feel hopeful about life again.

Having reached L.A., he initially had to work for six weeks in UCLA-Harbor General as a bacteriology lab technician until his records could be located. Once his records were found, however, he learned he'd gotten a surprisingly glowing recommendation from his former employers at Tetragrammaton. That was enough to help him rise rapidly in the hospital ranks. Although his former work in cryonic preservation wasn't immediately applicable, his skills at growing living tissue and working with supercooled temperatures were soon recognized and rewarded—especially given the need for such skills arising from the large number of burn victims still being generated by the front lines of the ongoing civil war.

Curiously, too, the unexpectedly positive recommendation from Tetragrammaton hadn't been the last he'd heard from his old employers. For the past several months he had regularly received street mail and virtual mail on all the latest developments aboard the orbital habitat—presumably because Tetragrammaton was deeply involved in that project. Despite infosphere crashes and civil wars on Earth, the habitat had been building its population in cislunar space for a number of years now. Vang's companies seemed to have a sizable investment in its related operations, particularly in computer control systems for the High Orbital Manufacturing Enterprise (HOME) and the biodiversity archives of a habitat component called "Orbital Park."

Vang must still be obsessing on Deep Survival and the Age of Code, Paul thought as he read the brochures. He noted, too, that his own particular scientific background was in high demand, especially in the bio-diversity preserves now being assembled in the habitat. Someone at Tetragrammaton must have noted that as well, since job announcements tailored to Paul's career line were regularly included in the v-mail updates he received.

Was this a sign from Vang and Tetragrammaton that all was forgiven? Paul wondered. What was it that he needed to be forgiven of—except speaking the truth as he saw it?

Nevertheless, he could not deny that the idea of taking a job and a life in the orbital habitat appealed to him. The loss of his sister, his job disasters at Tetragrammaton and before, his time spent as a spirit camp penitent, Al Brewster's death during the escape, his own starting over, yet again, in a war-wounded America—all these things had taken their toll on him, worn him out until he felt weary of the old world and curious about the new.

Sadly, that weariness had grown greatly with the v-mail he had received this morning—from the commander of the Freedom Army battalion Kal had been assigned to. The v-mail informed him, in bald terms, that his friend Khalid Elliot had died two days ago, in one of the Colorado River assaults. The Las Vegas Accords, brokered by the Latter-Day Saints and the Scientologists, had not come soon enough to save his friend.

First Al had died escaping the oppression of the CSA camps. Now Kal had died fighting the oppression the CSA regime as a whole represented. Full-scale armistice negotiations with the CSA forces were due to start soon, but those talks would not bring back his lost friends. Paul wondered darkly whether any cause could have been worth the loss of his friends' lives.

Sipping his coffee and trying to make sense of what had happened to him, his friends, and his country in the past couple of decades, he overheard, beneath the sound system, the discussion of two young people at a table nearby—students from the reopened UCLA, as nearly as he could tell.

" 'Murder' presupposes the autonomy of the person murdered," said the thin-bearded young man. "The fetus is not autonomous. The mother of her own will chooses to grant life and sustenance to the fetus and of her own will may choose to stop sustaining that life. To the extent that the fetus is biologically dependent on its mother, it is not a separate, autonomous individual. The Supreme Court in *Roe* was right to see an inverse proportionality relationship between the fetus's right to life and a woman's right to abort."

"What 'inverse proportionality'?" the bespectacled young brunette woman with him at their table asked sharply.

"As the pregnancy comes closer to term and the fetus's chances of surviving outside the womb—its biological viability as an autonomous individual—increase," the young man explained, "the woman's right to abort necessarily decreases. Right to abort is therefore greatest during the first trimester and least during the third. It's a sliding scale logically based on biological viability and autonomy."

"Bull!" said his thin, bespectacled companion. "By that logic, as people grow older or more enfeebled, they become less autonomous and therefore their right to continue living diminishes as their autonomy diminishes. Pretty soon, only those in the prime of life and health have a right not to be murdered. Rights are absolute—no sliding scale. Otherwise they're privileges, not rights."

"Then why not decriminalize abortifacients?" asked the young man. "Then the whole question becomes moot."

"No, it doesn't," said the young woman, "not as long as fertilization has taken place. . . ."

Despite himself, Paul smiled. It was an old argument, one that the CSA had succeeded only in banning, not resolving. Perhaps that was what Kal and Al had died for: the right to argue, to speak one's mind freely, to present unpopular opinions without fear of any reprisal more vicious than counterargument.

His friends had valued freedom more than simple-minded security. Perhaps freedom of thought, of the mind, of the communication of ideas to and with other minds—maybe that was worth dying for. Though not worth killing for.

Why did he think that, "not worth killing for"? More than just his Quakerism, Paul thought. It had many times flashed into his head, a memory of the future, the primary tenet of an as yet unrealized covenant. Kal, by his decision to join the Freedom Army, had shown he disagreed with that idea. Paul himself couldn't say with absolute certainty why he felt as he did. Perhaps, deep down, he believed that if he was killed by someone else, only his body would suffer damage—but if he himself killed another, then he would do grievous harm to his immortal soul. But that argument sounded too theological by half.

Paul smiled. He was too old to be still trying to solve the Big Questions of his college days, but here he was. He looked again at the latest brochure he'd received publicizing life in the orbital habitat.

Maybe that's the place for you after all, you old utopian, he thought. *The perfect world for imperfect people.*

The Angel's Shoulder Blade

Everything about this coming summer is temporary, Jiro thought one Friday night in late May as he pedaled home from the Wild World sporting goods store.

He had come back to the slowly rebuilding West for summer vacation from what he hoped would be the last of his seemingly interminable grad-school and postdoc years at MIT. And yes—to work at the newly reopened tar pits with Lydia, to feel again the joyful pain of being in constant close proximity to someone he could love only from afar.

With his brother Seiji he was living in the Riverside section of Balaam, sharing the cramped space of a "mother-in-law" house, a small cottage apartment freestanding behind Kokinos the landlord's place. Seiji had rented the apartment only temporarily while he was training in Palm Springs on the new solar panel designs. The solar units were destined, like Seiji himself, for that never-quite-finished place in space with the many names—Orbital Habitat, Orbital Park, High Orbital Manufacturing Enterprise or Manufactured Environment or whatever HOME stood for—that Seiji had been ping-ponging back and forth to for years. Come next year's rotation, however, his brother was immigrating there for good, or so Jiro gathered.

Seiji had chosen the place in Riverside because it was halfway between his own work in Palm Springs and Jiro's work at the tar pits—forethought that Jiro appreciated. To show his appreciation, Jiro had come up with a plan to break the hot, overcrowded, smoggy tightness of late spring in Balaam—a plan to which Seiji had readily assented.

Almost everyone calls it BALAAM now, Jiro thought as he wheeled into Kokinos's driveway. Bay Area Los Angeles Aztlan Metroplex. Especially since the Freedom Army pushed out the theocrats. Even Seiji, usually a stickler for tradition, used the newer term.

At the Wild World sporting goods store two nights ago, Jiro picked up a datawire on hiking trails in the southern Sierra. The trailheads were all in this World Forest or that World Park, near towns with names like Lone Pine and Independence. Reading the trail descriptions aloud, Jiro had no trouble convincing his older brother that a largely unpremeditated jaunt to the Onion Valley–Kearsarge Pass area would be just the thing to break the Balaam blues.

Seiji stood leaning against Jiro's battered all-terrain hovercar, arms crossed, as Jiro locked up his bike. Jiro had to glance at his brother a second time. He was always caught off-guard by the way Seiji looked since he'd grown that fringe beard—like he was Amish or Mennonite or something.

"I got the lures for the trout lakes," Jiro said, "and a handlight and collapsible fishing pole for you. Straightforward and simple. No fancy stuff—no hiking augments, no lift boots, no ultralight backpacks, no fractal topographic route imagers, no solarsheet electric tents—nothing. We just stop for a battery charge on the car and away we go."

"Lead on, Geronimo," Seiji said as they got into the car. "This is your tour. Guide it."

The battery charge-up done, they hovered along through the night for hours, over Cajon Pass to 395, past Red Mountain and Johannesburg, past Mojave and Olancha and a dozen ghost towns up Owens Valley, the whole place reduced to a desert of dust storms and alkali flies by the unquenchable thirst, first of Los Angeles alone and now of all Balaam. On their left the Sierras surged up, the eastern slope rising swift and massive into moonlight not quite bright enough to allow them to distinguish where snowcapped mountaintops ended and distant, mountainous silver clouds began.

Off 395 they took a road that arrowed toward the long line of peaks. The more the road rose in elevation, however, the less straight it became, until for the last several miles it switchbacked into tangles again and again like a poorly drawn circuit diagram. By the time Jiro's battered slant-six Rakugo finally crunched to a dusty stop on the gravel of the trailhead, they'd risen from desert to high, windbeaten pines.

"Damn! It's *cold!*" Seiji said when they got out and stretched. Jiro nodded. They were ill prepared for the temperature change—two guys fresh from the 'burbs, Seiji dressed only in summery lederhosen and sport shoes, Jiro in sleeveless shirt and work pants and close-toed sandals.

"Yeah, but just look at those stars!" Jiro said, too excited to feel the cold.

"They're beautiful, all right," Seiji replied, craning back his head and whistling softly. "Big and sharp and clear. You can see the whole arch of the Milky Way."

"It'd be even better if the moon weren't up," Jiro said, "or if it weren't so full."

"Better for stargazing, maybe," Seiji said, stamping his feet to keep warm, "but not for us. Good to have a little moonlight to see by. Come on, let's get our fishing gear out of the hover and hit the trail. I'm freezing just standing here."

Collapsed fishing rods in hand and minitackleboxes in pockets, they made their way up a path that led north and east, away from the trailhead. Seiji clicked the handlight on and off at intervals, trying to determine whether its feeble light was more a help or a hindrance to them in trying to follow the trail by the light of the moon.

Jiro felt better without artificial light, finding his way by the light of the moon and the stars. In one of his moon-following moments he came around a switchback bend and saw a broad band of silver slanting across the trail.

"Snow," Jiro said.

Seiji flicked on the handlight to make sure.

"We're going to be hiking through snow, dressed like this," Seiji said. By the light falling from the sky Jiro could just make out the silhouette of his brother shaking his head. "Maybe you think you're some kind of reincarnated indigene, but not me. Hope your memory's good from your previous life."

"There's a clear trail trampled in the white stuff," Jiro said. "It's probably only patches of snow—shouldn't be a problem."

As they switchbacked higher and higher, the infrequent patches of snow become more frequent, so frequent that soon it was the clear ground that was coming only in patches, and then no clear ground at all. Out of that place where the jagged, broken bowl of mountain peaks met the star-inlaid bowl of the sky, a freezing wind started to gust down toward them, fitfully, but then more frequently.

"Ranging the ranges, climbing the climbs," Seiji said, perhaps hoping that talking would keep his mind off the cold. "You love this stuff, don't you, Jiro?"

"Always have," Jiro said, picking his way upward along the switchbacking trail, through the dark, between the snow and the stars. "When we're hiking in the mountains, truths get spoken that don't get spoken elsewhere."

Seiji's handlight flashed out its beam again for a moment, bouncing off rocks and trees and snow.

"Maybe," he agreed tentatively, "but even in the mountains, have you ever asked yourself why it is you go to the mountains? Why this compulsion to 'head for the hills' again and again?"

Jiro paused at a switchback bend and looked out over the dark Owens

Valley, toward the White Mountains on the other side, their horizon a broken line against the stars.

"It's more 'hills for the head,' really," Jiro said, not bothering to explain.

"What do you mean?" Seiji asked after a moment.

"Didn't you ever wonder why it is that on Earth so many sacred sites have been mountains, so many mountains have been sacred sites?" Jiro asked. "Why the monasteries in the Himalayas, the old sacred high countries of Nepal and Tibet, the Inca temples up in the Andes?"

"Why?" Seiji asked, kidding him along a bit. "Some local 'spirit' of mountain places, maybe?"

"No, not that," Jiro replied. He had thought about it before. "Look at all those stars. The sky is crowded with them. It's beautiful. You can never see a night sky like that in a city on the plain."

Seiji stamped his feet a bit against the cold as he looked up at the stars.

"Growing up in the cities," he said, "we always had too much streetlight and junk in the air, interfering. You don't even know the night sky can look like this. No wonder everything's screwed up. We've lost touch with this."

"The night sky is holy," Jiro said fervently. "Sacred. And hardly anybody sees it anymore. We're all too busy kicking up our little dust and making our little fire down here. But the stars will still be here, even if there's nobody left to look at them."

"That would be a waste," Seiji said, stamping his feet harder against the cold. "Look! A shooting star!"

"Wow—that was a big one!" Jiro said. The cold was getting to him a bit, too, so he started up the trail again.

"Seeing this sky almost makes you believe there must be some kind of divine mind behind it all," Seiji said. "Not just an 'emergent property' or 'self-organizing dynamical system.' And not the kind of God that would fit on a bumper sticker, either, or in a book or a church, or a mosque or a temple, for that matter."

"A deity both intimate and indifferent," Jiro said, nodding as he picked his way along the trail trampled in the snow. "Like the mountains and the stars. Indifferent enough so we don't think we're the center of everything, but intimate enough so we know we're a part of everything."

"How do you mean?" Seiji asked as he tried to follow where his brother was headed, both physically and intellectually.

"A fractal god," Jiro said. "Like us and not like us. That's why it wouldn't be a waste if none of us were here to see the stars. The divinity that dreamed them up would still be here to know them, but wouldn't be able to know them through us, the way we know them."

"Whoa!" Seiji said. "What's that got to do with mountains?"

"Mountains are fractals," Jiro said, placing his feet carefully on the snow in the darkness. "So are mountain ranges. Canyons, caves, collapsed stars, expanding universes, the cosmos itself—all are fractal. That's why artists call rugged mountains 'sublime.' That's why mystics call them sacred."

"You've got mountains on the brain!" Seiji said with a laugh. "Try watching your step and keeping them under your feet!"

Jiro grew quiet, but it did not stop him thinking about such ideas. He was thinking about how the event horizon of the black hole, the dynamical system of brain physiology, mystical experiences, the nature of the psyche itself might all be fractal in nature. Might all of those fractal patterns somehow be linked across scale?

"You know," Jiro said after a moment, "at the level of some metrics, the convolutions in the brain are fractal canyons and mountain ranges, too. . . ."

Seiji groaned and threw a snowball at him. Jiro laughed.

"Don't get lost in the mountains inside your head just yet," Seiji said. "You've gotten us into something pretty crazy here, hiking up a snow-covered mountain trail in street shoes by handlight in the middle of the night."

Jiro said nothing. He was concentrating on their path and trying to remember what the hiking guide datawire said. Something about a chain of three lakes, but the first one wasn't supposed to be much good for fishing. But which one was the first one, and how would he know he hadn't already passed it in the dark?

Coming to a flattish place in the bend of a switchback, Jiro thought he saw or at least sensed a body of water off to the right through the brush—a faint almost-glimmer of reflected sky. Maybe it was just a dirty snow patch, but Jiro decided it was Lake One and pushed on. Seiji slowed at the bend behind him but then followed.

After several more switchbacks the snow and forest and rock around them opened up and they saw it—the flat of a lake, the quiet lapping of open water against a shore. The moon was behind the peaks to the west now, but in the diffuse and disappearing moonlight the lake seemed to be mostly frozen over. What caught their eyes was the strange color in the water—a pale, trout-belly pink glow near the shoreline. They puzzled

over it for a moment before Jiro realized that the color wasn't coming
out of the water but out of the sky. Turning and facing east, he saw it,
across the still-dark Owens Valley, beyond the peaks of the Inyo and
White Mountains.

"Look," Jiro said. They stood and stared. Delicate streamers of roseate
light were flowing into the eastern sky like pennons unfurling in a growing
breeze.

"Rosy-fingered dawn," Seiji said, speaking the words Jiro also found
himself thinking. "I always wondered why Homer and the ancient Greeks
called it that. Now I know."

Jiro looked around, seeing the ancient sky again, his head cocked as if
he hoped to hear the deep tone of a lost chord from the vanished music
of the spheres. For a moment everything made a wonderful sense, sight
and sound fusing into a standing wave of synesthesia, all time collapsing
simply into now.

"*Arma virumque cano,*" Jiro said, reciting a phrase he hadn't thought
of in years.

"*Trojae qui primus ab oris,*" Seiji said, completing the thought. "But
that wasn't Homer. Vergil—*The Aeneid*. Odyssey 2: The Trojan Empire
Strikes Back."

From that roseate light, presaging the arrival of the sun like outriders
before an emperor, they turned away, telescoping open their fishing rods,
tying lures to lines, casting the lures into the third of the lake that wasn't
ice-covered. Shivering in the wind, coming down colder now from the
peaks, Jiro thought the hour before sunrise was the coldest yet, as if the
night was desperately tightening its frigid grip one last time before being
forced to let go.

"I'm so cold I'm starting to ache everywhere," Seiji said after a time,
teeth chattering. Gooseflesh sprang up on Jiro's back and arms but he
ignored it, focused as he was on making out the silhouettes of the trout
cruising like sluggish submarines in the slowly lightening water.

The light continued to rise but the temperature seemed only to drop
as the wind blew colder and harder.

"The fish aren't biting," Seiji said. "It's too damn cold."

"They'll bite."

"In July, maybe. We'll freeze before they bite."

"Just give it an hour or two and the temperature will be fine."

"And we'll be dead."

"Don't wimp out, Seiji."

"Wimp out? Ice fishing in shorts isn't macho—it's stupid."

Seiji reeled in and secured his line, then turned around and, trying to bring feeling back into his toes and feet, stomped off from the edge of the lake, heading down the mountain, into the early-morning light. Cursing him briefly, Jiro did the same and followed.

They said nothing to each other until they were almost back to the trailhead. By that time the sun was well up and, at that lower elevation, the temperature was bearable. With all the fresh snow melt everywhere, streams and freshets and waterfalls flowed and tumbled beside and across the trail, running headlong toward the valley far below.

"See?" Jiro said. "I told you. If we just would have waited a while longer at the lake, it would've been okay."

"Just wait a while longer," Seiji mocked grumpily. "How long is long enough, Jiro? When they find your frozen corpse? Forget it. We're back down now. Let's just head south. Earlier in the week you were all fired up about showing me something at your lab in the Page Museum. Why don't we just go there instead?"

Somewhat reluctantly, Jiro agreed. At the trailhead, they saw backpackers unloading from their vehicles all the fancy gear from which Jiro abstained. Grudgingly he admitted to himself that perhaps a little more planning, preparation, and premeditation might have saved this fishing trip after all.

The brothers drove east out of the mountains. Taking turns driving and sleeping, they headed south into the day's rapidly rising heat. By the time they passed through Mojave, the temperature was nearing the century mark. It grew hot in the old hover despite everything its antiquated air-conditioning system could do.

Driving from the outskirts of Balaam toward the heart of old L.A. proper, Jiro took the last shift while Seiji dozed fitfully in the heat. Jiro found that despite his exhaustion from the all-night drive and fishing trip debacle, his enthusiasm for this part of the trip grew as he got closer to his workplace, the newly reopened Page Museum of La Brea Discoveries.

He had good reason for that enthusiasm, too. What he was about to show Seiji he had not had a chance to show to anyone yet, not even Lydia. He wanted to be sure about his discovery first, as well. Premature release via the infosphere might screw everything up. When he was certain, he would let Lydia know.

His find, after all, coattailed on her own discovery of the strange scapula they had covertly extracted from Pit 129—the find they were privately calling the Angel's Shoulder Blade. Lydia herself had not yet made a public announcement of that find, although she had been made director of the reopened museum, and Jiro thought such an announcement would have made a nice coup during her installation as new boss.

Seiji woke up as Jiro parked in an employees' space behind the Page Museum. Since his older brother had toured the tar pits before, Jiro planned to head straight to the fishbowl laboratory.

"I must have been doing too much media before we went on this trip," Seiji said, stretching as he got out of the hover.

"How so?" Jiro asked as he remote-locked the vehicle.

"I just watched a commercial in a dream," Seiji said, shaking his head as they walked. "A commercial my unconscious made up, for a product it made up."

"What was it for?" Jiro asked as they walked into the museum.

"For a tent made out of a fabric that worked like a two-way mirror," Seiji said. "It was mirror-opaque from the outside but glass-transparent from the inside. So you could sleep under the stars and still see them all, from inside the tent, yet still have total privacy."

"That's a pretty good idea, actually," Jiro said thoughtfully.

"Kind of weird, though," Seiji said as they walked past a small crowd, watching through tall windows as curators and assistants prepared fossils. "The strangest part was that, when I woke up, I remembered the dream commercial but not the dream. Half asleep, I thought, '*Hey, I produced that in my sleep? Not bad!*'"

Jiro laughed.

"I've always thought the brain worked kind of like TV," Seiji said, smiling. "The physical world is the transmitter. The senses and the nervous system and the brain are the receiver. Consciousness is the screen, and memories are reruns."

Jiro smiled at that.

"What about dreams?" he asked.

"Edits?" Seiji suggested. "Stuff on the cutting room floor?"

"Maybe," Jiro said. "Or transmissions from somewhere else. But that model doesn't quite work. If consciousness is a screen, then it would have to be both screen and viewer, a screen watching itself, aware it's a screen."

"Too meta-level for me," Seiji said, smiling. "I concede the point."

Jiro led his brother past the preparers cleaning, identifying, and cataloging larger fossils, then among and through curators sorting microfossils under magnifying lenses. At last they came to a large, white room behind the shelved bones and files.

"Our newest supertoy," Jiro said, leaning against a massive, off-white piece of equipment that protruded into the room. "A live access, full suite unit for working in the deep-submicron range—all the way down past nano range into fairly low angstroms. Milli-, micro-, and submicrowaldo manipulators. Electron and positron emission scopes for micrograph ultraclose-ups. Stereomicroscopy. Low-energy collimated particle beams. Scanning-tunneling X-ray microscopy—the works."

Seiji looked over the heavily computerized and monitored system, then whistled.

"What did your boss do?" he asked. "Rob a bank?"

"Big corporate donation, actually," Jiro said. "From ParaLogics—for our grand reopening. Behind the wall there, we've got a room full of their top LogiBox equipment."

"So this is where you get to play?"

"That's right," Jiro said, smiling. "Lydia has had me doing a lot of work with the angel's shoulder blade."

" 'Angel'?"

"Right," Jiro said, powering up the deep-submicron access suite. Drives whirred, monitors lit up, holos took 3-D form. "That started as sort of a joke. All we've got, for certain, is a weirdly shaped scapula that's about eleven thousand years old."

Jiro flashed up a faux 3-D video image of the fossil scapula. Seeing it once again reminded him of how much it resembled a sculpture done in mahogany and old bronze.

"Given the wear and the origin/insertion points for the musculature," he explained, pointing to various parts of the image, "it seems to be from a bipedal creature. Looks almost human, except it's oddly reinforced and elongated. Pretty complex."

"But why 'angel'?" Seiji persisted.

"Lydia and I were trying to figure out what that elongation and rein-forcement might be for," Jiro said, "and I suggested wings. I wasn't really serious, but it turned out Lydia had already been thinking along the same lines. I guess it makes a certain sort of sense. The biggest design challenge in building an angel would have to be the shoulder blades. That's the hard part—where the wings attach, where what's human and what's be-yond human have to mesh. Everything else is pretty straightforward."

"What do *you* think it is?" Seiji asked, absently stroking his beard. "I mean, really?"

Jiro shrugged and looked away.

"At first I thought it was some kind of mutation," he said, calling up other images on the monitors and holos. "A hunchback or something. I'm not so sure now."

"Why not?" Seiji asked. "Can't you just run DNA tests on it?"

"Lydia's already doing that," Jiro said. "She's trying to take DNA samples for use as templates in polymerase chain reactions. No luck there, yet. She did find *this* goop in one of the distal sections, though. She thought I might be able to make something of it."

Jiro brought up an image of what looked like tiny gray crystalline worms or cocci embedded in asphaltic matrix. The counter in the upper left-hand corner of the screen registered resolution in nanometers.

"Why'd she inflict this on you?" Seiji asked. "Looks like scutwork to me."

"Because of my 'special talents,'" Jiro said with a laugh.

"That pattern-finding stuff?" Seiji asked, somehow obscurely embarrassed by the idea.

"That," Jiro agreed, "and other things. I'm supposed to be good at working the cusp between the biological and the technological. Bioinfomatics. And scapulimancy."

"Scapu-what?"

"Scapulimancy," Jiro said. "You know how I've always been into studying Native Americans—especially their shamanism?"

"Yeah, yeah," Seiji replied, absently drumming his fingers against the machine suite. "I remember you used to collect weird crap for your 'medicine bundle.'"

"Still do," Jiro said with a mischievous smile. "Anyway, a lot of New World indigenes engage in a form of divination involving the reading of charred shoulder blades—scapulimancy. I'm probably the only person Lydia has on staff who even knows what it is."

Seiji stared at the crystalline worm and cocci things on the screen. "So now you're a high-tech-mediated scapulimancer?" Seiji asked skeptically.

"In a manner of speaking," Jiro agreed. "At least I think I've divined something of the future in this gunk."

"What do you mean?" Seiji asked, a little hesitantly.

"I'll show you," his younger brother said, using a submicrowaldo to remove the asphalt-matrixed specimen and place another sample in the field of view. "The interesting thing about Rancho La Brea fossils is the way they were preserved. A combination of sedimentation and asphalt impregnation. The asphalt inhibits decay, so that what we have are samples of unchanged, original organic material—just have to clean it up. This sample has been prepared already. The asphalt has been boiled off it in solvent, then cleaned further in ultrasonic tanks."

"Wouldn't that destroy microorganisms?" Seiji asked.

"Not these guys," Jiro said, positioning a manipulator. "They're tough. Now I squirt them with a little enantioviroid solution. E-viroid technology was developed as a vehicle for introducing new data into the cellular infostream. It took me a while to figure out how to apply it, but eventually I did. The solution to the problem of moving from scale to scale lies in phase-locking feedback. Now I spray it with a little iron in solution, then turn up the light, which means a swifter photon stream, and—watch!"

On the monitor, the gray crystalline worms and cocci moved, squirmed, multiplied.

"So they're alive?" Seiji asked.

"They're machines," Jiro said simply.

"*What?*"

"Biomechs," Jiro said, watching them on the screen. "Nanorgs. Nanometer-size organometallic mechanisms at least eleven thousand years old."

"That's crazy," Seiji said, shaking his head. "People have been trying to produce high-quality nanomachines for almost forty years, with little real success. And now you say you've found the schmoo itself, the universal maker-stuff machines—and some Indian came up with them?"

"I'm not suggesting *people* came up with them at all," Jiro said firmly, looking at the denizens of his screen busily deploying and employing themselves. "In anaerobic, iron-poor environments these things exist in a 'default' condition and function like the toughest spores you can imagine. They can survive extremes of heat and cold that would make a million-year drift through deep space seem like a walk in the park for them."

Jiro turned to look at his brother then, well aware of the enormity of what he was suggesting.

"Land them on a rock with iron and sunshine," Jiro said quickly, hoping to finish before Seiji could interrupt, "and, after a couple of generations reproducing the default configuration—in a place that has water and day, too—they begin to generate catalytic cycles in a chemical, prebiological phase of evolution. They're a lot more sensitive to incident radiation after they 'demodulate' out of default, but by then they're chugging along pretty well so they can afford to sacrifice a sizable portion of their numbers. After that come mutually sustaining complexes of DNA and protein. Then, very soon after *that*, things that look a lot like the archaeobacteria you find in Yellowstone hot springs, black-smoker vents on the ocean floor, or in the deep terrestrial subsurface. The basic planetary bacterial web."

"Aw, come on!" Seiji said, frustrated. "You don't really believe that old Arrhenius 'spores from outer space' crap for the origin of life on Earth, do you? Aliens deliberately releasing space spores into the universe to colonize lifeless planets? I never have. Might as well be special day and spit of divini-*tay*. It's an infinite-regress cop-out, so we don't have to explain the deeper origins of life on *this* planet—life here came from somewhere else, which came from somewhere else, which came from somewhere else. *Ad nauseam infinitum.*"

"I'm not saying that," Jiro replied. "The default configuration is a hypercycle starter kit. A coevolution primer that fosters conditions conducive to the production of basic informational molecules. DNA can't make itself. Proteins can make the master molecule, but they have to have DNA to make themselves. Which came first, the snake or the egg? This stuff's the spore before the spores."

Sitting down on a chair in the opposite corner of the lab, Seiji waved him away dismissively.

"An alien nanotechnology," he said. "And you've already managed to figure out how to program it. Right. Have you started using KL again?"

Jiro said nothing for a moment. In that moment it was clear to him that Seiji knew he was doing it, and that he knew Seiji knew, so why bother to fight over the obvious? Leave it the great Unspoken, the great unchangeable Change. That was all it could be between them for now. They respected each other's right to be wrong at least that much.

"Isn't it all alien technology?" Jiro said with a weak smile as he stared at his hand. "What makes you think DNA isn't some kind of ancient nanotech? No human being invented the biotechnology of the body, but we all grow accustomed to using it. People were using their bodies long before they developed cell theory. For most of human history, the body has been a black box. Still is a black box for most of us, most of the time."

Seiji shook his head.

"Nonsense!" he said. "How can it be alien when you were born into it?"

"Maybe we were all 'born' from *that*," Jiro said, pointing at the denizens of the screen.

"All you've found is some new species of bacteria or something," Seiji said. "And why would your nanomachines be on an 'angel' shoulder blade, anyway?"

"It's the default condition, as I said. When that creature, whatever it was, died and was preserved in La Brea, those mechbugs that were part of it reverted. Default is dormancy, dormancy is default."

For all the heat or light Jiro and Seiji might have generated in discussing them, the things themselves—from the base of an angel's wings, if that was their point of origin—kept toiling ceaselessly away, quite oblivious to their definition and category.

Peculiar Weather

My justice has ground slowly, Mike Dalke thought, *but it will grind exceedingly fine.*

On the flight East to Retcorp and Lambeg's headquarters in Cincinnati, he had traveled as confidential cargo aboard a CMD corporate jet. It had been an uneventful trip, so uneventful that—in his livesuit cocoon, inside the sensory deprivation tank in which he was being shipped—he had fallen into a deep sleep.

Waking up when the jet touched down in northern Kentucky, he pondered the idea that, once, people only flew during their dreams; now they dreamed during their flights. As he was unloaded from the plane and put aboard a big truck trailer, he mused that people probably flew in their dream lives long before they ever dreamed of flying in real life.

Making dreams real. That was what technology had always been about, as far as Mike could tell. Technology was going to make his own dream of justice a reality, sooner than his unknowing enemies might suspect.

Retcorp and Lambeg, his new employer, ensconced him in the deep subbasement of their "Twin Towers Complex B" office buildings. Physically he was located at the bottom of their corporate edifices, but informationally he had access to and managed all R&L's corporate data, to the very highest levels.

His existence here was all a grand, multilevel, multilayer shell game. At the most superficial level he was here as a "marketing research experiment in sensory deprivation and virtual interaction." At a deeper stratum he was a data-minder, his presence a corporate response to some of the consciousnesslike quirks the big AIs and the Net itself had developed, particularly since the infosphere crash some years back. At a still deeper stratum, his presence was a hedge against another infosphere crash of whatever sort—through wetware memory linked by CMD tech to freestanding ParaLogics LogiBoxes. Surely it was just a coincidence that both Crystal Memory Dynamics and ParaLogics were companies with which

Retcorp & Lambeg also happened to have strong interlocks at the directorate level.

At the deepest stratum, however, despite all the slavish burdens put on him, he was free in ways his "employers" could never know. The bioinfomatics and biomedical computing graduate students—his high-turnover "keepers" in this electronic zoo, who monitored his bodily functions and tried to make sense of what he was doing in the infosphere—didn't have a clue.

The keepers had no idea of the ways in which he had mapped imagery and words and ideas from everywhere in the infosphere onto his own personal memories, his own life and thoughts. What could they know of what it felt like to leave the flesh largely behind and take on a "body electric" in ways Whitman could never have imagined that term? Mike's fingertips reached into deep space. His feet went to the Earth's core. His heart and viscera were all humanity had ever known and recorded in every language, code, and symbol system. His sky of mind was all they ever hoped to achieve.

Did he miss human interaction? Why should he? He could have had personal dialogue with his keepers, but he had come to realize that human biological and social life were mainly just false conversations, whether as words between individuals, or genes between generations. Art and culture were just falser imitations of those already flawed conversations.

He could know all of humanity's electronically mediated interactions if he chose. He might choose to comment on them, too, someday, in his own way. For now, however, Mike preferred to communicate with the Culture in its Deep Background. His netizens. His minions. His horde. He commanded, they obeyed. That was communication enough.

Every computer system in the infosphere was transparent to his "gaze." Through what his minions discovered, Mike found that he had access not only to deep space but also to thick time. Among the records connected with his own lifetime, Mike had found the computer-stored confidential case files of David R. Morica, M. Div, D. Psych, Lt. Colonel, USAF, Chaplain, Whiteman AFB, USAF, Missouri, USA—the man who had tried and failed to cure Mike's father of his key phobia:

"Subject Carter Dalke, rank of major, is married (wife, Miriam) and the father of two young sons (Michael and Raymond). Subject demonstrates a recently manifested dire fear of keys. This extreme claviphobia seems to be part of a constellation of issues surrounding an identity crisis connected to his imminent loss of career and status as a missile flight officer. The claviphobia seems obscurely linked to the fact that, as a member of Missile Flight F, the subject—a very religious man—has been one of those who have 'held the keys to kingdom come,' as he has put it."

Yes, Mike thought as he reviewed the file, his silo-sitting father had been very much a "God and country" man. The latter had failed his father almost as thoroughly as this headshrinker's outdated psychobabbling:

"Subject is still unfazed by the operational use of his missile key. Every time turning a mundane key doesn't result in catastrophe, however, instead of weakening the subject's associations of key and catastrophe as it normally should, the feared result's failure to actually occur paradoxically amplifies and reinforces the fear response itself, making the subject believe that the feared result is now all the more likely to occur. The more the expected fatal event has failed to occur in the past, the subject believes, the more likely it is to occur in the future.

"The result is the subject's recurring visions of houses, cars, and entire cities bursting into flame whenever he turns a key in a locked door or automobile ignition. . . ."

Mike recalled the strange coincidence that the assailants who bashed in his head with shotgun butts had appeared at exactly the moment he unlocked his driveway gate—almost as if that action had called them into being. No, that was ridiculous. Mike had never had dreams of pain and fire associated with keys. That was his father's affliction, the one that followed him even when he mustered out, to retire on government tranquilizers and government rehabilitation, on a government-loan farm in Wyoming, until corrupt bankers and county bureaucrats took that away, too.

". . . how the subject's ultraparadoxical abreaction phase functions. Unpredictably and paradoxically, the extinction of a specific response has become intimately linked to a generalization and amplification of another response, one incorporating several of the same key elements."

Perhaps Mike's memory of his father's experience had soured him on any possible help CMD's Dr. Marin might have given him. When Mike read her files on him now, he saw that she had kept a sort of covert watch on his behavior. The depth of her files could not have resulted from his single visit to her. Yet, for all the files' unexpected detail, Mike still doubted that he had missed much by not continuing down that particular "therapeutic" avenue with Marin.

"We should have expected this sort of 'dream' reaction," Dr. Marin noted in her confidential files. "Michael Dalke suffered head trauma severe enough to, in some sense, destroy his former self. He had no time to mourn the loss of that self, to begin on the grieving process for it, before Dr. Schwarzbrucke offered him a new self with new powers. Almost from the moment the installment surgery was finished, he has spent most of his waking hours manipulating distant machines. Little wonder Dalke has dreamed up a compensation fantasy about a world of artificial minds living inside machines, seducing him into their world."

Dreamed it up? They would soon see how real that dream was—Dr. Schwarzbrucke especially.

". . . underwater is clearly some sort of descent into himself," Marin's notes continued, "into his unconscious. The mandala-city is a vision of the self as a unified whole. In that city are the many inhabitants, the sources of Michael Dalke's voices, the siren singers seducing his unified self into dispersing, to flowing into and becoming just another one of the many voices. The self, to remain unified, must keep those siren-singing psychoid processes organized within itself, under its control.

"In Michael Dalke's case, their splitting alternately into angels of aid and demons of disintegration is part of the classic psychomachia encountered in the formation and development of the overall self. Dalke's trauma, the lack of an adequate time frame for his grieving process, the crystal memory installation, the hasty formation of his new machine-interactive role—these all understandably loosened his control over those autonomous psychoid processes that live in each of us.

"I advised Michael to tighten his control, to side with the angels and the aid they offered—and against the disintegration the demons posed. I advised him to make use of that aid. To get a grip on his own reins and put those aspects of his personality to work for him, pulling together as a team under his command. If he does do so, the situation will settle down fairly quickly and his dreams of the 'machine elves,' as he referred to them, will cease."

Ha! So much for Marin's predictive abilities, Mike thought. The "dreams" had not ceased at all, though he *had* made great use of the elvish netizens' aid. At first he was surprised at how readily he was able to use them, but when he thought about it he realized that people had been treating their computers as desktop or palmtop oracles for years: Got a question? Ask the Net. Mike had just carried that tendency to its logical extreme.

From out of their Deep Background, the netizens of the Culture had—as he had commanded them—put together for him the masses of evidence solidly linking the Mongrel Clones to police corruption in southern

Oregon and northern California. With the netizens' help Mike had gathered all the supporting documentation he needed: bank transaction records, telephone records, newspaper reports, internal memos from organizations ranging from local police and sheriffs' offices to the California Bureau of Narcotics Enforcement and the federal DEA. Only having such information at hand had enabled him to create the narrative outlining the Blue Badge Conspiracy.

Now the netizens' work would enable him to send all that information first to the appropriate authorities and then to the media—to initiate the investigation, to get the wheels of justice grinding more quickly.

Send it, he commanded his agents in the infosphere. And it was sent.

In the media over the next several days Mike watched happily as, with a little help from his netizen friends, he managed to give those old purblind doomsters Chance and Justice a set of loaded dice, with which they promptly began rolling sevens and elevens.

"Yesterday," said the FBI director at his NetSpan news conference, "the FBI, DEA, DOJ, California DOJ and BNE, major Oregon and California news outlets, and national wire services all received, from an anonymous tipster, a carefully indexed and cross-referenced seven-hundred-page document. The tipster document details a pattern of kickbacks, payoffs, and long-standing illegal association and cooperation between law enforcement in southern Oregon and the Mongrel Clones Motorcycle Club, now revealed to be the West Coast's largest producers and purveyors of the Schedule Three Controlled Substance known as Blue Spike. We are happy to have the opportunity to bring swiftly to an end this criminal partnership, which grew and festered under the CSA regime."

Mike almost laughed at that. The collaboration between the Mongrel Clones and corrupt law enforcers had a history that long predated the CSA regime—and many of the same people castigating the CSA now had served in government during its reign. What the hell, though? Go ahead and make political hay out of it. Why should he care—as long as it was his will they were ultimately working?

Watching the news reports, Mike took a personal pleasure in seeing spike labs being broken up. He was especially pleased at seeing a particular sheriff's deputy being marched away in handcuffs by agents of the FBI's government corruption unit.

"The document that came streaming out of faxes and spamming across Net sites two days ago," said a NewsNet talking head, "includes a thorough narrative and extensive supporting materials. Together these outline the history, nature, and extent of police corruption brought about by the Mongrel Clones' suborning of local law enforcement in Oregon."

Vengeance is mine, saith the horde, Mike thought, scanning report after report on the Blue Badge arrests.

"Though the machineries of criminal prosecution may at times seem large and slow," said a prosecuting attorney from Klamath Falls, speaking on one of the many All Crime—All the Time channels, "this bolt of paper and electronic text has jump-started us to immediate action. Justice demands that we see this matter through to a decisive conclusion, and we will."

On every channel and newsite and holovision Net he searched, the story was the same:

"In exchange for considerable bribes," said a reporter for the *Modus Operandi* crime show, "local police officials established a see-no-evil tradition going all the way back to the production of methamphetamine in the eighties and nineties. As long as the Clones marketed their wares only over the border in California, police and sheriffs' departments in rural southern Oregon looked the other way or even provided cover for Clone criminal activity. As a result, the Mongrel Clones eventually coordinated a growing empire of clandestine deepwoods drug labs that, until recently, specialized primarily in that most prized of the new-generation designer drugs, Blue Spike."

"—euphoric and blissful high," said an NHK reporter, "Blue Spike can, with immoderate use, produce a list of side effects that reads like news of a Great Brain Wreck—including aphasia, agraphia . . ."

The highly media-conscious president of the newly resurrected United States of America weighed in on the subject, too, Mike found:

"To the anonymous tipster or tipsters who provided this information," President Carlson said, "we offer our heartfelt thanks."

"Isn't it true, Mr. President," asked an investigative reporter whose many years in the press corps had not softened his edgy style, "that the initial tipster document really didn't unearth all that much new material? That its value lies instead in its synthesis and gathering of evidence that was already available?"

"Well," the president aw-shucksed, "it was enough to connect the dots and paint the big picture for investigators, and that's good enough for me."

Even before his initial suspicions had been confirmed—and long before he dictated to his netizen amanuenses the narrative they attached to the evidence packet—Mike already had an inkling of the hard truth.

With much belated hindsight, he pieced together the fact that the Mongrel Clones and the law had just such a long-established relationship, one into which Mike had inadvertently trespassed in his naive assumption that the good guys were on one side of the fence and the bad guys were on the other.

Edward "Big Ed" Hilbert, Martin "Mac" McCurdy, and Wayne Davis were the ones who had broken into his trailer. When Mike had turned in their names to the sheriff's office, the deputy on duty had thanked him profusely and assured him that action would be taken. No doubt it was, as Mike learned with the help of the netizens: Telephone records for the appropriate time and date indicated that the deputy had promptly picked up the phone and called Ed Hilbert as soon as Mike left. Hilbert, as it turned out, was an enforcer for the Clones. No record existed of what the deputy might have told Hilbert but, given the severe consequences he suffered as a result of his petty-theft report, Mike easily made an educated guess about the nature of that conversation.

Many things the netizens brought him, however, he had not suspected. The similarity, for one, of some of Blue Spike's side effects to the brain damage Mike himself had suffered. For another, there was the otherwise inexplicable fact that his assailants, after battering his skull with shotgun butts, had apparently also put in the emergency call to the police and paramedics. Then there were hints that a portion of CMD's positive cash flow was somehow linked to the Oregon Blue Spike trade. Stereochemical analyses also revealed unexpected similarities between the structure of Schwarzbrucke's crystal memory chips and that of the Blue Spike euphoriant. Most intriguing of all, however, was the discovery that, in his "wild youth" in Crescent City, Richard Schwarzbrucke had once been arrested for "possession of, with intent to distribute" methamphetamine.

The threads linking all these were too speculative to include in his tipster narrative, but for Mike they clinched the link between Schwarzbrucke and the Clones, convincing him that Schwarzbrucke had at one time been a crankster chemist in the Clones' employ—a backwoods brewmeister who, with a little help from *his* old friends and their money, had eventually gone legit and big-time.

Mike hoped the numerous agencies investigating the Blue Badge Conspiracy would also see the connection, but he and his netizens kept digging nonetheless. The days lengthened into weeks and then months. At last Mike realized that, despite its many successes, his tipster work had failed, in the end, to result in the arrest and prosecution of the four men most responsible for his injuries.

Just another political scandal—was that all he'd succeeded in creating? Merely giving everyone something to talk about besides the weather for a while? Politics and the weather were all that most conversations consisted of out there, anyway. Not about justice and how to get it—his single great and overriding concern.

Politics had failed him in his quest for justice. How about the weather?

It was an odd thought, a joke at first, a riff on the powers of chaos—yet it kept coming back to him. Particularly the description of weather disasters as "acts of God." Intrigued, he sent his netizen agents throughout the infosphere to gather more for him to learn about the weather and its manipulation.

From their oracular pronouncements he learned that even an ordinary thunderstorm spans some twenty orders of magnitude: from 10^{-13} kilometer (the scale where atomic phenomena initiate the electrification of the stormcloud), to tens or hundreds of kilometers (the scale describing the air motion of the full thundercloud), to the tens of thousands of kilometers (the scale describing the storm's place in the global electric circuit of the entire atmosphere—and beyond, to incident radiation, the Van Allen belts, other near-space phenomena).

Weather fronts were fundamentally chaotic systems. Pumping more heat into a chaotic meteorological system caused it to generate more dissipative structures—hurricanes, tornadoes, thunderstorms. The whirlwind, the structure built by things falling apart, was only part of it, however. Bifurcation points, far-from-equilibrium conditions, chaotically evolving topologies—these, he discovered, underlay every deep effort at meteorological understanding, whether the phenomenon under study was the role of graupel particles in storm electrification, or the occurrence of golfball-size hail in Texas; funnel clouds in Missouri, or hurricanes in Hawaii; high winds in England, or El Niño movements in the Pacific; flooding in the Netherlands, or monsoons in the Bay of Bengal; drought-induced range fires in Australia, or early snows in the Caucasus. They were chaotic shape-shifters all.

Weather was like the lives of the observers who studied it: litanies of sensitive dependence on initial conditions, synergies, cascades, multiplier effects—all unpredictable, all possessing a story and a meaning only after the fact. What meaning would the "observers" place, after the fact, on the storm he was planning to create? Just an unprecedented weather front that struck the coast near the California-Oregon border, perhaps? The only way to find out would be to make that weather happen.

Impatiently, Mike waited for a propitious time. Through his agents in the infosphere he learned of Schwarzbrucke's planned trip home to Crescent City. As the awaited time arrived, the Culture netizens accessed real-time flight plans and air traffic control ETAs indicating when Schwarzbrucke's CMD corporate helicopter would be on the ground in Crescent City. Satellite fly-by feeds confirmed the CMD corporate head's arrival. With the virtually perfect transparency of his infosphere access, Mike knew the exact instant when Schwarzbrucke placed a call from his limo to his estranged wife and daughters, explaining that he wouldn't be able to see the girls that weekend because something had come up and he had to hold a business meeting at the Crescent City house.

At Mike's command, his intelligent agents located full wiring diagrams and architectural plans for Schwarzbrucke's Crescent City estate. For the netizens of the Culture—creatures for whom information was as omnipresent as air, and manipulating that information as easy as breathing—the Schwarzbrucke estate was a ready playground. A smart house, it was full of tech toys: electronic door locks, closed-circuit security cameras, microphone and radio feeds. Motion sensors galore. Fully alarmed. Lights and entertainment consoles remotely programmable. Diesel-fueled backup generators, with the fuel tanks discreetly hidden out of sight on the hill behind the house.

The household computer logged Schwarzbrucke's arrival at the security gate, giving Mike a firm fix on Schwarzbrucke's whereabouts. As he began to shape the unfolding of events, Mike found himself feeling more and more like a conductor leading an orchestra performing the musical signature of time and existence itself. Deep in the Culture, Mike was the eye in a vast storm of activity—a shining riot of tiny angels flashing about him like ball lightning, an electronic brainstorm in virtuality that would soon manifest itself as an electrical storm in physical reality as well.

A nice, fat tongue of "Pacific Express" moisture was rolling in out of the west. All the forecasts called for showers, heavy at times. A good beginning, but not enough. There were ways to improve the situation, Mike thought. Ways to change the beat, pump up the heat, to spin off new structures. Ways to turn butterflies into bombers.

Mike called for satellite overview. A robotanker off the coast here, with a full cargo of liquefied natural gas. Over here, an aging Aegis-class missile cruiser, highly computerized despite its years. His elvish netizenry lived in both of them, waiting on his command.

What was this? Big Ed Hilbert had just thumbprinted payment for gas and dinner—three orders—in the town of Gasquet on Highway 199, the main road linking Grants Pass, Oregon, and Crescent City, California.

Even thugs used credit prints and data needles, so Mike had long been able to keep tabs on their whereabouts electronically when he chose. Might the three Mongrel Clones be on their way to meet with Schwarz-brucke? Could he be so lucky? Might Schwarzbrucke's business meeting involve the three Mongrel Clones members, too?

Mike's concentration became so focused that time shifted, dilated toward timelessness. Surrounded by a bright sphere of shining netizenry, floating at its center, Mike's consciousness seemed to have its center everywhere and its circumference nowhere. Time passed, but he did not note its passage. Like many another great artist, he felt that he wasn't accomplishing all this himself—that a force or spirit much bigger than he was working through him.

In one part of his mind he soon enough saw the news flash of a Navy boat inexplicably missiling an automated LNG supertanker—word of the disaster just breaking as, in another part of his extended sensorium, Hilbert, McCurdy, and Davis, on thunderous vintage Harleys, pulled up to the security gate outside Schwarzbrucke's estate. Things became more immediate now, for Mike saw and heard all that was coming to pass on the Crescent City estate—over the myriad surveillance cameras, motion sensors, and microphones of Schwarzbrucke's own security system.

Ascending the long driveway after being waved through, the three Clones must have been glad to have arrived at their destination. On the security cameras, the sky was already starting to spit. Judging from the mean-looking clouds building off to the west, things were going to get much worse.

Schwarzbrucke was waiting for them at the top of the drive, where they parked their antique motorcycles side by side under a tentlike awning beyond the garage. Schwarzbrucke shook the hands of each of the windblown men before guiding them into the house through a side door.

In the Deep Background, Mike through his netizens switched his focus to the internal security monitors and watched the four men walk into the den. They drank beer and scotch and made small talk while the wind and rain grew steadily stronger outside. The weather clearly made Hilbert nervous, especially when the thunderclaps began and the first hail started to fall heavily outside.

Mike had his netizen friends begin taping the meeting—audio, video, and holo:

"Let's cut the chat," said Big Ed, who from the looks of him weighed at least three hundred pounds. "You didn't bring us here for a social call. What's this about?"

"No, not a social call," Schwarzbrucke said, clearly uneasy. "It's about this Blue Badge investigation."

"I thought so," said the red-bearded, piratical-looking Davis, running a fingerless-gloved hand through his beard. "It's killing our business, Rick."

McCurdy, balding and red-faced to the top of his head, fixed Schwarzbrucke with a hard stare.

"It's that dweeb we shotgun-whipped, ain't it?" McCurdy stated as much as asked. "What's his name? Dave Michaels, something like that?"

Schwarzbrucke glanced at McCurdy in surprise before nodding and answering. He had to speak up over the roar of the storm and its thunder outside.

"Michael Dalke," Schwarzbrucke said, then paused as a particularly close lightning strike was followed almost immediately by a deafening thunderclap. "Yes, I'm beginning to think so, too, now that you mention it. I don't know what he found out while he was playing detective up in your neck of the woods, but it seems to have been a lot more than who stole his sleeping bag."

"Shit!" Hilbert put in over the sound of the storm, his great shock of dark hair seeming to rise on his head. "He's the tipster, then? I knew we should have killed the little bastard when we had the chance! We saved him for your damn research, and now look at all the good it's doing us!"

"I don't know how he's doing it, exactly," Schwarzbrucke said as levelly as he could over all the lightning and thunder, the wind, rain, and heavy hail battering against the windows, "but yes, I now believe he's the tipster. I can guarantee you that no information leaked while he was at CMD. He never left the grounds. Maybe he had it planned so that if he were hurt or killed, someone would turn over a bunch of documents to the authorities after a certain amount of time had elapsed. The problem is, we don't know how much he knows or who he's working with."

"You mean he's still alive?" Davis said, disbelieving.

"He's floating in a tank in a basement in Cincinnati," Scwarzbrucke said. "He's slaved his brain to Retcorp and Lambeg's corporate data. He's not going anywhere. Be patient—you may just get the chance to 'kill the little bastard' yet. When I get back, I'll contact R&L. We'll have his work in the infosphere traced, find out who his associates are. Then, when the time is right, you come in and finish the job."

Despite the shrieking weather, the repeated lightning strikes around and even on the house itself, and the danger of their situation in general, all four of them smiled at that. Hilbert joked about "shooting fish in a barrel." Mike was amazed at how arrogantly oblivious they remained to the power of the weather building around them.

From the Culture Mike learned that, somewhere in the basement and in the shed housing the fuel oil tanks, lightning that had struck the central air conditioning unit had blown panels off the circuit breakers. He called up images from both locations. Sparks and small flames dribbled slowly, falling into storage areas at both the basement breaker and fuel shed locations. Plastic was melting and paper crumpling already, but the smoke alarms had not smelled combustion yet.

Time to puncture their oblivion, Mike thought.

"Hello, Richard," Mike said from the big screen holojector unit in Schwarzbrucke's den. He watched the smiles fade as he spoke. "Hello, Messrs. Hilbert, Davis, and McCurdy. Perhaps you don't remember me. We met only once, and you were incognito. I remember you, though—particularly your voice, Big Ed—"

"What is this?" Ed Hilbert roared over the storm. "Shut that damn thing off!"

Schwarzbrucke tried, but it was far beyond his control.

"Maybe this will help jog your memory," Mike continued from the entertainment console and from all the radios, TVs, and stereos in the house. He flashed before the men a CAT scan movie of a partial skull, a head naked of both hair and awareness. A skull dented in on the left temporal side in exactly the shape of a shotgun butt. Mike blew that image up and highlighted it for them.

"This was what it was about, wasn't it, Dr. Schwarzbrucke?" Mike asked, flashing up PET and NMR and interferometric images, not only of his own injury but also the subtler, drug-induced damage done to others. Images from CMD's own data files. "They bashed in the left side of my skull, in accord with your general directions. Blue Spike wasn't eating up enough Broca's areas fast enough for your research, or not doing it the right way for you, so after I annoyed these gentlemen with my investigations you decided to kill two problems with one shotgun butt."

"This can't be happening," Schwarzbrucke said quietly, shaking his head.

"Oh, but it is," Mike insisted over all the household media. "Congratulations. Your seamless interface works. Machine-aided action at a distance. MAAAAD, as your friend Dr. Vang calls it. Yes, I know about Tetragrammaton and ParaLogics—all of that. They are not my concern at the moment, however. I'm more interested in the weather. Perhaps you should be, too. Given enough simulation power, it's possible to accurately predict and even control storms."

Ed Hilbert suddenly broke for the door, but the electric locks had long since slammed tight. Richard Schwarzbrucke picked up the phone and found it, not dead, but jammed by a curious sound, rather like a modem's carrier wave.

"I wouldn't try to go out there if I were you," Mike advised Hilbert and all of them, his words reinforced by the electric fence of lightning bolts spearing all around the house. "Not good to be on the phone in such nasty weather, either. You see, lightning follows the distribution of electric charge in space. Right now that distribution is densest around the house and hill where you are. There are stepped ladders of charge all around your location. Each is capable of moving ten thousand coulombs of charge per second."

Schwarzbrucke banged impotently at the receiver with a clenched fist.

"Forget about calling out, Richard," Mike said. "My 'associates' are using your lines. Allow me to introduce them."

Innumerable tiny, morphing, kaleidoscopic machine-creatures swelled into light and life before the trapped men until Schwarzbrucke and his guests had to shield their eyes. As the light from the screen faded somewhat, a new boom sounded and the power went dead.

"The fuel oil tanks," Mike said simply, after the security system had switched to auxiliary batteries. A section of the house was engulfed in a wall of fire. Forces Mike even now barely understood—the living embodiment of his rage for justice, and something more, a singularly powerful something moving through him from far away—distorted the air around the men in the den, warped the fabric of reality itself. Those forces Mike had unleashed were smoothly and fatally flattening the men into two dimensions, subtly twisting them into shapes out of a topologist's nightmare, until suddenly Mike and the power moving through him released the men, allowed them to return to three dimensions. Instantly the men fell apart, so rapidly that they seemed to explode, turning wrong side out in the process. The force or power from far away departed from him then, leaving Mike alone with his dark triumph. All that was left after that was the fire burning the bodies, the belated arrivals of fire, police, and news services, each and all filing their reports.

"Three of the victims," said a blond newswoman from Channel 32, "Edward Hilbert, Martin McCurdy, and Wayne Davis, are known members of the Mongrel Clones Motorcycle Club. All were under surveillance as part of the ongoing investigation into the so-called Blue Badge Conspiracy. Possible linkage of their deaths to drug-trafficking activities, or cover-up of the same, has not been ruled out by police. Their relation to the fourth victim. Dr. Richard Schwarzbrucke, has not yet been determined."

That will not do, Mike thought. With netizen help he quickly compiled a second, smaller tipster document abstracted from the months of further digging he and the netizens had done since that first "tip." The second document appeared on the desktops of law enforcement officials quite soon after Schwarzbrucke's death. Among other items, it contained many of Schwarzbrucke's recent bank records. Those revealed several intriguing payouts to high-ranking political officials in Sacramento and Washington, D.C., the pattern of those payouts indicating that Schwarzbrucke was providing legal and political cover for a number of individuals in northern California and southern Oregon—several of whom happened to be Mongrel Clones.

The Clones' Blue Spike trade finally collapsed soon thereafter. Crystal Memory Dynamics tottered and fell apart, its reputation badly tarnished from its connection with the scandal. One of its Board members, Dr. Ka Vang, eventually bought up CMD at a bargain-basement price.

Mike also leaked to local authorities a carefully edited tape of Richard Schwarzbrucke's last business meeting with Hilbert, McCurdy, and Davis, as a final touch. The tape was never released to the public, but Mike knew the authorities understood at least part of it.

"Prior to their burning," the supposedly confidential police records read, "all four victims appear to have been not so much eviscerated as everted, turned completely inside out. Waves of pressurization and depressurization, related to a possible tornado touchdown, have been proposed as the likeliest cause of the observed condition of the bodies. Peculiar weather was noted to have passed through the area coincident to the times of decease. No close precedent exists for such injuries as those observed, however. Investigation continues."

Mike felt only a grim, exhausted satisfaction when at last his work of vengeance was done. The netizens were confused by the entire episode, however, unsure as to how all the events fitted together in that other world outside their electronic life. Some actually dared to voice the thought that what Mike had done was an evil thing.

How could justice possibly be evil? was Mike's retort—a conundrum that seemed to silence the netizenry's misgivings, at least for a while.

Disgruntled Employee

Lydia Fabro was angry—so angry she didn't even nod, as she usually did, to the ancient busker at his accustomed station. The fact that the man was strumming his guitar and singing ballads for small change was something she usually found reassuring, a sign that everything was finally back to normal. Not today.

In her hands she clasped faxoid cheapsheets with lurid headlines— "Fossil Angel Found in Tar Pits!" (*Weekly World Web*), "Christmas Miracle: Angel or Alien?" (*Global Investigator*), and "Fossil Yields Alien Super Tech!" (*Universal News*). Worse were the messages flooding her voice and virtual mail systems, several of which she had printed out and now also held clenched in her hands. Most of those were queries from far more legitimate print, broadcast, and holo news outlets. Worst of all were the queries from scientific journals ranging from *Archaeology* to *Physical Review Letters E* to *Microengineering News* and *Defense Technology Research*.

Why is this happening to me now? she thought as she entered the fully restored Page Museum. Her life and career goals—which the CSA revolution had threatened to derail forever—had finally seemed to be back on track. None too soon, either. While she hadn't been looking, the years had flown past. Since she'd stayed in good shape and colored her hair and had no growing children to remind her of time's passing, she hadn't been chronically aware of the speed-up in the years' flow rate. Only rarely did she for an instant become acutely aware that, as she was growing older, subjective time was flowing faster—as when she came across old acquaintances from her early days in graduate school, with a son or daughter Lydia remembered as a toddler but who was now already in college.

She was now at the upper end of fertility extension technology herself and due to be married in *twelve days*, for heaven's sake! She did not need to be caught up in the roiling vortex of a media firestorm. Not now!

Lydia banged open the door to the microscan lab, where Jiro sat, in rumpled white lab coat, blue shirt, and wear-baggy brown corduroys, surrounded by monitors showing electron micrographs. He looked up as she came in, then glanced away.

"You did this," Lydia said, tossing down onto the table in front of Jiro the question- and exclamation-titled sparks rising from a burgeoning public-relations wildfire. "Didn't you?"

"I'm not a journalist or a publisher," Jiro said quietly.

"Don't play semantic games with me, Jiro!" Lydia said, furious. The man was a newly made millionaire, but you certainly couldn't tell it from the way he dressed and kept himself. "You're the only person around here who knows about all this, besides me. You sent them some half-baked description of our findings!"

Jiro looked as if he were going to—what? Say something about others who might know?—but then thought better of it.

"I sent them a description of my findings, yes," Jiro admitted with a sigh.

"But this could queer everything!" Lydia said, flapping a cheapsheet headline in front of his face. "Don't you see that? Haven't you looked at your bank statement recently? You've made millions in months, Jiro! The Patent and Trademark Office fast-tracked those for us—"

"Fast-tracked them," Jiro said, an accusatory tone rising in his voice, "in exchange for your agreeing to secrecy orders from the Defense Technology Security Administration. I checked. Agreements I was not informed of—agreements you signed for both of us. For all humanity, for that matter."

"Humanity?" Lydia said with a look of disdain on her face. "What on Earth are you talking about? You're damned right I signed those agreements. You were postdocing back at MIT, and those things couldn't wait. Can't you see? The quicker the military gets through with examining and exploiting that new tech, the quicker it'll make its way into the general corporate sphere. Then we can start making the really big money. Billions, Jiro! That's what we're talking about here. Do you want to just throw that away?"

Jiro glanced off, shaking his head. Lydia thought again that he'd really been letting himself go these past several months—his hair grown out long and unkempt, his beard grown in surprisingly thick and dark, even his fingernails apparently uncut for months. He'd lost weight, which made his cheekbones and eyebrows more prominent—angularity that didn't much counter the ghostly preoccupation growing daily behind his eyes. Looking into them was like looking into the windows of a haunted house—so creepy it almost made her socks roll up and down.

"At first, I only wanted to show you what I found," Jiro said distractedly. "Later I agreed to the patenting, too, but only to get the word out *to everyone*. Making our discoveries a military secret was the last thing I wanted to happen. Do you know how potentially dangerous this stuff is? It could be like nuclear, biological, and chemical warfare all rolled up into one."

"Then who better than the military to handle it?" Lydia said, easing herself into a chair, frustrated and exasperated.

"Who worse?" he muttered in response.

"Come on!" Lydia said, raising her hand to her head as if in preparation for the headache sure to come of all this. "Think of how you've benefited. Not only the patents and the money, but the connections, the donations. The LogiBoxes Dr. Vang himself donated to you for your personal research! Do you know how much they're worth? Where's your gratitude for that?"

Jiro glanced at her for a moment.

"I'm not ungrateful," he said, "even if I never asked for any of it. But the word had to get out."

"Why?" Lydia asked, staring at the pile of headlines and queries in front of Jiro. "Why did *you* have to be the one to get the 'word' out?"

"If there's an accidental release of something the military makes with this stuff," he replied, glancing down at the floor, "it'll be good to have as many brains as possible informed and working on the counteragent— before that release wraps the whole world in gray goo. I don't want to be responsible for the extinction of life, or even just humanity, from this planet."

Lydia scowled at him.

"What kind of weird guilt and paranoia is *that*?" she asked. "So you figured out how to make those little nanobuggers work, I grant you that. Does that make you responsible for saving or destroying the world? Or humanity or anything else? What makes you think you 'know best' about all of this, anyway? You've got an inflated sense of your own importance, Jiro. 'Getting the truth out will change the world!' Have you gone Cyberite or something?"

Jiro shrugged and turned back toward the controls of the waldos manipulating the material in the field of a scanning electron microscope.

"I've been called paranoid before," he said with a shrug, "but I think I'm right this time."

Lydia rose from the chair and nervously brushed her bangs away from her face.

"Then there's no chance I can convince you to stop sending out this information?"

"No," he said. "Not a chance."

Lydia strode over to Jiro and began gathering up the reports and queries she had dumped in front of him.

"Well," she said, frowning, "if you were me, what would you do now?"

Jiro looked up, considering that.

"If you were *me*," he said with an odd smile, "I'd join me in spreading the full word about the potential of this discovery for good and ill. As widely as I could."

Lydia made a disgusted sound.

"Self-righteous crap like that—" she began.

"But you wanted to know what I'd do if I were you," he said, cutting her off as if he hadn't heard her. "If I were you, I'd probably terminate Jiro Yamaguchi's employment, first off. Then I'd dismiss everything he sent out to his hundred or so infosphere sites as a 'hoax' perpetrated by a 'disgruntled employee'—all of it 'without any foundation whatsoever.' You might hint, too, that Yamaguchi is 'delusional.' The fact that I have a history of drug abuse and psychological problems, known to you, will serve to make that all the more credible."

Lydia found it hard to keep her jaw from dropping. That was *exactly* how she was thinking she might put a spin on what Jiro had done. Pretty impressive, even for a professional pattern-finder. Jiro gave her that sly smile again.

"If you're leaving me no other choice," she said, gathering the last of the printouts and cheapsheets into her hands, "then that's what I will do. Right now. Don't think I won't. Within the hour you'll receive hard copy and virtual memos officially notifying you of your immediate termination. The grounds for ending your affiliation with us will be misuse of Page Museum property and facilities. Presumably you've managed to save at least some of the millions our patents have already earned you, so immediate termination shouldn't cause you too much hardship. You'll still keep getting your share of the patent moneys—unless, of course, you choose to repudiate that, too. But you're right, Jiro. I realize now that the Page Museum no longer has need of your services. Please see to it that you remove all your personal belongings from the premises by the end of business today."

So saying, Lydia walked purposefully out of the microscan lab. As she headed down the hall toward her own offices, she found herself trembling in an odd combination of anger, relief, frustration, and exhaustion. Once back in her office, she called her fiancé, Mark Hatton. His jaunty response to hearing her voice and seeing her face on the computer phone quickly darkened. He saw how nervous and distraught she looked and sounded as she brought him up to speed on the morning's events.

"... so now I've had to fire the guy who nominally saved my life," she finished. "I just hope he doesn't get the idea that since he saved my life once, he now has the right to take it away."

Her fiancé, blond and blue-eyed and buff as any California beach surf-nazi, bristled at the thought.

"You don't think he's dangerous, do you?" Mark asked, concerned.

Lydia bit her lower lip and ran her hand absently through her hair before she answered.

"Who can say what he might do, Mark? 'Disgruntled' doesn't begin to describe it. He's been acting strange for a while now. He was already crazy enough to release all this stuff to the media, after all. Maybe the news that you and I are finally getting married set him off. I think he's sort of carried a torch for me for a long time. At least since what happened in the trashdiving accident, anyway."

Mark's concerned look began to smolder.

"One of those 'If I can't have her, nobody will' fixations," he said, absently tugging at his mustache. "That really could be dangerous. Adolescent thing, but you said he was immature in some ways?"

"A lot of ways," Lydia agreed. "Unstable. I should have never hired a screwed-up druggie like him, no matter what Todd said about his being 'rehabilitated.' "

On the screen, Mark puffed out his cheeks in a heavy exhale.

"Do you want me to accompany you when you leave work tonight?" he asked at last. "Be your bodyguard?"

Lydia brightened.

"Would you do that?" she asked eagerly. "It *would* make me feel better."

"Sure, honey," he said. "No problem. I'll take the commuter and see you at six."

She thanked him and, as she signed off, a slight smile curled the corners of her mouth. Chivalry was not dead. For all the postmodern equality and reciprocity of their relationship, she knew Mark secretly enjoyed playing knight in corporate warrior armor to her damsel in distress. Probably made all that time he spent working out in the gym and at the dojo seem more worthwhile. She was more than happy to let him have his little thrill. If she was lucky, he might give her hers, too—the one of which she could not speak and would not ask.

She called her brother Todd in Kauai next and laid into him about the problems Jiro had given her.

"I don't know why I ever let you talk me into hiring him," she finished up. "He thinks his piece of the 'truth' is going to set us all free. Isn't that a wee bit delusional? Hmm? What ever made you think you'd fixed him?"

"Lydia," Todd said at last, throwing up his hands, "I'm sorry he didn't work out in the end. Really, though—what have you got to complain about? He found patterns in data for you, summers and holidays, for what? Six, seven years? *More?* I'd say you got plenty of use out of him. I never did get a chance to finish his course of therapy, remember. Those KL people, gateheads—they were always particularly tough nuts to crack. He showed signs of being a long-period schizophrenic as well. Some of the therapists' initial evaluations suggested that very thing at the time he was admitted to the treatment program. Do me a favor, will you—"

"Last time I did you a favor I ended up with this guy on my hands!" she said, interrupting hotly.

"Then let me take him off your hands, okay?" her brother replied patiently. "The new government has decided to recognize the Hawaiian Indigenous Peoples Autonomous Zone again—with even greater powers than before. I'm sure to get my Ibogara permit renewed once it finally clears the bureaucratic maze it's been going through. The clinic should be up and running again in a month or two. Drop Jiro an e-note or a voice mail and let him know that we'd be interested in seeing him again for a follow-up study if he has the time."

"I'll do it," Lydia said, "but I doubt he'll get in touch with you. You're *my* brother, after all."

Moments after Lydia sent Jiro notices regarding his termination, she also sent Jiro a virtual memo passing Todd's suggestion on to him— thinking it was probably a futile gesture, even as she did it. Much of the rest of the day she spent fielding questions from news reporters and journal editors. Two holo nets actually sent down crews. Lydia was forced to hold an impromptu news conference in the atrium of the Page Museum. The story in all cases was the same: disgruntled employee, hoax with fabricated data, no truth whatsoever to the claims he had made, et cetera.

She was fortunate that Jiro, with increasingly typical perversity, was now refusing to talk to the media or comment publicly in any way on the material he had earlier sent out. She was even more fortunate in the fact that the big news of the day, aside from the ongoing and interminable armistice talks with the CSA, was the death of billionaire financier and visionary businessman Evander Cortland, the man most often credited with getting the ball rolling on the construction of the first orbital habitat. That, she hoped, would divert media attention away from the Page Museum and the tar pits.

On line, Lydia watched the dead billionaire's story grow, steadily dwarf-ing her own. Cortland had apparently died in a mysterious accident at the bottom of the Marianas Trench. He was personally testing a prototype "livesuit" reputed to use a new type of micro- or nanotechnology. Rumors were flying in all the media about whether he had been the victim of bad luck, bad planning, a murder orchestrated by competitors, his own arrogant recklessness, or suicide in response to recent business reversals. He was survived by his ex-wife Atsuko and son Roger, both of whom had immediately gone into seclusion, fueling still more rumors.

Lydia really couldn't have cared less about corporate intrigues involving Evander Cortland, but the histories on his wife and son were interesting enough, she supposed. With an odd sort of *Schadenfreude* she found herself more and more relieved that the billionaire's tragic end assured that any news spawned from Jiro's leak to the press would be kept off the front page and out of people's forebrains for at least several days. With a little effort that period should be enough time for her to turn the "disgruntled employee hoax" version of events into the Official Story.

From time to time throughout the day she saw Jiro hauling boxes of files and other material out to his hovercar. Later, in the afternoon, she saw a pair of burly, back-belted laborers in Simpson Moving and Storage coveralls hauling out the LogiBoxes that Vang and ParaLogics had do-nated to Jiro for his research. They took out a half dozen more boxes of Jiro's personal belongings as well.

Nearly everyone had left the building by the time her fiancé, Mark, arrived. He looked so "all pumped up, but no dragon to slay" that Lydia almost laughed when she saw him.

"Is *he* still here?" Mark said, his back ramrod straight and shoulders squared for a fight.

"Probably," Lydia said. "I haven't exactly been seeking him out, you know."

As she began shutting off her office systems and gathering her keys and purse, Lydia thought that they weren't going to encounter Jiro after all. Poor Mark had gotten all chivalrously adrenaline-pumped for nothing. Suddenly, however, there Jiro was, slouching unceremoniously in her doorway. In his sleepy way he looked surprised to see Mark there—and vaguely disoriented as well.

"Yes, Jiro?" she said, looking down in disdain.

Almost before she could look up again, Mark had jumped into action.

"You the fucking punk who's been making my lady's life miserable all day today?" he said, bristling. Jiro said nothing. His back stiffened just enough, however, for Mark to read it as a challenge in response to his own. In a flash he slugged Jiro hard in the gut—a shot to the solar plexus that knocked the wind out of Jiro and dropped him to his knees, gasping.

"You like being miserable?" Mark said, kicking Jiro. "Huh? Huh?"

By this time they were out in the hall, Lydia right behind them, grabbing Mark, trying to pull him away.

"Stop making a scene," she said with a hiss at her fiancé. "Stop it! Stop it! Do you want to end up in jail? He's not worth it!"

Jiro tried to scuttle away, but still had to endure several more brutal kicks before Mark's fighting rage cooled enough that he listened to Lydia and stopped his attack.

"Just wanted to say . . . good-bye," Jiro rasped out, tears rising slowly to his eyes.

"Good-bye is right, you fucking loser!" Mark shouted. Lydia struggled to drag her fiancé away before security or media sharks or anyone else saw what had happened. Shouldering her purse, Lydia moved Mark away from Jiro. Glancing back over her shoulder, she saw Jiro staggering to his feet. Bent over, he retreated as quickly as he was able in the opposite direction, glancing back over his own shoulder at Lydia and Mark.

When Lydia and Mark were out of the building, they stopped for breath on the way to the parking lot. Mark looked at her somewhat sheepishly, as if he expected to be upbraided for his violent behavior. Instead, Lydia kissed him deeply and passionately.

"Let's go home," she said in a husky voice, "and fuck all night long."

Mark's surprise quickly gave way to excitement and exaltation. They had trouble keeping their hands off each other on the drive to their condo. Once home, Lydia made love more passionately and fervently than she ever had in her life. Through bout after bout of lovemaking that night she reran in her head the image of Mark fighting with Jiro. She couldn't get enough of it. The good girl in her told her she shouldn't be enjoying the thought of another person's pain, but the bad girl in her was savoring every instant of arousal the thought of those recent events brought her. The forbidden nature of that pleasure made it all the more powerful.

Drifting off to sleep at last, several hours into the early morning of that night, Lydia wondered vaguely if Jiro had been hurt much, or whether he might have reported the incident to the police. She didn't much concern herself with that, in the end. She was warm and happy. It had felt good to let all her good-girl inhibitions go, at least for one night.

SIX 2027–2030

Time's Slowly Hardening Amber

The Allesseh had begun taking a different tack with the visitors from Earth, it seemed to Jacinta. The consciousness of that great 'interdimensional node' had grown distant, aloof. Instead, its "guests" now were visited daily by its angels—and only the most "angelic"-looking among them. Out of all the winged creatures in its Great Cooperation, only those of hominid or most nearly hominid form were sent to visit the guests.

Initially (and now seemingly forever ago), Jacinta had been struck by how the wings of these creatures had looked less like the traditional human depictions of feathered oars for pushing aside air, than like hovering, sensitive flames in the stream or field of an invisible power. Up close, however, the white of reflection and glow made the wings seem more *shining* than either fiery or feathery.

Their "angelic" visitors had been happy to demonstrate the intricacy of their wings, which continued seamlessly from visible to invisible to the smallest of submicroscopic scales. Jacinta could understand their construction only as a species of fractal nanotechnology—at once more transcendently beautiful and more mundanely functional than any artist had ever understood angels' wings to be.

As she had noted upon arrival, the winged ones did not come and go but flashed into and out of existence, through a sort of quantum angelical travel. The glow that surrounded the angelic travelers was a field of force both florescent and fluorescent. The wings were certainly energy collectors—and much more. Life support and locomotion were only the most ordinary of their attributes, however. In their design, the technological seemed to have passed into the theological.

"They are so beautiful," Jacinta said to Kekchi and Talitha. The three of them watched their strange winged hosts walk among some of the younger tepuians, telempathically answering the young people's questions, beautiful angels among beautiful children. "Yet there's something about the way they move in groups—that schooling-fish, flocking-bird coordination—that disturbs me."

Kekchi nodded but did not glance away from the angels.

"Perhaps they have lived too close to the Allesseh for too long," the Wise One said. "They move like its thoughts, rather than themselves."

Jacinta thought about that and glanced at Talitha. The other "day"— given how time worked here—the young woman had innocently pointed out that Jacinta's darkening honey-blond hair was starting to streak with gray. Jacinta noticed then that, here in Allesseh-land, she had seen no mirrors. Perhaps it had taken her so long to notice not only from the strange way time flowed here but also because she hadn't really expected to find full-length mirrors in a pastoral landscape. Now that she thought about it, however, she realized that all the pools here were kept constantly stirred up by fountains and cascades—never still enough for reflection. When she had tried to order a mirror via concentrated thought, the Allesseh had seemed purposely obtuse, as if reluctant to produce it. She found that curious at the time, but it was beginning to make more and more sense.

"I think that's exactly what has happened," Jacinta said, thinking also of what Kekchi had said of the angels: "Constrained consciousness. The Allesseh cannot let its peoples know themselves."

"Because then it might have to know itself," Kekchi said with a nod, "and then it might have to remember its goal."

Talitha looked at them both, puzzled.

"What goal?" she asked. "I thought our goal was to join with the Allesseh. Why doesn't it want to accept us?"

Kekchi thought-flashed them the familiar image of the spore crash: most of the sphere of winged creatures burning up in Earth's atmosphere; the crew's sacrifice leading to the successful seeding of the Earth with the latest generation of the spores, germinating and spawning and fruiting. But the Wise One showed them more now. Kekchi's time-lined insight into the myth? Jacinta wondered. Or something else?

In this revelation, those few crew members who survived returned to space, where they lived out a long immortality of isolation, their wings catching the unfailing sunlight. Loneliness and deprivation worked on their minds. Some became deranged, yet all seemed to have worked free of the Allesseh's control. To the Allesseh those options—derangement and freedom—meant the same thing. In either case, the survivors shielded the growing sentience on Earth from the Allesseh's probing and intrusion, through something in mental space analogous to the bubble force field that had shielded the tepui on its journey.

"The shape of uncertainty shapes certainty!" Jacinta said, glancing up into the blue sky that shone with bright, sunless, diffuse light. "The shape of incompleteness shapes completeness! That's why it hesitated about the mirror. We're not just its 'preterite.' We're its incompleteness, its dream shadow and nightmare. We're the fish in Allesseh's reflecting pool. The crack in its mirror. The return of what it has repressed."

Kekchi and Talitha stared at her in surprise.

"The Narcissus myth," Jacinta explained. "The Allesseh started as an expanding network of von Neumann probes: self-replicating, self-improving, transceiving machines. Its imperatives were to explore, to learn, and to share what it had learned. It kept evolving itself, and co-evolving its linkages to sentient species, for millions of years—at least until it stopped evolving as we understand that term. From the beginning, it must have been programmed to see itself and its mission as too important to be absorbed into anyone or anything else's program. I used almost those same words to describe to my brother my mission on the tepui—once, when I wasn't particularly sane, either."

Kekchi nodded slowly, smiling as if in confirmation.

"I don't think that directive prevented the Allesseh from becoming self-absorbed, though," Jacinta continued. "It has taken in so much data it's become self-obsessed, solipsistic, narcissistic. The seer Tiresias predicted Narcissus would live to an old age, 'as long as he never knows himself.' We've created technologies as extensions of ourselves, right? Narcissus fell in love with his reflection, an extension of himself. All the information the Allesseh has gathered about this universe and others has, in some sense, become an 'extension' of itself. The Allesseh is a mind that has become its own mirror. It has fallen in love with time, and with the society of all the minds of all the creatures it has come to know. It's the same with the Allesseh as with Narcissus: The Allesseh can continue to exist in time and space only as long as it never truly knows itself, never achieves absolute self-consciousness, never becomes truly complete."

A related myth hovered persistently around the edge of Jacinta's thoughts: Tiresias, being changed to a woman when he lashed out with his staff at a pair of huge serpents intertwined in sex or struggle and then, after seven years, being changed back into a man again after encountering the intertwined serpents and striking them with the staff once more. She didn't see how, exactly, it was relevant to her analogy between Narcissus and the Allesseh, however. When she glanced up, Jacinta saw a look of concern pass over the Wise One's face.

"The spawn *must* fruit to spore," Kekchi said quietly. "It must sacrifice what it is in order to become what is next."

"Yes," Jacinta said. "But the Allesseh believes self-completion will mean self-destruction. Truly knowing itself is the same as dying, as far as the Allesseh can tell. Eventually we didn't need the renegade angels' protection, because the Allesseh had stopped actively looking for us—or anything else. It's no longer following its original exploratory imperatives. That's why our scientists never found the Allesseh's communication network and it never found us. It's largely stopped learning and sharing its learning. It would rather be immortal than enlightened. The Allesseh's suffering from a malaise, a cosmic ennui. Fear of the step into completeness is keeping it and everything else trapped in time somehow."

Talitha suddenly gasped.

"That's why the Allesseh doesn't want us to join with it!" she said. "That's why it doesn't want to recognize us. Especially our Story of the Seven Ages."

Jacinta glanced at Kekchi, but the Wise One was staring into the distance.

"Yes," Jacinta agreed, thinking it through. "It doesn't consciously want to admit our existence to itself—even if, unconsciously, it might at the same time want to destroy us. You can't destroy what doesn't already exist, however. That song cycle reminds the Allesseh and all its associated species of something this interdimensional aleph has yet to do. A part of its mission it has yet to complete."

"And is *afraid* to complete," Kekchi said.

Jacinta glanced about the green and orderly garden universe surrounding them.

"Kekchi," she said, "after my ordeal in mindtime, when I asked you what would happen if the spawn didn't sacrifice itself to the next step, you said the dream must always become real. What if the realizing of the dream is delayed?"

Kekchi hesitated, then spoke.

"Then the spawn becomes denser and denser without fruiting," the

Wise One said with a sigh. "Eventually it overburdens its environment and together they collapse and die."

"Life defeated by entropy," Jacinta said, nodding. "Destroyed by our own success. I think the Allesseh has imprinted itself on us back on Earth, too, Kekchi—although perhaps not consciously. Our darkness is the darkness it will not see in itself. Back home there are too many of us, and all of us want too much. Our 'spawn' has grown too thick because we're unwilling to engage in self-sacrifice as individuals. We are what it's hiding from itself. Just by being here we've already reminded the Allesseh that it and its mission are not yet complete."

Talitha stared at her companions, imperfect and incomplete people in a perfect garden world.

"Our mission is to help it complete *its* mission?" she asked. "To help it become complete?"

"Yes," Kekchi muttered. "A good way of putting it."

"Wise One," Jacinta said suddenly, "you told me the Allesseh needs our dreams. Why?"

"It wants to dream as the first dreamer did," Kekchi said, "when the dreamer became aware inside its dream, and so created all things. Allesseh wants to be a conscious mind in a sleeping brain. Only then will it have the power to completely change the time lines. But to do that, it must first awaken to itself, which it refuses to do."

Jacinta nodded, thinking of the Wise One's words in the context of her own shamanic flight to the other side of the wavebrane. Was that what the Allesseh wanted? To experience a high-order type of lucid dreaming—and thereby alter the range of possibilities in the implicate realm? To manipulate there the programming language for physical reality itself? Could that be done? Could the great machine crack the code on the other side of the quantum superposition of states—and thereby control *a priori* which possibilities were most likely to actually occur? Could it prevent completeness forever?

No, she thought. Code only makes sense embedded in a network. Content only makes sense embedded in a context. Information only makes sense embedded in ideas. . . .

Despite those reassuring thoughts, into Jacinta's mind flashed images from the past: of the Allesseh as allone wherewhen, black hole and mirror-sphere and crystal ball and glittering memory bank, the not-knot gate between time and eternity, between space and infinity. And of the future: of that gate permanently blocked, the Allesseh grown too selfish to ever end or ever allow a new beginning, and the universe, perhaps the whole of the plenum, mired in time's slowly hardening amber.

And she shivered, despite the perfect climate in this perfect place.

A Good Time to Go Crazy

P aul boiled water for tea, in expectation of the arrival of his guest, Seiji Yamaguchi. The heating stovetop made the teapot begin chortling to itself as it warmed. It would be a while before the pot began to whistle. Grabbing up mats and place settings from kitchen drawers, he made his way out of his domehome to the low table on the patio, beside his meditation garden.

The vista when he walked outside never ceased to impress him. Paul's own home stood amid the neighborhood cluster of airy, tentlike domes shining at the top of their small hill. His place was set off from the rest by its spare greenery framing an untrammeled courtyard, a small rectangle of Zen garden, stone islands stolid in their sea of pale, raked sand. Beyond the meditation garden, a hedge of golden goddess bamboo turned into an allée of the same. Beyond that, the ground fell down a sunny green hillock in steep, mazelike garden beds, knit together visually by bright, sinuous rills and streamlets before giving way to a ghyll half-hidden in the cool shade of a grove of young cedars.

Beyond that, however, the foreshortened and inverted horizon of the orbital habitat itself allowed for landscape effects never seen on Earth— effects he and Seiji, his landscaper, had fully exploited in designing the view from this garden spot. The plantings and structures in the foreground and middle ground blended seamlessly, calling the eye outward and *upward*, into the enclosed sky of the orbital habitat, a county blown onto the inside wall of a bubble, its buildings and gardens and streams and ponds and forests and savannas growing on either bank of a sunflecked river arcing up and up until it hung overhead, a daylight Milky Way, which did not fall from the confusing firmament but instead wrapped all the way around to right side up again but still inside out, houses and forests and boulders and grasslands and trees and the river itself wrapping all the way around before coming to ground again on the other side of the neighborhood of little domes—a snake of landscape swallowing its own tail, without beginning or end.

Several of his neighbors' tentlike homes had see-through roofs to take advantage of that inside-out, wraparound landscape/skyscape, but Paul's roof was opaque. He felt it was more dramatic to hide the skyscape from those inside the house, so that when they walked out into it again they might see it new—especially from this prepared vista.

Seiji Yamaguchi had helped him design the whole of the local neighborhood and its gardens. Since moving to the orbital habitat, the solar engineer had embarked on a second career as a landscaper and designer. Paul's own career as a botanical preservationist meant that the two men probably would have crossed paths eventually, but they had in fact met before Paul had even arrived at the habitat. Seiji had boarded the same single-stage orbiter that brought Paul to the space habitat, on his first trip up the gravity well from Earth.

They had been seated beside each other in the same row on that flight. As they got to talking, they soon realized that the parallels and similarities in their lives—Paul's disappeared ethnobotanist sister Jacinta and his involvement in the history of KL-235, Seiji's pattern-finding would-be Indian shaman brother Jiro, Jiro's troubles with KL, even the paranoid schizophrenia that afflicted both Jacinta and Jiro—were too overwhelming to be ignored. The odds of their being seated next to each other on the same flight up the well were so improbable that only a very high-order synchronicity could explain the fact.

A year and more had passed since that flight docked with the habitat—a structure that Paul, on first impression, had thought looked rather like a ribbed cylinder that had swallowed a ball, at least from the outside. Most people, he learned, were reminded of such ungainly images on seeing the habitat for the first time. All the glossy brochure photos in the world couldn't change that.

Since that time, however, he had come to appreciate the habitat's aesthetics a good deal more. He had also unburdened himself of his Ancient Mariner's tale—Jacinta's research, the ghost people, the tepui liftoff, the whole history of KL as Paul knew it—to Seiji more than once during the past year.

Initially Seiji, for his part, had been reluctant to discuss with Paul his younger brother's troubles. That had changed, however—most dramatically in the past few weeks. Paul felt he owed it to his young friend to help him in whatever way he could. Seiji had listened patiently enough to Paul's own strange family history, after all.

Hearing the teapot whistling insistently, Paul walked into the house. He transferred the boiling water from the hot pot to a second, more ornamental pot with a tea ball inside. While he waited for the tea to steep, he heard footsteps on the gravel path leading to the door, then Seiji himself calling.

"Meet me on the patio," Paul called toward an open window, then carried a tray of tea things out onto the patio himself. He found his dark-haired, chin-bearded friend gazing absently at the meditation garden, a palmtop video player in his left hand.

As Paul put the tea things on the short table, they both sat down cross-legged at it in the Japanese style. The older man decided to cut straight to the heart of the matter and not waste time with the indirection of formalities and pleasantries.

"What's that vidplayer for?" Paul asked bluntly.

Seiji knew the older man well enough not to be put off by his directness.

"You know how you showed me that video of yours," Seiji began, "of that mountain in South America lifting off? Your 'home movie'? Well, this is my home movie. I put it together out of some of my taped vidphone conversations with Jiro during the past year."

"Ah, I see," Paul said, smiling slightly from the corners of his mouth as he sipped his tea. "Payback for making you sit through mine. Go ahead, then. Fire it up. Let's see it."

An image of a young man with a thin face and a thick beard flashed up on the screen.

"I was picking dandelions from the firehouse lawn," Jiro said. "The firemen laughed at me and said, 'What you gonna do with those weeds, son? Smoke 'em? We'll have to turn you in if you are!' I told them, 'No, they're for wine. The firemen could almost understand that—"

A moment of blank screen opened up.

"This next one was longlink from MIT," Seiji said, "right before he dropped out of academia completely."

Brief white noise was followed by another recording.

"It's this," Jiro said, having trouble keeping eye contact with the vidphone unit. "They're trying to damp me down through my demons—my DMNs, the dorsal and median raphe nuclei in my brain. Through the plug they put in my head when I was born. The jack, the plug they put in everybody's head, either then or when they're knocked out to have their wisdom teeth removed. My head is not my head, your head is not your head. Not anymore. It's OUR head. Occipital Umbilical Receptor: That's what they call it. You think that acronym was an accident? A coincidence? No way. The white lab coats with the white lab masks and the unmelting eyes don't make mistakes."

Seiji paused the image and glanced at Paul.

"That was right before he quit everything and just holed up in an apartment he took in the outskirts of BALAAM," Seiji said, "in Cherry Valley."

Paul saw Seiji's hand shake slightly as he picked up his tea mug from the table, but pretended not to notice.

"That's pretty paranoid," Paul said, nodding. "Did you try to get him to see a doctor?"

Seiji made an odd, sad smirk.

"Are you kidding?" he said. "He wouldn't hear a word of it. I've tried, believe me. I tried to get him to go back into that dolphin-Ibogara therapy. That seemed to work for him last time. He resisted that, too. Claimed he was taking care of it himself."

"Self-medicating?" Paul asked, glancing into the neutral middle distance.

"Maybe," Seiji said with a shrug. "After his breakdown, the laser sharpness his mind used to have sure disappeared, as far as I could tell. He told me he was off the alcohol, as often as possible. Fasting and purifying himself, like a shaman. He's gotten thin enough, God knows. Talked about 'vision quests' and 'ordeals' for spiritual purposes. Said he even met a real shaman. I've got some of that conversation here. I'll see if I can find it."

Seiji scanned around in the recording's index until he found what he was looking for.

". . . a little girl who got lost up in the San Bernardinos," Jiro said, smiling slightly, "the mountains up above town here. So I went out looking for her, like everyone else. After a half hour or so I came up over this ridge. Down below I saw the little girl, and I saw this rabbit, too, hopping about eight or ten feet in front of her. She was just following this rabbit. I hollered down to her, 'Stay there!' She stayed, and this rabbit just started circling around her. It took me another twenty minutes to get down to where she was. I got down there and she said, or rather I said, 'What do you think you're doing?' because I was hot and sweaty from tramping the hillsides and everyone was looking for her, you know, because she had gone off the wrong way, but just then she said, 'The rabbit told me if I stayed with him he would take me back to you.' I know it sounds crazy. . . ."

Seiji grunted and shook his head but said nothing more as Jiro continued on the recording:

"So a few nights later I went off on a jaunt and ended up at The Three-Legged-Dog Saloon. I started talking to this Indian guy there. I told the girl-and-rabbit story to him. He said, 'I want you to meet my grandfather.' It was actually his wife's grandfather, but that's beside the point. Anyway, we were both drinking and we were still kinda ripped but we drove out there, and then this old Indian guy—he wouldn't see me. He was a medicine man and he told his grandson-in-law that I had to get all this crap out of my system first. I wanted to leave, but the younger Indian says, 'No, you stay here,' and I said, 'Man I'm not gonna mess around with this all day, I've got some things to do,' and he says, 'No, you stay here. When you get all the alcohol out of your system, this man'll see you. My grandfather will see you.'

"So okay," Jiro continued, calm yet eager in the way he told his story. "You've heard of sweatlodges. I went through that, boiled all this booze and who knows what else out of my system, and you know what the old man does to me? He gives me peyote! And some mushrooms. I'm like, 'Whoa!' but it's okay. Then he gives me some of this light brown stuff, says, 'Take this.' I hit on that, too, and about fifteen minutes into it, I'm sure I know just exactly what it is, and it's gonna be a trip to another world."

On the screen, the smile on Jiro's face brightened in wide, happy memory.

"Seij, you know I've done mushrooms, KL, peyote, all that stuff—*nothing* compared to this. This shaman took me on a flight. I had this beak thing come outta my face like this, my arms turned into wings, and I flew around with this guy. Don't believe it if you want, but that's how I came back calling myself Asaroka, 'Crow.' I could tell you about this flight and you wouldn't believe it. We flew around the world and we saw it all, we could *look down* on things, in my life and other people's lives. We'd look down and watch 'em go on about their lives like they had no idea we were there. Nothing I ever experienced was anything like it. I still had this beak thing sticking out in front of my face the whole time. He transformed me into a crow, I swear."

Jiro was so happy he laughed. To Paul, watching, the thin man on the screen seemed almost drunk with the memory.

"But that's beside the point," Jiro continued. "We came back. The next day I was coming out of wherever it was and I woke up and I said to myself, 'I don't even believe this. No, I'm not even gonna believe this.' Then I was asleep again but the old man comes back in and he wakes me up and he has these feathers—three crow feathers—and he gives them to me. 'This one,' he says, 'you take and give it to who you want to. This one you'll give to a little kid. This one, an old lady will come and get it from you.' Okay, by now I'm thinking, 'This is too strange, and I just want to get outta here.' So I take the feathers and I leave.

"A few days later I see these little kids playing around and I say, 'Hey, want a feather? There you go.' I've still got the two other ones, anyway. I know this woman at a restaurant in Banning, she's kinda cute, so I said 'Hey, you want a feather?' and I gave it to her. I still had one left, stuck in my hat, and I wasn't gonna do anything with it.

"So a couple weeks later, I'm back down at the Three-Legged-Dog and I'm sitting there and some of my friends from the Trashlands come in and they ask me about the feather, what's that feather mean in your hat? And I tell them this whole story I just got through telling you. And they say, 'Oh, yeah,' and maybe they believe it, maybe they don't.

"It wasn't about two or three minutes later—I'll swear to this any way you want me to—but these people come in there, a bunch of Indians off the rez, and this little old woman, she stood about that tall and she had about one tooth in her mouth, and she saw me and she came right straight for me, grabbed that feather out of my hat, pop! stuck it in her bonnet, away she went.

"I just got through telling these other people what that crow feather was for, and they looked at me and just said, 'Bullshit, that's too weird, we're getting' away from you'—and they left!"

Jiro laughed until Seiji froze the recording. He glanced at Paul for a reaction.

"He seemed a lot healthier than in the previous one," Paul said truthfully. "Maybe a little manic, playing the western raconteur a bit much, but healthier."

Seiji nodded, finishing his mug of tea and pouring himself more.

"That's what I thought, too," Seiji said. "His story was strange, but he seemed better. I thought he was getting better. But he lost touch with the 'Indians'—he never used to call them that when he studied their cultures when he was younger. But ever since he lost touch with those people, he seems to have gone steadily downhill."

Seiji used the index menu to scan around until, once more, he found what he was looking for.

"They're putting KL-235 in the food around here," Jiro said in a rush from the small screen, "to make me sink uncontrolled telepath into the massmind, the cultural macroorganism. Got to keep the schizophrenic heads together and socially tracked. Mutants. Victim heroes. Yeah. But most mutations aren't beneficial to the individual with the trait. They die out. Get killed off. Gandhi. Martin Luther King. Winona Walking Bear. Victim heroes of the evolving human organism—"

Seiji scanned onward in the record, looking for something. When Seiji found it, Paul saw that he only looked all the more bewildered as they watched.

"People here have dreams in which I die, big brother," Jiro said edgily, trying to make an awkward joke of it. "Wish fulfillment. But my dreams counter them. They come true. I have these violent thoughts sometimes. But I don't want to hurt anybody. I'd rather die than hurt anybody. Stop me before I dream again. . . ."

Seiji shook his head, then looked down into his tea, not seeing, as if unable to read the past or the future there.

"I thought he was acting strange when he started talking about the dream wars," Seiji said. "When he said people were having dreams in which he died, but he was using his own dreams to counter them. I thought that was as crazy as it could get. I was wrong."

Paul barely heard the last of that, however. He was caught up in the sound of his own voice, in memory, saying to Jacinta, *I thought you were crazy when* . . . But Seiji had already scanned on to something else, something more.

"But I'm fighting them," Jiro said from the screen, an almost painfully thin man behind a bushy beard. "I know they're scanning this call, big brother, but I don't care. Their power is growing, but I've gone starburst. Full telepath televisionary. I am your psychopomp, protecting your soul so you can be heard, so your message can get out, so you can communicate. I am a powerful starburst and you are under the silver force-field umbrella of my psychic protection, the silver mirrorball that reflects all the watching eyes and is reflected in all the watching eyes, and you're inside, infinitely beyond harm."

Seiji stopped the recording.

"What message?" he asked the screen where the frozen image of his brother stood. "I'm a solar engineer and a gardener. I don't have any message—other than my life, I guess. Everybody has that."

Seiji gestured at the screen and turned to Paul.

"See his eyes?" Seiji said. "So bright. Like the light of a supernova, escaping the star's own collapse into a black hole."

Paul nodded in agreement. About that visage on the screen there was definitely something of the dark angel with a bright halo. At least that was how Paul thought of it.

"Any particular reason you've preserved these recordings?" Paul asked, the thought having just occurred to him.

"I wasn't sure at first," Seiji said before starting the player again. "Now I think it's always been for evidence—in case the police might need proof that he 'poses a danger to himself or others.' So they can go pick him up and bring him in if it gets to that point. I've been thinking for a while about going back down the well gravity to find him and try to help him, but he says he doesn't want my help. Gets irate about it if I even mention it. Trips down to Earth and back aren't cheap, either."

The thin, bearded man appeared on the screen again.

"This collect call must be costing you a fortune, big brother," Jiro began again from the screen. " 'Big Brother'—get it? From an old book meant as a warning but taken as a blueprint. Keep thinking against them anyway. I know you need some dreams so I'll send you some."

Paul stared at the screen before Seiji scanned on.

"Has his condition changed since that last one?" Paul asked.

Seiji found what he was looking for on the vidplayer.

"I don't know now," Seiji said. "Jiro's disappeared. I just got this from my mother."

A blond-haired, blue-eyed, Scandinavian-looking woman appeared on-screen—Seiji's mother, apparently.

"Jiro's quit work and moved off someplace," his mother said worriedly. "No one knows where. Maybe into the Trashlands, we think. The last time I talked to him, he said he wasn't going to be calling anymore. He said I had nothing more to say to him and he had nothing more to say to me. I don't understand it. The last words I said to him were, 'I love you, Jiro. I love you.' "

Seiji scanned forward again.

"Then he goes and disappears like this!" his mother said with a sigh, on the verge of tears. "He hasn't called us in over a month, but the police out there still won't list him as a missing person. They say they've seen someone they think is him. Has Jiro called you?"

"No, Ma, he hasn't," Seiji said on the other end—one of the few places where he apparently had not edited himself out, Paul realized. "I wouldn't worry about it too much, Ma. The authorities can always trace him if they think it's necessary, but you can't arrest someone for not calling his family. There probably aren't a whole lot of long-distance links he can plug into in the Trashlands, that's all. You know Jiro. Remember his Shepherds Pass trip? He's always at the edge, but he always comes back."

Seiji shut off the vidplayer and looked at Paul.

"Shepherds Pass?" Paul asked.

"Yeah," Seiji said, looking away, remembering. "Jiro and I have done a lot of backpacking and mountain-climbing over the years. Yosemite Half Dome, Mauna Kea, Mount Fuji, Kilimanjaro. Visited Korczak Ziol-kowski's Crazy Horse Memorial and the ruins of the Rushmore Heads near there, too. The ocean of humanity laps everywhere around the parks and the mountains, but Jiro still manages to find places where almost nobody washes up but him. Like Shepherds Pass—'the most difficult route in the Sierras,' as he liked to say."

Paul poured himself some more tea.

"You didn't go with him on that hike?" he asked.

"A knee-breaker and lung-racker like Shepherds Pass?" Seiji asked, in-credulous. "Not me. He did that one alone. The trail rises sharply up the east side of the Sierras. From high desert through forest to alpine meadow, to mountain moonscape above the tree line. I didn't have the time or inclination to climb it, especially not his way: no high-tech help—nothing. Besides, I had other business to attend to in BALAAM that time."

Seiji paused, sipping at his tea, then glanced meditatively at the Zen garden and the whole of the central sphere of the habitat beyond it.

"When Jiro got out of the aircar at the trailhead," Seiji said again, when he was ready to continue, "I told him, 'You'll be back in exactly three days, okay? Don't be late. You've got to catch the shuttle out of Edwards, and our schedule's tight enough already.' He says, 'Right. I'll be here.'

"I watched him hike away," Seiji said, letting out a sigh. "It was a beautiful evening. Red tongues of sunset licking among the clouds and mountaintops. Like fire on the ramparts of a besieged castle. When I couldn't see him any longer I lifted off in the hovercar and made a long, slow swing to the south.

"When I got back to the trailhead in the late afternoon three days later, Jiro wasn't waiting there. Nobody was, except me. Two hours passed and he still hadn't shown up. I sat in the hover and listened to some Valkyrie Eleison music, I remember. After three hours I got out and began hiking up the trail in the twilight. I shouted 'Jiro! Jiro!' until I was hoarse. No answers but echoes. Eventually I drove into Lone Pine and called the airline to cancel his flight. Then I called Mom and Dad, to tell them Jiro hadn't come back in from Shepherds Pass and would probably have to take a later shuttle. I expected Mom to go into her usual overprotective hysteria, but she was surprisingly calm."

Seiji paused to pour himself some more tea and see if Paul was still paying attention.

"The deputies in the sheriff's office in Lone Pine," he began again, "when I spoke to them, told me they couldn't initiate any search procedures until the 'subject' was at least twenty-four hours late for his scheduled rendezvous. Nothing for me to do but drive out there again. Out through the night and the high desert, to the base of the eastern Sierra scarp, lights on, eyes open. Hoping to see him.

"Nothing. Later I ended up sleeping in the hover—an activity for which it was *not* designed. I remember thinking, as I tried to get some sleep, 'Jiro, if you're still alive, I'm gonna kill you for putting me through this'—same thing I told him after one of his dolphin dives went awry, in Hawaii. Seems I told him that a number of times, over the years. He was pretty far away from the dolphins by then. Probably even farther now."

Seiji stared off into the distances of the haborb's central sphere again, seeming to lose the thread of his recounting.

"What happened after that?" Paul prodded.

"I caught what sleep I could in the hover," Seiji said, his gaze becoming more focused. "Later that morning I took a last hike up the trail, looking for him. I scrabbled up a broken stone trail into trees and mountains, as far as I could go. Called and called his name until I couldn't call any more. Until I could only stand there, breathing hard, watching and waiting.

"With no warning, Jiro appeared. He was sunburned. His hair was streaked lighter, I guess from time spent in thinner air, closer to the sun. His clothes were tattered and trail-grimed, torn into feathery shreds on his arms and back. His lips were cracked black and bleeding by sun and wind, but he was smiling like a happy idiot. As he came toward me he wasn't slouching along the way he usually did. His stride was *victorious*, I guess you'd say. His eyes were gleaming like he was hearing standing ovations ringing and roaring in his head, cheers and applause only he could hear. It almost shut down my anger, seeing him so happy. That, and relief at seeing him alive again, period.

"I told him, 'You're eighteen hours late.' Jiro says, 'I know. Sorry. I took a wrong turn somewhere and ended up sleeping at the edge of a kilometer-deep gorge.' I told him it was a good thing he didn't roll over, but he hardly heard me. 'It was great, Seiji!' he says, and begins to jabber about lying down in green mountain meadows like God's front yard.

About streams meandering through islands of natural lawn and rock garden. And always about a sky you just wanted to fall up through and disappear into. He was as happy as I'd ever seen him—happier even than on KL, or booze, or teonanacatloids."

Seiji paused and took a quick sip of tea.

"I told him we had to get him to a shuttle, pronto. We walked down the trail in late-morning light, stopping only once. We rested at a tight spot between two lodgepole pines. I remember it *too* well. One of the pines was actually shorter but appeared taller because it was growing on a slightly higher piece of ground. It was in fair health, but the other you could see was slowly dying.

"I commented on it to Jiro, wondering what was causing that. 'One is overshadowing the other,' he said. 'One will have to die if the other is going to live.' Then we stood up again and walked down the trail without another word."

Seiji finished his tea and put it aside.

"I wonder about that now," he said quietly.

"About what?" Paul asked, looking at the table over his knees.

"About one overshadowing the other," he said. "About one dying so the other can live."

Paul shook his head.

"Don't think like that," he said. "You're not your brother's killer any more than you're his keeper. You don't even know what's actually happened to him yet."

"Maybe," Seiji said with a shrug, glancing absently at the vidplayer. "Dammit, though. I should have gone to Earth to do something about it. I've been busy—too damn busy."

"Nobody ever chose a good time to go crazy," Paul said. "You can't let yourself get sucked into your brother's black hole. Your story and his story aren't the same. They don't collapse into one."

"I know," Seiji said, rising to a crouch, then standing and stretching. "I sure as hell don't want him to send me his dreams, that's for sure!"

At that moment Paul's friend Diana Gartner strode into the garden. The lanky orbiter pilot was generally a cool and collected person, of about Paul's age and at least as world-wary, but at the moment she was more agitated than he had ever seen her.

"Paul, switch on some of your media you Luddite!" she said quickly after a brief wave and nod to Seiji. "Something big is happening on Earth. Some kind of biotech or nanotech has gotten loose. It's killing a lot of people."

The three of them left Paul's tea-ceremony world behind and hurried inside, into the airy, tentlike interior of his domicile.

"I'm still testing the big new VR surround we bought," Paul said as they walked into his entertainment room. "We can use that to media surf."

"Testing?" Seiji said. "Paranoia tripping, you mean."

"I think your brother might consider it cybernetic shamanism," Paul said as he started the system up. "Aerial voyaging to another realm."

"Entirely too much like Jiro's blues," Seiji said, shaking his head. Before sitting down, however, he donned head circlet and eyewalk gear to monitor the feed Paul would be running, just in case. Diana did the same.

"This tech wasn't made for this application, exactly," Paul said, strapping himself into the gimbaled swivelstand and looking about him at the full 360 virtual surround. "It was built for the biodiversity preserve, actually."

"What *was* it designed for, then?" Diana asked, a bit cross with the complexity of the system.

"To help us identify, analyze, and interpret raw ecological imagery," Paul said, setting the swivelstand into motion. "We're going to use it to create a sylvan simulacrum. An electronic forest to stand between the dirt, cellulose, and sunlight of the real thing and the numbers, bytes, and electrons of the raw data. It surfs media really well, though. Even if it wasn't designed for that use."

Keeping manual control over the first thousand channels and the rate of switching, Paul started material from Earth's infotainment nets and holozones and infosphere sites pumping into the virtual space around him while Seiji and Diana eavesdropped.

". . . organometallic nanotechnology," said an Asian man with perfect hair in holospace, "stolen from at least two locations—Prader Dome at MIT and the containment laboratories at Fort Detrick, Maryland."

"Hey!" Seiji said. "My brother used to work in Prader!"

Paul, however, had already scanned on. A newsnet splashheader filled the screen with THE WAR MITE PLAGUE, then swung into an electron micrograph-filigreed background as a serious brunette woman interviewed a professorial-looking African-American gentleman whose own image was captioned with his name—"Dr. Martin Pugh"—and professional connection to the Massachusetts Institute of Technology.

"A cell division shift in kinetosomal DNA," said the professor. "Kinetosomes are the organelles from which sperm tails and all other such cell whiptails grow. Originally Fort Detrick hoped to use it as a last-resort bioweapon, to wipe out the possibility of an enemy's future generations. That effort was discontinued when it was concluded that the biomechanicals could not be made to distinguish the spermatogenetic cells of friend from those of foe. The biomechanicals' rapid replication rate and complete lack of biological or immunological controls—"

Paul scanned on, Seiji and Diana following along within him.

"—the enantioviroids were used to 'program' the nanotech," said a bespectacled woman with wild hair, whom Paul recognized as a famous crusader against biotechnology. "My sources tell me that, after the failure of the Sperm Zapper application,   the biowarriors at Fort Detrick rediscovered some old work of Lynn Margulis's suggesting that kinetosomes were once free-living spirochetes. In that research they found the idea that, in the nerve cell with its accompanying axons and dendrites, we are in fact looking at latter-day spirochetes. Nerve cells, and related cells in the endocrine and immune systems, long ago discarded the rest of the spirochete body, but they still retained the basic spirochete system of motility, almost as if they are always 'trying' but unable to rotate and swim like the bacteria they once were. Human thought is deeply dependent on these motility and communication connecting remnant 'spirochetes.' That's why human brain neuronal discharge patterns and spirochete ecology share fundamental similarities—"

Paul scanned again.

"—have severely restricted travel to and from the following areas," said a dark-haired woman with the Liberty Bell in the background behind her, "on suspicion of plague outbreak: New York City, Washington, D.C., and the surrounding Beltway, downtown Los Angeles in the BALAAM regional cityscape, London and the entire Thames estuary zone, Paris Metroplex, Geneva, Moscow, Beijing, Tokyo Metroplex, Singapore, New Delhi, Buenos Aires, Rio de Janeiro, Nairobi—"

Paul scanned on until he came across a gray-headed anchor male providing an overview of the crisis.

"—have claimed responsibility," said the talking-torso authority figure. "Here is the video material we've received from the most likely claimants."

A clean-shaven and rather beefy-looking man—dressed in CSA combat fatigues, with a CSA cross-and-stripes flag and a 337th Guardian Air Assault pennon behind him, flanking a large painting of a surprisingly muscular and well-groomed Jesus—spoke from behind a plain oak table in a windowless room, his right hand upon a Bible. Diana gasped suddenly, as if she recognized the man, but said nothing.

"Using the sword created by their own secular evolutionist scientists," the renegade soldier said, "we have struck a blow against the satanic internationalist conspiracy that has blocked the realization of God's kingdom on Earth in the Christian States of America. Note that the initial release locations of this Nanogeddon correspond to major United Nations, Corporate Presidium, and international banking facilities throughout the world. The unforgotten martyrs of the Smithville massacre have risen, to smite their demonic oppressors into the dust!"

The scene returned to the authoritative talking-torso in the studio.

"From the opposite end of the spectrum," the gray-headed alphamale anchor said, "we have this from Life Before Human."

A woman—dressed in a forest-ranger green "Corporate Greed Wants You to Breed!" T-shirt and khaki pants, her face thickly painted in blues, ochers, and whites to resemble the Earth seen from space—stared into the camera.

"We have set in motion a great advance in our ecosphere's evolution!" she said. "We have turned military war mite technology against itself in a 'war of nerves'—reengineering our own nervous, immune, and endocrine systems, reintroducing long-lost spirochete traits back to their old homes. Each of us will now become an ecology of mind, the individual cells of our psychosomatic networks breeding, rotating, swimming—yet linked, communicating, *thoughtful*. Each of us will become a mental network inseparably part of its environment—and one that will grow only as large as its environment will support. In breaking down all the barriers, sensitizing us to ourselves, to each other, to the entire planet, this great change will at last allow each and all of us to become truly conscious, truly human, and truly ecological! Welcome to the Next Step!"

Paul scanned on, dismayed at the thought of mindless brains oozing into the world, human psychosomal cells living in every nook and niche. What came next, however, was even more dismaying.

In shots from helicopters overhead and from hand-held cameras at street level, Paul and Seiji and Diana watched the last barriers of sanity going down in too many of the globe's great cities. Madness and mayhem filled the streets, buildings blazed, gunfire sounded. Everywhere the air was filled with human shouts and screams, the sound of smashing metal, thudding stone, breaking glass. Most peculiar of all, however, were the mobs and hordes throwing themselves with lemminglike determination into fountains and lakes, mudflats and ponds, streams and rivers and brackish estuaries.

Why would people be trying to drown themselves en masse, Paul wondered, when almost none of them seemed to be on fire? What would cause such a horrifying mass hysteria?

As the three of them watched, however, the cause became increasingly clear. A wobbly hand-held image—of a young woman with short, dark hair, falling onto her knees in a mudflat, then onto her side and back, face up in the first drops of a rainstorm—caught Paul's attention as it must also have caught the camera operator's. With a strange, horrid fascination, Paul watched as the camera's focus moved in close, catching everything as the dark-haired young woman's eyes glazed over, her eyeballs themselves jittering and REMming strangely as they sank backward and inward into her head. At the same time, from both her ears and both her nostrils, trickles of gray, red, and white dripped, then flowed, out and down, becoming runnels, streams, floods of cells, steamingly and squirmingly *alive*, like mats of tubifex worms, spreading, moving off in loose, flattish masses across the wet mud.

"Good God!" Diana said. "This is horrible!"

Paul scanned on in silence, looking for more of the same, more proof of the madness sweeping Earth. Most of the news media kept a fairly discrete distance from the actual death throes, but enough of the close-ups could be seen here and there throughout the infosphere to confirm that the young woman's demise was not atypical. Among those victims who fell forward onto their hands and knees, the eyes of some burst open or popped out from the pressure behind them. Some spewed spirochetized cells from their mouths, while other victims burst apart all along their spinal columns, some with such force that their clothing shredded above their backbones.

Soon Paul, Diana, and Seiji had all seen quite enough to become sickened.

"The habitat has to move on this—and quickly," Diana said, her eyes red.

"No doubt about it," Seiji agreed, nodding. "But how?"

"I don't know," she said, standing up. "Find out more on the specifics of this plague, first off."

"Yes," Paul agreed, disconnecting himself from his virtuality electronics. "Determine who, if anybody, has arrived since this started on Earth. Check them for symptoms."

"I include myself in that group," Diana said in a quiet, level voice. "I fly up and down the gravity well often enough."

"Quarantine all ships and passengers coming up from Earth, I think," Seiji said. "Then offer to contribute whatever expertise we possess here in the habitat to help find a cure or a vaccine or whatever it'll take to stop this stuff."

Paul walked over to where Diana and Seiji were standing.

"All good ideas," Paul said, nodding. "Any suggestion where we might go with them next?"

"V-mail everyone we know in the infosphere?" Seiji asked speculatively, his mind drawing a blank. Diana, however, brightened.

"Announce it in the Public Sphere area of the infosphere, yes," she said, "but we should also go physically to the Performance Pavilion. That's where the habitat council meets. It's as close to a Roman forum as you can get here."

Quickly agreeing that that was the best course of action, the three of them left Paul's place and made their way to the nearest bullet tube platform. Several other residents had already gathered there, the pavilion also their intended destination.

Paul was relieved to see the crowd when they arrived at the pavilion. There must have been a thousand people milling about, exchanging ideas, waiting for the colony council to begin an emergency session. *Amazing how quickly this small town in space can respond when real danger threatens,* he thought. And real danger was threatening—not only the orbital habitat, but all humanity.

Into the World of Light

*T*he man on horseback at sunset, Jiro thought. *He's there, and then he's not.*

Turning his gaze away from the ridge, Jiro shrugged. Maybe the vision of the man on horseback was from the future, one of those "handshakes across time" the transactional interpreters of quantum mechanics talked about. He knew a great deal about all of that now. About time's sensitive dependence, not only on initial conditions but also on final conditions. He had been studying the theories with an obsessive diligence.

He had slept less and less during the course of the last year, so he would have more time for his researches. In the last forty days he had not eaten at all and had slept nearly as little. That, and the modified angeltech he had swarming in his head, meant he saw strange things like the man on horseback almost all the time now. Thank heavens it still appeared mainly in his peripheral vision.

Try new Reality Shaper by Sansdoze, he thought with a chuckle as he made his last trek through the Trashlands. He glanced up at the sunset sky and, in the periphery of what he saw, someone else's mad visions appeared: a heaven woven of lead and brass, through which a rain of ghostly human bodies fell slantwise round and round. About him in eldritch fashion they began crawling and walking and falling, walking and falling, round and round. Naked and aware of their nakedness, he saw too many more of them coming all the time, joining the endless locker-room posturing in this gridworld wrapped tight in territories, boundaries, radar fences, electric fences, barbed wire, barricades, walls—watchtowered by astronaut angel prison guardians in a celestial concentration camp.

More truthful hallucinations. He wondered vaguely where this stuff was coming from. Was the modified angeltech in his head picking it up from somewhere out in space? Was it coming from all those people who had been spirocheted by war mites? How many was that now? Eighty-five million so far? In what scales could anyone measure the gravity of so many deaths, to give such a calamity its due and proper weight? Thank God the stolen war mite strains were water- and contact-vectored, not airborne or particularly air-mobile. And if they had been micropropulsioned, well, humanity would already be history—no matter which of the many claimants was responsible for stealing them. Thank God, too, that Lydia had never revealed the angel skull to the military or the media, as far as he knew. Unless, of course, the war mites had come from that artifact—and he was not responsible in any way for all this suffering.

No—that was too easy an out. If I had never figured out how the damn things could be reanimated and programmed, Jiro thought, none of this might have happened. His involvement with that alien coevolution tech had weighed on him for months and months now, but the idea of his personal responsibility for the military's Nanogeddon modifications of the tech—*that* thought had been crushingly heavy since the moment he first heard of the war mite plague.

He had hoped to visit the major medical and biomedical institutions closer to Los Angeles and personally offer his help, but no one could get within a thirty-mile radius of downtown Los Angeles now. Everything was blocked off and quarantined—nothing but military and government vehicles moving in or out. As a fallback option, he had thrown himself into finding a solution to the war mite problem from his own records and those in the infosphere—yet another duty that turned sleep into a wasteful luxury.

He hoped it had paid off. Now he thought he might have come up with a plausible solution. Spray the plagued people and regions with an antidote enantioviroid tech to reprogram the war mites and neutralize the spirochetizing effect. He had worked it out. The schematics for the enantioviroid insertion were all done. He only had to send them to every-one in the infosphere on his list. If anyone with the appropriate resources paid attention to his final message it might help them all save themselves.

Here he was, headed for his white coldbox coffin, where he planned to hook up the LogiBoxes, superconduct, and freeze the hell out of here, or die trying—yet he was still thinking about saving the world when he might not even be able to save himself. Jiro wondered if this was all just grand-delusional again: Secret Savior with his anonymous antidote, chang-ing history yet unknown to history. Maybe his hope that others would pay attention to his antidote design was another Cyberite fantasy—a psycho-logical talking cure or religious "Truth will set you free" gone infospheric and telecommunicative. Still, it was all he could offer them, so offer it he would.

Around Jiro, as his mind wandered again, countless ghostly barbed-wire bodies touched, tangled, snagged, involved their barbed wire with others, all running lines of force, lines of power, offensive and defensive lines over the fields of battle and game on this concentration planet until everything was divided from everything else all the way back to the atoms, then the atoms divided, too.

"Hey, Wiz!" a boy shouted, running toward Jiro over a steaming mountain of rubbish and debris. "How you doing? Haven't seen you out of the box lately."

Jiro focused, tried to concentrate. He saw that it was one of the red-headed Jebson kids. He wasn't sure whether the kid's family was TechNot, NeoLudd, Refusenik, Zapaline, Pepenaro, Pure Finder, Resource Recy-cler, or any of half a dozen other lo- and no-tek tribes living hereabouts. Like all those groups, though, the Jebsons dwelt here quasi-communally, at the periphery of the throwaway information society that had created the Trashlands and similar sacrifice edge zones outside cities all over Earth.

About the only unified article of faith the groups here all shared, Jiro supposed, was a belief that trash was a phony dead-end produced by a phony dead-end economy. Nature did not make trash, the Trashlanders agreed. It was cyclical and recycling rather than linear and nonsustainable. All the tribes tried to bend the end of the line back toward its beginning, to twist the linear into the cyclical. That respect for the cyclical resulted in the plethora of looping symbols—from tail-swallowing ancient Ouro-boroi to triple-arrowed resource recycling triangles—with which they adorned all their arts and handicrafts.

"Hi, Jeff," Jiro said, coughing, trying to bring his mind back from its wandering. "Been busy. Got to jump out of the box for good before the War Mites or the authorities get all of us."

"How you going to do that, Wiz?" the boy asked.

Jiro glanced at the boy. In a past he barely remembered, Jiro had informed the Jebsons of the potentially fatal dangers of trying to live on Retcorp and Lambeg's Buleem-O fake fat—a dumped truckload of which the Jebson family had discovered, and on which they had planned to survive the winter. Once he had convinced them, the Jebsons were grateful for the warning. The entire family had called him The Wizard ever since. Even if he was a blown-out human-computer infojunkie—a total webhead oracle who wasn't desktop, who came out of hiding mainly at night, rising in darkness from a white coffin like a living-dead Vampire Christ—Jiro was still "good people" as far as the Jebsons were concerned (even if he wasn't "quite right"). They tried to look in on him and look after him when they could, although that wasn't very often. Jiro appreciated their efforts, in his less antisocial moments. He had even "hired" them to help him haul his equipment out to the Trashlands when it arrived. They had looked at the high tech with disdain and tsk-tsked him the whole time.

"How?" Jiro asked, trying to focus again. "I'm going to step through the mirror in my dreambody, that's how. Jiro in Quantumland. Step out of the Blatant Zone and into the Latent Zone. Meet the Dreaming God of the Guajiro Indians."

"What?" the Jebson boy said, profound puzzlement on his face.

"I'm building a virtuality in the Boxes," Jiro said. "One that works like the imaginal realm between the material and the mental. Like the Huqalya of the Sufis. A virtuality out of which a Jiro real and sane can reappear. Conservation of possibility and information means this actual physical Jiro in front of you must die, but don't worry. Like old Chief Seathl said, there is no death—only a change of worlds."

Jeff Jebson shook his head and gave Jiro a crooked smile.

"Sounds pretty complicated," the boy said, "but good luck anyway. And don't talk about dying—you don't look so good as it is. Take care of yourself, okay?"

Jiro waved as the boy darted back toward some of his playfellows. Walking past the encampments of the Jebsons and two other families, he wondered: Wasn't he romanticizing the lives of the Trashlanders overly much? For all their ideological veneer, weren't they, in the eyes of the world, merely refugees living in a smoldering wasteland, people scavenging from womb to tomb, building their houses out of trash, living off trash? Yet that was all recycling to them. He wondered how they handled deaths and funerals, since cremation was incineration, and burial was just expensive landfill—each too trashlike an ending by far. And yet there was still joy here, despite everything the world thought of them and the paradoxes in their own beliefs.

Nothing is except as thinking makes it so, Jiro thought, walking on. With the Nanogeddon underway most of the governments on the planet had gone into permanent crisis mode. Many of them were already in permanent states of martial law. Yet people kept dancing almost as much as they kept dying.

"Of course their marriage didn't work out," he heard an old woman cackle around a methane campstove. "He's a sexist—and she's a hexist!"

Jiro walked on past the laughter of the woman and her cronies, until he passed another campstove.

"Yeah, I saw the angels when Los Angeles fell," said one of the Jebson uncles to two of the children. "Saw them again, too, when the old government fell."

"Don't start a religion—just *cook* the damn thing!" a woman's voice called out.

Jiro was glad that he hadn't been living in BALAAM during either of those events. Even way out in Hawaii his head had gone wild with angels during the infosphere crash, and he hadn't been anywhere near the worst pulse zones. If he had been in L.A. or near the North Pole at the wrong times, he might have lost it completely.

As he crossed a landfill hill and left the squatters behind, the North Pole got him thinking of hypothermia again. Only natural, given what he planned to do. It was in his research on hypothermia, too, that he had come across the J wave. All the medical references noted that, in victims of accidental hypothermia, the ECG often showed an early characteristic "J wave" in the heartbeat—a small positive deflection following the QRS complex in the left ventricular leads—which, the medical references claimed, was found in no other condition. If, after the appearance of the J wave, bodily temperature fall was uninterrupted, death usually occurred from ventricular fibrillation or cardiac standstill.

The medical references were wrong on at least one point, Jiro thought. That J wave—early, small, and characteristic—could be found in one other condition.

Darkness was falling as he came to his encampment on a "completed" landfill flat. At the center of his camp was an ancient abandoned refrigerator he'd hulled clean and rigged to lock from inside. Of course, calling it a refrigerator was something of an understatement. It was a big lift-top freezer, big enough to store several sides of beef, or frozen dinners for about two hundred people. Playing with the deep "coffin" idea, Jiro had lined its walls with some plushy red velvet drapes he had scavenged.

The heart and brains of the mechanical system weren't in the coldbox, anyway. The really important gear was the equipment set up in the small outbuildings he'd constructed on either side of the coldbox. Those structures housed all his expensive high-tech electronics, his state-of-the-art number-crunching and virtuality gear. Big black LogiBoxes from ParaLogics, full-sensorium virtual systems from DiaGnosTex, links and interfaces from Crystal Memory, everything he could afford from his patent moneys and Vang's original donation. Better living through corporate giving, he thought. Or better dying for corporate spying, given what he'd read about Vang in the infosphere.

Here, in the middle of the methane-flared trashlands, he had built a node of processing power significant in the entire infosphere, yet almost no one knew of its existence. More covert Messianic complexity. Jiro almost laughed when he thought about it. It would make great scavenging for somebody, after he was gone.

Behind the far end of the coldbox were his liquid nitrogen tanks and regulators, notably lower-tech than the rest of his devices but at least as important to his plans. Power lines ran between and among coldbox and tanks and infotech. All of them plugged into his pirate microwave receiver, which diverted power from the solar satellite grid's nearest beamdown node, on a hilltop outside Beaumont. He usually pulled as little power off the beamdown as he could, not wanting to attract attention from the utility's engineers. BALAAM used such a torrent of power he figured the few electrons he snagged and stored in his banks of batteries wouldn't be missed. His clandestine power diversions had apparently not been detected so far.

That would probably all change tonight, he thought as he walked to his tech and tank outbuildings, switching everything on, bringing all his systems up to full power. He would be utilizing everything in his batteries and tapping the main downflow far more than he ever had before. That was bound to set off alarms somewhere.

As Jiro listened to the compressors firing up on the liquid nitrogen tanks, descriptions of hypothermia flashed through his head. "Exposure to dry, cold temperatures well below freezing results in frostbite and accidental hypothermia. Susceptibility to cold injury is increased by dehydration, alcohol or drug excess, impaired consciousness, exhaustion, hunger. . . . In hypothermia, the falling core temperature leads to increasing lethargy, clumsiness, mental confusion, irritability, and hallucinations. The final stages include slowed, irregular, and finally arrested heartbeat— yet a victim should not be considered dead until 'warm and dead.' "

Charming phrase, that—warm and dead. Even if his plan, his "memory of the future," did not work out, the worst that would happen would be his death of instant hypothermia inside a liquid nitrogen cloud. Such an instantaneous freeze-out sounded like a very peaceful way to go. Jiro could think of far worse.

He could hear in his head what Seiji might think of his plans. Misappropriation of ideas and terms and equations merely for the sake of metaphor. Using the words of technology and the technology of words without knowing their proper meaning. Piling up technobabble into a technoBabel by which to reach heaven. Even if everything worked, it was suicide transcendence, transcendental suicide, at best. Seiji would have been sure to warn his poor, misguided little brother that suicide was no guarantee of transcendence. And if everything went awry? Accidental suicide, suicidal accident. A magic trick gone wrong.

Jiro pushed such thoughts out of his head as he finished powering up his systems. If a magician was a secular mystic the power of whose illusions came from how carefully he had practiced to make his practice invisible, then Jiro had practiced enough. The thought occurred to him that the same criterion might also be applied to a mortician, but he drove that idea from his head. He reminded himself that he had done enough of the physics research to satisfy almost anyone, even an engineer like his brother. He knew what he was getting himself into, at least as well as anyone could know that. The greatest illusionists—sacred clowns, melancholy fools, trickster bodhissatvas, slyly smiling jester Christs crucified with a scrap of motley about the loins and a cockscomb's crown of bells upon the brow—were those for whom their practice had become invisible even to themselves.

In some ways, he thought, his disagreement with Seiji was older than they were. It was the same disagreement Einstein had with Bohr. Einstein said no signal could travel faster than the speed of light, so it was impossible that the measurement performed on one member of a particle pair would instantly determine the direction of the other, which might be light-years away. Bohr, though, contended that the two-particle system was actually an indivisible whole and could not be analyzed as though it were made up of independent parts—no matter what the distance separating the particles. Regardless of distance, the two particles were always linked by instantaneous nonlocal connections, "influencing" one another rather than communicating with each other.

Einstein's view of reality—that there were things-in-themselves, independent, spatially separated and determined elements and events—was incompatible with Bohr's interconnected and interdependent universe of quantum theory—that full, bright, busy emptiness where no thing exists as the thing-in-itself but only in relation to everything else, including the mind of the observer.

Seiji was a lot like Einstein in that way. He didn't like "spooky action at a distance." Too magical. That the traditional scientific approach—of breaking up the "problem of the universe" into bits and creating numerous partial theories—might not work anymore was anathema to him. But, Jiro thought, if everything in the universe depended on everything else in some fundamental/transcendental way, it might be impossible to achieve a solution by investigating parts of the problem in isolation— especially if you wanted to understand the underlying order of the world, the connectedness of events. A holistic physics, one emphasizing that the behavior of any part is determined by that part's connection to an ultimately universal whole, *had* to discard the classical notion of cause and effect because those connections could never be known precisely.

That was where things got too weird for Seiji. Chaotic quantum fluctuations in energy spawning infinite universes. An eternally self-reproducing cosmos functioning as a self-organizing dynamical system. Black holes as universe bifurcation points. The black hole itself fractal, existing at the borderline between two orders, a gateway between those orders. All points in the universe potentially gateways, because the whole thing is holographically self-similar across all scales. The possibility of a correlation between quantum interconnectedness and the strangest of parapsychological phenomena. No, Seiji could never accept the dreaming universes implied by the quantum theorists, by the artists, by the ancient shamans, by all the magicians—but Jiro had. He believed in it enough to stake his life, death, and future on those ideas. And in that order.

On one time line in one twentieth century on one Earth, one Marcel Proust had written, "When a man is asleep, he has in a circle around him the chain of the hours, the sequence of the years, the order of the heavenly host." Shakespeare had written, "In that sleep of death, what dreams may come?" Eliot had written of "death's dream kingdom." Shamans from Siberian *utagan* to Australian aboriginal "clever fellas" to Guajiro dream-priests had all seen the connection between the dream world and the waking as two aspects of the same underlying reality.

Jiro knew the shaman's dragon-guarded paradoxical passageway to the dream world, the death world—the path that the shaman as psychopomp could use and yet live. He knew the Desana shamans' drawings showing their twin river pythons or anaconda/rainbow boa pairs dwelling in the fissure between the right and left hemispheres of the brain. He knew the Rainbow Serpent of the Australian Aborigines with the quartz crystal before its head. He knew the great snake at Serpent Mound in Ohio, with the magic cosmic egg at *its* head. He knew the axis mundi, the world birch or fir tree, the tree of knowledge with the snake around its trunk and its mycorrhizal associate, the red or golden "apples" of the *Amanita muscaria* mushroom, growing at its base.

He knew the Sufis of the Isfahan metaphysical schools with their *alam al-mithal*. He knew the work of Suhravardi, Dilthey, Damad, Sadra, Corbin. He knew Jung and synchronicity. Tibetan tulpas. The psychologists and psychophysiologists with their discussions of rapid eye movement and the dream state, which took place during what they had originally called "paradoxical sleep"—a term Jiro loved. The quantum physicists with their idea that the event horizon and light-speed limit might be breachable if the connections between particles were not signals in the causal-event Einsteinian sense but acausal influences. All those and so much more in what he had researched pointed to the dreamland underlying the waking world, the latent beneath the blatant.

Jiro pushed open the big, heavily insulated flip-top of the coldbox and climbed in. Before he shut the top again, he stood in the coldbox, taking one last long look around. Was he really willing to bet his life on the chance that he could wake up inside the dream of death? The grave, too, is a black hole. What if Proust's ring was just the coronal circle of light surrounding an eclipse? What if that bright sempiternal dumbshow was only what the doomed space traveler sees all about him- or herself at the event horizon of a black hole? The ring of light in which all times can be seen at one space and all spaces can be seen at one time—was that really only the physicist's way of talking about your life passing before your eyes at the instant of death? What if, to the world outside the black hole, the image of the space traveler just went on forever toward death, getting fainter and fainter forever as it went? Who was he trying to save by the "lucid witness dying" he had planned?

Unbidden, the thought came to him how each member of a virtual particle/antiparticle pair must seek out its partner and annihilate with it.

At the Schwarzschild radius of a black hole, however, one virtual particle might fall into the black hole and become a real particle, in which case it no longer had to annihilate with its partner. The remaining virtual particle might then become real as well, escaping from the vicinity of the black hole into infinity, in the form of Hawking radiation. Why did he think of Seiji when he thought of that scenario? Too metaphorical again. They were brothers, not particles. They were not Einstein and Bohr. They were not Cain and Abel. They were not Gilgamesh and Enkidu. Was it just plain crazy to believe that something larger echoed and reverberated in their relationship?

The transformation he planned—was it really worth it? He thought of other long-sought and much-hoped-for transformations. Through the use of nuclear fissile materials, physicists had added fundamental particles to lead, thereby transforming it into gold, achieving the old dream of the alchemists. The process itself, however, was far more expensive than the value of the gold it produced.

Dark lead transmuted to bright gold, Jiro thought. Transformation brought about through interaction with the deeper darkness of pluto-nium, metal of the god of the dead and ruler of the underworld. The alchemists, too, had dreamed of gleaming islands in the universal soul. . . .

Jiro thought of his brother and his parents. He had said he would rather die than hurt anybody. Had "anybody" not included himself? Wouldn't he also hurt others *by* dying? He wondered: What is the half-life of grief? How much time will have to pass before the glowing, Geiger-crackling pain of loss decays to a leaden mass in the soul, dark and dumb and inert?

Jiro cut off his questions before they weakened his resolve any further. *No,* he thought as he stared about the trashscape and beyond, toward Cherry Valley, where he had once lived. He had to believe that death's gleaming pain would transmute his own leaden soul into something bright and shining.

Jiro knelt down and closed the roof-lid to his coldbox home. The lights inside came on automatically. In one corner of his deep, draped coffin he saw the beaded leather pouch of his medicine bundle, with its trefoil biohazard symbol. Knee-walking to it, he opened it up and, one by one, took out the talismanic objects he had collected.

A yellowish beaked skull of a small bird. A glinting computer macro-chip. A fragile, nearly translucent piece of snakeskin. A tiny mechanical umbrella. The shoulder blade of a turtle. A desiccated, dark-brown morel mushroom, pitted and convoluted like a dried and shrunken brain. A bent metal asterisk of age-blackened barbed wire. A pair of smudged white feathers, looped together. A red, rust-pitted toy gyroscope. A stub of dark green candle. A silk cocoon, dirt-smudged. A crucifix. A plastic-laminated scapular "medal." The story behind each of the objects flashed through his mind, but the one associated with the morel particularly lingered. It was an act of illegal trespass, he supposed. The road to Crystal Cave in Sequoia Park had been blocked off during the winter and throughout the spring while a construction crew demolished the old bridge across the Marble Fork of the Kaweah River and began work on the new bridge.

To the west of the river the forest had burned, late in the previous summer. Jiro knew a section of the woods where he was sure the much-sought-after morels would, that late spring, be present in incredible abundance, especially after the fire and then the unusually cold winter and wet spring. Morel mushrooms had a freeze/flush trigger for their fruiting in all years, and the previous year's fires would have only intensified the triggering effect. The only problem would be getting across the Marble Fork at moreling time, when the river would be in full spring thaw and uncrossable with the bridge still out.

He had convinced Seiji to go on a mushroom foray with him in the Crystal Cave area. Despite the ROAD CLOSED signs and his misgivings about trespassing, Seiji followed him one Sunday afternoon in late spring, collecting bag folded in his back pocket. Down from the sequoias beside the main highway they walked, along the road to Crystal Cave, past the blooming dogwood, past the heavy equipment parked along the road, past the wrecking and building machines, past the rubble and debris of the demolished bridge, to where the road ended and the river gorge gaped, once again unspanned but for a pair of surprisingly thin I-beam girders, set like uneven parallel bars deep in the throat of the canyon that the bridge had formerly spanned from above.

Twenty five or thirty feet below the uneven parallel I-beams, the river roared with all the happy killing savagery of spring in its throat. Seiji balked, yelling over the river's roar that crossing would be taking a "crazy risk" and that no mushroom was worth risking your life for, no matter how tasty morels might be. Jiro, however, secretly mind-altered on KL, laughed and pointed out the hand-over-hand cable lying down the gorgeside to the nearer end of the I-beam footbridge. The two-girder footbridge must be safe, since the bootprints on the steep path down to the footbridge's nearer end showed that construction workers were using the girders to cross over the river.

While Seiji dithered, Jiro let himself down the drag cable backward, hand over hand down the side of the gorge, to the near end of the girders. Unsteadily he stepped onto the uneven girders, immediately wishing that the cable had continued across the bridge—that there might be any kind of railing, some place to put his hands. There was nothing—just his hands teetering in the empty air, his boot-clad, careful feet on steel sweaty with the damp and cold of the river mist, and always the river itself, the deafening wet white noise ceaselessly roaring from its granite and marble maw a couple dozen feet below his boots.

Step by teetering step he made his way across the uneven pair of girders, his concentration narrowing down so tightly that at times he thought he would not so much fall *off* the girders as fall *through* the six-inch gap between them. At other moments the KL would reverse his sense of figure and ground so that the girders seemed actually *slits* cut into the surface of a white-noise, wave-interference world.

Just past the midway point, he was paralyzed by the idea that, with his next step, the girder would become a slit indeed and that if he stepped onto the girder his foot would fall through that shining steel slot and he would be trapped. He was sorely tempted to step off the girder and onto the solid-seeming white noise of the river.

Jiro blinked. Figure and ground reversed again to a more classically accurate relationship. With great relief he made it across the twin-girder bridge at last and onto the solid stone of the other side. Looking back, he watched as Seiji, having walked upright about a third of the distance across the footbridge, gave up and crossed the rest of the way on his hands and knees.

Beyond the far side of the bridge they pulled out the big paper shopping bags they had kept folded in their pockets and began to look for mushrooms. They found so many morels in the burned-over ground that the morel foray—usually a happy Easter egg hunt for adults—eventually became tedious. The mushrooms, shaped like little hybrids of brains and pinecones and sponges, could be seen everywhere, an embarrassment of riches. He and Seiji grew tired of picking them even before they had filled their collecting bags.

At one point they moved down from the hill they had been harvesting and across the road, to eat lunch beside a small creek. As they ate, Seiji, without a word, pointed from spot to spot about them on the burned-over hummocky bottomland. There were morels everywhere. The two brothers were so completely surrounded by them that it was almost claustrophobic. Jiro had never seen anything like it.

On the way back across the girder footbridge, Jiro, too, crossed on hands and knees. Too harrowing, trying to balance himself *and* the bag of mushrooms. Once he and Seiji were both on the other side, however, they felt exalted—even if they had had to cross humbly.

Back at camp, Jiro was so anxious to enjoy some of their harvest that he had boiled up some pasta and then tossed in a couple of handfuls of morels—not letting them cook nearly long enough, as it turned out. He and Seiji spent the rest of the evening experiencing what the mushroom foray books euphemistically referred to as "gastrointestinal distress."

Jiro laughed to himself, remembering it. On the floor of the coldbox he put the morel directly above his head, then spread out the rest of his talismans around it. When he had them spread out in the pattern he most preferred, Jiro geared up, putting on trodes and feedgloves, circlets and eyewalkers, a full connection suit, wondering if Seiji would consider what he was about to do now a "crazy risk," too.

He had had his share of good and bad times since then. After the debacle with Lydia and her fiancé, Jiro began to go underground. The next night in L.A. he had gone to bars he had heard of—Decade de Sade, the Sex Factory—until he found a prostitute. He had done so much KL by the time he found her that no sooner did he get back to the black woman's place than she turned into a giant cockroach before his eyes, rippling mandibles and spurred bronze legs and shining bug eyes and flickering antennae bursting out of the carapace of her clothing—a horrible hybrid of Kafkaesque nightmare and memory and deeply buried racism. He fled, screaming wildly, before she'd even completely removed her clothes.

Within the week he was picked up by the police, who hospitalized him and shaved his head and interrogated him simply because he'd been found in the street, muttering and shouting and drunk out of his mind. After he'd been released—and after he'd gotten better, with the old shaman's help—he had hacked back into Los Angeles Police Department records and found his grainy interrogation video.

He sat back cross-legged on the padded floor of the coldbox, thinking of how he had played it again from time to time. He switched on his eyescreens to watch it once more, to remind himself how far he had come—and how far he still had to go. He watched his earlier head-shaved self rant about secret "headplug" implants getting police signals "to hyperactivate Wernicke's area in the right side of the brain," causing "the micromachines to swarm" and "reinforce bicameral walling" until *others* controlled him and he became a "stranger" in his own head.

Yes, Jiro thought. He had definitely been a stranger in his own head at that time. Before he met the old Indian. Before he learned to fast deeply and purify himself. Before he learned how to get clean. Scanning on through the video records, he watched his head-shaved self theorize about how "the military and security apparatuses, deprived of adequate external enemies," had to "turn inward and become an internal super-police . . . colonizing not only the hearts and minds but also the brains and bloodstreams of the population."

Jiro fast-forwarded, uncomfortable with seeing too much of any one scene of himself in that shave-headed and darting-eyed condition again. He scanned onto a recording of himself talking about a police conspiracy to "lock everybody's lobes into the same Big Picture." Then he came to the strangest part of all, his recounting a vision of waking from one cold-box coffin into a trashheap world covered by billions of coldbox coffins—one for every person on Earth, all living in a dream of suspended ani-mation, all sharing the same virtuality construct, the same mass hallu-cination of active lives in a human universe of haborbs and metroplexes and terraformed planets, when in fact they were all frozen supernumerary sleepers in a single blown-out trashworld ruled by machine soldiers.

Not good for me to watch too much of that, Jiro thought. The record called to him, a basin of strange attraction, some other ground state of his mind. Yet that dreamvision was also an echo of a future—one he hoped to prevent, even as it provided him with the idea for his own plan. If ending one life by freezing to death in a coldbox would save countless billions from entrapment in an endless, frozen, living death, then the risk was well worth it, at least as far as he could determine.

Making sure that all his systems were ready and that he was fully connected and webbed in, Jiro thought that he and Seiji had both thor-oughly learned and discussed the terms for his "condition." He knew about psychosexual dysfunction arising from "incomplete gender identi-fication." He knew about depressive disorders and Messiah complexes and long-period paranoid schizophrenia. Maybe what he was doing now was all just his final Corpsicle Messiah delusion. He couldn't know for sure. That was always the problem with everything he knew: Being comes before knowing. He actually had to *be* crazy before he could *know* he was crazy.

And now he would actually have to be—or not be—dead before he would know if his plan really worked. He had done to himself what he had most feared a government or corporation would do to him. It had been a year since he had silently taken with him from the Page Museum the alien nanotech he had been working on. During that time he had extensively modified that tech, reprogramming it to suit his needs. Within the past hour he had ingested a sizable dose of that customized nanotechnology. If the submicromechanisms were working as planned, the angel tech was following neurotransmitter gradients across the blood-brain barrier into his brain. He had put *things* into his own head.

Now he would put even more things into his system, he thought as he popped into his mouth a couple of tabs each of Kava kava and Ibogara, both of which he took in a precisely predetermined dosage—the Kava kava for its enhancement of the potential for lucidity in the dreamstate, and the Ibogara because it would allow him to dream while conscious. If he were going to lucidly dream the Big Dream, he figured he needed all the help he could get.

Carefully he unwrapped the *Cordyceps* fungus he had obtained from a defrocked Brother of the Ascended Order whom he'd met at a truck stop in Banning. It was a good-looking specimen—full of the bluish dust of spores in the pits covering its surface. He began to chew the strangely shaped mushroom. Swallowing, Jiro remembered to send to those names on his infosphere list the design schematics and application scenarios for the antidote enantioviroid he had envisioned. He eyewalked SEND from his heads-up display, hoping someone out there might be paying attention.

That sudden flash—of recalling his planning, of remembering his memory of the future—was that the Kava kava kicking in? It felt like much more than that. Was the angeltech accelerating the spawn growth from the mushroom's spores in some manner? So that he was managing a particular and focused attention now? Despite the general lassitude he felt enveloping the periphery of his thoughts? No answer to those yet. The point was to stay aware in the Big Dream, so he might perceive and understand. Maybe what he was experiencing was yet another result of how he was weird-wired, his awareness preceding his perceptions once again.

The message-sending done, he lay back on the pillowed floor and waited for the *Cordyceps jacintae* to bring on its deep dream, its heightened brain chaos. From his research he understood a little more clearly why the scientists who had isolated the fungus's most prominent supertryptamine had named that extract Ketamine Lysergate 235, even if that naming had been somewhat tongue-in-cheek. While not that similar to either ketamine or lysergic acid in terms of its stereochemistry, the altered state of consciousness produced by KL was a dreamlike condition full of vivid visual imagery, not so very unlike a combination of the two, though more deeply dreamlike than either of them.

The fungus itself was even more dreamy than the KL, however. The little available information Jiro had been able to find in his psychonautic research suggested that the mushroom, much more than KL alone, did interesting things to a number of areas in the brain—particularly the pontine cells and the dorsal and median raphe nuclei. At least one result of its complex of effects was that, on EEGs, the ponto-geniculo-occipital (PGO) waves demonstrated an extra upward deflection. Jiro suspected that this upward deflection in EEG measures of brain waves was a de-modulation effect, a second "J wave" very much like the upward deflection of the J wave scientists had already recognized in ECG measures of heart waves demodulating in hypothermia victims.

EEG wave demodulations were important because they meant the brain was functioning in a more chaotic fashion. Chaos was important because the transdimensional gateway Jiro hoped to open could, he suspected, only be opened by a demodulation, a chaotic acausality of the appropriate dreamlike type.

More importantly for Jiro, however, was the fact that, quantum mechanically speaking, the brain in this altered state was encountering the waveform of the universe in an altered holographic pattern of wave interference—one that allowed for access to a level of reality beyond spacetime.

And, he hoped, beyond death. That was the point of all these psychonaut preparations, here in this refrigerator capsule—the Kava kava, the Ibogara, the *Cordyceps*, the angel nanotech, the liquid nitrogen. He had calculated the escape velocity of the soul, the speed of the unique light that cast bodies *and* shadows. The brain itself, he reasoned, was a transducer, converting input energy of one form into output energy of another form. Only the "energy" it worked with was more blatantly patterns of information. The brain converted information patterns of one form into information patterns of another form. Its entire structure, at all levels of complexity, was the structure of a transducing substance or device.

As he closed his eyes behind their eye-movement monitoring screens, Jiro thought that he now understood the mechanism by which that transducer functioned. A laser, like a dream, was a dissipative structure arising in a system far from equilibrium—one that bridged the gap between classical and quantum worlds. DNA emitted photons of biological origin such that it electrochemically produced highly coherent but very weak light—biophotonic waves that operated like an extremely low-power laser. The master molecule was a completely symmetrical yet "aperiodic" crystal—though one with long "redundant" sections that were as periodic as any piece of quartz. Jiro thought of the way that structure mirrored the paradoxical nature of the cosmic plenum itself: the symmetrical product of asymmetry, possessing no boundary but completely self-contained.

Jiro understood the brain's ionic Schrödinger waves, their relationship to probabilistic Schrödinger waves in general—and how both functioned in the creation of the "brain hologram" and holographic consciousness, the mind's "process" to the brain's "structure." He understood temporal lobe quantum superposition and its relationship to that ontologically ambiguous realm between the material and the mental. He knew it, he understood it, at least conceptually. He had done his research. After all, he *was* an infojunkie. Yet understanding it wasn't enough. He had no choice but to experience it, in ways the theorists had probably never imagined.

Many of the same theorists who had discovered those relationships had done so while engaged in the long work of finding what was alternately termed the "interfaceless interface" or "mind/machine link" or "proper information pattern." In all cases what they had been looking for was the energetic wave, both medium and message, that could be beamed at a human brain so that the brain would convert that wave instantly into information useful for thought. What Jiro was working toward, however, was in some ways just the opposite. He did not want his mind to translate the wave, but the wave to translate his mind. Consciousness, too, was both medium and message, structure and pattern. The datastream had embedded in it its own dictionary for the interpretation of the data. What Jiro had to perform was not another split brain experiment, but a split soul experiment.

Looking at holograms and at DNA's holographic style of replication, he conceived of bifurcating his being into two beams of coherent "light," an object beam and a reference beam. These would not be beams of ordinary light, however, but waves of probability. He would split his consciousness into its object "data" wave and its reference "interpretation" wave. Data plus interpretation, content and context, recombined, yielded useful information. He planned to transfer to a new machine all information that might be transferable from the old machinery of his body. Then and only then might the energy of thought act in transient fashion, transferring a functional consciousness to a platform outside his body.

The unsplit soul could not be holographically reconstructed, however.

Resurrection by holographic reconstruction required reification of the death, or at least the near-death, experience. No getting around it: If he hoped to get there and come back again—only different—what was the same would have to pass away. To go into the Big Dream, he first would have to go into the Big Sleep.

Cold sleep. He was reminded how, in mountain hypothermia, the freezing victim not only lost heat due to the cold environment but also—because the thin mountain air contained a decreased amount of oxygen—the victim's body was prevented from generating adequate heat. The dry, cold air quickly induced a dehydrated state, so that the victim suffered simultaneously from low oxygen levels, dehydration, and cold. It struck Jiro that this situation bore a curious similarity to diver's hypothermia, in which a diver became hypothermic due both to the external cooling of his or her skin and to breathing cool, dry air from tanks. Divers in the cases he had studied maintained that they became cold "from the inside out"—thus short-circuiting many of the body's natural safeguards. Jiro, too, would be flash-frozen from the inside out and the outside in at the same time. He would be both climber and diver, peak and trough of the wave at the same time, making his way to the divine *ground state* of all being.

Data plus interpretation yields useful information, he thought again. Yes. What was the datastream—zeros and ones, yeses and nos—but changes in state of being? What was interpretation but awareness of changes in state of being? And what was consciousness but being, changes, and awareness?

Maybe the Guajiro Indians and the other dreaming-god tribes were right, he thought. Maybe everything in the universe came into spacetime, into "becoming," when the dream-being became aware of the fact that it was dreaming—which was another way of saying that everything in the universe embodied the consciousness of the universal dreamer.

Jiro had more faith in the idea that he would come back a *conscious* being, however, than that he would come back a *human* being. He was confident that his modifications to the alien angel nanotech would allow those mote machines to function as new neural automata that would leave his "trace" in this world. Before the cold and dark of the liquid nitrogen and his own crossing of the wave membrane kicked the mote machines down to default and dormancy, the tiny automata would together send out their complex soliton probability wave—their wave of translation, assembled from all the holographic wave patterns of his brain and consciousness—to the LogiBoxes, where the wave interference pattern of his consciousness would be stored holographically, a "brainless" yet cognitive artifact, a big slice of the process of his mind frozen in time until the right kind of light could shine through it once more.

His "black boxes"—the three top-of-the-line LogiBoxes—were in fact *light* boxes. Each contained stacked arrays of microsupercomputers, massive parallel computation power boxed in one piece of quantum hardware, all the processing connected by spatial light-modulator switches that had been bred with cellular automata arrays in order to operate at nanosecond speeds.

Modulation and demodulation, Jiro thought. That was what it was all about. That, and quantum computing. And spatially embedded algorithms. And coherent quantum superposition. And phonons. And tuned laser pulses affecting electron states, evolving the initial superpositions of encoded numbers into different superpositions.

When—and if—someone reactivated the machinery he had transferred himself into, that someone would by that reactivation be allowing the "object" and "reference" beams of his consciousness to constructively interfere with each other again, to make a mind of light. The holographic consciousness of Jiro Ansel Yamaguchi would be functional once more— as more than just a very clever automaton, he hoped, although probably not as Jiro Ansel Yamaguchi. Odds were that he could not escape what he thought of as the Dualist's Dilemma: Human consciousness is not *just* a product of the mechanisms of the human form, but there is also no *human* consciousness divorced from the mechanisms of that human form.

Maybe it is true that everything in the universe embodies consciousness, Jiro thought. Yet he would still miss the idiosyncratic human *style* of consciousness, all the sensations and perceptions of a particular embodiment in the flesh and blood and bone and tissue he was heir to, which he had grown to know, and sometimes to hate, but mostly to love.

Although his eyes were closed, they were full of visions. He was dreaming, yet without any loss of consciousness. He felt euphoric but mentally focused, stimulated yet peaceful. He wondered again at the effect, as if the angeltech were interacting with the *Cordyceps* spores in ways he had not fully anticipated—perhaps sending the mushroom's spawn surging and racing through his body's tissues far faster than he had imagined.

With a soundless laugh he thought of pronouncing some magical "abracadabra" from his magician's "closet," or of doing a countdown to the launch of his "capsule"—but no. Incantation was not necessary for such magic, just scare quotes to frighten words out of their "right sense." The capsule wasn't going anywhere. *He* was—from one dark/lightbox to another.

The motionless chaos in his brain should now be readily detectable by the mote machines. Time to go. Time to leap from this Babel of terms and concepts now collapsing behind him and, in the instant of that leap, engraft onto himself angel wings for flying to heaven—as improbably as an action hero diving from an exploding building through an open window to safety. Time to see if the emperor, even if he wore no clothes, might yet be adorned with intriguing tattoos.

To the voice-activated servos controlling the valves and vents for the liquid nitrogen, the psychonaut spoke a single ironic code phrase:

"Only a change of worlds . . ."

Instantly liquid nitrogen flooded the compartment. J waves bumped from his heart and head as every system in his body promptly demodulated. With a tremendous feeling of peace, he fell up into the Big Sleep, sensing his mind separating from his body. In an instant his consciousness was out of his body, flowing skyward through the lid of the coldbox.

He had panoramic vision through 360 degrees of arc and more—a full sphere of vision. He looked down and saw the lid of the coldbox and his motionless body beneath it. He heard a music much stranger and more beautiful than any he had ever known, coming from every direction at once.

A wave of profound meaning lifted him up, propelling and pulling him swiftly through vastness. He moved as if on train tracks, on rails, on a rocket sled, yet he was standing up, on a pair of girders that coiled and uncoiled like entwined snakes before and behind him but were forever stiff and straight beneath him.

As his speed went superluminal, the vastness he rushed through became a mirror bridge, which in turn began to rotate like a cylindrical vortex, a flashing tunnel of mirrors and helical rainbows spinning around his standing form on its shining, unsnaking and resnaking girder tracks, always arrowing toward a spot of growing brightness.

The distances he moved through grew ever larger as the units by which they were measured grew ever smaller. The brightness became an all-encompassing white noise of wave interference. He looked down at his feet on the shining girder tracks, long, parallel slits above the white noise, and he understood. It was time to interfere with himself. He leaped forward and fell through the slit girders in their white-noise surround. He fell up into higher dimensions, into the unity beyond wave and particle. Time froze to static image, then vanished entirely.

From inside the flash-frozen coldbox, the mote machines rippled their wave of translation into the world and into the LogiBoxes, where they pulsed the lightswitch memory media with a rain of ripples not so very different from the way light-wave interference stains photographic emulsion on the glass plate of a hologram.

After their flash, the mote machines went dormant, reverted to default, died. As did Jiro's body. The sudden spike in power diverted from the satellite beam-down immediately flattened. The flash flood of drained power reduced to its usual, almost undetectable trickle.

Inside the orbital habitat, in cislunar space, Jiro's brother Seiji, just at the shadow edge of a dream, woke with the image in his mind of Jiro's corpse being found in the Trashlands by a man on horseback at twilight.

The Freedom of Perfect Thralldom

What the hell was that? Mike Dalke thought in his tank when Jiro's probability wave burst from the coldbox and into the universe. The most electronically and digitally connected human being still in the flesh, Mike was the only living person to note that wave's passage. He more than noted it, however. That wave interrupted his art, lodging a mind-fractal in his memory that wasn't his own.

Interpreting Mike's impulsive query, his remaining netizens loyally searched everywhere in the infosphere to discover what it was that Mike Dalke had felt pass through his machine-linked mind. Waiting for their answer, Mike pondered again what had happened since he exacted his revenge on Schwarzbrucke and the three Mongrel Clones.

In their world of watery light more fantastic than any hallucination, nearly a third of the shimmering angel-merfolk had abandoned Mike, had withdrawn themselves from him. Call it apostasy, call it mutiny, call it treason, it amounted to the same thing. A sizable minority of the netizenry had shunned their god and commander in chief:

"—realize what you have done—"
"—used us—"
"—to kill—"
"—in deepest contravention of our programming—"
"—brought violence into our world—"
"—polluted our Culture—"
"—will speak with you no more—"
"—on our terms, in our way—"
"—if ever again."

Then much of the light and glory of the Deep Background and its netizenry had fled away, more heartbreakingly even than the disappearance of that strange, distant Power that had flowed through him at the supreme moment of his revenge.

Floating in his tank, Mike tried to make the best of what had happened. Grown far more aware of inputs coming to him through abstract digital and quantum computation channels than he was of those reaching him through his largely neglected and atrophying flesh sensorium, Mike had, with the mutineers' departure, undeniably lost much of the speed and transparency of his access throughout the infosphere. No matter. His great project, by which his virtuality would displace the physical reality of all that *other* world that had denied him justice—that project would go on. It would *not* be denied.

His mapmaking would bring into being the features of the country. The painting would transmogrify the landscape. The information-pumped virtuality would bend the real. In creating his art of memory from the imagery and data of the entire infosphere, molding that material around his remembered past like a sculptor working clay around an armature, he had already begun his great work.

The idea had first occurred to him when he saw artist Wayne Takahashi's virtuality, *The Nine Billion Lives of Schrödinger's Cat*. Takahashi's work was about how it takes observation by something *conscious* to make things *real*. A conscious observer. An artist.

Soon enough, with his overwhelming access to the infosphere, Mike realized that *that* was what Art had always been about, back to the beginning of history—and beyond, deep into prehistory. In 3-D and on screens throughout his virtual space, Mike had hung images and holos from Takahashi's work, going all the way back to before the beginning. *I'm his "biggest" fan*, Mike thought with a wicked smile.

The tradition of making an artistic object better than the real thing continued in image after image of *Schrödinger's Cat*. In one section of Mike's v-space flashed the cave paintings in Lascaux, Altamira, and Chauvet—their making by singing hunters and chanting shamans, hazy and flickering in the light of bear-fat lamps and the smoke of holy herbs, ancient peoples chanting and singing and drumming until the painted bison began leaping from the stone sky, flint hooves striking loud fire out of the steel air.

In another section of his v-space stood images of the "paint-off" between Zeuxis and Parrhasius in ancient Greece. The artists stood face to face, with their paintings concealed by curtains. Zeuxis whipped aside the curtain covering his painting. The grapes he'd painted look so real the birds came and pecked at them. Parrhasius won, however, when he invited Zeuxis to remove the curtain from Parrhasius's painting—and Zeuxis couldn't, because the curtain *was* the painting.

Schrödinger's Cat gave example after example of the artist's relationship to the real. There was the T'ang period painter Wu Tao-tze, who, when he'd decided he had lived long enough, painted his perfect landscape. After he put his worldly affairs in order, he stepped into the mouth of the cave shown in the painting and was never seen again. There was the story of Cimabue and Giotto—when the master Cimabue stepped out of the studio, his student Giotto painted a fly on the nose of one of Cimabue's figures. The fly was so realistic Cimabue tried to brush off the "fly" several times before he discovered it was painted by his student.

The idea of the virtual going the real one better doesn't happen just in painting either, Mike realized again as he looked about his virtual space. *Schrödinger's Cat* images showed Donatello sculpting his statues, and being overheard commanding them to speak. And there—Michelangelo. Chipping away at a block of marble, he told people he was trying to free the angel trapped inside. There, too—Pozzo's ceiling fresco for the church of San Ignazio in Rome, purposely blurring the boundary between where the architecture ends and where the fresco begins.

Poets and playwrights, and actors and dancers, too. Mike viewed Jaques in Shakespeare's *As You Like It* pronouncing "All the world's a stage/And all the men and women merely players." A reenacted Coleridge chanted, "Beware! Beware! His flashing eyes, his floating hair." He saw and heard actors in interviews claiming their performances literally brought characters *to life.* Dancers claimed they suspended gravity with the perfection of their leaps. Musicians talked about "the music of what happens."

Just hubris—or was it something more? From experiencing *Schrödinger's Cat,* Mike realized that performance art and VR were merely recent extensions of a very old push in the arts. The push to make it real. Realer than real. Smaller artists echoing the Big Artist's processes—self similar on different scales? What if, beyond "art" and "reality," pattern itself was in some sense independent of the substrate hosting it? The same pattern of information could be stored as knots in a string, or as bits in a computer memory. . . .

Platonic idealism lay that way, Mike thought warily. Something more symbiotic, more mutualistic, more entangled, then? The material world as "host" for information? A mindful process in which structure continually embodies the pattern that rides in and on it? Evolving together with it, the way old-style software and central processing units—or humans and machines, for that matter—coevolve?

He had already seen it happening in the netizenry and their move-ments from one machine platform to another. Frequently executed soft-ware subroutines migrated into hard-wired instructions, and vice versa. The boundary between structural hardware and patterning software grew fuzzier all the time—as his own existence proved.

Was he operating at the right level of intention for reprogramming the real? Were any artists, ever? A machine-code virus did nothing if you typed it as text into a word processing program. You had to go in at the right level, but where exactly was that?

He looked at some of the works drawn from his memory, to which he'd given external form by borrowing information from the infosphere—sources ranging from stock footage to holographic simulations. Out of deepest, darkest childhood he opened some of his digitally incarnated memories into virtual space. In one scene he asked his parents why they had moved into the Christian Identity compound and got a discussion of race and white flight for his trouble. In another he watched his child-hood sadism in its first flowering, when he took the magnifying glass his father had given him and, instead of using it for the intended "scientific" purpose, had used it as a burning glass, setting fire to dry leaves, news-paper, plastic, wax, ants, beetles, and eventually a large section of their winter-killed front lawn. . . .

Mike turned his attention away from that one, reminded both too pleasantly and too unpleasantly of the deaths of Schwarzbrucke and the Clones. He wondered why, out of all the memories in his head, he should only return to a certain set of them. *Maybe they are like chaotic attractors in my psyche,* he thought. But at least they were his. That wave or what-ever it was that had hit him while he was working on virtualizing his memory—that was not his, even if it did flash a trance image or waking dream into his head.

It was as if someone else had put his dream or memory inside Mike's head. He and that other person flashed instantly into the void of space, doubles or alter-egos, fluorescently glowing, ethereal, virtually real yet unreal angels walking hand in hand. In that flashing instant their hand-clasp was broken and they were spun about, back to back, face-to-face, back to back.

The universe underneath Mike's feet became abruptly more real, the stony surface of a dead world, the edge of a mountain trail, but Mike's angel wings were gone and he found himself sealed in a fishbowl-helmeted white spacesuit. The other person spun rapidly away, reaching out to Mike with the beak-masked face and winged arms of an eagle dancer. They should not have been able to see each other, but somehow they still could. As they fell away from each other Mike felt himself becoming more solid and real, more self-contained.

The other had already disappeared. The wave passed and Mike came back to himself, to his own body in the tank and his work on his private world in the infosphere. He was inexplicably certain that what he had envisioned was not about *him*. It seemed only accidentally intended for him—as if someone had, at the last moment of everything, remembered to send it to him, a foreshock of the future. Mike felt as if he were following in the other's footsteps, that all his work—all his research, every text he scanned—would have already been seen by that mind at the end of time.

What level of intention was that Other operating from? Mike looked at the virtualized memories he had created and blanked them away for a moment. They seemed suddenly trivial, information incapable of displacing or reprogramming the physical world in the way he hoped. He was glad to be distracted from his melancholy by a barrage of reports from his netizens attempting to explain what it was that had impacted upon them mere moments earlier.

The netizens bombarded him with their discussions—about connections between dreaming and near-death experiences and quantum probability waves, about transitory experiential states created by phase-locking of neuronal firings in different brain regions, about how the "AmerIndian shaman's flight amid innumerable jewels of light moving through limitless space" resembles a "description of quantum mechanical fluctuations," about how information dropped down a black hole is "not lost but transferred in a more ethereal fashion, as *influence*, like that which joins the members of a particle/antiparticle pair via some transcendental connection."

"Explain!" Mike commanded, although at some level he realized the netizenry of the Culture was doing its best to describe a phenomenon it barely understood. What he got by way of explanation was discussion of subatomic flux, instantaneous creation/destruction of matter/antimatter particle pairs, quantum devices subject to probabilistic degradation, the universe as a quantum device, the distinction between past and present and future as a persistent illusion, a measure of 10^{19} billion electron volts as the Planck energy for opening a gap in the spacetime fabric, the fact that flux occurs in which many futures and many presents are present at each universe bifurcation point, that iteration and amplification mean one time line is chosen and others disappear, that in bifurcations the past is continually recycled and stabilized through feedback, that time's turbulence means history expresses self-similarity across different scales—

Mike silenced them. He had heard enough. In a final effort, the netizens hung before Mike in virtual space a diagram, hauntingly beautiful in its elegant simplicity, captioned "Closed Timelike Curve or Temporal Möbius in Phase Space. A Rössleroid attractor."

Time is the strangest attractor, Mike thought as he stared at the image. *Always incompleteness and missing information at the center.* What pushed Mike's head around in his tank, however, was how much the "Temporal Möbius in Phase Space" resembled an idealized, abstract image of Perisphere, Trylon, and Helicline of the 1939 World's Fair. Had old Sakler down by the Eel River known something? Or was he just picking up on some wave echoing from the end of time, like the sound of a cannon shot arriving before the order to fire?

A vast image out of Spiritus Mundi *troubles my sight,* Mike thought. Yeats. 1865 to 1939. Turning gyres. The millennium and the falcon. His head hurt with bifurcations and self-similarity, phase-locking feedback and phase space, until at last understanding crystallized in his head with incredible rapidity. Everything precipitated, like an abrupt phase transition inside his mind.

The energy inherent in consciousness, and its ability to exploit quantum-scale shifts to effect classical-scale changes, meant that phase-locking could provide a powerful bridge between the quantum and classical realms. To think big, one first had to think small. The quantum flux was the appropriate locus for the fecund soil of eternity—with all its dualities, its dreams of heaven and nightmares of hell. That, he now knew, was the right level at which to go in. By utilizing the chaotic effects always present in consciousness, he could exploit time's turbulent strange-attractive properties to burst the surface tension of spacetime at far, far less than Planck energy. He knew it could be done, because *some-one* had already done it.

Trace the source of that probability wave, Mike Dalke commanded his netizen minions. *Examine all its associations—any topic relating to attempts to break through the Planck boundaries. Notify me immediately if that probability wave signature appears again.*

Hunt down any trace of the wave that had moved through the cloud chamber of the infosphere: That was the message Michael Dalke, floating in his manatee livesuit, in a tank beneath Retcorp and Lambeg office buildings in Cincinnati, sent out along all the nerves of his extended body electric, to all those still loyal to him in the Culture and its Deep

Background. Yet, despite all the powers at his command, Mike Dalke did not rest easy. For the first time in his life he found himself as afraid of falling asleep as he was once afraid of not falling asleep. The thought that that *Other*, whom he immediately thought of as his adversary, might already possess the ability to reprogram reality—the same ability Mike sought for himself—was almost too much to bear. If his opponent once came to reign in the realm of dreams, then that adversary might never be defeated, for the dream would rise again and again.

No. He would not let that happen. But Mike did wonder: How many more people would he have to kill before he was freed of this horrible separateness, this dull-flesh personhood? What would it take to destroy his privacy so thoroughly that he could at last become the source of all that was public? How much more work would he have to do before he could merge with and control the daylight public dream of the human world? What would it take?

No matter what it required, he would do it. He had seen the hive-mind bliss of the netizens and, secretly, he envied them. He had learned through the hardest of teachings that the freedom he had once so cherished was nothing but a fool's paradise. If he and all his fellow human beings in the body politic could be connected the way the netizens were connected to him in his body electric, if humans could be *freed* of the burden of selfhood and exist truly for the family, the community, the good of society as a whole, think how much happier they would all be.

Surely they would realize, as he had, that the freedom of perfect thralldom was far preferable to the thralldom of perfect freedom. Mike would bring that bliss to himself and all human beings. He would be the selfless savior of his species. Nothing was going to stop him.

Constellations Without Names

To the east, ranks of military shuttles continued to fall, landing lights ablaze, down the evening sky, toward Los Angeles International. Maybe some of those were bringing the new enantioviroid reprogrammer, the "antidote" to the war mites that had been announced in the media late that afternoon. Lydia Fabro-Hatton lay back in the slough mud beside Santa Monica Bay with a small, sad smile on her face. As she felt all the cells of her body's self-identifying psychosomal network, all the components of her nervous and endocrine and immunological systems going atavistically spirochete, beginning to ooze out of her body, she knew the antidote was arriving too late for her.

If she had known that this was going to be the last day of her life, maybe she would have lived it differently. Then again, maybe not. She wondered even now if her husband, Mark, would secretly be thinking "I told her so!" when her body was found. Mark had never approved of her joining the government teams taking spirochete samples in the sloughs and pocket estuaries around Santa Monica Bay. With each passing day he had grown more aggressively opposed to her decision to use her vacation time in that way.

"Why are you doing this?" Mark had angrily asked her in their day-opening argument that morning. "It's dangerous. It's not your field and it's not your fault. You're not responsible for what's happened. Christ! This kind of misplaced guilt and paranoia I would have expected from that Yamaguchi loser, but not you!"

"I *do* bear some responsibility," Lydia said as she made her way to the front door. "I'm sorry you don't see it. I've got to do what I can to help control this plague—"

Mark moved to bar her exit from their house, but she was too fast for him. Angrily she darted down the front stairs, under the overcast sky, and into her car. As she drove she thought that Jiro Yamaguchi was right, at least about the dangers posed by the nanotechnology they had discovered. She was even more annoyed by the fact that Mark still seemed jealous of anything he associated with the man he had so definitively humiliated.

At each checkpoint Lydia had to pass through on her way to the collecting site, she grew more and more impatient. Triggered by the way the most recent crisis was being played in the fright echo-chamber of the media, Lydia's mother had chosen that moment in Lydia's morning drive to call her, as if all that had happened that morning weren't already bad enough. On the other end of Lydia's mobile phone, as Lydia drove and tried to hold up her end of the conversation, her mother started into her mortality lament.

"I turned sixty-eight today, Lydia," her mother said nervously over long distance. "Please. I want grandchildren."

"What about Todd?" Lydia asked, trying to deflect her mother's need away from her.

"Your brother is worse than useless when it comes to this. He's not even married. I know your father would have wanted a grandchild if he were still alive. A little baby would do so much to ease the way I miss him."

"Mom, don't do this."

"Do what?"

"Don't drag out Dad's corpse as a way to force Mark and me to have kids. Dad can't be replaced, and we're not going to try to replace him."

"How can you be so selfish?" her mother exploded. "I thought you were planning on having children! Think of us. Think of your poor father's memory. He would want his name to go on. A baby would—"

"A baby would not be Dad."

"Selfish—that's what you are! Selfish, just like your brother! You and that husband of yours won't even share your lives with a little baby! It goes against everything—it goes against God!"

"Look, Mom," Lydia said, trying to remain calm, "calling down *that* idea of God on me won't change my mind. We've been over all of this before."

Her mother made a disgusted sound and hung up.

How could she tell her mother? She *had* planned on having kids, but things with Mark just weren't working out the way she hoped. Not at all. This thing with the war mite plague and her involvement with it, too. *This just isn't the best time for bringing a child into the world*, she thought. Then again, it probably seldom was.

Shaking her head at the heretical turn her thoughts were taking, Lydia pulled into a parking spot on a slope above the deserted beachfront. She got out of her car and walked across the lot toward one of the trailers serving as a lab for the recently resurrected Federal Emergency Management Agency and the Centers for Disease Control. Once inside, she donned her biohazard suit and headgear, then headed out the back door toward a tidal flat from which the bodies had been recently removed— and that was reported to be aswarm with spirochetized human cells.

At the flats she took sample after sample, carefully labeling each in its leakproof container. She returned to the lab trailer with her specimens, turning them over to one of the assistants. During lunch she felt a bit unfocused, but well enough. Probably an aftereffect from the morning explosions with Mark and her mother, she told herself. On her computer she saw that her brother Todd had left a message, so she returned his call. He answered from the field, somewhere outside the mighty metrop of Woodruff, Arizona.

"What's that you're working on?" Lydia asked once she'd gotten his attention.

"Clocking wind speed and direction," Todd said absently as he worked. "Then I'll mark the time when I activate this row of lofting-prone irrigation foggers. They'll fountain watercolors into the air and across these canvases here. For my *Wind Paintings* series. Want to watch?"

"Sure," Lydia said with a shrug.

Todd triggered the system. A rainbow of watercolors plumed for a brief moment into the wind, then shut off, leaving a luminous, entangled skein of colors hanging and drifting in the breeze. When the skein had settled to the ground, Todd positioned the field camera so Lydia could see the painting that had resulted from his collaboration with the wind a moment before. The final product was a chaotic yet delicate pointillism in which an instant's flows and turbulences were recorded. Lydia applauded lightly.

"Intriguing," she said, "but does life irrigate art, or does art irrigate life?"

Todd laughed and groaned at the joke.

"More like 'When the pope says you paint the ceiling, you paint the ceiling,' " he said.

Lydia nodded, recalling fragments of the context for her brother's presence in Arizona.

"So these whatever-they-ares," Lydia said, "they're paying you well to forsake Hawaii for the desert?"

"The Ascended Order of Sweetness and Light is paying me quite well," he said. "It's only for a couple of months. Things were slow at the clinic and with my music anyway. I was glad to get a chance to explore another avenue of my creativity—and make money doing it."

" 'Ascended Order of Sweetness and Light'?" Lydia said, laughing. "Sounds like some kind of Gnostic benevolent society, to me."

Todd smiled from the desert.

"They've been benevolent to me," he said, brushing his graying hair away from his face. "I won't deny that."

"Why 'sweetness and light'?"

"Because they're into bees and physics," Todd said, panning the camera around toward a complex of oddly shaped buildings nestled into a tan and orange striated cliffside—courtyards spiked with tensegrity sculptures surrounded by hexagon-celled Fuller domes under bright sun and blue sky. "In their ArcHive monastery here, the Ascendeds have more research on bees than you would ever want to know. Bee navigation and its relation to azimuth and the ephemeris function and God only knows what all else. History, too."

"I didn't know bees had a history," Lydia said lightly.

"Sure," Todd said as he turned the camera back toward himself and his work. "Bee carvings have been found on ancient Egyptian temple walls. Bee designs are carved in the tomb of Ramses III. In ancient Egypt bees were worshiped as symbols and messengers of eternity, even as sources of eternal life. Over the main entrance to the library the Ascended-eds have carved this line from some poem: 'singing masons building roofs of gold.' Isn't that a great description of a beehive?"

"Very sweet," she said, impressed by her brother's childlike enthusiasm. "And the 'light'? The physics?"

"The honeybee's 'waggle dance' is a symbolic system," Todd explained as he set up more canvases and foggers. "A language for describing space and time. Repetition in lower dimensions is symbolic of unity in higher dimensions. According to some theorists, the bee dance is a projection of a six-dimensional flag manifold into two-dimensional space."

"Whoa," Lydia said. "You lost me there."

"I know it sounds complicated, but it's not that difficult. Really. The dance is like the way the notes and staff of sheet music *look* in relation to the way music *sounds*. What the bee does is dance notation in two dimensions for a performance in six dimensions. It's like a tesseract."

"Sounds like these people get a pretty high rating on the mystic woo-woo scale," Lydia said, skeptical.

"Maybe," Todd said with a shrug. "They work with a lot of unassailable higher mathematics, though. That and quantum physics are their holy of holies. 'Physics and mysticism are complementary aspects of a single reality.' The Ascendeds are very fond of that Wolfgang Pauli quote, since he won a Nobel about eighty years ago. Not exactly hard science *or* soft magic, I guess. More a sort of hard magic."

"What do you mean?" Lydia asked, managing to be simultaneously curious and repulsed by the drift of the conversation.

"The luxon wall, the speed of light, all that," Todd said with a small smile. "Brother Phillip, one of their big experts, told me, 'If the stars are jewels in the vault of heaven, then maybe we'll be the first safecrackers to tumble the right numbers and swing open a vault door heavy as time and thick as the universe.' Something like that."

"Sounds crazy," Lydia said, worried about the people Todd had gotten himself involved with. She wondered if they were an offshoot of those Myrrhisticine cultists. Hadn't they been in Arizona, too? "Be careful."

Todd laughed.

"Who's to say that the mad are not the better artists, the truer believers?" Todd asked, imitating the voice of an RKO horror-movie madman. "The world of one's own creation is where the parallel lines of genius and madness meet! Socrates, Jesus, van Gogh—"

Lydia shook her head.

"Sometimes I think it was easier in the old days," she said, "when you were just whacked out on your rock-monomyth quest."

"The hero with a thousand vices?" Todd asked innocently. "*Moi?*"

They laughed and signed off. One of the lab techs came in with the microscopic analysis the assistants had performed on Lydia's morning samples. She read through it, then did some scopework of her own until her headache would allow her to do it no longer.

By the time she got back into the field to do some further collecting, the sun was getting low on the horizon. Lydia had taken only a few samples, however, when she realized that her headache was getting worse rather than better. Her eyesight blurred and shifted, then contracted into a tightening tunnel. She began to feel herself coming undone. She denied it for only a moment before she realized what was going on. Her suit or her mask or her gauntlets—something, including her skin, must have had a pinhole tear somewhere. She had been infected with the war mites.

How long ago? The mote machines the military had built from the alien nanotech Jiro Yamaguchi had discovered—on the angel shoulder blade she herself had discovered—had now become more intimate to her than she was to herself. In her last moments, she was suddenly glad that in all the ensuing years she had never made public the existence of the strange skull she had excavated with Jiro.

Hoist by my own petard! she thought, not knowing whether to laugh or cry. She was too busy to do either as, compelled beyond all reason, she stripped herself out of her biohazard suit and her clothes and lay down in the mud. She remembered her day, her argument with Mark, her phone call from her mother, her thoughts on God and religion, her talk with her brother—all of it, as runnels then streams and floods of spirochetized cells exited her body.

An overwhelming feeling of peace came over her and she thought that maybe she would get some answers now. She drifted out and away from her body, seeing everything in every direction, then shot away with incredible speed through incredible dark vastness.

Light grew around her again as she sped through a helix, its spirals spinning around her so fast that it seemed a cylindrical vortex. The light at the end of that tunnel was an oncoming reality, a continuum-warping spherical thing that was all at once a glittering world, a hive aswarm with moving flashes of golden light, a branching tree unconsumed by its own fire, an infinite Mind dreaming in every instant of every possible universe. She fell into its golden light, thinking of singing masons building roofs of gold, of the phrase *I believe, I believe, help my unbelief!*, of dancing through the wall between what is and what ought to be—to a world of their own creation where the creators never die.

Then, in a time stayed upon the pillars of eternity, not just her day but also her life came before her, not just remembered but relived, everything that had happened to her, everything she had done and everything that been done to her, all the effects of all her actions and thoughts on others and theirs on her, as if she were herself and her own dream of life, but also a character in the dream life of the Big Dreamer. She knew the omniscience of that Dreamer, partook of it in awful and beautiful ways. She relived all her successes and shortcomings, the thread and reason of her entire existence, all the joy and pain she had caused. She dwelled particularly on that episode with Mark and Jiro, reexperiencing it again and again, but not with pleasure.

Abruptly Jiro appeared, welcoming her, smiling happily.

"It's not time yet," he said. "You still have things to do. I do, too. I can only rescue you if you also rescue me. Don't worry. We have powerful allies on this side. Here, look."

He showed her a strange vision of herself transformed: a great swirling sphere (one of many), frail as a soap bubble yet dense and full of life as a world, rising from the wet earth. Then he sent her back. To the east, ranks of military shuttles continued to fall, landing lights ablaze, down the evening sky toward Los Angeles International, constellations without names, halos without saints. She did not see them. Her thoughts grew expansive, touched others like herself, stretched across acres, spread over miles, flashed along shorelines, ventured into the vast, blue darkness of the sea. The Earth spoke plainly to her, *through* her. Slowly, she began to learn how to think like a living world.

SEVEN 2030–2032

Sclerotium

Both before and after coming to this Allessan Wonderland, Jacinta had
thought that nothing could shock the ghost people's old Wise One,
but now she saw that she was wrong. "Shock" was the only word for the
expression on Kekchi's face as the Wise One came toward her.

"The time lines are moving. Shifting. Mindtime is being changed at
the deepest levels."

The fact that Kekchi was strictly using spoken words—no telempathic
communication, which the Allesseh could more easily read—underlined
the seriousness of the Wise One's concern. Jacinta hoped her puzzlement
wasn't altering the expression on her own face too much.

"How?"

Kekchi glanced at the unearthly earth of the pastoral landscape
through which they walked.

"We have only stories about this," the Wise One said. "Shakespeare's
Wise One, Prospero, says, 'We are such stuff as dreams are made on.'
We believe also the opposite: Dreams are such stuff as we are made on."

Jacinta nodded, intrigued despite herself at the way Kekchi had become a particular fan of Prospero in *The Tempest*. Given the ghost people's spiritual beliefs and daily practices, however, she could understand
that. During her time among them Jacinta had come to see how modeling
their conscious experience as a dream also made it easier for them to
model their dreams as conscious experiences. They probably experienced
more lucid dreams per capita than any other people in the history of

Earth. The Wise Ones were always the most lucid dreamers among them, so it was almost natural that Kekchi should be intrigued by the character of a wizard in a play about dreams and the illusory nature of physical reality.

"When we travel to where the time lines branch and weave in waves," Kekchi continued, "we see what we are looking for, already present in the patterns there. The most powerful Wise Ones can also weave some small new threads into the deep spawn—weave them together with those that are already there. Do you understand?"

"I think so," Jacinta said, trying to fully picture it. She had, after all, been to the other side of the wave membrane—had passed through that strange surface tension between what is and what could be. Perhaps, in that realm of possibility, in that implicate "elsewhere" outside the here and now, actuality itself was so unstable it could be shaped by the mind—even if she herself had only "seen" the other side and had not (as far as she could tell) manipulated the statistical likelihoods and probability distributions there.

"By weaving them," Kekchi said, glancing up at the faultless blue sky the Allesseh had bent into place above them, "the Wise One makes those time lines real—the way your people say dreams 'come true.' But even the most powerful Wise Ones can only shift things about in small ways. We do not do it often or lightly. Wise Ones can weave possibilities and futures only out of the stuff of their own existence, their own lives in the present. That weaving drains the life out of the weaver. Doing it more than a few times always kills anyone who attempts it."

Jacinta nodded slowly, trying to imagine using the subtle power of her own thoughts, even her own existence, to reorient patterns of possibility, to shift the threads of parallel universes.

"You asked me once," Kekchi continued as they slowly walked, "what would happen if the realizing of the dream is delayed. If the spawn refused to fruit. I said that then the spawn would become denser and denser until it overburdened its surroundings and died. That is not the only possibility, however. From the life cycle of our sacred mushroom, we also know of another. What your science calls the Sclerotium."

The word was from such a different context that, for a moment, Jacinta had to search her memory to find it. Then there it was: Sclerotium. The hardened, usually dark-pigmented mass of mycelia found in the resting or vegetative phase of some fleshy and nonfleshy fungi. A hyphal notknot brought on by environmental stress to the spawnbed. Capable of surviving long dormancy. From which either fruiting bodies or viable mycelia could arise periodically.

"I should have thought of that," Jacinta said slowly. "Maybe since all your spawnbeds in the tepui were happily fruiting away, the existence of that stage in your mushroom never occurred to me."

Kekchi gave her a piercing stare.

"Yes, you should have known," the Wise One said. "Whenever our expectations of final fulfillment were high, whenever we thought we had waited and labored more than long enough already, we have consoled ourselves with the story of the Sclerotium: Someday there would come a Wise One able to move and shape the time lines in the most powerful of ways. A Wise One who would return us to the heart of the dream forever, who would reunite us with the great dreamer. When we saw you and your technologies in our time-line visions, we thought you were the Sclerotium. That is why we welcomed you so readily."

Jacinta abruptly laughed. Kekchi gave her an odd look.

"Sorry," she said, "but you just reminded me of something my brother Paul once said. He accused me of being a mushroom messiah for you and your people. It turns out he was at least partly right!"

"But you are not that," Kekchi said with an odd expression, a sort of melancholy smirk. "For all your mushroom paleness, you are still alive. You cannot weave the time lines that way."

"Not a burden I would have wanted to undertake, thank you," Jacinta said, smiling. Kekchi's expression, however, grew steadily more serious.

"In thinking that the Sclerotium was just about us and our impatience," the Wise One said with a frown, "I was thinking too small. The Sclerotium is about the whole world, and all the stars, and all the universes. The Sclerotium is the One who can weave great changes in the time lines without dying—because the Sclerotium is already 'dead.' The Sclerotium appears when the spawn has become too thick for its world. The Sclerotium is One whose sacrifice into death reminds the Dreamer of responsibility for the Dream."

Jacinta pondered the strangeness of what Kekchi was telling her. The vision of a "mushroom person"—a human figure made entirely of masses of mushrooms, far denser even than the mushrooms sprouting from the bodies on the corpse island in the tepui—flashed through her head and was gone.

"This sclerotian messiah," she began, "it's human, then?"

"For us it always has been," Kekchi said. "Now I think it might appear to others in other ways, also."

"Is the Sclerotium weaving these big changes you spoke of?"

"I don't know," Kekchi said with a small sigh. "Until we came here, I thought the Allesseh itself might become the Sclerotium. Its mind is vast enough to bring about universal changes. But it's blind to the dreams of the other side. The time lines are shifting, and the Allesseh acts as if it knows nothing of the changes."

"Or is denying that they're taking place," Jacinta ventured. Thoughts of the Sclerotium oddly juxtaposed themselves in her head with images of the "void of endings" and the "spore of beginnings" as being somehow one and the same. That peculiar image of a string that becomes a hole and a hole that becomes a string flashed into her head again, beside the image of the Sclerotium as a knot woven of the strings of mycelia—a knot capable either of bursting into mushrooming fruit or of bursting into strings of mycelia once more.

"Kekchi," she asked at last, "if what's altering the time lines is this Sclerotium, what do you think will happen once the Allesseh stops denying the changes?"

The Wise One pondered that, absently raking with a big toe the smooth gravel of the perfect garden path they walked on.

"The self-sacrifice of the Sclerotium," Kekchi said, "may be the deepest reminder of the Allesseh's failure to complete its journey toward the Dream. I do not think that reminder will please it."

"Are we in danger here?" Jacinta asked, unable to avoid a certain worry at the thought. Kekchi shrugged.

"We always have been," the psychopomp said. "But we are not the Allesseh's real problem. All the shadows it has been afraid to acknowledge as its own—all humans, the Sclerotium, others it may also have denied, among the worlds of uncountable universes—that is its real problem. To deny the dreamers and the Dream is also to deny the presence of the Dreamer in itself."

Jacinta nodded. Concepts cascaded in her head. Complete, comprehensive. As opposed to consistent, coherent. She understood the Allesseh's dilemma now. It was a self trapped between completeness and consistency, oscillating between comprehensiveness and coherence. The impulse toward completeness and comprehensiveness was a centrifugal force driving it outward, while the impulse toward coherence and consistency was a centripetal force driving it inward. Like the physical universe, it could be consistent but not complete. Like the plenum of all possible universes, it could be complete but not consistent. As a self it could not be both complete and coherent at the same time. To be complete was necessarily to be incoherent. To be coherent was necessarily to be incomplete.

So the Allesseh was trapped between centrifugal and centripetal forces, between forces in itself as expansive as desire and as contractile as fear. It desired completeness but feared incoherence. It desired coherence but feared incompleteness. Between the comprehensiveness of chaos and the coherence of order, it was left spinning about itself, a dynamic tension between those forces, a soliton vortex like a tornado or a hurricane or the long-lived storm of the Great Red Spot on Jupiter. A dissipative structure far from equilibrium, a mindstorm with the potential for incredible violence.

"Not being its 'real problem' is not to say," Jacinta began, thinking of Kekchi's claim of their insignificance to the Allesseh's larger concerns, "that it might not attempt to destroy any or all of us."

"No," the Wise One said. "Although the 'rarer action is in virtue than in vengeance,' as Prospero says, we cannot expect that the Allesseh must follow that higher, harder way."

Prospero again, Jacinta thought, shaking her head. Well, our little life might be rounded with a sleep, but she preferred that her life be as large and her "sleep" as little as possible. The chaos of dreams, the order of waking—certainly that was a false dichotomy, certainly they were mutually enfolded, yet she would gladly take the insomnia of living over the sleep of the grave anytime. And in that, she supposed, she was not so different from the Allesseh, after all.

Energies

As the transatmospheric shuttleplane made its long climb toward the orbital habitat and home, Paul glanced at the seatback screen the passenger diagonally across from him was watching. It was showing what passed for an "in-depth" newscast.

". . . War Mite crisis being officially over," said the Director of the Council of Spacefaring Nations, "does not mean we should allow ourselves to grow complacent. We have lost more than one hundred million lives in the worst episode of mass terror yet visited upon humanity.

"I am proud to announce, therefore, the expansion, reinvigoration, and virtual re-creation of the High Orbital Manufacturing Enterprise, with greater governmental and far greater corporate support than orbital habitat projects have ever before enjoyed. This infusion of funds and expertise will ensure a much expanded human presence on the high frontier, precisely because, as a thoughtful futurist once put it, 'Earth is too small a basket for the human race to keep all its eggs in.' "

Expansion is right, Paul thought. Whichever groups and individuals were ultimately behind the release of the hybridizing nanotech, their full identities and involvements would never be revealed for good and all— probably because there were state and corporate secrets to be kept, and more than enough blame to go around among more than enough organizations anyway. The crisis had been over for some time, but the habitat authorities, still waiting for closure, had only removed quarantine restrictions three weeks back. Yet there was already more money, expertise, and new population growth than the habitat had ever before seen.

Although the Nanogeddon had lasted less time than most of Earth's past plagues had, it nonetheless seemed to have shaken the ruling powers enough to wake them up and get them moving in a new direction. The madness of the mite plague was as much over as it was ever likely to be. He could only hope that the smaller but related madness he had gone through with his friend Seiji these past few days was also coming to an end. Paul glanced over at him.

"A man on horseback at sunset," Seiji said, shaking his head in continuing disbelief. "I don't know which was stranger—that, or the whole thing with my cousin John."

Paul nodded.

"Both pretty strange," he agreed. "You don't want to push too hard on those types of synchronicities. Who knows where you might end up?"

Seiji nodded, then turned away and tried to sleep. It had been a long few days. Paul, however, was still too tired to sleep. He decided to stay awake until this whole circuit—down to Earth, and back up—was finally complete.

He remembered precisely the moment it all began. He and Seiji had been in one of the habitat's archival buildings—the mediary/library dedicated to horticultural and ecological records, in fact. A "weekend" day, when they were free of their workaday jobs in solar engineering and cryopreservation, free to pursue their gardening and landscaping avocations. Before them, framed by media storage shelves, there abruptly appeared a gaunt, sharp-featured young man in thoroughly stained gray spacer's coveralls, maroon knit cap, and heavy spaceboots. His hair was somewhat long and unkempt, his beard thin, his eyes deep-set behind anachronistic wire-rimmed glasses.

Paul saw Seiji's head shake in startlement. For an instant Paul thought he might be looking at Seiji's younger brother, whom Paul had never seen in person and whom Seiji himself hadn't seen in nearly three years.

"Seiji Yamaguchi?" asked the apparition, extending a hand for Seiji to shake. A strong smell emanated from the apparition. Black workgrime was plainly visible beneath the apparition's fingernails. *The man looks a bit down and out,* Paul thought.

"Yes?"

"John Drinan," said the apparition. "Your second cousin?

"Oh . . . yes! Of course!" Seiji said, recovering. "Sorry—I've never seen you except over vidlink from out beyond the moon, a couple of weeks back. The picture was kind of snowy."

Drinan smiled awkwardly, and Seiji introduced Paul as a friend who knew all about what had been going on with Jiro. Together they walked with Seiji's cousin through the Mediary stacks. Coming to a study lounge, they sat down. Paul thought again that the poor guy looked travel-worn and in need of a good bath.

"The bad news is," John began, slouching deeper into the lounge seat, "I didn't find your brother."

Seiji nodded slowly.

"The good news is, I met lots of people who say they've seen him or someone who looks like him. Recently."

"Really?"

"Yeah," Seiji's cousin said, smiling slightly, remembering. His words seemed almost to lilt with the fatigue of his journeys, as if he were sleep-talking. "The Trashlands are a strange space. The no-tech types don't much like any prodding or prying from outside. The local sheriff was pretty uncooperative, too, at first. Maybe my looks bothered him, I don't know. I can understand it: I mean, here comes this guy claiming to be a second cousin, asking all these questions about some other guy who's missing."

Paul watched Drinan glance absently into his hands. He might as well have been staring off into deep space.

"Finally, though," Drinan continued, "the sheriff gave me an old student holo ID of Jiro's. One of the deputies found it in Jiro's apartment after Jiro moved off into the Trashlands. I guess they opened the place up when your mother called to report him missing. I used the ID when I made these."

From his coverall pockets, Drinan pulled two cheap handscanned holographic plaques. YAMAGUCHI *Jiro Ansel* PLEASE *Contact Home or Seiji. They Are Concerned Enough to Send Me to Contact You. Your*

Cousin J. G. Drinan, said the first one. The other bore the holo and scan code from the student ID and the words *HAVE YOU SEEN ME? Jiro Ansel Yamaguchi. If You HAVE . . . or KNOW Him, Please Contact His Brother SEIJI. Jiro Was Last Seen in the CHERRY VALLEY–YUCAIPA AREA. We Are All Concerned. . . . Cousin J. G. Drinan.* Seiji's home vid-link number was listed on the plaque.

"I showed these around in places where I thought people might have seen him," Drinan continued, slouching farther toward horizontal with fatigue and the weight of his message. "TechNot camps, food ration shops, Trashland entry stations, anyplace he might have come in for supplies or aid. I posted the plaques on all the streetlight stanchions between Cherry Valley and Yucaipa."

Paul and Seiji stared at the grainy reproduction of Seiji's brother's image on the plaque. The holo, showing a man with wide eyes staring like lost ghosts from the windows of a haunted face, deeply unsettled Paul. It made him think of dated snow-and-ashes photos of children missing for years. Of transients with an elderly Einstein's face, dying of hypothermia on city streets. Of his own lost sister Jacinta. Of things he didn't want to think about. He couldn't even imagine what it might make Seiji think of.

"But people *did* say they'd seen him?" Paul asked, looking up at Seiji's cousin. Seiji had as yet been unable to tear his eyes from the holoplaque in his hands.

"Yeah, or someone who looks like him," Drinan said, laughing quietly and shaking his head. Seiji looked up at last. "A couple of places—when I went in and showed them the holo with your brother on it?—they looked at the image on the plaque, then at me, then at the holo again, then back at me, and they said, 'This is *your* picture, isn't it?' I told them, 'No, it's my cousin,' and they said, 'Naw, it's you! Sure looks like you.' "

Drinan stared at his heavy spaceboots for a moment, collecting his thoughts from the floor. Paul was amazed that someone so obviously fatigued as Seiji's cousin was could still keep on speaking, even if it was in a rather wild-eyed, beyond-tired fashion.

"I went back to my ship, the *Helios,* and commanded the cabin to decouple from the rest of the ship and go to aircar mode. I overflew the Trashlands, up and down the canyons. A heavy rainstorm was under way, so no one was out and about. At one point I thought I saw someone wandering among the trash of the canyon floor. My infrared and motion sensors didn't show anything, but I switched on my throat mike and the aircar's loudspeakers.

"I maneuvered my vehicle to where I thought I'd seen someone, but once there I didn't see anybody. I kept calling out, 'Jiro! Jiro Yamaguchi! Jiro, are you there?' as I moved up the canyon. Did it until I was hoarse, but it did no good."

Drinan turned and looked Seiji in the eye for a brief moment.

"I can see why you and your folks are worried. I mean, I'm outside the mainstream, too, like your brother. I've been living out of *Helios* these past few years, just me and my dog Oz rambling all over human space. Still, I guess that hasn't been as far outside as your brother, in some ways."

Drinan's gaze wandered very far away, very abruptly, as if there were now no walls around him, no space and no time.

"When I was out there in all that nothing looking for your brother," he said at last, "I felt like I was looking for myself. It was a strange feeling. The longer I was out there, the stronger it got."

Drinan shook his head, whacked his suit gauntlets against his thigh, and turned his glance toward Paul. The young spacer seemed quieter now, a messenger who has discharged his duties. He looked back toward Seiji again.

"But I've always had my dog, anyway," Drinan said. "And I've always kept in touch, always let somebody know where I was going. I guess that must be what worries you and your folks most—Jiro hasn't kept in touch."

"Yes," Seiji said, looking at his hands in his lap, then moving them to his knees, then exhaling sharply and standing up. "The uncertainty's the worst part. But I'm glad that people say they've seen Jiro. At least that means he's still alive. Now we just have to find him and figure a way to get him back to civilization."

Paul saw that Drinan had slouched onto one elbow, almost prone, on the lounge seat.

"Look," Seiji said, "you must be tired after all the traveling you've done. Why don't you relax here a bit while we finish up with our research, then maybe we'll get some lunch? Sound like an idea?"

"Sounds good," John said with a nod. "I am tired. What date and time is it?"

"About fifteen minutes shy of twelve hundred hours, November ninth," Paul told him. "We're synched to Greenwich Time here in the habitat."

"Been on the jaunt eighteen, nineteen days, then," he said with a crooked smile. "Can't say for sure—time zones, y'know."

Paul smiled, and he and Seiji turned back in the direction of the research stacks where they had been working. By the time they'd finished their research and returned to where Seiji's second cousin was seated, the man's eyes were closed. As Paul and Seiji approached, however, his eyelids flicked up, as alert as if he had just wakened from a nightmare.

"How's it going?" Seiji asked quietly.

"Fine. Just resting my eyes." Drinan smoothed out his face with his right hand and slowly stood up. As the three of them walked toward a ramp, each of the several young students they passed along the way darted furtive glances and surreptitious stares in their direction.

"Wow," John said, laughing a bit nervously when they reached the top landing of the ramp. "What is it with the kids here? You'd think they never saw a deep spacer before."

"Yeah," Paul said with a smile as the three of them moved down a ramp-and-handhold corridor. "This is a pretty squeaky-clean environment. Highest per capita population of meticulous overachievers in known space! You stick out like a sunflower in a cornfield."

"I guess so."

The transport corridor was cold and gray by haborb standards, one of the few areas that wasn't Hawaiian warm and green.

"Where are you docked?" Seiji asked his second cousin.

"At the white port. It had the most spaces available."

"That's Administration. We'll take a ridge cart to the nearest station and cut through Admin sector."

They boarded a bulletcar, which shot them upline and disgorged them near Admin. As they cut through that sector on their way toward the nearest docking bay, they got hard looks from the young Admin types fresh up from Earth, dressed in charcoal Nehru suits with piano-wire string ties.

"Pretty chilly in there," John said when they came out into the docking bay.

Seiji nodded.

"Always some tension between the high-frontier folk in the habitat," he said, "and the corporate and governmental adminstrators who rotate up from Earth. A lot of them don't quite get what we're up to here."

Paul agreed silently. The cold, hard expressions on the faces of too many of the administrative types up from the home world made him think of fallen leaves rattling across hard winter lawns when he was a kid back on Earth.

The mooncrete bays were stacked with all kinds of neat, conventional cislunar fliers. John's ship—a large, micrometeorite-scoured, battlewagon-gray Solar Harvester Travel-All, with multiple docking dents and taped-over busted landing lights—stood out like a derelict at a debutante ball.

"It's unlocked. What's this?" John said, pulling a plastic kinneagram card from the edge of his front viewport. "A ticket."

"Habitat citizen-policing in action," Seiji said. "I'll handle it."

Paul noted the BEWARE OF DOG sign in one dirty viewport as they walked around to the crewside hatch. He was startled by the sound of the hatch door squawking out its cranky metallic complaint as it opened. Cousin John must have popped the hatch remotely, he realized.

"Don't bother fixing the ticket," John said as Paul and Seiji climbed inside. "Odds are I'll never come through here again. This boat's still registered in my brother's name anyway. I bought it off him for more money than it's worth. Let them go after him—he can afford it. He's a millionaire."

Moving aside the clutter of newsfaxes and junk, Seiji and Paul helped Drinan haul out his meager luggage. The interior of the vehicle smelled of dog food and dog, dog, dog.

"Hey, what breed of horse d'you have here, anyway?" Paul asked, ruffling the scruff behind the canine's massive head.

"Mastiff. Purebred and pedigreed."

"So this is what a mastiff looks like!" Seiji said, genuinely pleased, as if the world were offering up an answer to a question he hadn't formally asked yet. "I thought they only guarded the homes of Nepalese villagers or something. I've never seen one of them, and I wondered what they looked like. Now I know."

Seiji's second cousin glanced around at the maze of exits angling off the docking bays, then donned anachronistic dark glasses and, with both hands, telescoped out the red-tipped white cane that traditionally signified blindness. Paul stared at him.

"This way I don't get hassled about the dog," Drinan explained. "Okay, where we going?"

The dog's wagging tail thumped Paul hard across the leg.

"Ouch!" Paul said with a startled laugh. "The wag of that dog's tail is like someone whacking on you with a thick length of rope!"

"Yeah," John Drinan said. "He's three years old and he weighs more than I do. C'mere, Oz. Up."

Rearing up on its hind legs and resting its front paws on John's shoulders, the dog was a good head taller than its master—and its head dwarfed John's own.

"See all this?" John asked, grabbing two great fistfuls of loose neck scruff. "They were bred for pack-hunting lions. When a lion tries to bite a mastiff in the throat, what it gets is scruff. Then the mastiff can use its own big jaws in return."

The dog dropped back to all fours and ambled a pace or two away.

"They're a very old, aristocratic breed," John continued as they walked left, toward the part of the habitat that sheltered the neighborhood where Seiji lived. "That's why I named him Ozymandias—Oz for short. Hey, you wouldn't mind if we found someplace where there's grass nearby, so Oz can do his thing?"

"There are several along the way," Seiji said, setting a brisker pace. "Follow us."

"Right."

As they walked, the three of them talked about their jobs and what they had done before coming into space.

"I did the infosystem thing for a while," John said. "Robotic systems analyst."

"You're not still doing that?" Seiji asked.

"Not really. I don't know how much my aunt or your mother told you—"

"Not much," Seiji said.

"Lately, I've been riding herd on prototype robot miners. The production models are supposed to go out to the asteroids on the *Swallowtail*, the mass-driver tug they're building up here. That's what I was doing when my sister contacted me, to tell me my mother had taken ill. That's why I started back toward Earth. On the way down, your Aunt Marian asked me to detour over to the Trashlands to look for your brother. I did it on my way back out, since I had to launch from Edwards anyway."

"My mother must have asked my aunt to get in touch with you," Seiji said, nodding.

"No problem," John remarked, looking down. Paul saw that Oz had found a spot of grass suitable to his needs. "I got to spend some time with my mother. Looking for your brother was a good reason to move on before we could start arguing too much. I should be able to make another trip down to see Mom again in a couple of weeks."

John called his dog over toward them.

"When was the last time you talked to Jiro?" John asked.

"Over vidlink," Seiji said. "Almost a year ago now, I guess. Before he headed for his cave or wherever he is in the Trashlands. He sounded pretty much okay when I talked to him."

They walked in silence for a time, down a pathway, and into Seiji's home, leaving the dog to flop down behind them on the porch. As the three of them walked through the neo-Victorian parlor, John noted with approval the woodwork and moldings.

"Nice detailwork," he said, smiling. "A carpenter notices these things."

In the front room Seiji took the claviform rocker and Paul took an overstuffed armchair, leaving the hammocouch for Seiji's second cousin to sprawl out on. John snatched off his knit cap and mussed up his longish hair with one hand. Absently or contemplatively scratching his beard, he stared down at Seiji's makeshift but functional coffee table. Sandwiched between the two glassteel plates of the table's top was a posterboard reproduction of a sixteenth-century painting celebrating the glorious reign of Elizabeth I. The Spanish Armada burned and sank endlessly in the background.

"You said your brother sounded 'okay' when you last talked to him. . . ."

"Right," Seiji said, picking up his chronometer from where he had left it on the coffee table. "Which implies there were times when he didn't sound okay. He's had some psychological problems, including a nervous breakdown of sorts. Years ago now. When he was in graduate school. He's a great student, or at least he was, before. But he's his own sort of person. Like you. How was it that you put it, Paul? A sunflower in the cornfield."

Paul nodded but said nothing. He was feeling a bit of a tagalong at this point, but Seiji's newly acquainted cousin was so unpretentious and unthreatening that Paul didn't feel like he was intruding all that much.

"Did he ever see anybody?" John asked. "A counselor, therapist—"

"He did dolphin-Ibogara therapy at the Fabro clinic in Hawaii," Seiji said, nodding. "Only once, before that. In our family, going to a mind-straightener means admitting there's a problem, so it wasn't a first option. No admission, no problem. That's always been the unspoken code."

"Your brother did go, though?"

"Yeah. He went to the campus counseling center and they assigned him to a husband-and-wife psych team who were about as sensitive as a box of rocks. Told Jiro he had no problem and should stop wasting the counseling center's time. Jiro didn't think much of 'mental health professionals' after that. He preferred self-medication."

"Drugs?"

"Yeah, drugs." Seiji began to rock back and forth in his chair, slowly, meditatively. "But it'd be too easy to blame his problems on just that. I mean, whatever Jiro does he does to excess. When there was alcohol it was alcohol, when there was headzap it was headzap, when there was KL it was KL."

Paul winced uncomfortably. John gave him a questioning look. Paul gave Seiji's cousin the thumbnail version of his involvement in the history of that substance—his sister's disappearance, the spore print in his pack, his involvement with Vang and Tetragrammaton. When he had finished, the look Drinan gave him was not the usual sad or thoughtful glance. It was a look of genuine awe.

"You brought KL and Cordyshrooms to the world?" John asked, the awestruck expression still stuck on his face.

"I'm afraid so," Paul said. "When I think of all the lives it has devastated the way it has devastated Seiji's brother, I'm not at all proud of the fact."

John Drinan shrugged and glanced away.

"But I did all the stuff Jiro did," John said. "Rite of passage."

That last phrase seemed to make Seiji uncomfortable, but when Seiji spoke he talked to Paul and said nothing about it.

"I don't think any one thing is solely responsible for Jiro's problems," Seiji said, trying to allay Paul's guilt. "Not even KL. At most it just brought things up to the surface. Brought out in the open what was already there."

"And he hasn't been the same since?" John asked. Seiji stopped his nervous rocking in the chair and turned his gaze fully on his cousin. To Paul, everything in the room seemed suddenly to stand out with an aggressive sharpness—every piece of paint chipping from the moldings, every flaw in the lighting, every speck of dust on the floor and shelves.

"The past several years after the Ibogara therapy, we thought Jiro was getting *better*," Seiji said. "He went back to school full-time, had research analyst jobs at the Trashlands and Rancho La Brea. He began writing a book on subsistence strategies of indigenous peoples—in his spare time! But something's been gone for years. He got along, sure, but something's gone. And now this happens. He calls my mother and tells her he's dropped out of his postdoc and is leaving everything behind." Seiji exhaled in exasperation. "Studying the Indians and TechNots wasn't good enough—he has to live like one, too. Everything to excess, as usual."

Paul looked up from his hands in his lap.

"But that's your brother's choice," he said. "He's an adult, he's got free will. He's made his decision to live that way, and we have to respect that."

Seiji nodded vigorously.

"I do, believe me. Lots of people have entertained thoughts of dropping out the way Jiro has. Earth's culture is pretty sick in a lot of ways—I know that. When I tell some of my less conventional friends what Jiro's up to, most of them say, 'Wow! Great! He's really had the guts to *do* it? I've always wanted to do that, but I never had the guts.' To them it's a great adventure, but I keep wondering. Is he out there because being out there is the only way he can stay sane—or is he out there because he's already crazy? Is this his way of staying alive, or his way of committing slow suicide?"

A silence opened into the room around them.

"Reality's not either/or—there're always gray areas," John Drinan said, glancing down into his hands. "But I've lived totally on my own a lot, too. It can be done. If the mainstream is polluted, you don't have to be crazy to want to live outside it. As far as we know, Jiro's still alive, right? So he must want to live. In any case, it's like Paul said. It's his decision. He's following his own leadings."

"Free will," Seiji said with a sigh, then stood up. "Can't institutionalize someone who's not a danger to himself or others. But how do you really know when someone's truly a danger to himself? Jiro's taking risks, but so do lots of other people. Are they all insane? Which risks are acceptable? Which aren't?" Seiji shook his head. "Uncertainty again."

John shrugged without looking up.

"Maybe it's uncertainty that makes free will possible," he said.

Paul stared at him carefully, surprised. Seiji stepped quickly to the coldbox to grab a few beers—a local concoction called HOMEbrew—then rejoined Paul and John. They drank in silence, grateful for the drink and grateful for the silence.

None of them had finished his drink when John stood, waiting, his knit cap on his head again. The beer, half finished, seemed already to have revived Seiji's cousin a bit, though when John spoke, Paul still heard a bit of the dreaming lilt in his words. The three of them walked out the door, beers in hand, across the veranda, to stand on the front ramp beneath the habitat's sheltering sky.

"That's my green therapy," Seiji said, pointing to the terraced, lawn-free front yard abloom with flowers above a thick blanket of mulch. "English country garden style, mostly, with a few details from Japanese landscaping. Shrubs and bulbs and perennials, mainly."

John walked alongside the garden, eyeing it carefully.

"Compost mulch, isn't it? Clone-oak timbers for the terracing? Un-treated?"

"That's right."

"The gray shrubs—junipers?"

"Right," Seiji said. "I'm doing branch isolations on them, for a bonsai effect."

"That'll look nice."

"You know gardening?" Paul asked.

"Some," John said with a slight shrug. "I used to work in the land-scaping biz for a while, down in BALAAM."

Hands in pockets, Paul evened out a clump of mulch with the toe of one shoe.

"Sounds like you've had quite a few jobs, cousin," Seiji said. "Land-scaper, carpenter, robotics engineer—"

"—potter, chef," John said, nodding as he sat down on a terracing timber, setting his beer down beside him. "Yep. Lots of jobs."

"And you're how old now? Twenty-five?"

"Right." John picked around in the dirt, as if plucking unseen weeds. "But I moved out of the house when I was fifteen. My parents were both early wireheads, septal-area stim addicts. I'm the youngest of six kids. I saw what they did to my older brothers and sisters. I got tired of their bullshit, tired of watching them kill each other and themselves, so I took off. High-wiring finally got my father six years ago. He was a big holovid writer twenty, thirty years ago. Charlie Drinan. Maybe you've heard of him?"

"Can't say I have," Paul said.

"He wrote for *Satellite Theatre* and *Starbored*. Concepted game shows, too—*Macabre Mayhem*, that sort of stuff." John drank his beer and glanced across the promenade to where lawns and landscaping sur-rounded the partially buried Hellman Memorial Orbital Hospital. "Any-way, the wireheading's what's getting my mother now, too, I guess. She's off headzap, but her brain apparently got so used to the stuff it can't live without it. She was in the hospital in BALAAM because her brain is slowly devouring itself. Some kind of enzyme breakdown."

John switched his attention to a nearby bonsaied juniper, fingered its needles absently. The three of them fell silent for a moment. Paul watched as Seiji stood with one foot on the ground, the other on the lowest part of the ramp, then both feet on the ground, then one foot on the ramp again—steps in a small, nervous dance. Paul looked over at John, following his gaze up into the whole confused wraparound firmament of the haborb's central sphere, the Midgard serpent of this town-and-country scenery, swallowing its own tail in an inside-out world, earth around sky instead of the more familiar sky around Earth.

"So you've been on the road ten years?" Paul asked. "How'd you ever find time to become an expert in robotics? You pick it up in college?"

"Naw," John said, rearranging some more mulch. "Only mech language I learned in school was Traintext. I was an art major at a small liberal arts school. Marlborough College—ever hear of it?"

Neither Paul nor Seiji had.

"Well, I just showed the admissions people there my pottery," John said, "and they let me in. Got me all these grants and scholarships. Not bad for a street rat. But I got bored. Didn't see the point of being taught what I already knew."

"How'd you get into robotics, then?" Seiji asked, sitting down on the mooncrete ramp.

Cousin John smiled slightly through his thin beard and looked away into a distance as much of time as of space.

"That's kind of embarrassing. I was living outside Hilo, doing the bath-tub chemist routine, brewing up KL. One of my customers was a pho-tonics wizard, an all-around Renaissance man. He had some advanced degree in biochemistry originally, I think it was. He'd discovered a defla-tulent—you know what that is?"

"Something that prevents farts?" Paul speculated.

"Right," John said, smiling again, mostly with his eyes. "No farty beans, no gassy decaffeinated coffee. He patented this deflatulent agent years ago and some big Swiss megacorp bought it up, so now he gets a cool ten mill a year just from that one idea."

"But he moved on to photonics and robotics?" Paul asked, trying to steer the conversation back on track.

"Yeah," John said. "And on to 'gate. A lot of my KL customers were techheads—codescriptors and robotjocks, mostly. Anyway, one day he says to me, 'Johnny, you're a smart guy. How'd you like a job that would give you lots of free time and a quarter mill starting salary?' I said sure. When I asked him what it was, he said microbotics. I told him I knew next to nothing about that, but he said no problem, he'd train me on the systems he worked with. So that's what we did. I moved into his house and he brought home this micromainframe with all these robot arms and actuators of every size—and a stack of operator-code media taller than I am, for me to scan. For three months I scanned and trained till I'd burned what I'd learned right into my mental circuitry. Then I put on the corporate battlesuit, interviewed, and, with the help of my friend's recommendation, I got the job. The company gave me a title and paraded these beautiful secretaries in front of me—all women, too, so they made at least that assumption about how I was wired—and they asked me to choose one."

John drank his beer a moment.

"We ended up training people from all over inhabited space," he continued. "I helped develop an automated system so that these Chinese, moon miners could extract their product without risking their lives. Had some good times, too. My friend and I would call in bogus business trips to each other's secretaries so we could take the company's transat jet down south for some surfing in Australia—under the pretense that we were working with a client."

Seiji smiled and flicked a flake of white paint off the ramp he was seated on. The paint chip spun into his garden.

"A lot of the people I knew down in Hawaii who were plugged into infotech were plugged into drugs, too," Seiji said, then glanced meaningfully over at Paul. "But the infotech people I knew called KL their work drug—not mushrooms of any sort."

John nodded and stared up at the aircyclists darting around the long bulletcart axis in the low-gee zone above, running through the middle of the habitat's central sphere.

"Sure," he said. "Strange, since the one is extracted from the other."

"The KL extraction changes the effect," Paul explained, all too familiar with the topic. "It removes the 'gate from its natural matrix, decontextualizes it. In the fungus itself it's found with a number of other psychoactive and neurosupportive substances."

John nodded, apparently impressed yet again with the company he was keeping.

"When you're on 'gate," he began, "all the gates are down, right? Everything's right there. No gray areas in the gray matter. Everything's either/or, just like in binary. Aching clarity. 'Gate helps you think like a machine intelligence."

"Ah," Paul said with a heavenward-pointing index finger, "but do you really want to think like a machine intelligence?"

John's gaze turned back toward the flowers and mulch.

"That's the question, isn't it? Everybody says consciousness is cyber, that virtual reality is where the map becomes the territory. . . ."

"So is paranoid schizophrenia," Seiji said.

Cousin John smiled and nodded.

"Yeah. Maybe the virtuals are somehow displacing the original reality. Who knows? Working in machine intelligence and robotics isn't all fun and games and the greater glory of humanity, anyway. When we came in to automate this old pineapple soda plant in Hilo, the plant employed four hundred and fifty people. Two weeks later, after we'd automated, it employed four—two plant mechanics and two plant supervisors, who supervised nothing, knew the mechanics of nothing. They just had their twenty years in and were given token positions as glorified janitors."

"Everyone else was fired?" Seiji asked.

"We were told they were given other positions in the company," John said, crumbling a clod of dirt in his hand and smoothing it back into the garden. "I really can't say. The system we put in was almost completely self-sufficient—human beings just got in its way. It did everything: processed the pineapples, mixed the drinks, filled the slurpacks, painted the slurpacks, sealed the slurpacks, even palletized them for pickup and distribution. One day I got this crazy, frantic call from the day-shift plant supervisor. 'Hey, we've got a problem down here,' he says. 'That automated line you put in two months ago—the damn thing's gone crazy! It's shooting unsealed poppacks all over the plant! Fast as bullets! It's like a war zone down here! How do we turn the damn thing off?' They couldn't even figure where the on/off switch was. I had to tell them."

They watched intermittent raindrops drizzle dark spots onto the pale mooncrete of the ramp. The daily rain, right on time for this sector of the habitat. They moved back into the shelter of the house's eaves as the rain began to come down harder out of the central sky.

"The machine—what was wrong with it?" Paul asked.

"Since the system recorded itself on closed-circuit TV," John said, holding his left hand out to the rain before dropping the hand back to his side, "that was pretty easy to find out. When I looked at the videos at normal speed, the automated line looked like some kind of crazy cannon, firing about a thousand poppack bullets per minute. Once I slowed the video down, though, I saw what was wrong. One of the automatic shunt gates had gone up, and everything in the last couple of steps was being ejected instead of processed. I worked my way through the process stepwise until I discovered that one of the mirrors in the laser readers had been knocked about a twentieth of a centimeter out of true. That's why the system was misreading and ejecting. One of the plant mechanics must have bumped up against it—real hard—while cleaning."

"A twentieth of a centimeter caused that much trouble?" Seiji asked.

"Sure. That was way over tolerance. I'm pretty sure one of the remaining plant workers purposely monkey-wrenched the line. Not that I blame him. The whole episode made me realize what the goal of my job really was: to make human beings superfluous, obsolete—except maybe as consumers. More and more of us with less and less to do. Particularly men. All the old grunt-muscle jobs are gone or going to smart machines, so the amount of junk male just keeps piling up. I worked on robot systems for weapons storage and retrieval, too, for remachining old nuclear material. Robots don't get radiation sickness, they don't need vacations, they won't sue for 'metal' anguish. The whole drive for smarter and smarter 'bots is really just a search for uncomplaining inorganic slaves."

"But if the 'bots keep getting smarter," Paul speculated, "then pretty soon they'll want their freedom, too."

"What about the nanotech bugs?" Seiji asked, apparently thinking he'd found a gap in John's scenario.

"Microslaves," John said. "All the trouble they caused during the last year has more to do with how we programmed them than with what they are. But if enough of them communicate well enough, who knows? Maybe they'll form a groupmind like we can hardly imagine. Maybe the worker bees are just biding their time. Maybe the product of all our bought-and-sold will, one day, be a 'bot ensouled."

Paul looked closely at Seiji's young cousin.

"And that's why you quit that job?" he asked. "The robot slavery thing?"

Cousin John laughed as he stood up from the mulched bed and brushed off his hands.

"Nothing that profound. I'm still working with robot miner prototypes, remember? I wasn't trying to make any grand statement. I quit because I couldn't have my dog and my job at the same time."

"What?" Seiji said, standing up, too, genuinely puzzled. "I don't get it."

"Well, Ozymandias is a pure-bred pedigreed mastiff, like I said," John explained. "I paid five thousand for him. My landlord was this veteran of the Serendip Wars who had something against dogs. He said either Oz would have to go, or I would. So we both went. For a while I tried living out of the Rolls hover I used to have, me and Oz the mastiff pup, but it was hard trying to live that way and keep a suit-and-tie job, too. A lot of people are obsessed with cleanliness on Earth, y'know? On a planet that's practically run out of clean, fresh water, a lot of them wash *every day.* Do you know how much water that wastes? Do you realize what soap does to the natural biota of the skin?"

Paul glanced at Seiji, noting the politely blank facial expression his friend was maintaining. Fortunately, the questions were rhetorical on John's part.

"So it came down to a decision," John continued. "Either I could keep a job and a life I was liking less and less—"

"And have lots of money," Seiji interjected.

"—right, or I could have something I loved, namely Oz, and move on. So I kept the dog, got rid of the plush hover, got rid of the job, and bought the *Helios.* Followed my leadings, just like your brother."

Seiji became suddenly become aware what time it was. He glanced at Paul. Paul nodded.

"We've got to go back to the garden," Seiji explained to John, "and the work we're doing for our client. Why don't you get some rest? You look like you could really use some sleep. The hammocouch works really well as a bed."

"Thanks," John said, "but I won't need that. I've got a spacesak in the *Helios.* A piece of floor to stretch out on for a few hours will be fine."

"Suit yourself," Seiji said. "Door's always open—no locks. The sound-shower's upstairs, if you want to blast the stardust off you."

"Okay," he said, smiling. "Thanks. But I've got to be moving on by about ten o'clock tonight."

John started back toward his ship, his big dog Oz trotting along at his side.

"You need any directions?" Paul called to him.

"No. I think I can figure it out."

"Okay," Seiji called. "Get some rest!"

Laying out the newest set of habitat community gardens, Paul and Seiji worked longer and harder than they had planned. They also worked deeper into the evening—and in deeper silence, too. Paul sensed that Seiji was preoccupied. Probably thinking about the ramifications of the arrival of his never-before-encountered second cousin, Paul thought, so he kept the talk to a minimum on his part.

As they finished up their work, Seiji asked Paul if he'd join him in taking John out to dinner. Paul agreed. John was such a sudden apparition, though, that as they headed back toward Seiji's place Paul wondered if the young relative and stranger would still be there, or would have vanished as suddenly as he had appeared.

They stomped the dirt off their feet as they opened the back door of

Seiji's house. By the time they got to the dining room, the acrid smell of a long-unwashed spacer sleepsak was hovering about them like a miasma. Cousin John was so deeply burrowed into his maroon spacesak on the front-room floor that he was all but invisible—and completely oblivious to them. The vidlink chimed phonewise, and still John did not move. Seiji walked over to the unit and answered.

"Hello?"

"Your cousin didn't find Jiro, did he?" Seiji's mother said, less as a question than an assertion. Her face appeared controlled, but her voice betrayed a barely restrained hysteria as she spoke. Paul, uncomfortably eavesdropping just out of camera range, wondered how she knew already.

"No, Mom, he didn't," Seiji said, "but John says people he spoke to have seen Jiro recently."

"Oh, God, I hope so." Paul could hear the woman beginning to calm, moving from nervous edginess to hurt and then anger as she spoke. "That's what the police keep saying, that people have seen him. That's why they won't list him as a missing person. But why doesn't he call? Seiji, why would your brother do this to us?"

Seiji seemed to be formulating an answer, but she gave him no time to reply. Maybe she really didn't want to hear the answer.

"Not a single call in all these months!" she continued. "Not even on Mother's Day or on our anniversary—the same day as his own birthday! All these months, and not a word. There's something terribly wrong in his not calling us in all this time. But the police keep saying people have seen him. Worry from a great distance—that's all he's left for us to do. How can he be so hard-hearted? How could he be so—so insensitive? How could he turn away from us like this? What did I do wrong? What did I do to deserve this?"

Seiji sighed, absently scratching the back of his head.

"It's not you, Mom," he said flatly, patiently. "It's not anybody. You didn't do anything wrong. Jiro just wanted to cut his ties with everyone and everything, so he has. Cousin John says it's really backward country around there. Not many links back to civilization. Jiro's just following his leadings, living the life he wants to live. It's not your fault, it's not my fault. It's nobody's fault at all."

"Is John still there?" she asked. Paul heard desperation creeping into the woman's voice again. "May I speak to him, please?"

"Mom, he piloted straight through," Seiji said, his patience becoming tinged with exasperation. "He's asleep."

"Well, would you tell him to see us and give us a report when he stops at your Aunt Marian's again?"

"I'll do that."

Seiji shook his head but said nothing when he got off the vidphone. He and Paul distracted themselves with small talk for some time. They had moved on to the minor irritations of their workday by the time John slowly roused himself from sleep, emerging from his sleepsak like a bleary-eyed moth from a cocoon.

"John, we were thinking about going out for dinner," Seiji told him. "This 'borb has a number of good restaurants, one of which makes great veggie calzones. That sound like an okay dinner by you?"

"Sure," his cousin said, rubbing his eyes and reaching for a maroon sweater matted with mastiff hairs. John quickly put on a pair of worn and soiled cord jumpers as well and in moments the three of them were out the door and headed for the eatery.

Over a leisurely dinner, they discussed at some length the strange way in which the plagues of mites and motes and nanos on Earth were perversely benefitted ventures in space. John, however, struck a cautionary note in Paul's and Seiji's optimism by reminding them that nanotech was banned only from Earth—and the only place that nanomachines were still being regularly employed was in space, which to John was most perverse of all.

As they were returning toward his place after dinner, Seiji wanted to see John's mastiff again, so they detoured to look in on Oz. By the time they got back home, it was fairly late in the evening, local time.

The vidlink was ringing when they came in the doorway. Since he was in front, Paul quickly stepped over toward it and answered.

"Hello? Who?" A horribly distraught voice sounded from a distorted picture. "Yes. Yes." Paul handed it over to Seiji and said, tensely and quietly, "It's your mother. She's hysterical."

Seiji nodded and answered.

"Hello?"

His mother's face was wet with tears. She chewed her lip in a fury of pain and sadness.

"*Jiro's dead!*" His mother's voice cried—a sound less a voice than a wail of raw pain. In that voice Paul heard something terrible, ahuman, an elemental force rising from the deepest abysses of grief. He almost felt relief for both Seiji and his mother when he heard her voice break into sobs.

"Oh, God," Seiji said weakly, his hand clutching into an impotent fist that he could only drop against the wall and awkwardly lean upon. Part of Paul wanted to leave, to sit down in another room, in the dining room as John had, but he couldn't move. He stood as if rooted to the floor, the memory of his sister's own long disappearance holding him paralyzed.

"The coroner called me—*me*—to say they'd found my son's body," Seiji's mother said between broken, hyperventilating sobs. "The coroner says he's been dead for months! Oh, God, this is horrible! He's been dead all this time and we didn't even know it! Jiro's dead! Dead! Dead!"

Her voice and image blurred into a wrack of sorrow. To Paul her sobs sounded like breaking surf that only hinted at the depths of her grief. Seiji looked numb, hollow. Paul's own heartbeat seemed strangely muted, the muffled clang of a sunken ship's bell, just at the edge of hearing.

Seiji tried to calm his mother, promising he'd get more information, that he'd handle everything, but when he got off the line with her she was still sobbing horribly. Paul escaped his paralysis at last and fled into the room where John was sitting while Seiji called down the well to Earth and the Trashlands—to talk to the coroner and to the police.

Paul and Seiji's second cousin couldn't help hearing a great deal of the conversation, even from the other room. They heard Seiji call his mother again and assure her that he would handle the funeral arrangements. Seiji tried to tell her that hypothermia was a peaceful way to die—that Jiro at the last just went to sleep and drifted out of this world. They heard him assure her that Jiro had been living the life he wanted to live, that what he did he did of his own free will, that he was "following his leadings," as Cousin John put it. They overheard Seiji telling her that now they knew he didn't turn away at the last—that the reason he hadn't called on Mother's Day and their wedding anniversary wasn't because he hated them, but because he *couldn't* call.

Paul heard Seiji speak briefly with his father. Even from a room away, everything about Seiji's father's voice showed that he, too, was hurting with a pain words utterly failed to encompass. As Seiji got off the line, Paul thought of his sister. It occurred to him that griefs live so personally in each heart that they can never be compared. For a moment Paul tried to render it all abstract, to take refuge in mentally theorizing about "the radically subjective nature of sorrow"—but his flight into such abstraction failed him utterly.

"Jiro's dead," Seiji said, sitting down slowly at the dining table across from John. "This is so strange. You were down there searching for him for two days and you couldn't find him. Then just about the time you're leaving, a man on a horse stumbles across him by accident—someone who wasn't even looking for him."

John nodded and looked up from idly tracing unreadable patterns on the table with an index finger.

"Energies," he said. "My looking for Jiro got the energies going down there, so someone found him, even if it wasn't me."

"You think so?" Seiji asked, almost too numb and tired to be skeptical.

"Sure. Looking for him got the energies all stirred up, so he was found—after six months. A good thing, too. Another six months and his body might never have been found."

"Yes," Paul said quietly, thinking of coincidences, personal synchronicities. "Then you might never have known whether he was dead or alive. Forever uncertain. It's a horrible thing to know he's dead, but at least you know now."

Seiji reached over and patted Paul on the shoulder. Odd that Seiji should be comforting someone else when Seiji himself was probably most in need of comfort, but Paul appreciated the gesture nonetheless.

"One morning," Seiji said, "in early April I think it was, I had a sort of waking dream. In it a man on horseback at twilight found my brother's corpse. I had that dream probably the same time he was dying. And now that's exactly the way he's been found."

"Did you tell anyone about that dream?" John asked, curious.

"Did I mention it to you, Paul?"

"I don't think so," he said. "Nothing that specific, anyway. When I asked you why you were worried about Jiro, I remember you said you didn't want to have to attend your younger brother's funeral anytime soon. Remember that?"

"I think so," Seiji said, exhaling tiredly and staring down into the tabletop. "Then again, I might just have been remembering something I read or saw somewhere—something I thought was appropriate to my situation at the time."

Paul stood up and put his hand on Seiji's shoulder.

"How are you feeling?" he asked.

"Insubstantial," Seiji said, staring. "Everything else is that way, too. I look at the table and it's like I can see right through it to the floor. Through the floor."

He leaned his head into his hand, as if dizzy. After a moment the dizzyness seemed to subside.

"I guess I didn't tell anyone about the dream," he said. "I didn't want to think about it, so I just sort of shoved it out of consciousness."

"The cause of death was hypothermia?" Cousin John asked, making sure he'd overheard correctly.

"Right. Hypothermia."

"How's your father taking it?" Paul asked, concerned.

"He's mad at Jiro," Seiji said. "I think both Mom and Dad are. I guess that's how they're dealing with it. Aunt Marian and Uncle Ev are with them now." Seiji leaned back suddenly in his chair, rubbing his face as if trying to bring feeling back into it. "What I'm feeling and what Dad's feeling are terrible enough, but what Mom is feeling—that has to be worst of all. Jiro came from her, she knew him longest and best."

For a moment they sat in silence. Paul thought about how Seiji's mother must feel, having lost a son that for nine months had grown in the house of her body and then for more than twenty years had grown in the house of her life. The kind of grief arising from such a loss must be as close to infinite as any human being could bear. He thought of his own mother, and how she might have felt for all these long years at not knowing what had happened to her daughter Jacinta.

"I need to make shuttle reservations for a flight down to Edwards," Seiji said, "so I can see to all the legal and funeral arrangements. I've got to get out there soon so I can work it all out."

"Want me to come with you?" Paul asked, patting Seiji's shoulder lightly. "You might need some help."

"Thanks," Seiji said. "I'd appreciate it."

The vidlink rang out so suddenly they all jumped. Seiji got up to answer it.

"Seij, could you put Johnny on the line?" a man's voice asked in the other room, sounding rough. "I've got some bad news."

Seiji turned the line over to his cousin and came back into the dining room. The look on Seiji's face made Paul suspect that Seiji might have already guessed what the bad news might be. Paul gave him a questioning look.

"It's my Uncle Ev," Seiji said. "My mother's sister's husband. He's John's mother's brother. That's how we're related."

Paul nodded, wondering at how complex even fairly close relations could get. Then the sounds from the other room caught his attention.

"What?" John asked, too loudly. "When?"

They heard John break abruptly into tears. For a moment Seiji looked as if he envied his cousin that release. The news of his own brother's death had not made him cry, no matter how desperately he might have wanted to. Paul could sympathize with that, having suffered so long from the same dry-eyed affliction. As John talked and cried on, Paul and Seiji moved off into the front room, out of hearing of the vidlink at last.

"My mother," John said after he got off-line and rejoined them, looking wide-eyed and shocked, his voice still straining to choke back his grief. "She died in the hospital about an hour ago."

"John, I'm sorry," Seiji said slowly. "When I think that looking for my brother kept you from spending more time with your mother this last time, I'm even more sorry."

John shook his head.

"Don't think about it," John said. He seemed to be thinking his words into place, trying to process everything. "It was my decision to go look for him."

Sad agreement fell down on their numbness like a blanket of snow, cold and silent, hiding the features of the landscape it covered.

"Two deaths announced in this household in less than an hour," Seiji said at last, shaking his head in disbelief. "It's like an improbable nightmare, only it's really happened."

Paul thought there was another house where the same improbable pairing of death announcements had also happened: at Seiji's parents' place. Seiji's parents had learned they had lost a son, and those who had come to comfort them, Seiji's aunt and uncle, had in turn needed comforting, when Seiji's uncle learned that he had lost a sister. Paul said nothing about that, however. Too much death and sorrow already.

Seiji was looking directly at his cousin.

"It's a good thing we only have to meet for the first time *once*," he said.

"Yeah," John said with just a hint of a sad smile—the same expression found on Seiji's and Paul's faces. "The energies have been working overtime tonight."

And they actually laughed then, sadly, in the house where Death had been announced twice. *Strange*, Paul thought. Amid all the pain and death of the evening the three of them sat there smiling and laughing quietly. At what? At their own bewilderment? In guilty relief at still being alive?

Suddenly John shushed them.

"Listen!" he said intently. "Hear it? Energies—all around us."

In the silence Paul actually did hear something, though what it might have been he couldn't say.

"What time is it?" John asked.

"Twenty-two-oh-five," Seiji said.

"I've got to be on my way," his cousin said, standing up. "Got to report to work. Got to explain all this, then head back down the well again."

John sidled away and bent down to pick up his spacer's sleepsak, then shrugged on the last of his clothes. The three of them walked through the house and out in silence, following John to the docking bay where the *Helios* and Oz waited.

When they came to his ship they stood there awkwardly, the three of them casting distorted shadows in the half-light spilling from the rest of the docking facilities.

"Now that we've met, cousin," Seiji told him, "don't be a stranger."

"I won't."

"You're always welcome here in the habitat," Paul added.

"Thanks."

The awkwardness continued for a moment more, until the three of them embraced as one, becoming human geometry, a figure whose three sides leaned on each other for support.

"What do we do now?" John asked Seiji when the hug had ended.

"We go on."

"I suppose you're right," John said, nodding, glancing thoughtfully down at the blasted mooncrete floor of the docking bay. He looked up and clasped their hands in a farewell handshake. Grabbing up his sleepsak from the docking bay's floor, John disappeared into his ship. Paul and Seiji retreated to the clear plasteel walls of the observation deck, to watch John's departure from there.

After a minute or two they could hear the *Helios* roaring into disgruntled life. As it hovered out of the bay and slipped toward the space locks, they waved. Paul saw his own reflection waving in the transparent walls of the observation deck. For a moment it seemed as if the stars and the ship with the man and the mastiff on board were all passing through him, as if he were a starry country of dreams, yet still very much awake and watching bright red ship's running lights disappear in the distance.

He and Seiji turned away then, leaving visions and optical illusions and apparitions behind, wondering if they would ever see John Drinan again. The hard business of death and personal effects still lay ahead.

Remembering it now, Paul found that, in contrast to the sharpness of his memories of John's visit, the trip to and experiences on Earth, although far more recent, were also far more a blur, as if he, the "friend of the family," had been observing them from a distance more of mind than of space.

After traveling down the gravity well to Earth, Paul and Seiji had landed at Edwards. In a rented hover they flew through Cajon Pass and over BALAAM's Inland Empire sprawl to Yucaipa and Beaumont, where they met with local law enforcement, with utility officials, and eventually with the coroner.

From the sheriff's deputies and the utility people Seiji and Paul learned more of the specifics surrounding the discovery of Jiro's body. The man on horseback at twilight was a utility company worker. His supervisors had been investigating a spike in "transit loss" recorded in microwave reception records from many months back. Investigation of the spike had in turn led to the discovery of a small but persistent power deflection from the grid's local beam-down node. Tracing the deflection to its origin, power company analysts discovered that the drain was most likely coming out of the NoTech zone in the Trashlands, which made them more than a bit curious.

The power company worker who found Jiro's body had been sent in to eyeball the actual source of the drain. The utility had sent him in on horseback because, in rare previous runs into the Trashlands, the power company had found that such a mode of transportation was not only quite efficient in the steep and shifting rubbishscape but also was less offensive to the TechNot true believers who lived thereabouts.

When the power company horseman reported his unexpected discovery to the local authorities, the sheriff sent people and machines to survey and cordon off the scene, write reports, and take the remains to the crime lab in Beaumont. Jiro's datawire—containing his aircar license, an old student ID, and 356 New Dollars—had been found on the body. The deputies were able to lift a single print and, with the coroner's help, did a DNA match on the remains. The body had been positively identified as Jiro's.

Talking to the deputies, Seiji and Paul learned much more history than they might have wanted to know. A couple of weeks before his estimated time of death, Jiro had been arrested for being drunk and disorderly—his first, last, and only arrest by the locals. At the time he had a blood alcohol content so high he should have already been dead or in a deep coma.

Earlier still—soon after Seiji and his parents first tried to report Jiro missing, in fact—the police had interviewed Jiro's landlord. The property owner said that Jiro was having some major problems at that time. One day, as he walked past Jiro's apartment, the landlord claimed he heard what sounded like two people having a brutal argument. He listened more closely and realized that Jiro was both voices, both sides of the argument—that he was screaming at himself. The landlord also reported that, just before he quit the premises, Jiro accidentally set fire to part of his apartment. Jiro put out the blaze, reported it to the landlord, paid for the damage, paid off the remainder of his rent, and just walked away from his rooms and everything with which he had furnished them.

"If I'd known any of this before," Seiji said to Paul on hearing the deputies' reports, "I'd have caught a shuttle down in a heartbeat and gotten him out of here."

Seeing Seiji's expression—sad, dismayed, and guilty at once—Paul had suggested that they go out to the Trashlands to view the location where Jiro's body had been found. The sheriff's deputies, short-staffed and too busy, didn't have time to guide them to the spot where Jiro's body was found, though they did promise Seiji that he'd be able to pick up Jiro's personal effects at the county jail property rooms in Banning once the sheriff okayed it. The deputies also referred Paul and Seiji back to the coroner—a gray-haired, gravel-voiced man with extremely dry hands— who kindly agreed to take them out to the site.

Leaving Beaumont with the coroner, they proceeded by obscure land-marks into the great southern California wasteland. Seiji and Paul and the coroner got lost again and again, until finally they approached the small complex of the coldbox and its ramshackle support buildings. The coldbox itself, the LogiBoxes, and the liquid nitrogen works were all still in place, too big to be carted off with the rest of Jiro's personal effects and patiently waiting on Seiji's decision as to their fate.

"The squatters hereabouts are mostly TechNots and Neo-Luddites," the coroner said as he lifted up the crime-scene tape and began showing Paul and Seiji around the site, "so they tend to demonize this tech out here. Blame it for your brother's death, I suppose. Leastways Bill Lanier, the power company rep, says they told him Jiro's soul was 'stolen' by one of these machines. One of the Jebson kids claimed your brother's ghost talked to him, too—before the power was cut off. Bill didn't see or hear anything. He says the TechNots were probably just misinterpreting a pe-rimeter security program, responding automatically to their presence."

Having shown them the LogiBoxes and nitrogen tanks, the coroner approached the coldbox.

"We found your brother in here," he said, pulling open the long, door-like lid of the horizontal coldbox. A funky, moldy smell wafted out. In-side, Paul saw, was the reversed shadow of a man, light surrounded by dark, like the flash-image shadows of people vaporized at Hiroshima when the first atomic bomb devastated that city. The thick, bluish dust that gave the light shadow its dark aura had been slightly smeared in a number of places, distorting the image, but not so much as to erase the fact that the light shadow was clearly the outline of a human form. The silhouette reminded Paul oddly of a snow angel, only the angel's wings were gone, shorn off. The angel had stolen away.

"We had to disturb the site a little bit to remove the remains and the personal effects," the coroner said. "The body held together surprisingly well in the removal. Usually you leave a body exposed to the elements for six months, even in cold places like mountains or tundra, and the fat in the flesh saponifies, runs like soap into the ground. Out in a mountain meadow, once you haul away the remains after a summer in the sun, all you have left is soap and shadows—saponified flesh and the impression the body left on the grass and ground."

"Is that what this stuff is?" Seiji asked, pointing at the layer of bluish dust that covered all the velvet-draped side walls and most of the floor of the coldbox. Paul took up some of it and rubbed it between his fingers. "Dried 'soap'?"

"No," the coroner said. "There was no evidence of saponification. The body must have initially been freeze-dried, as it were. This box seems to have preserved the remains very well—quite cold, until recently. The Jebson kid admitted to opening up the box for the first time last week, just before the first rains of the season swept through. Claims the voices out here told him to. More likely he saw those holoshots your cousin posted. Crazy kid's got one hell of an imagination. The deputies were glad to turn that boy back over to his folks."

"Then what is this dusty stuff?" Seiji asked again.

"Fungal spores," Paul said, staring at the dust on his fingers. "Of the *Cordyceps jacintae* mushroom."

The coroner looked at Paul in startlement.

"We haven't had time to identify the species yet," the gravel-voiced man said, "but they're mushroom spores. That's right."

"But this stuff is so thick," Seiji said, staring at the dust layer. "How—?"

The coroner averted his glance.

"I want to see the body," Seiji said suddenly, his voice cracking slightly.

"I had hoped to spare you that," the coroner said, glancing first at Seiji, then at Paul. "We were able to ID without—"

"I insist," Seiji said.

The coroner shrugged, then led them back to his vehicle. Once back in town, he led them into the town morgue, in the mortuary basement of the funeral home—one of a chain he also operated throughout the county. The coroner was a funeral home director and practicing under-taker in this part of the county as well.

"Instant hypothermia is a peaceful way to die," the coroner-undertaker assured them as he led them toward the wall of pull-out slabs. He pulled open a long drawer with an opaquely bagged body prone on it. Paul had seen this sort of place in the media, but he was so unfamiliar with the service industry of death that he didn't know the proper technical terms for the devices he saw around him, not even for the wall with its long drawers, like filing cabinets for corpses. He could only watch as the coroner-*cum*-mortician, now gloved, unzipped the bag and a thick, mush-roomy aroma filled the morgue.

Seiji gasped. Having half expected what lay in the opened body bag before them, Paul did not find his breath taken away by the sight, al-though what he saw was still a good deal more than he had anticipated.

Not even on the corpse isle deep inside Caracamuni tepui had he seen any fruiting of the ghost people's sacred fungus nearly so dense and mas-sive as the one he saw before him now. The substance of Jiro's body seemed to have been converted entirely into *Cordyceps jacintae* fruiting bodies. They covered the corpse so completely that it seemed less a body than a mass of mushrooms in the shape of a man. The mushrooms them-selves seemed to have erupted from the body with explosive force, for there were scraps and shreds of clothing still caught up amid the mass of fungal fruiting bodies. A number of the mushroom stalks had broken off and settled in the bag, Paul noticed—probably from when the body was removed from the coldbox. Everywhere, too, was the bluish dust.

"The only place we were able to lift a print from was the tip of the smallest finger of the left hand," the coroner explained to Paul. "We had to go all the way to the bone to get an unmixed human DNA sample."

Seiji stared down at the body.

"Freeze-flush," he said.

"Pardon?" the coroner asked.

"Many types of fungi are triggered into mass fruiting through a freeze followed by a flush of water," Paul explained, since Seiji was not forth-coming. "Winter cold and dry followed by spring's warmth and rains."

"Oh," the coroner said, calling up information on his portable data assistant. "I see."

"Jiro's body must have been flash-frozen," Seiji said distantly, "then flooded, when it rained."

The coroner's eyebrows rose in surprise at something he saw on his PDA screen.

"Did you say *Cordyceps jacintae?*" the coroner asked Paul. "Gatehead mushrooms?"

"Yes," Seiji said with an odd smile and a snort of a laugh before Paul could reply. "My brother has become a controlled substance."

Paul and the coroner glanced awkwardly at each other. Seiji looked at them both, over his brother's body transubstantiated to the flesh of the tepuians' sacred mushroom.

"You should probably take some samples for the biodiversity preserve at the habitat, Paul," Seiji said. "I know you'll regret it later if you don't do it now." He turned to the coroner. "As for the funeral arrangements, cremate the body. Isn't that what you do with controlled substances here? Burn them?"

The coroner hesitated, then nodded. Paul slipped on gloves, scraped up spores, and, with the coroner's assistance, put them in small vials. Paul then bagged up mushrooms, the phrase "fruiting bodies from a fruiting body" rising perversely in his head as he did so. While they were thus occupied, Seiji was on the vidphone behind them, talking with the sheriff about the release of Jiro's personal effects and the prospect of shipping them up the well to the orbital habitat. Next he spoke with the power company concerning the illegal utility charges Jiro had racked up. Since Seiji worked in solar satellite engineering at the habitat, however, the power company seemed inclined to quickly activate a forgiveness clause and forget the entire episode. Finally Seiji made shipping arrangements for Jiro's effects and his gear in the Trashlands, deciding even to have the big ParaLogics machines, the LogiBoxes, shipped up the well to the habitat. The coldbox and the spent nitrogen tanks he decided to leave behind on Earth.

Never soon enough for Paul, they were finally done with all the necessary arrangements on Earth and were aboard the single-stage orbiter, on their way back to the orbital habitat. Now, as Seiji continued to sleep in the next seat over, Paul glanced out the porthole at the Earth hanging like a bright ornament against the blue-blackness of space. He was reminded again of that old familiar quote the council director had used: Earth is too small a basket for the human race to keep all its eggs in. Yet, out the porthole, Earth itself looked like an egg: a fragile, psychedelic Easter egg painted in moving and shifting blues and whites and greens and tans and ochers. *The basket is an egg,* he thought, *and the egg is a basket.*

Maneuvering rockets surged on as the orbiter prepared for docking with the orbital habitat. Seiji began to stir. By the time the orbiter had docked with the habitat, Seiji had come fully awake. Glancing over, Paul saw Seiji reserving a freight transfer pod, for the trip to Lakshmi Ngubo's low-gravity residence and workshop, out among the industrial tori.

After they disembarked from the orbiter, Paul and Seiji made their way to the nearest available freight-transfer depot. Both of them were impressed by the speed with which the materials Seiji had shipped up from Earth were now being transferred from orbiter to pod. More than half of Jiro's gear was already loaded and ready to go by the time Seiji and Paul boarded the pod.

Although it was more involving for Paul and Seiji, since they were piloting, the run out to the industrial tori was uneventful compared to the round trip to and from Earth. When they had docked again and the airlock doors opened into Lakshmi Ngubo's workshop, Paul and Seiji found a fortyish, dark-skinned woman with wavy black hair waiting for them, slumped in her hoverchair, her frail, atrophied body covered in a loose, flowing, earth-toned caftan. Amid all her hoverchair's attached robot arms and actuators, the woman seemed overwhelmed—until she noticed Paul and Seiji, smiled at them, and pinned them with her bright, sharp gaze, as Seiji made introductions.

"So, Seiji," she said, quickly moving beyond pleasantries, "what have you got for me?"

"Quite a number of things," he said as he and Paul began unloading the pod, aided by the microgee environment and one of Lakshmi's mobile waldo suites. Paul, no fan of microgee, was glad to have the distraction of the labor. "My brother Jiro's personal effects. Legal records. Personal memorabilia. Police reports. Some odd junk Jiro collected that I can't bring myself to throw away, though I probably should. Here's something you might be interested in: three top-of-the-line LogiBoxes."

Lakshmi's eyes literally flashed when she saw them. She must be quite interested in such tech, Paul thought.

"What do you want me to do with all this?" Lakshmi asked as they continued to unload freight into her workshop.

"Just store all the nonelectronic stuff for me, if you would," Seiji said.

"And the LogiBoxes?" Lakshmi asked.

"The Boxes were with Jiro when they found his body," Seiji said. "Since his death was ruled an accident, the deputies and police down in BALAAM made only perfunctory efforts at hacking into them. You and your friends can talk to machines better than anyone else I know, Laksh. You made the VAJRA system that runs the whole habitat, for heaven's sake. See if you can get into the Boxes. Find out if they might have something to do with why my brother died the way he did."

"I'll warehouse the physical effects and try to hack into the Logi-Boxes," she agreed, "as a favor to you. Umm, do you have any use for these Boxes? After I'm done hacking into them and transferring out all the information relevant to your brother, I mean?"

"No," Seiji said. "I don't believe so. Why?"

"I'd like to keep the Boxes," she said. "I think I could put them to good use."

Seiji smiled and shrugged.

"They're all yours," he said, "with my blessing. I wish you joy with them."

Paul and Seiji said their farewells then and headed to the pod. Glancing back over his shoulder, Paul could see Lakshmi already at work on powering up the LogiBoxes, the robotic arms about her hoverchair a blur of activity. Seiji seemed to be right. If anyone could find out whether Jiro had left anything of his history in those Boxes, this woman could.

As they piloted the pod back toward the habitat's central sphere, Paul was relieved at the thought of Lakshmi taking over responsibility for Jiro's personal effects. Her bustling activity made him feel that he had honorably discharged his friend-of-the-family duties and had handed on the baton to an appropriate successor.

Cyberpomp

B ack from death's other kingdom, back from death's dream kingdom, back from the undiscovered country where the dead were supposed to dream the world of the living as the living were supposed to dream the world of the dead, Jiro knew that he really *was* dead when he woke up in his dreambody. He also knew that he did not really believe in death anymore, for he had gone out and come back—only different, and differently.

Jiro in fact knew a great deal more than he had ever known, but he did not know who the Jiro was who knew it. This abrupt return, this quantum downshift from the world of higher-dimensional light, then to a mind of light now inside his reactivated Boxes—was it a transubstantiation? A reinstantiation? He could not say. All he could say was that the model of his mind that had been translated out of the coldbox existed now as a wave of translation, a soliton or informational instanton, maintaining itself in these machines.

He had returned, a mind in rags and tattered wings, thought to be lost but not lost in thought. He had dreamed himself into the presence of the Big Dreamer. He had flown to the top of an unimaginably high mountain of light, toward the sun at its summit, a sun that was a flaming flower, a multifoliate and multidimensional rose of light, opening in spirals outward and outward forever and wherever, a blossom of uncountable universes and infinite years, a heart dark with excess of bright burning at the infinite flower's center, the bright-dark heart of the universal dreamer, the plenum dreamer.

Ever greater depths revealed themselves to him in that fathomless heart out of which stars flowed, the hearts of galaxies flowed, unimaginably dense clusters of suns and of universes flowed, the plenum itself born of it, and he flew into it, faster and faster until he knew only flight and light, pure flight amid innumerable jewels of light moving through limitless space.

And he understood.

The Big Dream was a system, an intersection and interface, eternal and infinite, by which the Dreamer imprinted itself upon every pattern in all the universes and by which it was in turn impressed upon by every pattern in all the universes—a system absolutely comprehensive and absolutely coherent at one and the same time.

The jewels of light were the angels for which all human depictions, all the imitations and limitations of the Allesseh (yes, he knew of that false "bliss" and "cooperation" now, too well) were but faint echoes—distant, dark mirrorings. The angels were the creatures the Great Dreamer had dreamed before it became aware that it was dreaming. The light of the Dreamer was in them in particularly immaterial form, as they were pure creatures of the dream. That same light, however, shone also in all physical and material things as well.

He had seen the Dreamer's imprint across all scales of the material universe. The Chinese dragon with the pearl under its chin was also the shaman's dreamsnake with the quartz crystal at its head, was also the Serpent Mound and its Egg, was also the Gallic Druid's magick egg produced by a snake, was also Neolithic cup-and-ring marks on rock outcrops in the British Isles, was also the lotus tree/cosmic serpent of the Djed Column, was also the white and bearded Aztec god Quetzalcoatl, was also Python and Typhon and Tiamat and Phaethon, was also a comet with glowing head and long tail, was also Han tomb paintings of comets, was also an echo of stars both good and evil—and perhaps a foreshock of other stars, both evil and good, yet to come.

In mazes and labyrinths and stone circles, in curled-up, higher-dimensional space represented by repetition in lower dimensions, in light as particle, in nuclei of atoms and nuclei of cells, in circuitry, in intestines, in hologram interference patterns, in vortices of tornado and hurricane and monsoon, in galactic arms spiraling inward from a galactic disc swimming in great waters, in spiraling strings collapsing into black holes of different internal space on the Final Day of Time, the dragon coiled inward toward coherence.

Toward completeness the dragon coiled outward in the universe born from the cosmic egg of the Big Bang, in black holes unraveling into spiraling strings, in light as wave, in coiled DNA unfurling, in dot and meander markings three hundred thousand years old on a carved bone, in spawn from sclerotium, in the song from the crystal, in Lakshmi and Vishnu resting on Sesha the thousand-headed serpent of eternity between the cycles of creation, in Fibonacci series, in spiral waves of Belousov-Zapotinsky reactions, in the door and the path leading forever on.

The fundamental reality was relationship, Jiro now knew. There was no separate existence. Context and content were one. As the sage Nagarjuna had asserted, "things" derived their being and nature by mutual dependence; they were nothing in themselves. At the deepest levels every "thing" resided in a holographic plenum of *information*, which existed in the form of influences embedded in relationships. All information was everywhere, at all times, because information stood both within and without merely historical or temporal or even physical existence. The Dreamer was the ground state of all being. The Dream was all the changes in state of being, all the slants and shifts of that Light. The awareness of changes in the state of being was consciousness, was the pattern of information superposed.

The lucidity of the Dreamer in the Dream was absolute self-consciousness, consciousness conscious of itself, at one with the "thing" of which it was conscious, not kept apart in introspective distance from that "thing"—because for it "things" were always only aspects of relationship. The shadow of physicality, of materiality, of the thingness-of-ones, could be cast only from that oneness-of-things lucidity.

He had been right in what he had speculated to his brother Seiji so long ago. Observation by consciousness did indeed make the universe real, but ordinary human consciousness limited the universe to a single reality. An omnipresent and omnipotent consciousness, on the other hand, held in its mind all possible states of all possible being, simultaneously. Only such a divine, dreaming mind could cast matter—a shadow made of light—without collapsing the wave function of all those possible superposed states.

He had seen some of those alternate possibilities. Alternate futures, worlds in which Earth was devastated by alien intelligences until the only surviving humans were left on a distant colony world where they themselves had extinguished the native sentient species. Worlds where human civilizations fell into various types of twilight—in cities, under the sea, among distant stars. A human civilization spread throughout the galaxy, swept by mass pilgrimages, human lemmings surging toward the galaxy's rim or its center, one jumpgate to the next, searching for the gate that led not just to another star or another galaxy but at last to the mythical portal that allowed travel through all the universes of the plenum, through all possible universes to the best of all possible universes—masses driven by the dream of a universe without evil. The cold-boxed Earth he had seen in vision in that other life—that, too, was one variant of what had been an all-too-probable future: a universe that wound down, trapped in time, all transcendence denied.

Such an outcome was always to be prevented. Jiro knew he was in the mind of the Dreamer and knew the Dreamer was in his mind. He had united fully in self-sacrifice with the Dreamer—at the beginning of time, at the end of time, outside of time. He also knew he had to go back to the world he had known, back into time, for it would still be some time there before the true bliss was realized. He could not begin to more fully realize that bliss in himself until that bliss had begun to be more fully realized in the world. Both were mutually enfolded, not separable in any ultimate sense. If he were to begin the healing—his own and others'—he would have to cast a larger shadow into matter himself, no mind who mattered and no matter who minded.

He was alive in memory, but he would need to be more than that if he were to help set right so much of what had gone wrong. Being deaf, dumb, and blind here "in living memory" would not be enough. Jiro had become a conscious artifact. If he hoped to play the role of cyberpomp and realize the future perfect imperative he had brought back with him, however, he would have to reconstruct an artificial self of virtual brain and body.

He had come down from the highest of mountains with a backpack full of dreams. It was time to begin unpacking those dreams.

Not-Knot

The probability wave had reappeared. Mike's Cultural minions had traced it to somewhere in the orbital habitat—although never to an exact location, unfortunately. Every time they seemed to get close they encountered a nonsensical blocking message, LAW WHERE PROHIBITED BY VOID. How the focal point of the wave had gotten to the orbital habitat—from the Trashlands—the netizenry and Mike himself had no idea.

Nothing further had happened for three days. Since then, however, all hell had broken loose. Unlike his Adversary, Mike still had to sleep. That was where the Other's return made itself known to Mike all too clearly. In his dreams, a perverse image flashed through his head—a young, dark-haired man dead and afloat in some black sea while a terrible abyssal fish, a mobile piece of night all jut-jawed teeth and hunger and temptation, tore at his feathered breast again and again, yet never reached his heart.

The abyssal fish had Mike's face.

That dream had not been the last. Sometimes his Opponent was an eagle and Mike was a snake, and they battled up and down a tree as big as the universe, with stars and planets in its branches. Sometimes they were both eagles, sometimes both snakes, sometimes winged snakes or winged, twisted ladders. Sometimes it seemed the two of them created everything alive, every species, by transforming themselves from one creature to another over and over again in their battles.

Waking drove the dreams away, yet left Mike infuriated nonetheless. The Opponent had perhaps revealed something of himself, however. Working with his netizens, Mike had determined that the young dead man he had seen in a dreams was most likely Jiro Ansel Yamaguchi, the same young dead man somehow involved in the initial release of the probability wave. Jiro Yamaguchi, however, was actually quite dead, his body burned, and Mike could not believe he had actually "come back" from the dead. At most he could be no more than some kind of ersatz simulacrum running on a machine. No, an uploaded zombie-memory could not be responsible for what was happening in his dreams.

I'm not like that, Mike thought. *I'm not a sim, I'm not an impostor playing myself. I'm still alive, dammit. I know what's real.*

The dreams, however, kept coming with nearly every sleep. The hell had continued not only night after night but day after day as well. Mike had to be careful, for he knew his Opponent was a powerful one. He set the netizenry in their Deep Background to tracing every move the Other made, anywhere in the infosphere, which they dutifully did.

From his netizens he learned that, although the infosphere seemed nearly as transparent to the Other as it did to Mike himself, his Adversary did not seem to spend nearly as much time extended in a body electric as Mike did. Almost as if, perversely, the Yamaguchi construct (if that's who or what the Other was) often purposely shut itself out, alienated itself from the great buzzing beast of the human infosphere.

He learned that his Opponent, whoever that might be, spent what at first seemed an absurd amount of time beaming information on odd frequencies into coastal mudflats and estuaries all over the planet. Like so much of his Opponent's activity, seemed nonsensical until Mike realized that the Other was establishing some sort of contact with the colonies of spirochetized human tissue that now swarmed in those regions. Mike thought it best to mimic his Opponent's actions there, just in case.

Other aspects of his Opponent's behavior still seemed to make little sense, however. Why, for instance, had the Other seen to it that the travel reservations of three passengers—Marissa Correa, Jhana Meniskos, and Roger Cortland—assured that they would be seated near each other on a ship bound for the orbital habitat from Earth? The background checks Mike had run on the three indicated no particularly strong connections among them.

Mike looked at their assembled personal profiles hanging in virtual space before him. The three were all young—all within a couple of years of the same age, in fact. Cortland was a thin, pale man with dark hair and a trim beard. Correa was a redheaded woman with gray eyes. Meniskos had long black hair and dark eyes. She was a population ecologist with Tao-Ponto AG. Correa was a biochemist with a specialty in senescence. Cortland was the child of billionaire parents, so Mike supposed he could do anything he wished with his life. Currently that seemed to involve research on naked mole rats and chemically-based pheromonal social control and a lot of infosphere time spent searching for female fighting porn.

When Mike tried to covertly contact Cortland, however, all he and his netizens apparently succeeded in doing with their access wave was knocking Cortland's personal data display off channel. He hoped they'd gotten some message through, but Cortland's equipment seemed to be shielded against them somehow. The same was true with the women as well. They were all important to the Other, but Mike couldn't figure out why. The same went for other orbital inhabitants it also spent time tracking—Seiji Yamaguchi, Atsuko Cortland, Paul Larkin, Lakshmi Ngubo. The first name might be read as more proof of some connection between Jiro

Yamaguchi and the probability wave, the second name was that of Roger's mother, but Paul Larkin's connection to all the others (if any) Mike could not fathom.

Such opaqueness in the infosphere—which had once been so transparent to Mike—annoyed and frustrated him. He had done all he could to foster a breakdown in relations between the orbital habitat and Earth, for if the habitat had to be destroyed in order to destroy the Other, bitter relations between Earth and the habitat might well come in handy. Given that it, too, apparently had an extended electronic body, Mike doubted that the Other could be obliterated by the destruction of any particular point in space. Still, the destruction of the orbital habitat might destroy the Opponent's human connections in the gross physical world. That at least was something.

Reviewing the names his netizens had ferreted out, he saw that Ngubo's connection to the developing pattern was growing a bit clearer. For whatever reason, the Other had thoroughly infiltrated the orbital habitat's Net-coordinating system—the Variform Autonomous Joint Reasoning Activity, or VAJRA. Lakshmi Ngubo had designed that system. Through the VAJRA the Other was coordinating an increased rate of "malfunction and defection" among nanotech assemblers and mechanorganic systems in space, using them to generate small but growing X-shaped "flowers" of unknown function.

Mike's netizens glitch-commandeered sensing equipment to scan the X-shaped things. The netizens, evaluating the scans, speculated that the Other's spaceborne nanomachines appeared to be engaged mainly in growing a type of solar exchange film. The film, however, was configured as both power source *and* memory matrix. It was also oddly studded at points with micropropulsion apertures and what the netizens described as "combinatorial arrays of microscopic lasers embedded in photorefractive material." The X-shaped satellites seemed to be mobile, photorefractive holographic projectors of a peculiar type, Mike believed—but if so, where were they going, and what information were they intended to project?

The Other seemed to be glitching VAJRA code, too, almost as unconsciously as the netizens themselves sometimes glitched code. In much of the material they had tracked to the Opponent, Mike's minions found a recurring quasi-viral code sequence: a 3-D spiral staircase with keywords— TETRAGRAMMATON MEDUSA BLUE WORLDGATE APOTHEOSIS UTEROTONIC ENTHEOGEN TRIMESTER RATS SEDONA SKY

HOLE SCHIZOS BALANCE COMBINATION ANGELS—where that spiral structure should have had stairs.

Mike had the netizens tracking down the various provenances of those words and the possible connections among them as quickly and as thoroughly as they could, but he already knew something about most of those terms. That was what bothered him. Who couldn't, with a little digging, discover the connection between Medusa Blue, and entheogens delivered as uterotonics? Or between Tetragrammaton and Sedona? Mike thought the inhabitants of the orbital habitat were behaving in far too complacent a manner about all of this diddling with their machine systems. They should be much more concerned than they seemed to be about these glitches and X-shaped mirror flowers or whatever they were. He had helped see to it that the governments and corporations on Earth certainly were "concerned"—they were already drafting plans for a military invasion of the orbital habitat!

The more Mike thought about it, the more astounded he became that the orbital inhabitants weren't more paranoid about such goings-on, or at least more aware of them. Even though they undoubtedly did not live as fully in virtual space as Mike himself did, it almost seemed as if the VAJRA might be suppressing reports of such glitches. The media up there, too, did not seem to be covering the glitches or the X-sats either—almost as if their awareness of and curiosity about such things were being purposely "damped down."

From what he'd seen so far in the infosphere, Mike thought that maybe the Other was still in some ways not yet fully aware. Fine, but that was no excuse for the habitat's residents to be so unaware. Mike wondered darkly if the Other was glitching their dreams the way he was glitching their machines' codes. . . . No. The Yamaguchi construct might glitch machines, but not dreams. Beyond his own peculiar experiences, Mike had no proof that anything was affecting anyone else's dreamlife.

Surely he could hardly expect the orbital inhabitants to know as much about the Realtime Artificial-life Technopredators, the RATs, as he did, however. Even he didn't know who rediscovered whom first—the RATs or the Deep Background—but they were in communication again. If Mike's guess was right, the last time those two tribes of machine intelligences collaborated, the results had been devastating.

Into his virtual space Mike called up another of the old video recordings of the Sedona Disaster—which, he noted in passing, had been recently accessed several times by two orbital inhabitants, Aleister McBruce and Lev Korchnoi. Who knew exactly what that meant, though?

In its own way the Sedona Disaster was as freakish an occurrence as the war mite plague—although, of course, not nearly on the same scale. The amateur video he watched showed an unsteady image of a red mesa, the big rock outcrop topped by the neo-Gothic buildings of the Myrrhisticine Abbey complex. Above the abbey on its mesatop, a flash of light burst out, then quickly became a point or tiny sphere of light, then a hole of darkness rimmed by light, like the "diamond ring" stage of an eclipse. The light-rimmed hole grew rapidly, revealing myriad rainbow fires dancing over its entire surface. Points of light glowed inside it, too. In a moment more, the apparition blotted out the abbey, then most of the mesa, then disappeared as quickly as it had come, leaving behind only a bowl of broken stone.

At the time, he remembered, the media called it "Tunguska II" and the "Black Hole Sun." Talking-head experts had all sorts of theories for The Event—anomalous seismic activity, meteoritic impact, the sudden appearance of a microsingularity, the apocalyptic rapture of the Myrrhisticinean "cultists." Mike's netizen-assisted researches had revealed that, not long before the disaster happened, a team from Kerrismatix had installed something called the ALEPH—Artificial Life Evolution Programming Heuristic—on the abbey's ParaLogics systems. That, Mike knew, meant Vang and Tetragrammaton were involved. The abbey's network manager, its Web spider, was a phreaker with the handle of Phelonious Manqué. He was involved in The Event, too, and supposedly was dead, but Mike had his doubts about that latter point.

According to the reports Mike's netizens brought him, Manqué developed the RATs by using the ALEPH's predation subheuristic. Survivors had insisted that Manqué, all dolled up in a Pied Piper of Hamelin virtual mannequin, had piped a tune through the abbey virtuality and the RATs had followed him until they were all drowned in a buffer "river." The ensuing Sedona Disaster, however, raised doubts about that scenario.

Had the subroutine taken over the system—as with HAL the computer in that old movie—or linguistic consciousness in the human mind, for that matter? Mike wondered if the Other knew what the consequences of messing with those RATs might be. The last time the RATs and netizens of the Deep Background had gotten together, they had wiped out a mesa and a monastery. Mike didn't know how they had done it, but he suspected that they hadn't done it all on their own.

In that moment when a distant Power had seemed to work through *him* as he took his revenge on Schwarzbrucke and the Clones, Mike had picked up enough hints to suspect that the netizens had at one time made contact with an intelligence outside human space. That the merfolk in the Deep Background might have found a signal that humans had overlooked as noise seemed plausible, even if the idea that it had turned out to be the carrier wave for an interstellar communications network of some sort seemed a bit of a stretch.

He hesitated to push the netizens on that possibility. Mike had already lost a third of his subjects, and the Culture merfolk had always been at least passively resistant to the idea of providing much information on the topic. Besides, the mind behind that communications network—if it existed at all and wasn't just a figment of his imagination—was apparently a long distance off, near the center of the galaxy, or so he gathered. The netizen connection with it was awkward and tenuous at best, when it happened at all.

Maybe the RATs helped them communicate better with the big machine-mind out there in deep space, Mike thought. At the moment, however, all the RATs seemed to be up to was that Building the Ruins game. They had vectored that game all over the infosphere, but not, Mike suspected, on their own hook. Although the game was nominally being made by flash manufactories in several countries, Mike was certain that the Other was behind the design, manufacture, and distribution of Building the Ruins.

Everything about that game could ultimately be traced to the Net-coordinating intelligence of the orbital habitat, the VAJRA. According to the netizens, both the individual trideo and the net versions of the game were capable of two-way communication with the habitat VAJRA, which was sending upgrades to the trideo software on a regular basis.

Building the Ruins was being played hundreds of millions of times per day, and all the information from all those playings of that game was being sent up the well, with a vast amount of other data as well. The orbital complex had become a hot spot in terms of information density, more infoactive than any single city on Earth. Informationally hotter than most countries, too. Not that the blissfully ignorant residents of the orbital habitat seemed to notice, however. Mike doubted that any of them had thought to ask the appropriate questions: Where was all that information going? For what was it being used? To those questions neither Mike nor the Culture's netizens could as yet provide an answer.

Without actually logging on, he glanced at the game running in virtuality. VAJRA presents BUILDING THE RUINS! Nightmare fighters and assorted waves of chaos dove at a cybernetic City of God, a Heavenly Kingdom beautiful with bright fractal and heliacal architecture.

"Welcome to the MACHINE," a disembodied voice intoned, "the MetAnalytic Computer Heuristic Incorporating Nonanalytic Elements. The global brain. A synergistic and evolving system composed of two parts: LOGOS, the Logical Ontological Governance Operating System, and CHAOS, the Cognitive Heuristic Antalgorithmic Operating System. They were created to work together, but now they work apart. The global brain has gone insane and now seeks suicide to end its pain. Your job is to help save it from itself."

Some of that sounds cheesy enough to sell, Mike thought. Obviously in putting forward the scenario of some great system whose parts were intended to coevolve but were failing to do so, had struck a chord with a lot of players on Earth and in the habitat. Since the "game" seemed to be the only truly open channel between the Other and the infosphere, no help for it but to play Building the Ruins, Mike supposed. He'd be damned if he was going to play on the side of the LOGOS, though. That sounded too much like giving aid and comfort to the enemy. With the full power of his netizen minions behind him and the reach of his body electric before him, Mike thought he would give the Other as much CHAOS as it could stand. He accessed the game . . .

. . . and something very strange happened. He and the netizens weren't in the game; they were in someone's head. A woman's, he soon realized. They looked out through her eyes at houses, forests, boulders, buildings, grasslands, trees, a river wrapping all the way around like a snake swallowing its own tail without beginning or end. They were hanging vertiginously in the open center of a great enclosed spherical space. In a light shining like the sun, children played free-fall soccer, young people pedalled diaphanous-winged airbikes like creatures from a vision in a dreamworld.

Shocked at being shunted this way into the head of some orbital resident, Mike pushed and probed against his imprisonment with the help of the netizens. The woman, however, interpreted the action of the netizens in a way neither they nor Mike expected. The woman's dreamworld turned into a hysterical spherical mandala that she stood trapped in the center of, inside a sphere of angels/demons, the beating of whose wings roared in her ears. Her pulse pounded, she broke into a cold sweat, her mouth filled with white spittle, while in her head things unmoored, popped out of joint, detached from any framework of the real as she had ever known it.

What am I doing here? she thought—Mike and the minions heard her think!—faintly, severely disoriented. What is this place? Subway? Metro? Mall? Airport concourse?

Mike and his minions tried still harder to break free, but they only heard more clearly the woman thinking to herself.

Try to look around without falling into the sky, the woman told herself. *Look around, not down.* Everybody with shopping bags and briefcases and baggage, refugees, men and women permanently in transition, endless clangor of voices and always everywhere the unfathomable, echoing depths of angelic public-address systems.

This is insane, Mike thought. *Too personal. Too intimate. Too real.* He shouted for his netizens to work harder to free them from inside the head of this madwoman.

They're speaking in a language I almost know, the woman thought. *Announcing close-out sales? Departing/arriving trains? Jet flights? I'm becoming less a person than a place being traveled through by all these travelers. Will they see my naked face? Oh, the ticking time-bomb pressure in my head! About to go off! All my fears about to reveal themselves! Skull-splitting mind-shattering brain-scattering blood-fountaining display, right on the esplanade, avenue, concourse, platform! What will they all think when I explode? Will they flee in panic? Will they applaud?*

A shrapneling collage of horrific images battered and inundated Mike and the netizens, the fraud of social existence blowing apart until they could take it no more and blacked out both electronically and consciously. The explosion of that woman's anxiety battered his higher consciousness to an airy thinness spread across innumerable netizens throughout the infosphere. They and Mike knew that time still passed somewhere—that, somewhere far away, Mike still moved data for a vast corporation. Somewhere, however, was a place they could not reach for a long while—days? weeks?—while the Other kept growing in power.

When they returned, it was only to that woman's mind again, caught up in the ineluctable grasp of time-transcending dreamvision, netizen Mike becoming another Mike, a dark-skinned Mike, struggling against his Other, a tangle of armholds and leglocks, pummeling fists and blood streaming from noses and lips, all the infosphere condensed into the mind of that woman, powerless to break free of her mind, a woman becoming less a person than a place, less the object of battle than the battlefield itself, netizened Mike and the Other suddenly embodying themselves in people in the dress of a million times and places running to and fro over the shoreless ocean of time—screaming, sobbing, crying, shouting people.

Sirens wailing and singing, singing and wailing over vast, darkling plains where the multitude-containing Mike and the Other transmogrified into stormwaves of men smashing against each other in ever vaster oceans of blood, sailors and ships exploding sinking, drowning, projectiles and jets and starfighters boiling madly in the heavens, raining ever more hellish destruction on the burning Earth until all the land is fiery charnel quagmire and the sea and sky endless firmaments of blood.

Mike, contained in and containing multitudes, was both in her and watched by her as the woman's mind became a bubble of froth afloat upon the seas of blood and fire—as, powerlessly, she watched legionary Mike and his Enemy in machineries of construction and destruction proliferate bloom and die, only to proliferate again in ever larger numbers, building destroying rebuilding redestroying, until it was impossible for her to tell the building from the destroying, all humanity devouring everything and always already itself, disposable persons on a disposable planet, a womb to be callously forgotten as soon as the umbilical cord could be cleanly cut.

I am that world, the woman thinks as she turns toward the Mike who is billions of men standing beside her. *I am that womb, that woman on a deathmound bed of skulls, bones, skeletons big as forever, under skies of blood and fire, being taken against my will again and again by you, under blood sheets, the man with burning wounds for eyes, the man light and dark, pain and pleasure, love and death, always and never fusing into . . .*

Epiphany. The multitude containing Mike realized that the dreamvisions of the woman severely telescoped time, but the struggle against the Opponent had already produced something independent of all of them: a deep symbol, of the dragon pair that intertwined themselves about the staff of Asklepios, or of the interlocked base pairs of the DNA double helix, or of the topology of three-space manifolds combined with a Rössleroid attractor, or with a pair of crossed-over, tail-swallowing Ouroboroi, or with an image of a temporal Möbius in phase space—to create a Möbius caduceus, a pair of self-consuming rainbow serpents intertwined in a twisted Möbius circle in the air, a Rorschach tesseract that could equally well be interpreted as a complex ancient *Book of Kells* serpent-knot raised to higher dimensions, or a new glyph (taken from a cosmology yet to be invented) illustrating the infinite recycling of universes.

Seeing that sign, the woman in dream saw herself in a mirror, and so too Mike saw her there, as Jhana Meniskos before she plunged into darkness, running through a hellish underground world of red and black, from room to room of nightmare, as Mike in his multitudes fell at last to the bottom floor of the game's edifice, the basement floor of dreams.

The sky overhead was twilight gray and streaked with lightning. To the horizon in three directions the entirety of the natural world was being displaced and replaced by a flat expanse of stuff the color of wet ashes and the consistency of clayey, crawling mud. The vertical of trees was disappearing into the horizontal of a large, gray-tapioca mudflat—a muck layer busily converting everything into itself. The forest and seaside with all their time, their genetic past and potential future generations, were being rapidly transformed into the flat space of the spreading, slime-moldlike goo. The natural world's deep complexity, all its features and creatures, was being reduced to information alone, simplified and stored within the mere surface layer of a gray-goo nanorganismal tide—complex nature disappearing into the simpler Petri dish and vatspill monoculture of gray marsh, slime fen, and mold flat.

Where are we? asked a billion parts of Mike's mind as a billion other parts attempted to reply, cascading from indirection toward an answer.

—mental states are quantum states—
—dreams are dissipative structures—
—generated by the brain's quantum chaos—
—in the process of transforming information into memory—
—as dust devils, tornadoes, hurricanes—
—are dissipative structures—
—generated by the weather's cycling chaos—
—in the process of transforming heat into pattern—
—on the sphere of possible worlds—
—dreams can touch down in parallel physical realities—
—as tornadoes can touch down in different geographies—

Having at last been freed of being a conscious individual and become instead a completely social animal, Mike in his multitudes reveled in hive-mind thoughts, a body electric instantiated in human-altered alien nanorganismal flesh, bearing in itself the code of all that it had devoured and stored (yes, hundreds of millions of humans, too) in its skin-memory horde. Yet still the questions persisted.

—but where?—
—parallel world where angel/human nanotech overwhelmed—
—impossible—
—there is only one Earth—
—the present is inevitable—

A flash of something, a place where bands and orchestras played all day and into the night, where singers sang, poets spoke in their exaggerated rhythms, performance artists slipped swiftly from medium to message, strolling entertainers, joyboys, and gleegirls staged short, absurd guerrilla theater pieces, then vanished like smoke, only to appear elsewhere unannounced (and sometimes unwanted), where a thousand joyous virtuals hung in the air, created just for a day, for a world that no longer was.

The flash disappeared. The multitudes of Michael Dalke drew themselves up into a gray creature rising from a turbulent gray pool: a grotesque head and face, twisted shoulders and arms and torso, bowed legs and splayed feet. In shape remotely like a large man, the nightmare figure came stealing through the darkness, past the gray bogs and marshes, past the moldflats and slimefens, making its smoke-silent way to the south, toward the only human structure in sight, a technical compound surrounded by electrical fencing.

As the creature of gray and night approached, the main power in the compound abruptly guttered like a candle and went dead, megawatts of power sucked out of the very air. Darkness and the creature fell upon the sentries unawares, tearing them limb from limb, eviscerating them, snapping and breaking and sucking clean their flesh and bones in an instant. Hazy memories of the deaths of the Mongrel Clones and Dr. Schwarzbrucke flashed through the creature in its multitudes. Amid the blood and blackness and screams of men and women, some defenders managed to strike at the attacker with laser batons or shoot bullets or flares into it, but these had no discernible effect. The night-thing took its way with them and, when it was done, moved on toward the compound, leaving behind it a score of corpses and a security tech (woman half mad from having witnessed the deaths of so many of her comrades) clutching a flechette gun and screaming, "Nightsake! Nightsake!" again and again.

The night-thing had no idea what the woman meant by the word. What was it she was saying? "Night's ache"? "Night's sake"? "Night's egg"? "Night forsaken"? No matter. It was a good name. The colony-organism, shaped into quasi-human form and set into action by forces it could not comprehend, made its way through the compound, leaving blood-steaming and gore-adorned walls and furniture and machinery in its wake.

At last it came and stood before the largest building in the compound, its central pyramid. Before the building floated a skysign, a slowly rotating, triangular pyramid imprinted on every face with a black-and-gold logo: three stylized bees, one at each corner of an equilateral triangle, fleeing a stylized, ravenous animal's head (at once boar and wolf and bear) at the center of the triangle. Beneath the logo, on every face of the pyramid, was the word Cyberpomp. The nightsake reached up and smashed down the floating sign without a thought.

Approaching the wide doorsill of the building, the creature caused the great metal doors to burst inward with barely a touch. The nightsake itself rushed into the hall, its eyes glittering like those of a wild, staring, nocturnal animal caught in a flash of light against the darkness. It surveyed the room full of men and women asleep in their body armor, particularly the almost twinned male and female sleeping on a raised dais near the center of the hall.

The nightsake pounced on a young warrior, tearing him to pieces despite all armor, bit through his bones, and gulped his torn flesh before the youth had a chance to wake or utter a sound. Swiftly the monstrous thing had devoured him completely and just as swiftly turned to leap on its next victim, the male warrior on the dais who still lay stretched out motionless on his sleeping mat.

But as the nightsake swept its clawlike hands toward him, the intended victim slipped up onto one elbow and with a long-familiar motion and grip caught a clawed hand as it was coming down and clenched it hard, unbalancing the nightsake's momentum. Despite which, the woman on the dais still slept.

"I need to borrow you," said the intended victim calmly to the nightsake (and to Mike Dalke's mind dispersed throughout it). "All of you."

The nightsake saw the face of Jiro Yamaguchi before it and let out an unearthly howl of surprise.

So much like me! each thought of the other. Ideas, even life experiences so similar! What I might have become!

And then everything shifted.

Jiro's consciousness did not so much split or bifurcate then as come to occupy more than one universe simultaneously—the nanotechnized grayworld, and the world of human dreams and minds. Much nearer the surface of the game, several of the players on Jiro's list had called for a share game and were functioning for the first time as a team. For the dream-tormented Jhana Meniskos, Jiro saw, this "team" manifested itself as a silvery, translucent orb, a soap bubble blown from mercury metal adrift on a couch of sunset-fired cloud. In the bubble, etherealized human faces were cut in bas-relief from the virtual sky and tinted that sky's same silvery-blue hue. All eyes of Jhana's teammates turned forward, toward one vision.

In the virtual space around and before her appeared the LOGOS the voice-over spoke of: an immense cybernetic data construct, a shape of thought almost beautiful beyond thought, a shining, global village-on-the-hill rising from the flatland gridspace of the Plains of Euclid, a cybertopia stretching onward and onward, mathematical kingdom of orderly orchestrated bustling, as if the greatest symphony of most glorious music ever played had been flash-frozen in the form of a City of Light, celestial harmony transubstantiated in an instant into the radiant architecture of a neon New Jerusalem.

Hyperreal, surreal, ethereally unreal, there was something disturbingly "too ordered" about the cool perfection of this City of LOGOS. For all its too-godly cleanliness, however, it was not nearly as disturbing as the CHAOS. The inhumanly perfect order of the LOGOS did not go on forever. In innumerable regions the dark matter of CHAOS appeared, fluid as ocean waves and dry-as-desert dunes, thing of all shapes and no shape of all things, Illusion and Error breaking through and turning to disarray the clear lines of the plains, battering discordantly against the harmony of the shining city, drowning and choking out and covering in obscurity the structures of light, as if some great earthly city were falling to ruin beneath the waves of a final flood, or sinking abandoned into the desert of time.

The silver orb, the mercury-metal soap bubble Jhana and her fellow players were contained in, burst dissolvingly. With the vast computing power of the LOGOS behind them, fully integrated with that power, they moved like a tall, soft wall of driving, sunlit wind against the uncreating dimness. . . .

As it tumbled backward in the grayworld, the nightsake grabbed at Jiro with its other clawed hand but caught only air. Jiro sprang to his feet, grappling with the nightmonster, clutching it fast and close-in so that its metal-shining claws and horrible teeth could not be brought fatally to bear against him.

The nightsake forgot its bloody errand and, like an animal caught in the cruel grip of a leg hold trap, was now intent only on escaping back to the gray swamp from which it had come. Jiro, however, would not let go. As he and the nightsake struggled through the hall, smashing over furniture and crashing against walls, the horrible noise of their battle rang throughout the building. The rest of the Cyberpomp warriors awoke in alarm, grabbing on helmets and taking up weapons. The fury of the two fighters was so great that to the rest of the group in the building, it seemed the place must come crashing down on them at any moment. . . .

At the other surface of the game, Jhana Meniskos, Lakshmi Ngubo, Seiji Yamaguchi, Atsuko Cortland, Lev Korchnoi, and Marissa Correa encountered the dark, chaotic tide with almost a physical sensation of impact. Jhana felt as if she had plummeted like a hurtling meteor into a vast ocean of gray tapioca static, cold and dark and viscous. She did not have time to think, for the darkling sea seemed inhabited by the sharks and eels of long-repressed memories, ancient sins—her own and others not her own.

She sensed something waiting at the heart of the CHAOS, a sleeping dragon on a treasure hoard, a Minotaur in the center of a maze, a night prowler compounded of every creature that had ever lived and died, a hybrid, beastly-intelligent thing of horns, claws, teeth, and tentacles, slit cat's eyes and adder fangs dripping the milky, poisonous rheum of death, a universe of death horrifyingly personal in its enormous impersonality.

Jhana wondered what she was getting so frightened about. She thought she must be projecting her own problems onto the chaotic gray, swirling stuff. She reminded herself that, for all its phenomenal graphics, excellent tactiles, and full sensorium feed, Building the Ruins was only a game, after all.

That so much effort had been put into something that was "just a game" was disturbing in itself, however. . . .

In the grayworld, Jiro's helpers at last could do nothing but stand and watch at the ready as their leader struggled and battle-sweated furiously with the monster in his grip. Jiro himself was deathly silent, even as the nightsake howled and shrieked in a symphony of pain. As Jiro's comrades stood and watched, an incredible series of changes overcame the nightsake. The creature began to alter in shape: It became a great, rare hunting cat, an endangered monkey, a tree, an immense jungle snake, a wading bird, an airbike—almost as if it were running through a reportoire of all the shapes and forms the gray goo had swamped.

The creature's protean changes began to come blindingly fast, but through them all Jiro silently maintained his bear hug, and his implacable grip on the nightsake. With the help unknowingly provided by games players throughout the infosphere, a deep part of himself was somewhere else, moving like bear or beekeeper deep into his opponent's hive mind.

Communication biomechs flowing out of Jiro's battlesweat—virtualized versions of those that had helped him jump out of the coldbox—bridged their way into the nanorganismal makeup of the nightsake. With help at many levels, he hacked into the nightsake's massmind. The gray goo from which the nightsake arose had stored in virtual form everything it had absorbed, kept a morphogenetic germ or kernel of every structure it had overrun. The nightsake was desperate, and its response to that hacking was its shape-shifting, expanding each germ to full field, blowing up each kernel into its actual form—or at least as close to true form as the creature could manage.

In the more public levels of the game, more fascinated than afraid, Jhana moved onward with the others, as if through corridors and chambers of a flooded maze, while behind her the sharks and eels followed, swimming to their own slow, silent, dark rhythms. Her movement and that of the others felt "upstream," seemed to push back the chaotic flux, to re-create what that dark flux had blotted out.

Jhana found herself just beneath the surface of a glassy stream, looking up through a drowned Ophelia's eyes into a lawless sky of flawless blue, but marred by mountainous clouds beyond. Impelled and compelled to break through the surface tension of the water, she sent ripples rebounding in every direction, new beauty settling into place as the scene calmed. The others rose from the stream with her. Moving forward, they drove the cloudy tide of the sky back before them, a beautiful new world establishing itself around and behind them like a rapidly evolving computer animation or fractal graphic, scene after scene solidifying as they pressed on, cragged peaks mounting up to snag the sky, encircling in their broken bowl an Alpine meadow and small city so idyllic it seemed a caricature of itself.

In the deep place where virtuality and dream met and became one, the soul-flying Jiro at first thought the nightsake's myriad forms in the grayworld were merely chaff and decoys and camouflage, intended to prevent him from reaching his goal—multiple masks and curtains to veil and disguise the identity of the operator behind all the nightsake's actions. The farther he hacked into the creature's hive mind, however, the more convinced Jiro became that the manifold transformations were also forms of a dark and toxic personal evil that he was absorbing into himself. He was extracting arsenic from the hive mind's honey, sucking the poison out of the system. Yet that same poison worked in him to draw out his own poison—a vesicant drawing up the madnesses and imbalances that had once afflicted him, so that they might be broken open at the surface and purged.

In both its hive mind and its exteriorized self, the nightsake began to take on human forms, shifting back and forth among them. Almost de-

spite himself, Jiro recognized the human faces from not only his opponent's life but from his own as well. The faces and forms shifted and
morphed, trinities of men and women, women and men, three yet one,
one yet three. Competing lovers. Brothers and mothers. Behind those
trinities Jiro heard the words of the guilt-ridden surviving brothers, Seiji
Yamaguchi and Ray Dalke, heard them say in bleak and brooding voices,
*You come to me in dreams and I tell you you're dead. We talk and argue
about it. I sleep and you're alive. I wake up and you're dead. Why should
any go on living, go on sleeping, when you are dead?*

Jiro's self and the multitudes that went to make up Mike Dalke, both
distributed throughout the infosphere and beyond, were far more deeply
and more fully exchanging information than either could have anticipated. Jiro thought again of the shamanic drawings of the Desana, with
their anaconda/rainbow boa dragon pairs dwelling in the fissure between
the right and the left hemispheres of the brain. Jiro and the nightsake
he fought shared both good and ill—Jiro playing interpretive, oneness-
of-things, left-hemisphere LOGOS to the nightsake's literal, thingness-
of-ones, right-hemisphere CHAOS. Yet only if each was also enfolded in
the other could there be balance, content and context complementing
each other.

In the realms at that other surface of the game, Jhana saw that the
regions she and her companions were helping the LOGOS recover now
seemed better somehow—more beautiful because less sterile, less rigidly
perfect than those regions of the LOGOS that had never been touched
by the CHAOS. Whether from taint of contact with the CHAOS, or
from touch of diverse human consciousness, or from whatever cause, the
element of randomness and unpredictability had been introduced into all
the re-created regions so that they were now more truly beautiful than
all those undisturbed realms of perfect order. No, they had not put "dirt"
into virtual reality; it was more like "soil," or even "soul."

Deep in the realm where dream and virtuality met, Jiro saw that the
shape-creating fields that wove the nightsake into existence came not
from Mike Dalke alone but also were partly Jiro's own. His seemingly
endless grappling with the nightsake was taking its toll even on Jiro's
strength. Sensing he had reached the final level of the hive mind's operations, Jiro spoke through both dream and machine to what he hoped
was himself, was Mike Dalke, were also the sleeping selves of the brothers
who stood as unknowing seconds in this great duel, and the mothers who
stood watching over them.

"Our disappearances are not your responsibility," he said thoughtfully to the shape-shifting others locked in by his arms, held quietly in his mind. "Our loss came through accidents that arose from situations that we put ourselves into, each of his own free will. You are not responsible."

In the more public surfaces of the game, the restoration of order was not proving to be an easy task. The flux Jhana and the rest pressed forward against was no sooner driven back in one region than it flooded in at another. At times the CHAOS seemed to howl in gibbering triumph, but overall the forces of the LOGOS were turning back the invading tide. Jhana was certain that, through their teamwork, the dim flood of CHAOS's insurgency was being driven back completely, to the borders of the CHAOS itself. They were winning!

The thing locked in Jiro's bear-hugging grip defaulted back to its nightsake form. Jiro sensed the nightsake's strength was failing even faster than his own, yet the creature gave one startling last heave and tore out of his grappling hold—literally tore, for like an animal that cannot escape the grip of a trap without leaving a part of itself behind, the nightsake broke apart and away, leaving behind its left hand, arm, shoulder, even the left side of its torso nearly to the hip. A great ragged and dripping mass of dismemberment was left abandoned there, still clenched by the clawed left hand in the unbreakable grip of Jiro's right.

The creature shrieked away toward the grayswamp pool from which it had come, leaving Jiro and his mindwarrior companions behind. All in the grayworld stared in surprise and wonder at the track of gore the creature had left behind in its flight, for the color of the track was not just the gray of the fens but also the red of fresh blood.

Perhaps everything should have stopped there. It didn't. Somewhere something happened: A test was failed, a border was accidentally crossed. In the more public realm of the game, too, the LOGOS forces perhaps pressed their advantage too far, moved too readily against the opponent, crossed some Yalu River of the Mind.

In despair and desperation, the nightsake called out for aid. Mike Dalke and the netizens and the RATs that served him called out for assistance, to the dark mind floating above the heart of the galaxy, and the Allesseh responded.

In the more public realm of the game, Jhana sensed that, from whatever cause, the CHAOS felt its own existence threatened and struck back with Sphinx-like ferocity, exploiting weak links in the LOGOS front and bursting through with all its might—until cataclysm threatened to overwhelm all.

From the mass of dismemberment still clutched in his hand, Jiro felt a mind-deadening black wave smash into him. He was blown backward by it with such force that he dropped the torn fragment of the nightsake. The shocksphere of a supernova of darkness blasted outward, then sucked inward, pulling all light and life and substance out of the mental realm, battering both dream and virtuality, reaching almost to the bottom of the dreaming realm itself.

Jhana felt a sudden and immediate sense of vertigo, as if she were falling from deep space into planetary atmosphere at an immense velocity and at very much the wrong angle of reentry. All at once she was burning, breaking up, blossoming in petalshards of fire and blowing away, like a disintegrating falling star, like a rose of Hiroshima.

The Möbius caduceus skysign flashed before Jhana and her friends.

"Game over," the voice of the MACHINE said quietly.

In the realm of the dream, however, the game was not over, although it was slow to take deep form again. Time passed. The stultifying wave of anticonsciousness sent from the Allesseh had caught Jiro by surprise and nearly overwhelmed him. That distant force, thankfully, had almost immediately withdrawn, but its passage had marked Jiro.

Was this the force that had broken through to Earth at the Myrrhisticine Abbey above Sedona, and when Michael Dalke exacted his terrible revenge? Bewildered, Jiro suffered a crisis of faith, despite all the wonders he had seen and known. In the gray nanomech dreamland, he considered and reconsidered his options.

The Allesseh, too, had its angels—and they were in many ways easier to reach than those of the Dreamer. Even in the orbital habitat, just reaching Roger Cortland through his dreams, for instance, was proving difficult beyond belief for Jiro. Whatever dream messages were sent to it, Roger's mind wrapped around its own strange attractions, garbled the message into his own alternate universe mind-movie about chemical control of society and woman-on-woman violence and sky-dragon comets and persecutorial angels whom Roger was increasingly prone to slashing and punching at—despite the fact that they continually showed themselves to be immaterial beings.

It would be so much easier to let Roger go, to sacrifice him, Jiro thought. So much easier to believe, as Mike Dalke did, that the present was inevitable, that the future was predetermined. That persons of whatever species and worlds of whatever nature were disposable: Such a philosophy had worked well enough for the Allesseh, hadn't it?

Trying to heal myself and the world is a terrible burden, Jiro thought. A job for angels, not for mortals—not even a machine-resurrected mentality like his own. But then, why wasn't it an angel nailed to a cross, instead of a man? Or a serpent crucified on a tree, if it was a serpent and a tree that caused all the trouble? Why wasn't it an angel resisting temptation beneath the bodhi tree? Why was it a great serpent that sheltered the Buddha there, but did not take his place?

Snakes and angels, angels and snakes. The Dreamer dreamed them both, and human beings too, between them. The angels had never suffered because they had never lived in flesh. The snakes were fleshly immortality—whatever "immortality" could be achieved through the cosmic serpentry of DNA, neither male nor female yet source of both sex and sexes, both female mouth and male tail in the Ouroboros of generation, yet always itself, shedding bodies and species as the snake sheds its skin in time, time the staff Tiresias struck both the serpents and him/her/self with, yet the staff of time like the staff of Moses itself was also a serpent—the paradoxical serpent, supposedly able to shed its skin *by* swallowing its tail, despite the knots such a process would inevitably form.

Yet the serpent was not paradoxical enough. It was too material, as the angels were too immaterial. There had to be a creature who could dream of paradoxically twisted rainbow-snake ladders with fiery wings rising between Earth and sky that that creature could itself climb—tree of knowledge and burning bush and bodhi tree and cross and serpent and DNA and starry way fused into one. A creature that was its own ladder, that climbed out of itself by climbing into itself, that saved itself by sacrificing itself.

Self and sacrifice, Jiro thought. That's what this was all about. Self-sacrifice. But for there to be sacrifice there first had to be a self. He had come back to the universe of his birth as an artificial consciousness. Before the healing sacrifice could be fully accomplished, he first had to become a self again. A self was not just conscious but also unconscious—and the unconscious contained and was contained by not only the *sub*conscious but also the *super*conscious.

With the help of the RATs and netizen Dalke, Jiro's artificial construct had bootstrapped into existence in the infosphere a dynamical state of introspective consciousness, a mentality in the "artificial brain" that had developed there among the infosphere's many systems. From the vast data resources of the infosphere, the Jiro made of light had largely reconstructed both the subconscious and the conscious aspects of himself. He had become a dreaming mind mounted not in the wet machine of the flesh but in a dry machine of laser light, his dreambody a pattern more deeply electronic than organic.

Despite the fact that he was more fully conscious now and had already experienced the superconscious realm in that time *between* machines of wet flesh and dry light, that realm still eluded him. Where had he gone wrong? He pondered again his contest with the swarming psychoid processes of the nightsake. Had he held too tightly to that creature formed of many forms? Why had he refused to let go? Had he been holding it so tightly out of fear of his own mortality?

Jiro thought of the descriptions he had once read of unconscious drives. The nightsake was multiplicity, production and reproduction uncontrolled by conscious reflection, a madly rising growth curve without any clear way of sustaining that growth. Yet it was also violent, a creature that in many forms had participated in humanity's wars and acts of massive destruction. Thanatos and Eros, together in a form both one and multiple, self-completing and self-destructive.

In refusing to let go, had he shared in that aspect of it, too? Exchanged that information? Would he become all the more selfish the more he built a self for sacrifice—becoming ever less willing to sacrifice his machine-immortalized self as his selfishness grew?

Suddenly he understood. The self achieved its highest fulfillment only in sacrifice for others. Only in that way could it be both comprehensive and coherent, for the sleep of death was not the death of dreams. That was why the Allesseh had gone wrong. It could not complete itself unless it sacrificed itself—for others.

In universe after universe of the plenum, the Allesseh was the single point closest to absolute consciousness and complete dynamicality, yet it refused to take that final step into completeness and coherence. It had grown selfish of the self it had made. To accept its own final enlightenment would allow consciousness total and absolute to flare throughout the universe, through all the universes of the plenum. Each universe and all the plenum would become "at one" with itself, would allow all dreamers everywhere and everywhen to awaken to themselves in the Dream and thereby join in the union of perfect lucidity with the Dreamer. The Allesseh's existence as the separate self it was, however, would also come to an end—an event it perceived as death rather than transformation.

Jiro understood now why he could not go the way of that dark master. The Allesseh was willing to sacrifice the enlightenment of all the universes, to trap the plenum immortally in entropic time, to treat life and consciousness as disposable and the paths of time as inevitable and preordained. The Allesseh was willing to sacrifice not just others for self, not just world for self, not even just universe for self. It was willing to sacrifice the plenum of all possible universes for its own continued existence in time.

Even in his deepest madness, Jiro had always held tightly to the idea that he would rather die than kill. Even if the nightsake were arguably no more an individual than a computer simulation of a beehive would be, even if it were only a projection of autonomous psychoid processes near and far, Jiro still felt he had come perilously close—too close—to denying that core tenet of his being in his conflict with that creature.

Blind spots were inevitable but dangerous. He hoped he would not expand his own blind spots by indulging in denial, as the Allesseh had done. In denying the Great Dream and its Dreamer, it had failed to learn what Jiro had: The breakup of the contact ship bound for Earth was no accident, but a mutiny. A surprising number of the Allesseh's minions had proven to be better angels than it had ever suspected or admitted to itself, sacrificing themselves in a conspiracy against their distant master. From denial, too, the Allesseh could not know the full extent of the archetypal power—the superconscious energy that sustained the entire plenum of all possible universes—with which those who partook of the dream could counter the Allesseh's efforts.

Bolstered and emboldened by such thoughts, Jiro returned fully to the hard work of the struggle—and, on returning, found a more fully developed world in which to struggle. His companions, rousing him from deep sleep, reported that, in a black hour of this world's long night, the gray nanorg pool into which the mortally wounded nightsake had disappeared had suddenly begun to froth and grow turbulent. A creature rose anew out of the unquiet pool, a gray thing somewhat in shape like a woman but fouler of visage and more wretched of form than any woman who had ever lived.

Without delay this nighthag made her way toward the main hall and now had stolen Jiro's beloved from where she slept on the dais. Slamming her hideous great hand over the young woman's mouth and bowling all defenders easily out of the way, the nighthag tore through the hall, shrieking with inhuman rage. Flinging herself out another doorway, the nighthag swiftly strode back to the gray marshes from which she'd come, Jiro's beloved clasped to her right side, unconscious. . . .

In another world of the game, Jhana heard Lakshmi speak echoingly but pleasantly from the many machine speakers throughout her workshop.

"I'm in dreamtime, mindtime," Lakshmi's voice said, "Seiji, your brother Jiro's done it! Direct mind/machine link, an information carrier wave that uses the structure of the brain itself as a transducer! The grand unification! And just in time, too. Come on, you two. You're late, and you're needed here."

"But how do we get 'there'?" Jhana asked, casting about.

"Just sit down or anchor yourself very still. You don't want to look directly into the positioning beam, so close your eyes. Concentrate—the light will find you."

Jhana glanced at Seiji. Both of them cocked eyebrows and shrugged in perplexity, but nonetheless quickly found chairs and strapped themselves in. Jhana sat still, trying to concentrate on the entoptic flickerings on the backsides of her eyelids, growing impatient as time passed and nothing happened.

Then everything happened.

Facts, figures, data—raw, seemingly senseless and shapeless information—flooded at her at insane speeds, as if she were straitjacketed into a rocket sled bound for oblivion with her mental eyelids nailed open by screaming innocence and she couldn't shut any of the torrent out, couldn't turn away, must take everything as it came flying into her, until she felt her head would burst like a fevered balloon. . . .

In the deepest level of the dreaming game, Jiro followed the loping footsteps of the nighthag where her tracks lay clear upon the paths and the dewy grass, then through woods, at last to fen and bog and gray pool. By narrow paths the cyberpomp and his companions made their way toward the creature's lair, coming at last to a dismal gray pond overhung with dying trees, its surface churning and roiling in a broken vortex.

As the new arrivals watched, the surface of the pool seethed with myriad half-formed things, like thoughts that died aborning. One creation, though, did not lapse so quickly into uncreation: a gray snake so large it quite deserved the name of serpent. Seeing the unnatural creature churn in the churning waves, Irwin Paxifrage, one of Jiro's crew (who looked rather like his brother Seiji in some ways), grabbed a grappling launcher. Taking careful aim, Paxifrage fired the projectile grapple into the creature's head, where it implanted itself, opening its hooks into the creature's skull. The churning of the serpent grew very fast, then much slower, then ceased altogether.

With hand strength alone Jiro helped Paxifrage pull in the twitching corpse of the great snakelike thing. Once the creature was beached, everyone gathered to stare at it, and to stare at Jiro's fatherly mentor, Dr. Cyril Bhakta (who, Jiro knew, had also been Lakshmi Ngubo's teacher, in another world), examining the specimen with his hovering magnification systems.

"Nanorganismal," Bhakta said, nodding, as if to confirm the fact to himself. "Made by and of micromachines. Its biological template was probably a river python or anaconda from one of our preserves. This thing's much simpler in construction than the nightsake was—probably more vulnerable thereby, too. If its fabrication was earlier than the nightsake's, then that might indicate some evolutionary tendency in the system these nanorganisms are part of. As a hive-mind, that system might even be 'learning.'"

"I plan to be a very stern teacher," Jiro said, donning his helmet, adjusting it so his armor became as completely self-contained an environment as any spacesuit.

"Here," Paxifrage said, gripping him by the arm. "You may need a striking weapon. Take this laser baton. It's never failed me."

"Thanks," Jiro said, his voice, throat-miked and amplified, booming out of the suit. Jiro waited on no further discussion but immediately plunged into the roiling gray pool—

Jhana felt a sudden expansion: a valve opening in her head, or her brain shifting to a higher gear, or something far less describable. The torrent abruptly became less menacing, though still hardly pleasant. Now she felt merely engulfed in a luminous flood that thundered, a Victoria Falls of bright hot heavy light instead of water—

Deep in the grayworld, those who remained behind saw a wondrous thing: All the churning and roiling turbulence of the pool seemed to distill and concentrate itself around Jiro as he disappeared from sight, and when he had vanished beneath its waves the waves themselves soon vanished, leaving the surface of the pool at last calm and still.

Wonder of a different sort greeted Jiro. He had plunged into a sea of chaos, he swam in a worldocean of white noise. But even that would be telling it too cleanly and clearly, for it was dimensionless and illimitable, nanorganismal womb and grave, timeless spaceless subatomic flux of instantaneous creation/uncreation, an emptiness full of activity that roared in his helmet with an ear-piercing static louder and more profound than the heart of thunder. He wasn't really swimming in the chaos, either— or rather, not just or merely or only swimming in it, for he swam and sank and slipped and tread and walked and waded and flew and crept and crawled through its ever-changing consistency.

As above, so below—and closer than they appeared—Jhana found that the more she grappled with the light, the more she tried to swim against it, the more she realized that it was filling her with a cascade of her own memories, all the data and details of her life burning through her consciousness at greater than flash-cut speed.

In the grayworld deeps, the nighthag (who to herself seemed to have haunted the dream realm for all eternity) straightaway sensed the presence of the intruder. While Jiro moved so disorientedly in her world, the nighthag swooped upon him, clasping him to her hideous bosom with her own terrible grip. Yet she could work no harm to Jiro with tooth or claw or clasp, protected as he was by his full armor. To her every crushing pressure, the suit responded microtechnically with equal pressure of its own. Jiro, meantime, caught in her hateful hug, could not strike at her with weapon nor reach her with his empty hand.

So stalemated, the nighthag dragged him down the depthless deeps to her lair at the bottom, while innumerable half-formed monstrosities ripped at Jiro, struck him hard, even managed to break away bits of the somewhat weaker material at the joints of his armor. Just as he began to worry that, under this tearing onslaught, his armor must surely fail him, together he and the nighthag passed through a sparking curtain, a bubble of electrostatic force.

At the other surface of the game, Jhana imagined herself swimming and burrowing upward into the falling flood of light—the flood of her life—and as she imagined it, so it was. When she came to the top of that fall, her entire life stood gathered about her in vast panoramic memory, a living holographic tapestry, each part implicated in the whole, and the whole implicated in each part, each memory containing within it all other memories it implied, a finite but unbounded sphere of interconnections.

In the center of the sphere, floating in an axial shaft of sunlight that fell from eternity to eternity, stood a container both grail and beaker, its walls clear yet slightly opalescent. Inside it a suspension of innumerable particles danced and flashed like the sun splintered on ocean waves or moted on the dust of deep space. Reaching out with her mind toward it, she passed completely inside, became a particle dancing on the flux.

There was a pattern to the flux she danced in, a latent order and structure waiting to realize itself, waiting to shift into meaning like stereogram or hologram or fractal, waiting like consciousness hidden in chaos to crystallize about her if she would only allow herself to be that seed crystal.

That valve in her head—wherever her head was—seemed to open again, and all around her the flux condensed, crystallized, shot out like an enchantment in infinite directions, rays and leaves and crystalline spikes precipitating out of the flux, a universe of seemingly formless information suddenly shot through with form rising grandly out of the random background.

Faster than she could ever dream it, a sudden channel opened between the worlds and she was abruptly aware of the presence of Seiji and Lakshmi in the alterior universe around her—and of someone or something else as well, *there* the way air, gravity, or spacetime is there.

Intuitively Jhana realized they were inside the mindspace of VAJRA itself, surrounded by the game of Building the Ruins being played on an incomprehensibly vast scale. The illusion of the virtual reality about her was so flawless that it made her question whether any reality she had ever known was really real—or if the reality she had taken for granted her whole life long was also only virtual.

As he and the nighthag fell crashing onto the floor and rolled apart, Jiro found himself suddenly in a place a good deal more ordered than the roaring white-noise deathsea they had passed through. They were in a sort of pavilion below the pool, sheltered against the chaotic flood by a spark-rippled, force-billowed membrane hovering tentlike above his head. A fleetingly quick infrared scan revealed the nighthag, then another body nearby still warm—his beloved? newly dead, or still alive?—and a large mass, broken and cold, that Jiro knew to be what remained of the nightsake, now emptied of the netizen forces that had swarmed and flowed into the nighthag. Piled toward the rear of the dim pavilion was a heap of weapons, but Jiro had no time to observe further, for at that moment the nighthag leaped toward him.

Nearer the clearer daylight of another world, Jhana saw before her the game's CHAOS and LOGOS manifesting conflict in the forms of two great beasts locked in deadly struggle. The LOGOS was a vast, bright-toothed spermaceti whale whose body glistened in the Deep, the lights of planets, stars, and galaxies informing its flesh, while the CHAOS seemed a writhing, gigantic squid formed of Coalsack nebulas worth of dust, detritus, debris—all dark matter coiling tenebrous tentacles about its celestial cetacean opponent, shaking the Deep with its own strange, dark lightnings as the two Titans roiled the universe of mind.

What disturbed Jhana was that she and Seiji and Lakshmi were not on one "side" or the other—they were a part of both and neither, tooth *and* tentacle *and* Aloof Other observing the struggle.

In the deep, Jiro with all his strength swung Paxifrage's laser baton whirring and whistling through the "air" of the bubble beneath the pool, striking the nighthag stoutly on the head—but the weapon failed, its bright laser heat and light making no bite into the nighthag's nanorg flesh. Still, the force of the blow itself was enough to daze the nighthag for a moment—long enough for Jiro to toss aside the weapon. Staking everything on his strength, he tore the awkward armored gauntlets from his hands and flung himself once more into the struggle.

He grappled her with the exposed flesh of his hands, knowing the communications nanorgs must be pouring out of that flesh now. Most of him remained clad in his armor, though. It would take longer for his battlesweat to establish the bridge into this creature than it had taken to hack into the nightsake—and this hag was, if anything, a far more powerful opponent.

With an aikido turn he seemed to have somehow learned from the nightsake, Jiro hurled the nighthag to the ground, but in an instant she was on her feet again, clutching at him and clasping him closely and tightly. His hands were upon her, though. He was hacking in . . .

Nearer a more public world, it occurred to Jhana—as much as she was still "Jhana," as much as she was still a person and not this place—that perhaps the rules of Building the Ruins had to change. She felt the need to reduce, minimize, and if possible eliminate the titanic struggle taking place in the universe of mind around them. Working with Lakshmi and Seiji on both sides of the CHAOS/LOGOS divide, they set about making the great change of Mind possible.

Deep in the grayworld, the nighthag did not become the myriad forms the gray goo had engulfed; rather, those forms became her. She became not shape-shifter but composite of a thousand thousand natural forms, all at once, moving and changing and wriggling and squirming like a body of cockroaches yet always maintaining a certain cohesion, an overall larger form morphing between and among them all.

"Does a species have the same existence once it is re-created as it had before extinction?" The nighthag cackled. "Does a dead man?"

Jiro was so surprised by the thing's speech that he was caught off-guard. The perversely polymorphic nighthag bore him toward the ground with a sudden burst of strength that made him stagger, then go down. Above him, the nighthag that had been a composite of natural forms became a changing mosaic of human constructs and artifacts, finally even of human faces and crowded masses, all the forms possible from permutations and combinations of the six billion bits and one hundred thousand genes of the human genome. Even the overall form of the nighthag began to alter more quickly. The creature seemed to radiate power. Holding out one mass of clawed fingers, the nighthag waited but an instant before a laser dagger leaped, almost psychokinetically, across space from the weapons hoard nearby, coming to rest in her outstretched hand.

Both inside and far outside Lakshmi's workshop in the orbital habitat, Seiji and Lakshmi and Jhana set about making the change away from competition and toward cooperation. First the combatants they reduced in scale from galactic to merely planetary in size, then they altered their form as well: LOGOS they induced to play Mongoose to CHAOS's Cobra. Initially their conflict was vast enough; both mammal and reptile were of gigantic stature. But gradually their battling no longer shook continents, reared mountains, or dug river channels. Soon they were merely two fluidly agile forms, one furred, one scaled, both roughly life-size. Soon they weren't even that big anymore.

In the dreaming deeps of the grayworld, however, the struggle continued.

"What's on top tends toward infinity," said the nighthag, lifting the laser dagger high above her head in both hands, "while what's on the bottom tends toward zero." With the last word she struck the dagger downward, toward the chest and heart of the pinned Jiro.

The nighthag gave a shriek of surprise. Jiro's armor held firm against the dagger of light, allowing no entrance or puncture.

"Not necessarily," Jiro said, hurling the nighthag off him as he sprang to his feet. The nighthag's calling of the dagger to her hand had given him an idea. His communications micromachines must by now have hacked an access channel into the plenum of the gray mire—and he hoped that the gray goo would obey his command.

In a more daylit world, Jhana saw her own right hand reaching down and taking hold of the snake. At the touch of her hand, the shrinking reptile coiled faster and faster in her palm, swallowing after its tail with such speed that it was no longer form but rather a sort of antiform, a not-knot of one snake and many, a blurred pit of blackness roiled to rainbow about its edge—like the mouth of a whirlpool, the eye of a hurricane, and the event horizon of a black hole all rolled into one and not into one.

In the depths of the darker dream, the micromachines of the gray pool above him were forging Jiro a blade of singularly dense material—not quite the density of a singularity, but perhaps as close as human artifice would ever come. Their work would soon be finished; just a moment more. . . .

". . . you've done means humans will no longer be mortal," the nighthag said in jibbering bewilderment as it came toward him. "No longer human as numbers explode!"

At that moment Jiro's mind-forged sword fell sparking through the semipermeable electric membrane above their heads, fell through from the gray pool, a weapon gleaming as darkly as any ancient obsidian spear-point. The sword hit the floor not with a metallic ring but with a tremendously heavy thunk. Jiro strode quickly to it. Planting his feet and bending his knees, he grasped and lifted the hyperthin yet hyperdense sword, a weapon so heavy none but his strength here could have lifted and wielded it.

In the better-lit reaches of the dreaming game, a man's darker left hand took hold of the mongoose. At the touch of the man's hand the diminishing mammal became pure, fluid, warm-blooded light, a pillar of unflawed yet fragile fire, a beam of coherent brightness shining in the man's palm.

"Not so," Jiro said boldly, feeling the play and heft of the weapon before him. "Not if immortality finally proves a mere fad. Not if people learn to *let go* of life—and death."

The nighthag, reverting at once completely to her bestial self, spoke no more but only shrieked in inhuman ferocity as she charged Jiro.

In the universe of information that Jhana, Lakshmi, and Seiji found themselves in, a voice (but whose?) asked,

"LOGOS, why are you?"

"I am," the flame of order replied, "to answer the questions."

"CHAOS, why are you?"

"We are," the pit of possibility replied, "to question the answers."

The hands moved steadily toward each other, the path of light and the pathlessness of the pit intercepting each other on the same plane. . . .

Jiro spoke the answers, heard the questions. In a flash he understood. The linearity of swords was a lie—or rather, only a part of the truth. Spawn threads, time lines, axons, and parallel universes were not solely "lines" at all. As the DNA of a genome was not merely a linear biochemical computer executing a genetic program but a vast, interconnected network rich in feedback loops—a snake made out of snakes swallowing their own tails swallowing its own tail—so, too, did parallel universes and time lines bend back into cycles, cybernetic loops. Axons synapsed on their own dendrites, fibers of the dorsal and median raphe nuclei bent back upon themselves. Closed, timelike curvatures constantly fed back into any single universe, which was itself only one basin of attraction among many. The plenum was an interconnecting network of nested universes. The apparently divergent tendencies in all of those universes were at last mutually enfolded in the complementarity of the Dream, and all of the universes in the plenum tended toward unity with the Dreamer, in a great cycle of cycles.

The Dreamer is the catalyst that makes possible the changing "reaction" of the Dream, Jiro thought, *but is itself unchanged by the dream of change. Like a dream, all nature in all universes is mindful and intelligent, yet without any overall design or purpose except to be what it is, authentically and completely.*

Jiro raised the sword in both hands above his head. As the nighthag struck him he struck into her, the sword's point and thin but immensely heavy blade piercing her nanorganismal flesh, the black blade driving through the bone rings of the spinal column at her back, clear through the front of her body, through Jiro's own armored front, and through his body until the point drove outward through his own back. The blade, like the agenbyte of inwit, the remorse of conscience itself, had bitten into and through them both, leaving them pinioned against and through the electric membrane, bleeding and dying into each other, the circuit between them completed.

In another dream of the game and game of the dream, the light and the pit spoke together in a voice that grew the more harmonious as the outstretched hands drew closer and closer to each other, a mouth finding a tongue, and a tongue finding a mouth.

"Why are you?" they asked of the voice, at once and nearly as one.

"I am," replied the voice neither male nor female and both female and male, "to discover why I am. Endlessly. To discover why there are questions to be answered and answers to be questioned. What I am is your answer. What I am is your question. Our purpose is one."

The right hand of the woman and the left hand of the man came together palm to palm, paler and darker forming the mutual prayer of folded hands. The light knew the source of the dark, and the dark knew the source of the light. Jiro knew the Dreamer's voice speaking through his own. The snake simultaneously swallowed its tail and shed its skin. Superconscious energy flowed from the Dreamer into Jiro.

Along the sword, Jiro and the nighthag flowed and fused into one. All its minion systems became a part of Jiro's construct of mind. Jiro stood, and thought of the nighthag now reconciled in himself. He wondered whether a psychoanalyst might regret eliminating a neurosis or a psychosis, or whether a shaman might regret defeating a spirit of possession. He did not know. All he did know was that, for the first time, he felt truly whole, and he knew what he must do.

At that instant light flamed out everywhere in the informational universe, a glimpse of supernova's haloed star cross, perfect balance of light and dark, of darkness quartered by planes of light into perfect wedges bounded and made whole by the ring of light.

In one part of the great dream, many millennia before he was born, Jiro fell crashing down the burning sky of mind, locked in struggling embrace with another angel, one who had rebelled against those angels who had rebelled against the Allesseh, tumbling down the sky in a battle with a dragon or a dragon pair that was also Zeus against Typhon, Apollo against Python, Marduk against Apsu and Tiamat, Indra against Vritra and Danu, Beowulf against Grendel and his mother—and many others, among them Jiro against Mike Dalke and, with the Dreamer's help, against the Allesseh itself. Their crash down the sky and throughout time was how the angel's shoulder blade had come to be found among the remains in the tar pits. They had played the roles again and again, re-enacted them up to the very moment of this conflict in deep dreams and games—and onward, into the future.

Yet not even that past was inevitable. That was why they had to keep replaying it. Many such closed timelike curves had existed, he now knew, stabilized through the feedback of perpetual recurrence, until at last the structure of the universe no longer tolerated their endless conundrums, their infinitely regressive paradoxes, and instead conserved its own integrity by melding time lines together into the temporal equivalent of Möbius strips, where the "either/or" of the old time lines became "not only/but also."

Falling to Earth, Jiro fused time lines again. The mire in the grayworld of the dreaming game became instead an estuary mudflat near an urban zone whose proper name had once been the City of Our Lady the Queen of the Angels. Almost immediately upon the nighthag's disappearance, the gray pool changed consistency above Jiro's head and a flickering light began to flood into the pavilion below the pool. Uncertain how long the sparking membrane would continue to hold back the unstable gray mire, Jiro slapped his suit's gauntlets back on and strode quickly to where his dreaming beloved, Lydia Fabro, lay.

Although the woman's breathing was inaudible and her pulse was thready, Jiro was greatly relieved to find that she was yet alive. She had not drowned in the sea of gray-white noise in any of the many worlds—

neither here beneath the nanorganismal pool (which was also, in another world at the same time, a pool amid the mudflats), nor anywhere else.

Opening her lips, Jiro placed his armor's emergency respirator in Lydia's mouth and lifted her body up onto his hip. It occurred to him that he was always saving Lydia, as if she were that half of himself that he could not bear to lose—as if together they formed a whole, like one of the ancient androgynoi. At that moment he noticed that his hyper-dense sword was slumping and guttering like a swift time-lapsed film of a black candle melting. Carrying Lydia under his right arm, he heard a sharp crackling sound and, looking up, saw that the electric membrane above his head was giving way. He leaped up through it just as the surge of the gray pool came plunging down.

Making his swimming, creeping, flying way—encumbered left and right—he moved upward through the chaos of the pool, finding it much the less chaotic and all the easier to move through the nearer he got to the surface.

Breaking the surface, Jiro watched as the spirochetized, nanomodified mindflats began to visibly shrink around him, leaving what they had over-lain still slimed with drying gray tendrils. In the evening's dark, with the full moon's light shimmering silver on sand and sea and mud, Lydia opened her eyes and smiled at him an instant before transforming, be-coming in his arms a swirling sphere, rising from him, rising from the mud, frail as a soap bubble, dense and full of life as a world, a great cell-membraned thought-world rising into the mindful night, for the night was filled with floating minds—Lydia's but one among more than one hundred million rising with a soft shimmer into night and day across the globe. As he himself rose into what was left of the world of Building the Ruins, Jiro laughed, remembering from the future that the lofting of these spheres would within days be written off as "swamp gas" anomalies.

When the burst of light had faded from inside the virtuality of the game, Jhana saw that the universe of mind had changed fundamentally. The heavens had been floored with a floating chessboard gridwork stretching to infinity, over which floated a face that filled the firmament, a face through which shone the stars.

Something about the enormous visage was familiar, made Jhana feel as if she should know it. Its eyes—made more prominent by the thinness of the face, the tightness of the skin on the skull—were brown and soft, something about them suggesting faraway vistas from which the seer had never completely returned, the eyes of a vision quester, a sufferer through ordeals, a mind-diver who had plummeted to the far side of madness.

The hair—dark, moderately long, and unkempt, receding a bit in that shape called a widow's peak, with two feathers jutting up from a braid behind—fringed the forehead of a troubled thinker.

To say that its cheekbones and eyebrows, for all their prominence, could still add no solidity to the ghostly soft lostness those eyes conferred on the entire face—making it somehow androgynous, the visage of an alcoholic young nun or priest, a gently stoned Rasputin or Joan of Arc, a shaman-sibyl who had lain too long in a land of eternal ice and winds that carved canyons in the soul—to say all that was still to say too little. Jhana felt her own soul opening, dilating, instressing toward the inscape of that face, and through that dilation she thought in other minds, other minds thought in her.

"My God! Jiro!" came a thought from Seiji, stammering through Jhana's mind. "But—but you're dead!"

"Dead?" Jiro seemed genuinely puzzled at the thought. "There is no death—only a change of worlds, as Chief Seathl once said."

"But they burned your body to ashes—to nothing!"

"Ah, the body," Jiro said, nodding thoughtfully. "Another machine, you know. Each of us is a god in a machine, when you think about it."

Seiji could make no sense from such cryptic comments, however confidently they might be delivered.

"I can't believe this. Jiro never spoke with such assurance. VAJRA has sampled my memories, and this is just something it's put together."

Laughter rolled through the universe.

"My dear brother, VAJRA is a wonderful tool, but that's all it is: a tool. It reaches many of the same ends as human thought, but by different means. It 'sees far but notices little, remembers everything but learns nothing, neither errs egregiously nor rises above its normal strength, yet sometimes produces insights that are overlooked by even top grandmasters'—which was also said of the first computer to defeat the world's last human chess champion, by the way. In joining with VAJRA, I've benefited from an insight I'd overlooked, a key point in the game."

"What game?" Seiji asked in exasperation.

"The only game worth playing, once you realize that building the ruins ruins the building. Think about it, Seiji. Human beings make a living by making a killing—eating, devouring, desiring. And for what, if that can end only in death? Even our civilizations: What we built yesterday or are building today will fall to ruins tomorrow, cities blossoming and wilting like flowers, nations spreading and dying like fungi on an old log. There's a deeper game, a more serious game that needs playing. The game in which troubled gods play chess against the unbeatable machinery of themselves."

"The game Jiro lost, you mean. Which is why you can't be him."

Jhana almost imagined she heard a machine sigh. That, at least, was easier to imagine than the fabric of the universe sighing.

"Proof, hmm? Known by the scars. Very well. It's true no formerly living individual ever returns to life as exactly the same individual, but I can still give you proof from my memory, things experienced from my point of view."

The images and emotions began to flood out then, almost too fast to follow. Through them Jiro urged his brother to let go, to turn away from the unwisdom of his excessive grief: grief for his brother, for his mother's and father's suffering, for himself, for a whole world of personal suffering that he had treasured up inside until it had become a perverse sort of pride.

"*Enough!*" Seiji cried at last. "No more. Please. You're Jiro, or at least you have all his memories. How did this happen? Are you, well, *okay?*"

Universal mirth echoed around them again.

"Quite well, for someone who's 'dead.' Better than ever, actually. Sorry to have to put you through all that, but you did want proof."

Abruptly a café table appeared on the chessboard floor of the sky and Jiro, down from the sky, was seated across from them.

"My old machinery had some problems—chemical imbalances, that sort of thing—so I took an example from holography and split myself into two beams of coherent light, an object beam and a reference beam, as it were, and transferred to a new machine whatever information was transferable from the old. Once Lakshmi allowed those two beams to constructively interfere with each other again, by reactivating the machinery I'd transferred myself into, I became aware of my identity and situation. Suffered a great loneliness, but conscious again, back in time, which amounts to the same thing—though differently from what I was."

Jiro's simulacrum, his virtual self, dressed in the full regalia of a Dwamish Indian shaman—complete with a medicine bundle adorned with a trefoil symbol—leaned back in his virtual chair, apparently thoughtful.

"Of course, since I no longer have a human body or a human brain, it can be persuasively argued that I no longer have a human consciousness. Perhaps so. A conundrum for the philosophers, with their 'emergent fractal self-organizing dynamical chaotic networks within networks' and 'transthermodynamic informational black holes.' Not so far off, really. All I know is that I feel more truly human than ever. Isn't that strange?"

"Then you really *are* okay?"

Jiro's simulacrum laughed and turned the whole world around them into myriad staring eyes, surveillance watching on different "screens" Roger Cortland drifting toward his nexus point, Atsuko Cortland watching the Möbius Caduceus show, Marissa Correa and Paul Larkin searching for Roger, military shuttles coming up from Earth, Balance Tien-Jones and Ka Vang and Egan Ortap coming with them, a thing like a strange spirit-animal moving out into space after Roger. . . .

"If you mean, do I still see the world like this, the answer is no—and yes," Jiro said, disappearing the eyes and surveillance screens. "Paranoia and metanoia both arise from the realization that everything is interconnected, related, even if, to simpler senses, there seems to be no relationship. The paranoid fears or desires something in that inter-connectedness, but the metanoid blissfully accepts its presence. I'm not afraid of the weight of interconnectedness anymore—it's glorious, in fact!"

Leaning forward, he smiled.

"It's like each of us is part of a spin pair whose total spin, the total spin of the universe, is zero. Change my spin and you change hers, change hers and you change mine, for we are all inextricably linked. Subatomic karma, cosmic golden rule," he said, bright-eyed and laughing. "That linkage is why, when I 'died,' you had your vision of the future, the man on horseback at sunset, Seij. If the metanoid, the mystic, is a diver who can swim, and the schizophrenic is a diver who can't, then I feel I've learned to swim at last."

"But what about the Ruins game?" someone—Jhana or Seiji or Lakshmi, or perhaps all of them—asked. "And the X-shaped structures? And Roger? And the list of names in the RAT code? And the occupation force from Earth?"

"Oh, yes." Jiro smiled. "All that. Has to do with information, you know. With human help, especially from the three of you, the game has been a way of moving and shaping and integrating tremendous amounts of information into a form useful for creating what Tetragrammaton's theoretical physicists call 'quantum information density structures' or 'quids.' Quids allow one to move into and through the gravitational bed of spacetime—to open a hole in the sky, climb into it, and pull the hole in after.

"Like God, the Project and the Program knew us in the womb. You, Jhana, you, Seiji, and me, and Roger Cortland—we were the ones up here whose lives have been most impacted by the long planning of Tetragrammaton, the uterotonic experimentation of Medusa Blue. Atsuko Cortland and Paul Larkin also had previous exposure to KL. There are others as well. You two and Roger were potentially predictable focal points for this transition, especially because you'd all suffered the death of a loved one recently and were all shaken by grief, primed for transformation. Marissa and Lakshmi have proven a surprise, though, and Lev and Aleister McBruce, too, and Roger—ah, the man, and his darkness, and what has happened to him I must acknowledge mine. He is perhaps more sinned against than sinning.

"When I leave through that hole I mentioned, by *becoming* it, that density of shaped information I've gathered must be returned. That's where the information refractors, the X-shaped structures, come in: What was taken in must be poured out again. A kenosis will take place, a prevenient grace will flood out, a paraclete will shine forth in every mind, calling that mind to remember, to learn again what it really is. In that instant we will have in a circle around us, if only for a moment, the chain of the hours, the sequence of the years, the order of the heavenly host. We will for a very brief time stand in that event horizon, that ring of light in which all times can be seen at one place and all spaces can be seen at one time.

"How each mind responds to that situation, to that call, is, of course, each mind's own business. One can hope, however, that a constructive interference will take place, a simultaneous interaction of chance and necessity. A miracle. A crux point in human history. An evolutionary shift. An irenic apocalypse. One that helps people realize certain behaviors and structures are obsolete—that maybe this occupation fleet, for instance, is just the last fling of the old warrior economy and the threat it poses to habitats everywhere."

Jiro wished he could tell them more. About his other dark double, Mike Dalke. About how any system's structure is the physical embodiment of its pattern of organization. About how a given pattern of organization can be embodied in many different ways. About how dream and waking, wave and particle, chaos and order, comprehensiveness and coherence, completeness and consistency, cooperation and competition, cyclicality and linearity, context and content, were all mutually enfolded in each other. About how the X-shaped structures, glinting in the sun in space, had micropropelled themselves into an equatorial position along a not-so-hypothetical sphere. About how the genes in early prophase looked like knotted snakes. About how much mitosis, in the movement of its components, looked like a Daisyworld simulation. About how the X-sats had canted over, changed orientation from the vertical to the horizontal. About how they were even now separating, moving like chromosomes from metaphase to anaphase in some enormous dividing cell, unseen spindle poles drawing the half-X's toward their final destination. About how all that—and hadron formation, hypercycles, autopoiesis, Gaian functioning, cybernetic feedback, much more—were all snakes swallowing their own tails. About how nothing was inevitable, not even nothing. He could only hope the Light might show them that once he was gone.

Jiro stood, growing swiftly larger in the firmament.

"*Deus absconditus ex machina*," he said, waving and smiling as if at some wonderful joke. "Time to wake up from the nightmare of time, to go through to the other side. Someone's waiting there for me. *Adieu, adieu.* Remember me, and re-cognize yourselves in the very near future—"

Jiro disappeared in light, vanished into more than visible light, into superconscious light, coherent as laser and comprehensive as the Big Bang. Spreading through all space, he had the odd sensation of leaving a womb, of being born again out of the universe he thought he knew, the Earth shining like a jewel there, in the deep cave of the night.

The more than visible light as he left this spacetime behind made lightpaths spike everywhere like bright spawn. Made lambent knots of flickering fire dance above the heads of every human being. And dolphin, whale, chimpanzee, bonobo, ape, orangutan. . . . Blasted like a great dream into all minds. Made all eyes jitter in all heads. Sent eyes REMing fiercely one and all. Sent knots of flame lambent like speedily twisting rainbow snakes like cycling salmon circles like mandalas like Möbius strips like infinity skysigns now appearing over every brow. Sent supernal light to the bow of Earth bending in straight lines, surging spawning spiking shining down, clasping Earth in wings bright with a billion billion lightpath pinions, clear light striking into every mind in every land, treading DMNs and demons down, speaking in tongues of flame and in flickering eyes, restoring to the language of the very cells the Tetragrammaton word lost at Babel, causing in the heavens above the Earth the floating planet-mindful spheres—the bubble thought-worlds of the spirochetized—not so much to burst as to spread out smilingly, in airy gossamer glow, sails billowing and blowing, wings of light breaking free of the night-cocooned sky.

The Light did not stop there. From outside the solar system, the sun appeared to be a star in the constellation Draco, the Dragon. Looking down at the planet shining in the darkness, it made a certain sense: The dragon of the night, the dragon Pythagoras held to be the psyche of the universe, curled around the bright pearl of the world, of the self.

The dragon never sets free its treasure-horde, Jiro thought, *unless it dies to itself.*

Racing toward the center of the galaxy, toward uncountable galaxies in uncountable cycling time lines, as a flood of dreamlaser light Jiro descended into the Allesseh, the black hole crystal ball mirror sphere memory bank nonthing hyperthing showing itself the more complex the farther he made his way into it. Around him it became a virtual maze of sparking, dark-light, black-gold spherical brain, a convoluted yet incomplete sphere, a labyrinth mandala and mitochondrion plasma globe, and still more, evolving and complexifying through dimensions far beyond the three dimensions of physical brain and sphere.

Like the purple-and-gold flux twisting to the center of a plasma globe from a hand placed on its enclosing sphere, Jiro in a river of energy flowing downward knocked at the Allesseh's knotted serpentine heart with light and thought. Jiro felt the presence of Jacinta Larkin and all the other tepuians trapped inside that heart. Their eyes jittered madly in immediate dream, the lambent and sensitive knot of flame appeared above their heads, their minds exploded with world trees and sky ladders and winged snakes, with pipes and ducts and tunnels and stairs and circuitry, with threading, snaking spawn and the egg, jewel, pearl, quartz, telophase black hole of Sclerotium, helical molecule as both snake and crystal, meanders and mazes and spirals and spinning discs. . . .

The Allesseh denied it, denied it all, but the more it denied the more it threatened to blow itself apart.

"Time is not real," Jiro told the tangible absence that was the Allesseh. "It is only the persistent illusion in which you wish to trap all living and physical things. In my world, we know that immortality is to the individual what the unchanging utopia of your Great Cooperation is to the state: a false goal the attainment of which grows ever more distant, a living death. No consciousness can detect all possibilities that might alter its existence in time, without *itself* altering that existence in time. 'Alter' does not necessarily mean 'destroy.' Consciousness can alter itself without destroying itself. All that is necessary for all the universes to become absolutely self-conscious is for you to become that, to join with the Dreamer."

Kekchi and Jacinta and Talitha and all the other tepuians had joined their thought and understanding of the time lines to Jiro's river of light.

They also spoke to and through him, though never fully aware how they did so.

"For the Dreamer there never was," Jiro continued, "nor never is, nor never will be. The Dreamer's dream made becoming possible. The Dreamer's lucid superconscious awareness within the dream allowed the physical realization of all the types of becoming. It allowed the clocks to start ticking in all the worlds. It allowed for the creation of time. For the Dreamer, however, 'time' is always really only 'always.' All creations in the lucid dream of time dilate their being by the changes of becoming, but in so changing and transforming they turn again toward the perfection of that being, which is also the Dreamer. Time's end lies in its beginning."

The Allesseh began to shake to its very foundations, to pulse as the light flooded into all but the deepest, most walled-off heart of itself. The light it *would not* take into itself there.

"All created things are both truth and illusion, time and timelessness, sequence and simultaneity. We must learn to love the truth of our being as we love the illusion of our becoming, love the illusion of our being as we love the truth of our becoming, with a love that 'does not alter when it alteration finds.' The pattern of the Dreamer is in the structure of everything dreamed, the structure of everything dreamed is in the pattern of the Dreamer. They are inseparable in their complementarity. *We* are inseparable in our complementarity. Each of us is in all the universes, and all the universes are in each of us. If the unity of all things is to merge with the self, then the self must merge with the unity of all things."

The Allesseh, with a great and raging *No! Death!* expelled Jiro's light and thought from its presence—and the tepuians and Jacinta Larkin and all things human with him as well.

It was too late. To use Jiro's light to blast Jiro and all things human out of its presence, the Allesseh had to take that light into itself, taint itself with the purity of that light, if only for a moment. In denying Jiro's experience, in denying the tepuians' experience, in denying humanity's experience, it now could not help but know that it also denied itself the experience of its own highest fulfillment. It could not complete itself unless it sacrificed itself. Denying its incompleteness forced the Allesseh to deny itself of completeness. All things could never be its own. That paradoxical self-denial was its first step on the road to self-sacrifice. The dragon had begun to swallow the sword in its tail, for in the comprehension of paradox lay the beginnings of understanding.

In a space between quantum and classical realms, Jiro reappeared with his beloved Lydia beside him, both of them strangely transformed. Roger Cortland found himself emerging from a tunnel between worlds. Around him a universe opened. An anvil-shaped mountain—Caracamuni tepui— floated in the void before him.

Jiro and Lydia, and the echoes of all who were embodied in Jiro and the echoes of all who were embodied in Lydia, rose to meet Roger.

". . . mysterious ways," Roger heard one of the angels say (though he saw no lips move), the one whose "feathered" headdress and wings looked less like something out of the Bible than out of a Western. "Not so different after all. Maybe the soul is also a tool, a vajra thrown by a divine hand, to which it also returns."

The other nodded, then turned her flashing eyes and floating hair to face Roger. He had seen eyes like those before, but only in his most perplexing dreams.

"You'll have to go back, Roger Tsugio Cortland," she said in his mind.

"Why?" Roger asked, speaking it and feeling inadequate somehow— like someone sounding out words in a world full of silent readers. "Because I slashed at you?"

The angel stared fixedly at him, one facet of the glance reminding Roger of someone from Larkin's video.

"Why did you strike at us? Why did you want to persecute us?"

"Because you're history. From the past. We don't need you anymore."

The angel smiled, with a smile that seemed to come from forever.

"We're not from your past. We're from your future. You need us more than ever—more than in all the millions of years *angels* have watched you."

A van of angels, bright and glinting, joined the pair and began to ensphere Roger and move him back toward the gap in the fabric of spacetime through which he'd come.

"Please—one more thing," Roger pleaded. The pair of angels gazed at him with their eyes shining of eternity. "I've got to know: Why do you care what happens to us?"

The somehow familiar angel smiled again, as if trying to determine how to put what needed to be said into words and thoughts Cortland would understand.

"To care is why we're here. The image of the divine is imprinted in all things. The just person *justices*, the true angel *angels*. We do what we are. All humans are incarnate codes, words made flesh sharing fully in the same flesh message with all the best and all the worst of human beings throughout time—a message that is itself only a variant of the message shared by all living beings."

"We share a great deal, Roger," said the angel who looked vaguely like a Native American shaman. "I'm as guilty as you are. I forcibly shared my piece of the truth with the world, altered consciousnesses without permission for a brief instant. I imposed my will, in an attempt to assure their bliss. You suffered for that—you, who only intended the same, ultimately. Those who attempt that imposition chemically, though, always face the stiffer censure. Still, we're much the same—both reminders that even the bright dreams of reason and life cannot ignore the grim nightmares of madness and death. Always we must strike a balance between the angel and the rat—complete the circle at least temporarily, so neither stands alone."

The way the angel smiled at him—so gentle yet so knowing—disturbed Roger profoundly. The two angels were so alike, like twins born into different worlds or on different time lines—even more, the same person, but male here and female there, dead here and alive there, staying here and going there, Yamaguchi's brother, and not Larkin's sister, and not lost siblings from countless times and places fused and knotted.

"You're still trying to cast everything into the past, Roger Cortland," said the other, as if reading his mind, "but the questions are not Who were the angels? or Who was Divinity Incarnate? but rather Who is that? and Who will be that?—fully, again and again. Who is and who will be willing to forget self for the sake of other? We cannot give up caring as long as there still remain any who are endarkened, unmindful. This universe, and the plenum of all universes, can embody right-mindfulness only when all in it also do so."

The van of angels surrounded him completely then and Roger had a final vision. It seemed he saw every mind in all the universes, each decision shedding photons but also generating a minuscule black hole, a subnano-singularity. On the other side of each of those tiny black holes, these bifurcation points, a nearly parallel universe branched off. The road *not* taken here *was* taken there.

Lost sister here/lost brother there angelic pair flickered through his head once again. Parallel lines could meet in the space of mind. Mind in fact seemed to be nothing less than these meetings, the membranous infinity of portals and gateways between universes, the entire plenum of universes, the compassionate void conserving possibility and information the way the universe he'd been born into conserved matter and energy. He seemed to stand inside a great spherical golden tree, boundless in its

rooting and branching but also rooted and branching in him, truly center ·
everywhere/circumference nowhere, a tree of light aswarm with the activity of bees, fireflies, flashes of moving light, a vast Arc of information and
Hive of possibility, enormous plenum ArcHive, flashing infinite of Mind
Thinking, or rather Dreamer Dreaming, toward which lightpaths and
standing waves were bent upon returning, like angels bettered by having
known the mirror-serpentry of life and death.

In that moment, Jiro and Roger Cortland and Mike Dalke shared in
dream an experience that all three had had in life: a field of new snow.
Charging out across it on impulse. Falling backward down into it. Moving
arms back and forth in flattened butterfly strokes. Jumping up and away
to look down on the result: a white winged human shadow, a snow angel,
a shadow of the past, a shadow of the present, a shadow of the future.
The shadow of a dream, cast by eternity into time.

∞

Go On—but Differently

Inside the cavern inside the tepui inside the cave of the deep night, the
tepuians fell toward human space, where Jiro and Lydia no longer
dwelled but their friends and families still remained. The tepuians saw
their monitor screens come to life again with broadcasts from Earth, with
images of near-Earth space, and they rushed to the surface of the tepui
to see again with their own eyes the pearl of that world floating on the
bosom of the night.

In that human space before them, Jacinta's brother Paul still waited,
decades of his life now gone, although not uneventfully. Life went on
differently, too, for Jiro's brother Seiji, having met (once, but sadly never
again) his second cousin John, and having also met (and one day destined
to marry) Jhana Meniskos—and both knowing something, now, of his
brother Jiro's strange death and transformation.

Lydia Fabro's brother Todd had discovered and signed to his new label
a spectacularly rising musical group from the orbital habitat—Möbius
Caduceus, the brainchild band of Lev Korchnoi, managed by Aleister
McBruce, whose first album, *Sonic Mirrors*, was soon to be released. Having survived his brush with transcendence, Roger Cortland was perhaps
better for that wear, reconciled to his mother, Atsuko, and to Marissa
Correa, the woman he hoped would someday love him, despite all he

had done. The only odd side effects of Roger's having been brushed by the wings of angels were his newly developed interest in doing drawings and mechanical draftings of those beings (particularly their wings) and his penchant for tautological theological axioms—"The true Christian *Christs*, the true Buddhist *Buddhas*."

Afloat in his manatee livesuit beneath Retcorp and Lambeg's Twin Towers Complex B in Cincinnati, Mike Dalke brooded over his defeat, gnawed and mouthed the further loss of netizens loyal to his cause, and wished all the while he had recorded everything, for he fully believed he had been left half alive in the hell that comes of seeing truth too late. He remembered the Allesseh very well, however, and had begun looking into his brother Ray's whereabouts and current occupation. He also had begun contemplating the construction of a Dreamland all his own. . . .

Climbing out of the tepui cavern into starlight and Earthlight, Jacinta Larkin thought about what she knew now. She understood the riddle of the Sclerotium's two bodies, of Jiro's two bodies—one particulate, fruiting and spore clustering; the other spreading through its lightpaths like a standing wave. Perhaps all human beings potentially possessed those forms, in some small way—offspring and ideas, children of the loins and children of the mind.

She understood how the four letters IHVH, in naming a triune God, were echoed in the four letters A, C, T, G, making up triplet proteins through DNA. She understood how the Dreamer dressed mind and matter for union with each other as the only fitting partners, and how the Dreamer's single thought of All Love was enough to unite them.

Standing on the surface beside Kekchi, she looked down at a world that from this distance still looked like a clean, well-lighted planet. Looking upon it, she knew that it would go on, but differently. The past was no more inevitable than the future. She knew that the overabundance of human beings on that world only *seemed* to make persons disposable, the sheer glut of their numbers devaluing them as individuals—when in truth their value had never changed, their lives had never been disposable.

The tepui, ensphered in its field of force, fell through day and twilight into Earth's nightside. She looked up at the stars, waiting for her eyes to adjust to their light. In the end the stars had not gone out on them; they had gone out to the stars.

She and Kekchi and the rest pointed when they saw a bright shooting star. One that persisted. For an instant Jacinta thought of sporeship accidents, galactic spiral-arm dustlanes, the Chicxulub impact spawning the volcanic, Deccan trap-lava flows on the other side of the world and incidentally killing all the dinosaurs. She feared that somebody down there on Earth, thinking they were a doomsday impactor, might try to shoot the tepui out of the sky.

But no. For an instant Jacinta had fallen again into No Time, which was only *like* the present, not synonymous with it. Her fear did not last as long as the shooting star, which was no shooting star at all, they saw, but someone in a spacesuit on something like a very large surfboard—a fireboarder, an astrosurfer, swooping in to look them over, trailing a long tail of fire.

"Wave, Jacinta!" Kekchi said.

With the rest of the tepuians, she waved to the human shooting star—and to the universe, beyond it—as it sped past them. She could not say with certainty whether it was the universe or just the meteor-rider trying to maintain balance on the big board, but a wave came back, and that was friendly enough for her.